The WEIGHT of NUMBERS

SIMON INGS

Atlantic Books
London

First published in Great Britain as a trade paperback in 2006
by Atlantic Books, an imprint of Grove Atlantic Ltd.

This paperback edition published in Great Britain by Atlantic Books
in 2006.

9 8 7 6 5 4 3

A CIP catalogue record for this book is available from the British Library.

ISBN 10: 1 84354 464 4
ISBN 13: 978 1 84354 463 0

Text design: www.carrstudio.co.uk
Printed in Great Britain by
Clays Ltd, St Ives plc

Atlantic Books
An imprint of Grove Atlantic Ltd
Ormond House
26–27 Boswell Street
London WC1N 3JZ

www.groveatlantic.co.uk

For Anna

It will be an inhuman, an atrocious performance, but these are the facts.

General Giuilo Douhet, *Il Dominio dell'Aria*

The WEIGHT of NUMBERS

PROLOGUE

Lake Kissimmee, Florida

Monday, 25 October 1965

Marilyn, Jim's wife of thirteen years, pours out his second Coke, takes up her own and clinks his glass with ceremony as though it were champagne. Her eyes are big and black in the candlelight, wet with the unnamable emotions pilots' wives acquire in proximity to Canaveral.

Through the window of the restaurant, the night sky is speckled – had they but eyes to see – with spillage from the afternoon's catastrophe: a fuel explosion massive enough to shred a final stage to so much kitchen foil. For Jim the worst part is that at six minutes past three that afternoon, six minutes after the launch and at the very moment the Agena's engine turned over and choked on six tonnes of liquid fuel, he had been gaping, like some fool kid, eyes upturned on a calm sky.

'It'd have reached orbit,' he says, shaking his head.

'Tonight,' their waiter explains, 'our bass comes with a macadamia nut butter.'

'Well, whoop-de-doo,' says Marilyn.

'Ma-am?'

Marilyn blinks. 'I really have no idea why I said that.' She lays her hand on the boy's arm. 'I do apologize. Really.'

Perhaps she felt it, too, today. At six minutes past three, a wrinkle in things.

When they are alone: 'Marilyn?'

Marilyn giggles. This is the girl he fell in love with in high school. 'No idea at all. Sorry. Odd day today.'

Jim sets about his meal, determined to shake off bad thoughts. 'This fish,' he says.

The fish is really very good.

'Yes,' says Marilyn.

He's been told about this place: the best largemouth bass in the county, the tables small, unfussy, few, the air sweet off Lake Kissimmee – all this barely an hour from the Cape. Come December, Jim Lovell is riding shotgun with Frank Borman in Gemini Seven. An unprecedentedly long mission, two whole weeks, Seven is meant to test the shirt-sleeve environment the engineers have planned for the Apollo spacecraft. There's other, rather more gung-ho business for Frank and Jim to perform – for instance, they'll be demonstrating a new, more accurate form of controlled re-entry – but the core of their mission is 'station-keeping', NASA's word for staying clean and tidy and alive for 200 orbits of the Earth. One of the more damn-fool experiments dreamed up for them requires that Jim weigh every mouthful that enters his system before, during and after the flight. Although there are still six weeks to go before the launch, this will be, for Jim, his last unfussed-up meal for some while. To mark the fact, tonight he has arranged babysitters so he can take his wife out to dinner.

He says, 'I was standing on the crawlerway.' A pause. 'This afternoon. I watched it take off from the crawlerway.'

The main body of the rocket, the launch vehicle proper, was an Atlas, the machine that put John Glenn, America's first astronaut, into space. Today's Atlas worked perfectly, as far as he's aware. It was the final stage, the Agena Target Vehicle that exploded, one minute after separation, the very moment it tried to start its engine. Without a target vehicle for them to pursue, astronauts Wally Schirra and the rookie Thomas Stafford are even now slouching their way through the most disappointed night of their careers: the launch of Gemini Six, scheduled for tomorrow, is scratched.

'What will they do with Tom and Wally?' Marilyn's thoughts are tracking Jim's own with a niceness they had all expected of Gemini Six and its ill-fated target. 'Could they run their mission and yours together in any way that makes sense?'

James Lovell looks out the window at the lake. The sky is clear tonight. The water is so still, he can see the brighter stars reflected in the water. 'Probably,' he says. 'We'd at least be able to practise the alignment manoeuvres.' The Geminis are meant to lead to Apollo, and a bid for the moon. They are the only real practice the crews are going to get before the big push. Every Gemini failure makes Apollo that bit more daunting. 'It's not docking practice, but it'd be something.' Jim turns back to his wife, aware that in his preoccupation he is hardly giving her interest its due.

Every couple caught up in NASA's folly has its own way of dealing with the dangers and disappointments. Each solution is personal, its secrecy carefully guarded. It is impossible to know if Marilyn's careful, intelligent curiosity about Gemini is shared by any of the other wives. In public, and even among themselves, there can be no breach of the women's etiquette. This has less to do with class and custom – though that is part of it – so much as their common need to bootstrap a workable life out of the demands and sacrifices of the Cape. The artificiality of that life – Sunday clambakes in the shadow of the Vertical Assembly Building – is a given. That life *is* artificial, something you have to construct for yourself, like a shed or a car motor or a Thanksgiving dinner, is the great, soon-to-be-forgotten lesson of these days.

'They let you on the crawlerway?' says Marilyn, double-taking his earlier remark.

'That's where I watched it from.'

The crawlerway is, like any construction site, out of bounds. But there was no danger, watching a launch from there.

Practically speaking, the crawlerway is a four-lane highway connecting the launch complexes to the Vertical Assembly Building, where Apollo's colossal Saturn rockets will be built. But the lanes are deceptive. They are built, not for ordinary traffic at all, but for the giant caterpillar tracks of a single vehicle: the 500ft-high mobile launcher.

Standing there today, watching as the Atlas-Agena assembly rose out of its own exhaust cloud, high above Complex 14, Jim felt as though he were standing among giants, in a giant's footprint. He felt smaller than a child and infinitely less significant among these towering machines. He felt more like a rat: something tolerated and expendable.

'It seems to me now that I felt it.' This is something Jim Lovell absolutely will *not* say to his wife. 'It seems to me that there was a wrinkle in things. At six minutes past three this afternoon, and with nothing left to see besides the contrail, all of a sudden I became aware of a wrongness in the sky's fabric; a wrongness so intimate, at first I was afraid there was something the matter with my eyes.'

'What are you thinking?' Marilyn is asking him.

Drawn back to the present, Jim is startled to find himself already behind the wheel of their car. Marilyn is next to him, their meal is done, and Camp Mack Lane is already rumbling beneath their wheels. They are part-way home.

'Wait,' he says. 'Wait a minute.'

'What?'

'This isn't right.'

A wrinkle in things. Surfaces are bent and drawn into accidental contact. A short circuit, and the evening comes apart, skipping and hopping like a scratched record. 'Wait,' he says. He slows the car. 'Hang on.' He checks his rear-view mirror, slows them almost to a stop and turns them around.

He cannot rewind the evening. All those minutes wasted in introspection. He has to do something; this is their last easy evening together.

'What is it?' Marilyn asks. 'Did you forget something?'

'Everything is going to be fine,' he says, and he switches on the radio: a clue for her.

He drives them deeper and deeper into Florida's rural dark, under canopies of post oak and hickory, through pastures abandoned to mesquite. One by one, the stations peter out: WWBC out of Cocoa;

WKGF from Kissimmee. Wayne Fontana and The Mindbenders drift in and away and a silence descends, with an eerie, out-of-range sensation that Marilyn remembers now. 'You old fool,' she laughs, guessing his game. 'You fool, you.'

At a sign for a fishing lodge, he rolls the car down a dirt track. There are no lights, no other vehicles. Woods hug the shore. Between the tree trunks, moonlight glistens on Lake Kissimmee.

She leans over and slips into his arms. 'What about the babysitter?' she asks him.

'What about tomorrow's early start?'

'Did I switch the oven off?'

'Did I lock the door?'

A goofy routine to propitiate the ageing process: they understand that they are too old for this. After their first kiss, Jim draws away and turns off the ignition: it would be just like him to knee the stick into Drive and land them in the lake. The headlights die, the night is blue, they kiss again.

An orphan cloud covers the moon. Blue turns to black. The car's surfaces, tin frame and plastic fascia, close in around them. His scream is silent, wracking him out of her arms. He arches back as though electrocuted and cracks his head against the door column. *'Fuck—'*

'Jim!'

'Shit.'

'Not much better.'

'Sorry. *Darn.*'

She tries to laugh. 'What?'

'Nothing.'

'Jim.'

'Nothing. A rabbit ran over my grave.'

She thinks this over.

'Pesky rabbits,' she says.

She leans over and kisses him again. But the moment has passed. 'I'm going for a smoke,' she says, a minute later. She pecks him on the cheek and climbs from the car. He watches her go. He sits back, lays his hands on the steering wheel and forces himself, by main effort, to calm down. A second cloud hides the moon and the night swallows her. He leans forward and peers up at the sky: what is happening to the weather?

One by one, between the slowly stirring branches, stars are going out.

The waters off Japan, February 1954.

This is shortly after the Korean War and two years into Jim's marriage to Marilyn, effected just a couple of hours after graduating from the Naval Academy at Annapolis. At this point in his career, Jim is just a humble aviator, assigned to the SS *Shangri-La* from Moffet Field. He's flying McDonnell F2H Banshees: brutal turbo-powered monsters that cheerfully nudge the stratosphere.

The airframe wraps around him in the night, the dark itself turned metal, stuffing eyes and mouth, as he takes stock. What he's been following all these hours, burning up his fuel, what he thought was his homing beacon – well, it turns out that it wasn't. He's been following the wrong signal for – how long is it now? – and there are no ground lights, no ships in the vicinity, to help him find his way back on course. Neither are there any stars. He can't afford to waste fuel punching the cloud layer, because any navigation reading he takes will be meaningless by the time he descends again, and anyway he hasn't the fuel. Thank God the instrument lights are working. Without them, how could he be sure which way is up? It is at this point that he thinks to plug in the little geegaw he's made to boost the cockpit illumination – and in doing so, he fuses every light in the cockpit.

In a lonely bubble, bobbing above the Pacific, Jim Lovell, navy pilot, looks out from his blacked-out Banshee at the sky. If it is the sky. There are no stars. His instruments are out and his lights are out and there are no stars and there is no carrier, there is no *Shangri-La*. Where is the goddamn *Shangri-La*?

Jim Lovell, astronaut, climbs from the car. He misses the path and pushes through the undergrowth to the shore of Lake Kissimmee. Marilyn is stood at the end of a narrow wooden jetty, facing away from him. A red flare arcs and gutters as she tosses her cigarette into the water.

The screws of the carrier *Shangri-La* agitate the waters of the Pacific. The water, rich in plankton, glows. In the extremity of his failure, Jim Lovell, navy pilot, sees a green light: the wake of a ship. He follows the wake. It leads him home.

He steps onto the jetty. He walks up to his wife. An F2H Banshee stays in the air using two Westinghouse J34-WE-30 turbojets, each rated at 3,150 pounds of thrust. It takes off by means of a rubber catapult. It comes to rest by means of a grappling hook. It is very important for him to control his speed at this point. It is vital that he not overshoot and topple off the end of the jetty into the bass-rich waters of Lake Kissimmee. He bites his lip against laughter. The day has shaken loose so many bits of himself, all the joy and fear of what he does. He touches Marilyn on the shoulder.

She turns. 'Oh,' she says, looking straight into his eyes. 'You again.' She lets his laughter roll on a little way, then stops it with a kiss. 'Time to go home.'

BANSHEE

Beira, Mozambique

November 1992

In 1992, Mozambique's seventeen-year-old civil war was ended by the worst drought in living memory. Even fertile Gorongosa, in the interior of the country, found itself dependent on food aid. From trains grinding their way west along the contested Beira–Machipanda rail-line, armed men rolled sacks of grain into the dust. The sacks split. It could be days since the last train and I would still find boys from my class crawling about the embankments, sifting grains from fistfuls of gravel.

With the region in such disarray, I found it relatively easy to desert my post. So I returned to the coast and settled in Beira, Mozambique's second city.

Beira was a port town. It depended for its income on Mozambique's landlocked neighbours to the west, and on the busy overland corridor through which their trade was conducted. Attacks on this corridor by RENAMO, the apartheid-backed faction in this war, had rendered Beira redundant, and today's famine relief effort, shipping grain for onward distribution, was too little and too hesitant to revive the city's fortunes. Consequently, the streets had acquired a timelessness that was not romantic. There was no light, no water, no food, no sanitation. There were only people.

Shelter was at a premium. In my building whole families lived out diagonal lives in the stairwell. There was no electricity to run elevators, so the cheapest apartments in the city were on the upper floors of the tower blocks. None of the blocks was especially high by Western standards, so my tenth-floor eyrie gave me views across the whole city.

It was the piano, rather than the views, which first sold the apartment to me. I hadn't had a piano since I was a child. It was an antique upright from colonial days, shipped from Portugal and abandoned during the exodus. Its lid was locked, so I couldn't try it out, but once I'd established that it came with the apartment, I agreed to take the place, overpriced as it was.

For the most part of each day, I would sit out on my handkerchief-sized balcony and watch the city consume itself. There was no firewood to be had, and since most of the windows in town were mesh, not glass, people had decided that it was an easy and a relatively harmless thing to chip out the window frames for fuel. When that supply was exhausted, people turned on their furniture. Those who had run out of furniture pulled up sections of floor. By evening, the woodsmoke from 10,000 *braiis* made my eyes smart, and I went indoors. Usually I went to bed around this time. There was little else to do. The radio was useless as batteries were hard to come by.

The piano was a different story.

The day I moved in, the first thing I did was break open the keyboard. I sat down to play. The instrument emitted a dreadful dead thumping and wheezing. I pulled off the top and looked in.

The strings had been cut.

The piano came with a piano stool; lifting up the lid, I discovered that it was full of sheet music. Bach's *Well-Tempered Clavier*. I managed, with a deal of effort, to wheel the unstrung piano onto the balcony, and there I sat down and played: clippety-clop, clippety-clop – *bonk*. As the weeks went by, so my coordination improved to the point where I could hear the shape of the music and the pattern of the parts. At last the piano's hammers found their mark, tapping, ever so lightly, the strings inside my head.

I stopped my playing and looked over the city to the old holiday camps sprawled along the seafront. Beach huts were being adapted to accommodate refugees flooding to the coast from the parched interior. It seemed to me that, with this latest influx, Beira would achieve a critical mass. All it had going for it was the size of its population, but maybe this was enough. After twenty years of this bare existence, the city had learned how to feed off its own refuse for ever. I imagined it spreading in a chain reaction across the whole world: a self-sustaining half-life.

Communications were unreliable. The city had decayed to the point where it had learned to do without the outside world. There was little in the way of entertainment. A handful of bottle stores operated out of mud-brick houses along the shore, and it was to these that I thumbed my way, come late afternoon – or drove sometimes, if there was fuel enough for the pick-up.

With transport so hard to come by, every vehicle on the road was an unofficial bus; driving without passengers attracted the attention of the police. One afternoon, out on the coastal road, one of the men I had picked up rapped on the roof of the cabin and pointed me down a track towards a bit of beach I had not explored before. Several others seemed to know of the place, so once I had let off the onward travellers I rolled the pick-up down to the beach. At the tree-line, an enclosure fenced off with rushes marked the site of a new bottle store. The place had an ambitious layout. The tables and benches in the enclosure were cast concrete, but their surfaces were decorated with inset fragments of pottery and mirror. Under a raised veranda, I saw the walls of the store had fresh murals.

Inside, a white kid with a slurred Austrian accent was giving the girl behind the bar a hard time.

'I know every fucking owner on this coast,' he said, more or less, his speech a druggy mishmash of German and Portuguese.

Dumb, impassive, the girl shook her head.

'Fucking *bitch*.'

From out the back a white man – a real bruiser – joined the girl. 'Out,' he said, barely bothering to make eye contact. He and Austrian Boy must have run into each other before, because the kid began straight away to retreat towards the veranda. 'You're *fucked*,' he shouted. 'You'd better watch your back. I know people.'

The barman blinked. He was a big man, clean-shaven, crew-cut, built for a fight. His eyes were mean and set close together. His mouth let him down: small and pursed above a weakling chin. 'What crap was *that*?' he asked no one in particular, in English, when the boy was gone. I was surprised to hear the man's Norfolk burr: I had assumed, from the sheer size of him, that he was a Boer.

By way of conversation, I translated the boy's German.

'Really.'

'Or words to that effect,' I said.

All the other bottle stores were locally run and I wondered what had driven a European to set up in so unrewarding a business. The drinks here were the usual trio – orange Fanta, green-label Carlsberg and *chibuku*, a locally produced granular swill I had never got used to. I supposed he must be, like me, an ideological recruit to FRELIMO, the country's beleaguered socialist government. I couldn't think what else would bring an Englishman to such a miserable pass. He was about my age: a middle-aged drifter for whom home was by now a distant memory. He was happy to talk to a countryman and, when I offered to buy him a beer, he plucked a Carlsberg off the shelf and led me to an outdoor table.

His name was Nick Jenkins. I told him something about myself. I mentioned Gorongosa, and it surprised me how much I was prepared to relive of that time, merely to feed a casual chat.

We talked about the war, and when I explained how, in spite of my politics, I had come to work as a teacher in RENAMO's apartheid-funded heartland – how I had fomented Marxist revolution among my seven- and eight-year-olds under the very noses of the party hierarchy – Jenkins chuckled.

My own life, eventful as it might have appeared from the outside, had been dictated by the sweep of political events. Nick Jenkins, on the other hand, like all true adventurers, had somehow sidestepped the big events of his day. This was his second time in Mozambique. The first, the late sixties, had seen him working the merchant lines out of Maputo when it was still

Lourenço Marques, the colonial capital. From there he'd gone to the Caribbean, where he'd built up a small import-export concern. 'It was my second time there, and all,' he laughed. 'I can't seem to make up my mind.'

I did a quick mental calculation. 'You must have been young the first time, then. Your first time in the Caribbean. When was that? Early sixties?'

'Damn right.' He nodded. 'A bloody kid.'

It was when he told me about Cuba that I began to doubt his tale.

'Six bloody battalions,' he sighed, reminiscing. 'Fifteen hundred men. Christ!'

'You were in the Bay of Pigs landing?'

'Not "in" it. We just happened to be berthed in Puerto Cabezas for a refit. The boat was chartered. We came with the boat. We were deckhands, not squaddies.'

The enormity of this new anecdote, artfully shaped out of hints and hesitations and the occasional buzz-word, took my breath away. That a seventeen-year-old boy from the fens should have washed up on the beaches of Havana in 1961 seemed incredible.

He did not stop there. A couple of years later, he told me, one night in October 1963, he found himself washing glasses in the very nightclub where Yuri Gagarin, hero of the Soviet Union and the first man in space, was celebrating the first leg of yet another world friendship tour. Jenkins had a gift for detail. The motley quality of Gagarin's official retinue – every suit an arms supplier or party dilettante – was lent added spice by the invective he had saved up for their wives: monstrous, shot-putting hags obsessed with translating Neruda and Borges into Russian. He even had it in mind that the Playa Girón – the bay where a band of coral had, he said, been fatally mistaken for seaweed – later gave its name to the national honour the Cuban president Fidel Castro awarded Gagarin during this goodwill trip.

'He showed it to me, right there in the bar. Yuri did. His medal. And I showed him my scar. And Yuri laughed and told me, "You too wear the Order of Playa Girón!"'

I was tempted to ask what language they had used, that Jenkins could converse so freely with a Russian cosmonaut. Together with his highbrow literary references, so lovingly mispronounced ('Georgie Borkiss'), his story convinced me that I was in the company of a gifted imposter.

It was night by the time we were done, and the kerosene was running low in the lamp. I waited for Jenkins to lock up, and walked with him to where our vehicles were parked. My deepening silence should have warned him that the evening's game was up, but Jenkins could not resist further embroidery.

'Seaweed!' he laughed. 'Fuckers in American intelligence had it down for seaweed. Fucking *coral*, more like. I felt the deck lurch, the whole bloody boat started to roll, and I didn't hang around, I can tell you. I jumped, and it's a bloody miracle I didn't spit myself on the reef.' He thought about this and added, 'Some did.'

Jenkins's Land Rover was drawn up a few feet from where I had parked the Toyota. The moon came out from behind a cloud, and I saw that the Land Rover was leaning drunkenly to the right. Before I thought to stop him, Jenkins had walked over to investigate. He was still spinning his tale as he vanished into shadow. 'I heard them screaming in the dark. I tasted their blood in the water—'

There then came the sound I imagine a cricket bat makes as it strikes a cabbage, a thud as of a body falling into sand, and Jenkins was silent.

I charged like an idiot into the darkness.

I couldn't see a thing. Arms upraised, I swung about, hoping I might collide usefully with Jenkins's attacker. I stumbled and fell headlong. I tried to get up. Something buried itself in the sand by my right ear. I grabbed it. The stick came free without a struggle. I scrambled to my feet. I was afraid to swing the stick blindly, but then the assailant, disarmed, stumbled out of the vehicle's shadow into the moonlight. Austrian Boy, of course. I ran at him with the stick held point-first. It was a flimsy sort of weapon – the best the boy's fool mind could come up with in all the hours Jenkins and I had been drinking. I did what I could with it, punching him deep under his ribcage. Winded, he fell back another couple of paces. Jenkins was already up on his feet. He blundered past me and swung his clenched fist back and forth in front of the boy's face: his features disappeared in a splash of black blood.

'Jesus,' I said.

Jenkins turned past me. The boy was staggering blindly about the track, hands pressed to his face, holding it together.

I followed Jenkins across the sand. It was a magnificent night, the sky white with stars. At the water's edge, each wave gave a faint burst of greenish light as it rolled into the sand. Jenkins kneeled, oblivious to the water swilling round his knees, and washed the blood off his Stanley knife. He dried it fastidiously on his shirt.

I said to him, 'Don't do things by halves, do you?'

He ignored me, scooped up seawater in handfuls and threw it over his face, washing off the blood dribbling from the scratch on his scalp.

When he was done bathing his head he sank back on the sand. 'We never stood a fucking chance,' he said, his face empty of all feeling. I couldn't tell whether he meant tonight, or 16 April 1961. I didn't much care, either. The war had acclimatized me to Jenkins's brand of cheap violence, but it had not got rid of my distaste.

I helped him up and back towards the vehicles. The boy had vanished again. Once I had got Jenkins into the passenger seat of the Toyota, I turned on the cabin light and examined his cut. There was still blood running behind his ear and into the collar of his shirt, but the cut itself was trivial; the seawater had already begun to staunch the flow. I studied his pupils, and got him to hold out his hands for me. I found no sign of concussion. 'Sit tight,' I said.

Taking the flashlight with me, I went to check what damage the boy had done to his Land Rover. The worst I found were a couple of deflated tyres, but, when I returned to the pick-up, Jenkins had disappeared. I called and, when I got no reply, I seriously considered driving off and leaving him there. Every instinct told me I should leave this evening behind as quickly as possible.

Then I heard Jenkins ranting in bad Portuguese: 'What the bloody hell is the point?' His angry exclamation came to me muffled by distance. 'If I was a burglar you'd be dead by now!' Jenkins was fairly screaming. I turned my flashlight back on and shone it towards the bottle store. He must have gone round the back.

Another, unfamiliar voice replied, '*Eeh? Eeh, chiyani?* What? Where are they? I have a club! Look, I have a club!'

For the second time that evening, it sounded as though my host was being threatened. With a heavy heart, I approached the back of the bottle store. I found Jenkins towering over a small man by the side of a watchman's hut not much bigger than a kennel.

'Why don't you use the bloody *light*?' Jenkins shouted. 'You should be round the *front*.'

His watchman laughed at such absurdity. 'To light the burglar's way? They can't see in the dark, you know.'

'How are you meant to spot them, then? Wait till they trip over you? Look, you fucking idiot, *there's one out there now*. What are you going to do about him, eh?'

'The hut is here! I have my gun! I never sleep, I listen all the time.'

'Get out the front. He won't do you any harm, not now I've done your bloody job for you. Find him and get him to clear off.'

Jenkins noticed me waiting for him, and suddenly lost interest in his watchman. 'Oh, stay where you are, then. Get your throat cut, why should I worry?' Mumbling, nursing his head, Jenkins joined me and together we returned to my truck.

I mentioned his flat tyres, and since there had been no other visible damage to his vehicle, Jenkins, much recovered, took this as good news.

'It was so bloody dark we couldn't see a thing,' he said, as I dug about for my keys. He was picking up where he left off, practically mid-sentence. 'We were running into each other. Knocking each other down. Everyone was screaming. Most of us couldn't swim.'

After all that had happened tonight, I was losing my patience. 'If you were captured after the Bay of Pigs fiasco, if you were a convicted contra, how come a couple of years later you were working in a Havana nightclub?'

'That was the length of my sentence,' he said, surprised, as if the answer were self-evident. 'Twenty-two months in La Cabaña. Come on, I was only a kid, anyone could see that.'

He curled forward and bent his head for me to examine his shorn scalp, presenting me with incontrovertible proof of his story. 'There,' he said, playing his fingers over the cut the boy had dealt him. He wanted me to see something else, something beneath: the scar from a wound inflicted by an oar wielded by an outraged Cuban fisherman, twenty-six years before, on the day CIA-backed Cuban contras came to grief in the Bay of Pigs. 'Tottery old fucker, he was. Found me hiding in his boathouse.' Jenkins laughed, head still bent for my inspection. 'A sinking ship to escape from in the middle of the night, a fucking *reef* to climb over, couldn't see a thing, shells and bullets and God knows what whizzing everywhere, and this is my one and only battle scar.'

I could see that he needed a couple of stitches after tonight. What I couldn't see was any old war wound.

Jenkins sat up too fast, groaned and held his head. 'The shit must have clobbered me in the same place. Bloody feels like it, too – *there* he is...'

I had just that moment turned on my headlights. Austrian Boy was slumped some distance up the track, covered in blood. His eyes shone out of the mess of his face like two blue stones.

I drove towards him. Shock had made him stupid: he just sat there, waiting to be run over. I braked. 'Now what?' I said.

'All right, give me a hand.' We got out and went over to the boy. Jenkins took his arms and I took his feet. We ignored his keening and manhandled him into the bed of the Toyota. There were a couple of NGOs newly opened on the highway into town; if we dumped him in front of the right gate, some well-meaning Swedish doctor would see to him soon enough.

London – Johannesburg

September 1998

Heathrow. The airliner makes a lumbering turn, engages its engines and pushes TV and movie actress Stacey Chavez back in her seat.

The acceleration is oddly comforting, as the upholstery enfolds her stick-thin body, wrapping it away from harm, but the moment the plane leaves the ground, all this is lost and Stacey realizes she has made a terrible mistake.

(*'I wonder how you are,'* her father wrote to her recently, a quarter-century too late. How did he get her email address? *'The clinic didn't tell me anything. They just send me the bills.'* Moisés Chavez – a wanted man.)

Stacey is flying to Mozambique to film a short documentary about landmine clearance. Three years ago there were about three million landmines seeded across the country. How many remain to blow off a farmer's genitals here, an inquisitive toddler's head there, is uncertain; her producer Owen has already conducted interviews with a couple of the half-dozen organizations employed in mine clearance, and they have said that the problem will never entirely go away.

(Stacey claws at the armrests as the plane punches through pocket after pocket of dead air. She is afraid, not of flying, but of this sensation, this lurching and dropping which she associates, after years of illness, with the flutters of her starved heart.)

In twenty-four hours or less, Stacey Chavez will be standing in front of a camera, got up in the sort of protective gear – kevlar tabard, plastic visor – sported just last year in Angola by Princess Diana. Disaster is assured. She can see the tabloids now, feasting on the conjunction between her clothes-hanger body and a continent's starvation. (Her knowledge of Africa hardly extends beyond the Live Aid concert, and she imagines everyone there is chronically short of food.) She can rehearse in her own head, long before they are written, the ugly comparisons that will be drawn between her and Saint Diana. 'Who does she think she is?' they will say and people will snigger.

(*'I see your name in magazines but I don't believe them, I just look at the pictures. It looks to me like you're better now. Are you?'*)

There is, after ten years of self-starvation, no possibility of Stacey making a full recovery. If she is careful, her heart will not fail her just yet. But it *will* fail. A neat irony, this: the very moment you decide that you want to live, they tell you how many years you have shaved off your life. Yes, she has made a terrible mistake, and not even the attentions of Ewan McGregor can soothe away the fact.

He touches her wrist for the briefest of moments and gives her one of those how-are-you? smiles. His good looks are an affront. By his touch he has made her aware of her hand, and she rather wishes he hadn't: her hand, this pallid claw that is somehow attached to her and is, for some reason, her responsibility, its nails dug deep in the armrest's plastic padding. She lifts it, turns it, examines it: an unfamiliar domestic implement. McGregor, taking its movements for an invitation, takes her hand in his.

McGregor, the star of *Trainspotting* and tipped to play Obi-Wan Kenobi in Lucas's new *Star Wars* trilogy, is flying with Stacey as far as Johannesburg. Stacey Chavez has a three-hour stopover there before flying South African Airways to Maputo, the capital of Mozambique. Over the next couple of months, nine other celebrities will be flying to locations all over Africa. Their punchy, insistently upbeat documentaries will go to support a popular annual TV appeal.

A week before, Stacey's producer Owen sent her the rushes of their initial to-camera. The footage was worse than she'd feared. Who was that dead-eyed brat with her shock-white hair and her chemical tan? Could this really be her? Could those really be her thoughts? Every opinion she spouted came larded with junk words like 'exclusion' and 'branding'.

Owen's pre-fabricated style of documentary is ruthlessly efficient. Over gin and tonics in Blacks on Dean Street, Owen and Benjamin, their cameraman, have talked her through every shot. Each one of Stacey's sentiments and reactions is to be manufactured according to an already written plan. The technique will save a lot of time but this hurried style of rehearsal reminds her, ironically enough, of *Grange Hill*, the children's school soap opera which first launched her acting career. Stacey had been looking forward to something different.

The clearance programmes have lent a boom-town atmosphere to Manhiça, the town where they are filming. With all these foreigners around, Dutch and English and American, Benjamin wondered aloud, over his second G&T, how he was going to keep them out of his footage.

Stacey was slightly scandalized – she is unused to documentary and its compromises – and wondered aloud if this really mattered.

'One random white face and the whole thing's buggered,' Owen assured her, passing his expenses card to the waitress.

A television set domesticates whatever you happen to be watching. This is his theory. The exotic has to be pointed up, exaggerated, even manufactured, or the foreignness of their location – so obvious to them – will simply not translate to the screen. Neither Owen nor Benjamin expressed the slightest faith in the camera's ability to tell the truth.

The drinks trolley passes. McGregor insists they share one of those mini-bottles of champagne and, making conversation, slides unwisely into shop-talk. He asks her, 'Weren't you doing something for Amiel?'

Jon Amiel: director of *The Singing Detective*, back in the eighties. Look closely during the rendition of 'Dry Bones' in episode three and you will spot Stacey kick-stepping her way out of her five-year *Grange Hill* gig in a nurse's hat, white fishnets and a smile. Now Amiel is reinventing himself as a Hollywood action director. Stacey was his first choice for the part of the insurance investigator in *Entrapment*, a role since snapped up by Catherine Zeta-Jones.

'Events got in the way,' Stacey tells McGregor, fixing him with wide, black, mischievous eyes that, though sunken, have not lost all their glamour.

It is all a terrible, grotesque mistake, her being here, her doing this, and what makes it worse, she can't even blame her agent. Did she not burst into the offices of ICM, days after her return from Los Angeles and the eating disorders clinic, to demand work, exposure, media coverage, face-time? Begging for a second shot at the very life that knocked her down?

Looking back on her oh-so-promising past, Stacey senses its sterility. Even before she went to Hollywood, she had reduced her every passion to an ambition, every ambition to a career plan. By the time of her collapse she had stripped her life down so far it felt as though she had run her every permutation a hundred, a thousand times. No wonder death had seemed a welcome novelty; in that state of mind nothing, least of all success, could ever seem fresh or new or exciting.

(*'I want to be something to you now. You were doing so well before, I was only a liability. I hope you see that. I hope you see that things are different now.'*)

She has to find something else to do with her life. Something less fatuous.

'Who's having the special meal, then?'

The stewardess's interruption is fortunate. It is hard to know, otherwise, what response McGregor could have made to Stacey's candid reference to 'events'. He cannot possibly have remained ignorant of them. From *Variety* to *Hello!*, rags of every hue have anatomized the fall of Stacey Chavez, child star turned gymslip pin-up turned LA wannabe. Her collapse. The half-minute she lay flatlined on the gurney.

'The special? Ooh, that will be me.'

What saved her? If she knew that, then maybe this word 'recovery' would hold more meaning for her. If she had 'recovered her faith', for example. But she is not aware of recovering any sort of faith in anything.

It feels to her as if she simply woke up one day, found herself in hospital and decided that she was, after all, still afraid of death. Everything else – her gains in weight, her improved blood pressure, the ketones vanished from her urine – seem to have followed logically from that reawoken fear.

What kind of victory is that? It does not feel at all as though she is 'winning out over her condition'. It is rather as though she has simply swapped her love of death – so grand, so romantic – for the common-or-garden terror of it.

This sense of anticlimax is, she knows, part of her life now: a necessary consequence of her recovery from addiction. How shameful though, how embarrassing, to have to acknowledge that what she has been hooked on all this time is neither drink nor smack nor sex, but simply the glamour of her own will. Dying to please herself, she was larger than life. Actually having to live with herself, day after day – this is a harder, more humbling proposition.

(*Of course I heard about Deborah. I am truly sorry for everything. Not a day went by I did not think of her and of you.*' Moisés Chavez, absent husband, absent father, playing catch-up after all these years. '*I believe your mother had the very best care. Is there anything I can do for you?*' Though wanted by law enforcement on three continents, Moisés still contrives to pay his family's medical bills.)

'Is it special, then?' McGregor is still trying to get her into conversation.

'I'm sorry?'

'Is it a special meal?'

'Oh...' She cannot think how to respond. She casts around her compartmented plastic plate, looking for clues. She cannot think of a single thing to say that will not either embarrass or discomfort him. For instance, how the food on aeroplanes reminds her of the meals in the hospital, each portion so carefully presented, under foil, under plastic, the way a transplant surgeon might receive a donor's organ.

'Yes,' she says, and tries to laugh.

Her special meal. Stacey's circulation is geared by now to the meagre wants of a five-stone body, and her programme of weight-gain, painfully circumspect as it is, makes difficult demands of her ill-used vital organs. She will eat everything they put in front of her. This is the deal. She will neither toy, nor conceal, nor rearrange. Not that it is likely, so soon after treatment, that she will slide into her old, obsessive-compulsive behaviours.

('Call me. Please.')

It is much more probable, at this point in her recovery, that her shrivelled heart will explode.

Glasgow, UK

—

Friday, 12 March 1999

The receptionist wore an orange Jimmy-wig, a propeller tie and a big red nose. As I came in the door, he squeezed his nose at me. It squeaked.

I told him, 'I have a room booked. Saul Cogan.' I had gone back to using my real identity. I was beyond aliases.

'I am afraid your room is not quite ready, sir.' He made to squeeze his nose at me again, then thought better of it.

I said to him, 'Is this an airport hotel?'

'I am terribly sorry, sir.'

'Have you any idea how long I have been awake?'

'Your room would normally be ready for you, sir, only the staff are taking a little longer this morning.'

'Let me guess,' I said, 'the maids are wearing gigantic clown shoes.'

'Yes, sir!' he agreed, brightly. 'If you would care to wear a hooter today, sir,' he pointed to a cardboard tray piled with squeaky joke-shop noses, 'we undertake to contribute five per cent of your final bill to—'

'Look at my face.'

'It should only be a matter of minutes, sir. The breakfast bar is now open.'

I had spent almost a year working in places where the only food was *nsima*, a kind of gruel, with – as an occasional treat – Maggi instant noodles ('Asam Laksa Flavour'). I had had twenty hours or so of airline food with which to sate my yearning for all the tastes I had been going without. I had eaten everything the stewardesses had put in front of me. I licked the butter raw out of its tiny plastic ramekin. It was not enough. As soon as I entered that room and saw the laden tables, the fresh fruit, the ten different kinds of cereal, the serving bowls of prunes, dried figs, banana chips, mixed nuts, the cold-meat selection, the cheese-board, the tray of fruit-flavoured yoghurts, plain yoghurt, Greek yoghurt, I knew I was going to have to put all of it, everything, at the very least a little bit of everything, into my mouth.

Afterwards there was no point even trying to sleep, and I looked around for some amusement. There was a swimming pool; I liked the notion of standing about in warm water, relieved of my own weight. I could as easily have gone up to my room, assuming it was ready, and run a bath, but I was afraid I might fall asleep. I pictured myself choking on my own swill.

By the door to the pool area there was a keep-fit franchise. Though the hotel staff were bowed beneath the kosh of Comic Relief's Red Nose Day, the girl serving in the franchise had left her circus gear at home. The only swimming trunks she had left in stock were size XXL. They were fluorescent pink. 'Christ,' I said, handing her my card.

The pool was enclosed in a glass dome, the panes held in place by a complex spider-web of white-painted steel struts. The pool was an amoeboid shape that made 'lengths' impossible and off-putting displays of jock athleticism unlikely. The remaining space was filled with white plastic recliners and potted palms. There was one other guest, sat with her feet up on a recliner at the far end of the space, holding the hotel's standard-issue white terry robe tightly to her chin. Every so often she would take a moment to peck intently, one-handed, at a heavy black laptop computer.

I took a bathsheet from the pile by the door and tossed it onto a recliner far away from hers. Once I had found a deepish-looking corner I slipped into the water. The tiles beneath my feet were pimpled, anti-slip affairs that tickled all my cuts and sore places. Underwater light glanced off my trunks and lent the water a pleasant blush.

The water was so hot – practically bath heat – I could not stay in for long. After a desultory paddle or two I heaved myself none too elegantly out of the water. As I got to my feet I caught my neighbour's eye. The defensive way she was clutching her robe was belied by her smile.

I said, 'I just want to make it clear, these were the only trunks they had.'

She took a moment to study them. 'They do not necessarily reflect your opinions?'

'That's correct.'

'I am reassured.'

'I wouldn't want you to think that these trunks speak for me in any way.'

It began to rain. Raindrops driven against the hexagons and pentagons of the dome caused the structure to ring slightly. It was an exhilarating effect, and one the designers had probably not anticipated. 'I'm going to call for a drink. Do you want anything?'

She shook her head.

When my gin and tonic arrived she raised her eyebrows at me.

'It may be your morning,' I said, 'it certainly isn't mine.' I crossed to the recliner next to hers. The crow's feet at her eyes suggested a woman in her forties, and she had one of those perfectly preserved figures that childlessness gives some women.

She adjusted the fold of her robe and took her hand away from her neck. I set my drink down on the table between us and glimpsed, between her collar-bones, the start of a deep and beautiful scar.

She pretended to concentrate.

'What is that you're working on? Beyond the obvious.'

'As if I would stoop to a cheap gag like that.'

'As if.'

'It's a laptop.'

'You could not resist.'

'I felt a terrible compunction.' She set her laptop down beside my drink, loosened her robe and turned – all this in one fluid action. She headed for the pool and performed a goofy little dive: anything more dramatic, and she would have cracked her head on the bottom. She moved well through the water; her movements were so economical it was hard to see how they managed to propel her. When she was done, she pushed herself out on her arms. Her body had the sallow sheen one gets from regular indoor exercise. She walked back to her chair. The scar extended beyond the cut of her one-piece. It was a well-healed thing, perhaps from childhood. I wanted to trace it.

She dried herself off and belted herself into her terry robe. 'Can I have that back now?'

I was tapping at her keyboard, scrolling through the presentation she had been working on. 'Wait. I've nearly worked it out.'

'Really.'

'What this thing is.'

'Give it back.'

I lifted the laptop into her hands.

She closed the machine down and shut the lid.

I finished my drink. 'My room will be ready now,' I said.

'Is that some sort of invitation?'

'I like your aura of calm authority,' I said. 'I like how you move in water.'

'You want to know me better.'

'I can't ask you out for a drink, it's only ten in the morning. Anyway, you'll be gone in a few hours.' I gestured at the black box on her lap. 'According to your calendar.'

We left for our respective changing areas. I collected my card key from reception and went up to my room. There was a minisystem, but only one CD by Phil Collins. I tried tuning the radio, without success. When I turned on the TV it flashed up a greeting for Saul Coogan, whoever he was. I didn't expect her to knock.

When I found her there outside my door I said, 'You forgot your laptop.'

'I thought it might distract you.' She was dressed for leaving. She told me her luggage was already at the desk. It became clear that she was more practised at these encounters than I was.

She asked me what I did. I told her, with some necessary elisions, about the past year. About the camp at Al Ghahain, in the Yemen. About the Somali refugees I had befriended, and their plight. At some point her hand, which had slid from my knee to the crotch of my pants, ceased to move. She did not understand. Struggling to find some point of connection, she told me, 'In my sports centre, they let asylum-seekers in *for free*.'

'Asylum-seekers are not allowed to work,' I pointed out.

'*Exactly*,' she said.

I moved us onto safer ground. 'Your laptop,' I said, and while she talked I took off her clothes.

'It crawls from connection to connection,' she said. 'It closes the gaps between things.'

It learns who you are, she told me, and intuits the things you most desire. Which bottle of wine. Which book. Which holiday. Which human being. I took off her bra and took each nipple into my mouth.

The thing on her laptop was a search engine. This was her work, her reason for being. The crowning glory of a life of project management. Though she told me the project's name, I never saw it again, and I imagine both it and she fell victim to the stock crash which consumed her industry, just a few months later.

I laid her flat on the bed and lifted her arms above her head to stretch her scar. It ran at a slight diagonal from her throat to a point below her rib-cage. She told me they had cracked her chest when she was a baby, to plug a hole in her heart.

The cut had healed very well: the casual stroke of a tailor's chalk, splitting her in half. I knelt down to taste her, and, when she came, the scar flushed suddenly, a streak of red lightning under her skin. I traced it with my finger.

'The heart's signal,' I said.

She laughed. 'I can never fake.'

'A message from the heart.' I was determined to have my meaningful moment.

She told me some men wouldn't kiss her scar; or they would kiss it in a manner they fancied would not be noticed. Some pretended not to notice it at all. I understood why, when I first saw her, she had held her robe closed so tightly around her throat. It was to attract my attention.

I told her I wanted to pull her scar open. That I had this desire to touch what was inside.

Apparently I was not the first to say that, either.

We played each other like instruments, a finger here, lips there, with very little passion. She drew my foreskin down, wetted me with her mouth, and while she ran the palm of her hand in slow circles over me, she told me about her work and its philosophy. (She wanted me to know her work had a philosophy.) About webs and matrices. How things and people are bound together. About the shadow separating a desire and its satisfaction, and how that shadow is banished in the white glare of modern information technology.

'Now I want to fuck you.'

'Do you, now?' she said.

I reached over to the bedside table and fished a condom out of the packet. 'Make me wet,' I said. I held the back of her head while she did it, and then I put on the rubber and climbed on top of her. I wanted to see that white line go red again. I wanted to see that subtle, subterranean eruption along the old fault line: the halves of her yearning to separate. I slid inside her.

The door to the corridor opened and in walked a maid wearing a green fright-wig, a red nose, striped pantaloons and metre-long plastic overshoes.

'For Christ's sake,' I said.

The maid mumbled something about the door being open and hurried to leave. Her feet wouldn't let her turn around. She kept treading on them. Humiliated, she had to edge backwards through the doorway.

The interruption had ruined any chance that lightning might run through that scar a second time. Patting each other, reassuring each other, we abandoned the attempt. 'I need to freshen up,' I said, and locked myself in the bathroom, hoping that by the time I came out, she would be dressed again.

She was faster than I was: the room was empty when I emerged. I returned to the bed. She had straightened the duvet for me: a gesture with so little redeemable meaning, in the end I had to throw the thing off and lie on the bare sheet, just so I could stop thinking about *what it meant*.

I got out my mobile phone and laid it on the pillow beside me. There was still no call from Nick Jinks – Nick Jenkins, as I had first known him. (By the sixth month of our unlikely and profitable partnership, Jinks had drunkenly revealed his real name to me – but not his reason for changing it. That revelation would come later, and until then I more or less assumed that it was a seafarer's superstition that had made him keep Jinks a secret.)

I looked at my watch: why was I worrying? It was still far too early; the ferry wouldn't even have docked. I closed my eyes and tried a relaxing breathing exercise – something I had picked up, in spite of myself, from my long-haul's wakey-wakey prior-to-landing video.

She had told me how everything is architecture.

People, she had said, are the patterns they make.

People are rhythms, reverberating along the strands of an all-encompassing web.

I imagined myself embedded in her web of global connections, the futile syncopations of my gluey little feet, and fell asleep.

Portsmouth, UK

the same day

Fifty-seven-year-old former merchant seaman Nick Jinks rolls his juggernaut off the ferry and up the narrow causeway – tarmac over steel; the whole structure trembles – to the Portsmouth Harbour customs area. He shuts off the container's ventilation so as not to arouse the officers' suspicion, presents his paperwork, and waits.

Nick Jinks has travelled all over the world. In Havana, he has swapped jokes in bad Spanish with Yuri Gagarin. As he celebrated his twenty-eighth birthday alone in a jazz bar by the docks in Port-au-Prince, a man claiming to be John Kennedy's real assassin stood him a *mojito*, lacing it generously with cocaine from a silver spoon. He was in Port Canaveral, December 1972, closing the deal on a Cuban exile's sport fishing boat, in time to see a Saturn V booster carry Apollo Seventeen, the last ever manned moonshot, into orbit. He was in Auckland harbour in 1985, actually staggering along Marsden Wharf with a beer tin in his hand, the night the French secret service blew up the *Rainbow Warrior*. He has been brushed by newsworthy events. He has had more than his share of luck. But Nick Jinks has never acquired the knack of accumulation. What he earns, he spends.

Now, in his late fifties, Jinks wants an end to his seafaring life. He is weary of hard work and difficult hours, the identikit familiarity of ports, the insincerity of port women. He is nettled by the insolence of the young as they scamper up the merchant marine career ladder ahead of him, who never could be bothered to climb. He wants his boyhood before the mast to come to a stop before it is too late. He wants to put away childish things. He wants a wife. A kid. Even someone else's kid, whatever, he is not fussy. He wants to come home.

Saul Cogan, his long-standing business partner, has seen to it that he can return, without fear of arrest. Saul has even made it possible for him to enter the country under his own name.

The way is open to him, and Nick is beginning to wonder what, exactly, he is coming home to. Last time he was in the UK – trying on his real name for size, after nearly forty years of aliases; of Jenkinses and Jenningses, a Jiggins, a Jeves, a Jessup – he took the time to drive, in a rented car, past his boyhood home. The garage and the tea shop were gone, razed, a greenfield Tesco in their place, and the road that led him to the site of the erasure was itself a new thing: smooth, lit, signed, marked, cambered, mathematically curved, like the race-track on a computer game.

He pulled up in Tesco's car park and tried to get his bearings.

Curses perturb only those who are sensitive to them. It was impossible to believe that Tesco's greengrocery section would ever be troubled, as he and his father Dick had been, by fat, shit-coloured flies, wasps, rats, mysterious white galls. It was a different world.

As evening descends, Nick Jinks drives his juggernaut into the lorry park of a service station outside Carlisle. Three magic letters hang off the back of Jinks's lorry: T.I.R., 'Transport International Routier'. By international agreement, rigs with a T.I.R. certificate are exempt from customs inspections at national borders. It is generally agreed that there is little point chilling expensive foodstuffs down to a tidy minus five, if some bureaucrat with a clipboard is just going to open up the back of the van and let everything spoil in the dusty heat of the Spanish–Portuguese border. 'T.I.R.' is the people smuggler's favourite. Uncomfortable, but effective.

Jinks is practised enough at his business to know that he should not leave his vehicle unattended, so once he's washed and fed himself he leaves the service station, crosses the parking area and climbs back on board. In truth, spending a night on the lorry is not such a hardship. The driver's cabin is fitted for long-haul comfort. Nick turns the heater up full, draws the blinds over the insect-spatted windows and settles back to watch TV. There's a little colour set mounted off to one side of the cab. Reception is surprisingly good. The decent programmes haven't begun yet. It's still *London Tonight*. Nick is too exhausted to read (Juan Rulfo's *Pedro Páramo*; his Spanish has fallen away with disuse and he is finding the going very hard) and there is nothing else to do.

The early-evening magazine programmes offer up the usual mix of crime horror, community news and celebrity froth, and around 7.30 p.m. they segue, with disconcerting ease, into the antics of Red Nose Day's charity programming. On the promise of 'one hundred and one game lads and lasses going starkers for the nation', Nick Jinks holds fast to BBC1. He weathers Richard Wilson, and a Kate Bush medley. He even weathers Stephen Fry and Geri Halliwell in Uganda. After Boyzone's 'When the Going Gets Tough, The Tough Get Going' he is reaching for the off-switch when the screen goes dark for a moment and comes back to life on a place he knows: Manhiça, north of Maputo. He spent a while in hiding here, following the fiasco of 1969. Little seems to have changed, except that some scrawnier-than-usual celebrity is now picking her way along its dirt lanes and fly-ridden market.

Time to sleep.

Nick Jinks snaps off his portable television. He turns the powerful cabin heater down one notch, undresses, turns off the lights and climbs stiffly up into his bunk. He closes his eyes.

Nothing happens.

His eyes open.

His whole body is wired.

This is nothing new. Without a woman, he has never found sleep easy – not since he was struck on the head with an oar, the day he came ashore, a hapless seventeen-year-old, at Playa Girón. With weary resignation, he reaches down. He thinks of Manhiça, and the girls there. He thinks back to a time before his muscle turned to fat. Before fear of disease drew his zipper permanently shut. Before he lost his hair, and before his partnership with Saul expanded to its present, burdensome scale. He thinks about tits, comes, and closes his eyes.

Nothing happens.

Too tired to sleep, he figures. A long day. A rough crossing, and a busy road. Tomorrow shouldn't be so bad.

He closes his eyes.

There is a sound in the cab.

Movement. Scampering.

He struggles up onto his elbows to listen.

Nothing.

He lies back down again.

The sound is gone.

He still can't sleep. He reaches down a second time. His cock is slippery and disgusting. He manages somehow and lies back, waiting for a sour second wave of endorphins to carry him away.

Nothing happens.

He cannot remember when sleep finally overtook him. He wakes from troubled dreams, fingers aside the blind by his head. Sodium orange spills over his pillow. It is still dark out. What time is it? He has his watch on. He turns on the cabin light. Christ. Has he slept at all?

There is a sound in the cab. A scratching. Then, a thumping. Then, a scratching again.

He knows, now, what has kept him awake.

The familiar sound takes him back to his childhood home and his father, the old sea-dog Dick Jinks; back to the accident, and the terrible death at his hands which first drove him into exile.

It is the curse.

Even after all this time, the curse is alive. All these long years of his madcap absence, it has been waiting here for him.

Nick Jinks struggles into his clothes, lifts the blinds and takes his seat at the wheel. He turns the key in the ignition. He has to wait, agonizing seconds, for the diesel to warm. A thready keening fills his head. He stuffs fingers into hirsute ears. The light on the dash goes out. He turns the key, and the rig rumbles into life, drowning out the rat-sound of his curse. Roughly, wrestling the wheel, Nick Jinks hauls his rig back onto the A74. How far is Fort William? Eighty miles; a hundred at most. He will not stop again.

His foot comes down hard on the accelerator, though Nick Jinks should know by now that this is something he cannot outrun.

Chicago, Illinois

—

2.30 p.m., Saturday, 11 March 2000

Nineteen ninety-nine had been a bad year. Following Jinks's disappearance in March, I had had no choice but to dismantle the British end of the business. This inevitably meant that I owed favours. Relocating to the States, I had hoped to revive the fortunes of my moribund employment agency. But competition had grown fierce and word of my problems had arrived before me.

Blessing and Femi, my housekeepers for the northern states, fell foul of US Immigration at the beginning of March 2000, and there was no one on the books I really trusted to take their place. I debated whether to bring Chisulo and Happiness over from London. But they had their daughter to look after, and I had already asked too much of them.

Until I found somebody new, then, it fell to me to meet the arrivals we had already booked in for the spring. Arrivals like Felix Mutangi: I was there to greet him at the gate. It was a risky business, but no riskier than letting this son of the African soil wander alone through all the snares and brakes of late Western capitalism. I was pleased to hear that the paperwork I had prepared for him had seen him past the desk without a hitch. In the car, driving him to his motel and subjected to his boyish burbling, relief was added to pleasure: if he had had to open his mouth for any extended period he would surely have found himself on the first flight home.

He seemed hearty enough when I left him that evening, but the next morning when I picked him up he sneezed almost the moment he got in the car. I thought nothing of it at first; long-haul travel always leaves you feeling depleted. The sneezes did not stop. He was in his mid-twenties and, according to the medical report I had ordered, he was in good health. Still, even a head-cold could delay, by precious days, what we had planned for him. 'How are you feeling?'

'Fine, fine,' he grinned. He pulled out a packet of 555s and offered me one.

'They didn't tell me you were a smoker,' I said, waving it away. Where he came from, what twenty-something man didn't smoke? But I wanted to disconcert him a little; I wanted him to think about what we were doing, and what it would mean for him. The opportunities it represented. 'I don't know that the clinic's going to like you doing that,' I said.

Felix's smile was irrepressible. He wound down his window to let out the smoke. It was freezing outside. Literally: minus one according to the dashboard. He sneezed, spat and noisily inhaled the gasoline fumes of the promised land. Blood and urine tests were booked for 11 a.m. Assuming the authors of the medical report had not been altogether fraudulent, the operation would take place that night and by Monday Felix would be on a plane home.

The Stevenson expressway had other ideas: after half an hour's driving, just as we were passing under the Gilbert Road flyover, everything ground to a halt. I couldn't believe our ill-luck. The Tri-State Tollway was right ahead of us, straddling the expressway on an inclined curve. The whole arrangement of structures, piles and embankments here looked like something sculpted by the sea. We couldn't get near it. The feedlanes were barely half a mile away, and they might as well have been on the other side of Lake Michigan.

We were there so long we started picking up radio bulletins about the tailback building behind us, stretching far along the canal. It was a clear day, bitterly cold. The radio said something about a spilled load, and a couple of fire trucks, with lights but no sirens, slid sedately past us on the hard shoulder. I got out of the car, found my parka in the back and zipped myself up. I glanced around, looking for newscopters. This close to Chicago Midway it probably wasn't worth their while negotiating such a busy airspace. Domestic jets howled over our heads.

'Hiya.'

The voice seemed to come from above me; it made me start. I turned around. Beside my own rental there was a van. Not a pickup, or a people-mover; an honest-to-God van, with scratched blue panels and a faded campaign sticker: 'Vote John Gridley for US Senate'. Which was ironic, given that Gridley's lawyer was in the clinic even now, paying, in cash, for the senator's life-saving operation.

The woman in the passenger seat leaned out to speak to me. Her shock of short white hair was dazzling, her face was strangely sunken. At first I thought she was young – twenty-five or thirty – then that she was much older.

'I don't suppose you've got a cigarette?'

I leaned in through my window and got Felix to hand me his packet of 555s. I opened the packet and offered it to her.

'What are these?' she said. However unfamiliar she was with the brand, it wasn't going to stop her taking one.

There was a lighter inside the pack so I fired up her cigarette for her, cup-handed, shielding the flame from the wind. I handed it over. She smoked. Where it emerged from the cuff of her coat, her wrist was as thin as a child's. She did not cough, but she certainly changed colour. 'Jesus,' she said. She climbed down from the cab. Now I saw why I had not been able to guess her age. Her bright yellow North Face jacket hung off her as though from a peg. She was terrifyingly thin. It had to be an illness.

I glanced through the windscreen and glimpsed her driver: a porcine woman with a double-chin and dykish hair. I thought to myself: Laurel and Hardy.

'The radio said something spilled,' said the girl.

'Yes,' I said, teeth chattering. I lit a cigarette for myself, breaking a twenty-year pledge.

Felix got out the car and walked around, smiling his smile.

Things were in danger of degenerating into a social occasion. I tried to relax. I looked at my watch. Eleven fifteen.

'You're English,' she said.

Her own accent was a mid-Atlantic thing I couldn't pin down.

My Englishness seemed to fascinate her; I couldn't work out why. Poor Felix didn't get a look-in. She seemed to want me to reciprocate her interest and, since it was a good way of not talking about myself or my passenger, I asked her where she was going. This was all the prompting she needed. She leaned back into the truck and came out again with a couple of flyers for us. 'I'm opening tonight,' she said, 'if we ever bloody get there.'

Was the English swear-word for my benefit?

It was only as she climbed back into her van that it occurred to me: she was familiar for some reason.

The flyer was headed *SCTV02*, and underneath there was a picture of a bubble. There was something odd about that bubble. I unfolded the flyer, revealing the rest of the photograph: a hand was holding a disposable cup, and a trail of misshapen bubbles had spilled from the rim of the cup and were hanging in the air.

The bubbles were water, floating in air.

The photograph had been taken in space.

I went to see her show. There were no films I especially wanted to see, Jonny Lang had sold out at the Rialto Square weeks before and I couldn't think what else to do with my time. Felix was in good hands, and I would be seeing him in the morning.

If the venue for *SCTV02* had been some left-field place I might not have gone, but back at the hotel I read the flyer properly and discovered it was playing early at the Museum of Contemporary Art opposite Jan Svankmeyer's *Alice*. I figured if I didn't like the one I could go and watch the other and still have time to hunt down a decent meal.

The woman's name was Stacey Chavez and I understood why my Englishness had intrigued her. From her potted biography I learned that she had been a British TV star. Hearing my accent, she had expected me to recognize her.

Perhaps this was arrogant of her, perhaps not: I had found her vaguely familiar, after all, even though her active years coincided with my time in Mozambique. I had never seen *The Singing Detective*. I had never seen *The Moth*. I had no idea, come to that – beyond the none-too-subtle clues buried in *SCTV02* – how or why a mainstream actress came to be creating intricate, difficult and (for my money) downright unenjoyable performance art for a Chicago museum.

The premise was simple: in space, everything floats, so it is very difficult to eat and drink. Afterwards I couldn't tell whether Stacey's performance, a weird fusion of mime and dance and gesture, had gone over my head, or whether what I had seen was really all there was to get: the sterile white set, part hospital, part spaceship interior; plates that would slip out from under her hand; cups that hovered above her, just out of reach; the pink 'space food' she squeezed into her mouth from an upended detergent bottle.

I had had a belly-full of art for one evening, and rather than repair to the MCA bar – wall-to-wall twenty-somethings in tea-cosy hats – I braved a snow flurry and walked the couple of blocks to the nearest dive.

There was an old episode of *Cheers* running on a TV above the plasticated bar, as if to emphasize the degree to which this watering hole failed to live up to tourist expectation: characterless beer, sterile wood-effect surroundings, bar staff who bore all the behavioural stigmata – bright smiles, gimlet eyes – of some sort of customer-service boot camp. Everything designed and arranged so as to convince us that nothing bad was going to happen. No wonder the people around us were hardly drinking.

The door opened, letting in the cold. I glanced around, and there was Stacey Chavez. When she got to the bar I pointed to the show on the TV

– Kelsey Grammer sparring with Rhea Perlman – and said to her, 'In Rio, meanwhile, the swimsuit boutiques have "The Girl from Ipanema" on a tape loop.'

It took her a moment to remember me. 'Did you see the show?' she asked me.

'I saw the show.'

'You didn't like it.'

I shrugged. 'Was I supposed to?'

'Oof,' she said, miming a blow to the head.

I was growing used to her thinness. I was able to look beyond it, to fill in the gaps, as it were. To see the skin above the skull. This made her seem more familiar. She had a big-featured face, hawkish, striking more than beautiful. Not very kissable. A TV face – distinctive enough to survive the flattening effect of the lens, symmetrical enough not to repulse.

She said, 'I was walking down Southampton Row – Bloomsbury – you know London at all? I passed this place: "Virginia Woolf's Burgers, Kebabs and Grills".'

'Where's your driver?' I asked her.

'Back at the hotel. We're not a couple.'

'Do people assume that?'

'People have dirty minds.'

I had stolen Felix's pack of cigarettes – I figured he had plenty more – and offered her one.

'I remember these,' she said. 'Aren't they African?'

'Among other places.'

'I tried smoking these in Mozambique one time.'

Had I met her in Mozambique? Surely I would have remembered. But the truth turned out to be more banal. She told me about a documentary she had gone out there to make, a mine-clearance appeal, and I remembered that I had, after all, seen her on TV, exactly a year before, as I lay on my bed in a Glasgow hotel room, draining the mini-bar, waiting for Comic Relief to be over and for Nick Jinks to ring. Not a night to remember with great fondness – though it maybe explained why her image should have lodged with me.

We talked about Chicago, and she explained how she had timed her tour so that she could sort out legal wrangles to do with her mother's estate. 'She was only forty-six,' she told me, out of nowhere. She had things she needed to tell somebody.

I listened, or I appeared to be listening – I had my own troubles at this time – and afterwards I was rewarded with a dinner invitation at a place Stacey had learned about on the internet.

It seemed incongruous, her inviting me out to eat. First there was the age difference: I was nearly sixty by then. Second, there was the whole, vexed business of Stacey and food. Her fingers, curled for support around her whiskey glass, were knobbled and grey. When she gestured, the sleeves of her knitted shrug flapped as though hung off wires. Still, she made the place's huckster style sound inviting. 'Then there's Halley's Comet,' she said.

'Halley's Comet?'

'Gin martini. But I prefer their Super Nova.'

'Which is?'

'Vodka martini. Only they stuff the olive with blue cheese.'

'Jesus Christ.'

So it was, later that same evening, that we made our entrance – a starlet and her sugar-daddy – down the carpeted stairs of Lovell's of Lake Forest.

At the bottom of the stairs a small, athletic man glad-handed the patrons as they arrived. Any urge I might have had to giggle at the restaurant's gen-you-wine NASA memorabilia or its novelty martini menu was hereby instantly quashed: this was James Lovell, in the flesh, the veteran of Apollos Eight and infamous Thirteen.

The Ron Howard film had come out a few years before, the one with Tom Hanks as Lovell. I'd seen it on a long-haul flight someplace –

I don't remember where. Since then, Stacey told me, the locals had been queuing up to gobble down his son Jay's modern American cuisine, in hope of meeting Dad. Lovell, for his part, showed his face every few days so as not to disappoint; as we entered the bar he was guiding a family of Gary Larson characters to a coffee table made out of a relief map of an Apollo landing site. A chore for him, or a pleasure? His laugh was higher pitched than I would have imagined. Infectious. But you can't go by smiles or body language; these men are professionals.

Jim Lovell: the man had survived explosion and asphyxia and risked abandonment and slow death in deep space, but had never set foot on the moon. According to Stacey, the fact still rankled with him, even after all these years. (She had read his book, among many others, doing research for her show, and spoke as though she had some knowledge of him.)

I watched Lovell moving about the room, marrying the man to Stacey's words. Yes, it rang true, that here was a man prepared to admit to a single, defining regret. I did not know what attracted her to this idea, or how true it was. But I approved of it, on principle as it were. To compare Lovell's experiences with mine would be pointless, even laughable. Still, I fancied I too knew something about survival; about the double-edgedness of it, and the hollow feeling that comes over you sometimes, on sleepless nights, that you are living beyond your time.

Lake Forest, Illinois

—

the same day

·

In the dining room of Lovell's in Lake Forest, just outside Chicago, an alarmingly thin girl shares a candle-lit dinner with a man old enough to be her father. Jim Lovell has seen her before; is she a model? Her companion, a taciturn Englishman with a weathered face and uneasy eyes, has ordered the trio of pâtés with jellied onions and cornichons followed by sliced duck atop a vivid huckleberry reduction. She has ordered – nothing. She has brought in her own food. There it is on her plate: a muffin, as brown and unappetizing as a turd.

Watching her eat is like watching somebody drown. It's all Jim can do not to go over and shake her. Hard. Snap her out of it somehow. And he can imagine the headlines in the *Sun-Times* if he did: 'APOLLO VETERAN ASSAULT SHOCKER'.

Jim Lovell steers himself out of the restaurant. Let the poor folks eat their meals in peace. He heads for the office and moves his chair from behind the desk, over to the radiator. Just looking at her makes him feel cold. Chilled right through. Not a metaphor. He's really shivering.

Don't anyone tell him it's his age, neither. You don't play the 'You are Old, Father William' card on a man who's only just got back from the Antarctic. Five weeks at -10°F – and that was the temperature *inside* the tent – all to find bugs that might flourish on Mars. Really, he is too old for this shit.

Her shrunken face. Her claw-like hands. Jesus, no, he doesn't want to shake her, they'd be picking pieces of her out of the carpet for weeks. Whatever's holding her together must be as weak as wet cardboard by now. What should be wires under the skin turned to taffy. He doesn't want to think about it.

How does she manage to sleep? The waiter had to bring her a cushion, her rear end was too bony for the chairs. What does she lie on at night, that her bones don't jangle her awake? How does she keep warm?

Jim climbs out of his chair, pushes it away and sits on the floor, leaning his back against the radiator. It's scalding hot, and even through his clothes, the skin of his back puckers. He luxuriates: leans away, settles back, leans away, settles back. Should take a shower, he thinks. Warm up properly. But he can't bear the thought of having to take off his clothes.

He shakes his head. Pathetic. A month ago he was braving white-outs in the Patriot Hills. What is up with him? What has changed in him since he returned, that the cold seems to come at him, not from the outside any more, but from within, from his own bones?

Jay, his son, has a theory. (And incidentally, how on earth did the kid persuade him to buy into the restaurant business? Was there ever an occupation so grinding, so thankless?) Jay reckons he still hasn't got over the corpse they found in the ice.

Jim struggles to his feet. As if this was the worst he had ever faced! Jay should know better than to spout the philosophy of daytime TV at him. Yet…

Jim makes his excuses to the staff, finds his coat, heads outside, gets in his car, turns the heater up full, starts the engine, begins the journey home.

And yet.

(Darkness strobed by streetlights. This might be anywhere. The streetlights stop. No stars. All dark. He is thinking: Where is my ship? Where is the *Shangri-La*?)

Ever since Antarctica, things and people have started to acquire a family resemblance. Nothing is just itself any more; everything suggests an unconnected something else. The last time he experienced this muddy sort of thinking was following a particularly brutal centrifuge exercise. (The memory comes cluttered with medical buzzwords:

carbon dioxide poisoning; G-strain anoxia.) It's like the world is melting around him. Why should a girl with an eating problem remind him of a dead sailor, any more than a dead sailor should remind him of a live sailor, a sailor he met, large as life and definitely living, on the streets of Punta Arenas?

This was their jumping-off point: a sterile little township at Chile's southern tip. The polar microbe hunters had a week in Punta Arenas to arrange their gear, to check and recheck their supplies and equipment; above all, to wait. Jim didn't mind. It felt good to be working towards a target again. Missions are like charmed little lives: their purpose is pre-ordained, they are rich in intense experience and (God willing) they end happily. More happily than real life ever can.

The sailor, muffled against the cold in a threadbare black parka and thin knitted gloves, noticed him from across the snowbound street and recognized him for all his winter clothing. He just shambled right on up to Jim in the street and spoke to him, big-eyed and awestruck.

He was a big man so when Jim shook his hand the feel of it – its smallness and fragility – frightened him. The man's features were small, too. They were a woman's features – no, a doll's. Beautiful and cruel. Jinks, he introduced himself, in an English accent.

Nick Jinks.

They made, to begin with, a sort of over-serious smalltalk typical to extreme places. In Punta Arenas, everybody seems to be making a documentary about everybody else, and even the sportsmen and climbers couch their hiking plans in the rhetoric of the study trip. Jinks knew all the teams, but he didn't seem to belong to any of them. He claimed to have drifted in one day – and he didn't seem in any hurry to leave. The man seemed a throwback to the Antarctic's brutal beginnings, years of whaling and sealing, frostbite and trench foot and filthy cabins lit by penguin oil.

Jinks wanted to know if there were any rats on board Apollo Thirteen.

'Come again?'

How did they keep the rats off the ship?

'Well, I don't think—'

That main B bus undervolt which was the start of all their peril – could it have been the work of a rat?

Jim extricated himself as fast and as pleasantly as he could.

In Ellsworth Land, Antarctica, and especially on the Patriot Hills, you can find bubbles in solid ice, sometimes in strings like a diver's air bubbles, and in the summer, when the sun shines continuously, a liquid film forms on the inside of the bubbles, and things in the water begin to grow.

It is -20°F without windchill and Jim Lovell is out here looking for *bubbles*. He feels as clumsy as an infant in his cheery standard-issue red parka, and his hands, snug in layers of polyfleece and wool and leather, feel as useless as paws, when a sudden, unbelievably chill gust nearly takes him off his feet.

Instinctively the team huddle together like penguins under the onslaught of the wind.

Wind whips snow into the air. It is old snow: Antarctica is a desert, and precipitation falls as rarely here as it falls on the Sahara. The granules, ground against each other over decades, are so tiny they will penetrate the weave of rucksacks and the walls of tents. The team leader has them rope themselves together. Any second now, visibility is going to vanish. Really vanish. (Back in Chile, during their familiarization programme, the instructor had them put white plastic buckets on their heads to simulate the effects of white-out.)

Careful, groping, blind mice, the team edge down the slope towards their camp.

How they missed the body on the way out is no mystery. A thin skein of snow would have been enough to conceal him completely. The fierce wind has revealed ice that would be blue were there any sun. Now it is as black as jet.

There he is, inside the ice.

Jim's cry is inaudible in the gale. Katabatic winds – flash floods of cold thick air, spilling from rocky pockets in the highlands, fierce as waters and unimaginably colder – steal his words away. Finally the rope translates his sudden stop to the others of his team. Careful, purblind, they gather round. Jim kneels.

It makes no sense. This man here in the ice. Each inch of ice is an eon of human time. How can this man be buried here, arms spread as though he were treading water, head straining for the surface, eyes open, a trail of bubbles from his screaming lips?

They have to leave him, then. Nothing they can do in this wind. Nothing they can do, period. The next day, they cannot retrace him. They do not try hard, or for long. No way can they dig him out from under all that ice and anyway, what would be the point? In the fug and fabric-whip of their igloo-like Scott tents, the men talk out what they have seen. It must be the body of some early casualty of exploration, interred now in a grander coffin than any undertaker can provide.

A week later, in the relative warmth and comfort of the Amundsen–Scott station at the Pole, Jim Lovell and Skylab astronaut Owen Garriott sing for their supper; they glad-hand the residents and give talks about their experiences. Shouldering his burden ('veteran astronaut and motivational speaker') Jim stands and, without notes, begins his address.

But to be upright in the ice, one knee up and one knee straight, head tilted back like that, the ice so clear?

Jim, standing there before them all – the ultimate captive audience – falls silent. To cover his confusion, he takes a drink of coffee. Where is he up to? What was he talking about? Apollo Eight? Thirteen? It's Thirteen everybody wants to hear about, not least because of the movie. He doesn't mind. It's a decent movie. Is he so precious that he should look such a gift-horse in the mouth? Heck, no, the film's put him back in demand. Would he be here without Ron Howard? Well, yes, for certain – but the expedition sure wouldn't have gotten a plug from CNN.

They have logged the body, as well as they can, with the search and rescue people, and together they have agreed not to rehash the episode in front of the press. Besides, death and dereliction rarely make it out of the back pages this far south of the sixtieth parallel.

Now where was he?

Apollo Eight? Apollo Thirteen?

His audience wait expectantly.

Jim fakes a cough and takes another sip of coffee.

Gemini Seven maybe. Nobody's very interested in Gemini Seven. Not when the talk is only an hour long and they know that Thirteen, the explosion and NASA's most testing hour is still to come. It's not cynicism that makes him think this. He's been at this racket long enough to know what makes a good story and what doesn't. The sad fact is that it's very hard to make Gemini Seven exciting. The way everything, but everything, started packing up around them. Thrusters. Fuel cells. Poor Frank Borman, with a commander's tunnel vision, just itching to twist that abort handle, and who could blame him? Still, they hung in there, waiting for Stafford and Schirra to turn up in Six. Fourteen days in a capsule that, hour by hour, malfunction after malfunction, came to resemble a floating toilet cubicle.

Gemini Seven. The one he never gets to talk about. The one, therefore, that has come to haunt him more and more.

Rising through a calm black ocean, this steel bubble of ape life.

Winter comes. The sun is gone in now. Blue ice turns black. The film of water round each air bubble freezes solid, killing everything inside. There is no colour anywhere. Life stops.

Hoar-frost on the rations in the *Odyssey* command module. Conditions aren't much better in *Aquarius*. (Is this where he is now? Is this where he is up to – Apollo Thirteen, the lunar module their lifeboat, and nothing to do but wait?) He is speaking. The audience is leaning forward, rapt. Now and again, there is laughter. He wishes he could grasp the meaning of the words as they slide, smooth and practised, out of his mouth.

Nick Jinks, the strange Englishman who had approached him on the street in Punta Arenas, was gone by the time they returned, five weeks later, on the first leg of their long journey home. Nobody in town knew of him or remembered him.

So Jim, unable to find any evidence to contradict it, has had to carry this impossible image around with him ever since, unable to shake it free, unable to discount it: that the man in the ice *was* Nick Jinks. That Nick Jinks somehow fell into the ice. Which is the same as saying, that he fell into time. Jinks's pretty, cruel, close-set eyes stare out at Jim from the unimaginable past. His mouth, in rictus, mimes a ghastly *Eeeee!* In boots that look modern – not seal-skin, but plastic – Nick's right foot is raised to step on a sabre-toothed tiger's tail; the left, toe pointed, tests the warm waters of the Cambrian.

There is no *Shangri-La*. Where is the fucking *Shangri-La*?

Jim fumbles behind the steering wheel for the light switch and fills the unlit Lake Forest road with light. The dashboard comes alive, a soft green glow. Windscreen wipers squeal back and forth. Jim snaps them off with a curse that becomes an instant chuckle: in his eighth decade, he can freely admit that he's never been particularly good around buttons and switches. (He'll never forget the dirty look Frank shot him in Apollo Eight, the time he accidentally inflated his life jacket.)

Beyond the immediate splash of illumination cast by his head-lamps, the world is a ghostly grey, no colour anywhere. But Jim Lovell is a professional. With a set smile and eyes tuned to the colours of the world, the greens and the reds, the instruments and signs, Jim Lovell, bubbled in steel, steers his way home as he has steered his way home before, across unimaginable distances, across oceans of night, through the deep black calm of death.

THE GIFT

1

Summer 1939.

The British government believes that an air war will destroy civilization.

It has forecast the number of casualties likely to be sustained following a Luftwaffe attack on London. The numbers are apocalyptic. Bleaker still is Whitehall's estimate of the city's psychological resilience. Analysts believe the experience of bombardment will send the survivors mad.

Hospitals surrounding the capital have sent home their non-urgent cases. They are making up beds ready for tens of thousands of 'nervous cases'.

The government believes that following an air attack, survivors who make it into the city's tunnels will refuse to emerge; that they will turn their backs on the devastated Overground, preferring to live and breed beneath the earth, a Morlock terror to the Eloi above. In London, the Underground is locked at night against those who would seek shelter, come the raids.

Nineteen-year-old former abattoir clerk Kathleen Hosken knows better. She has inside information. With halting fingers, Kathleen has typed up data which even the government has yet to read. She has worked with the government's own specialist on a project to assess the physiological effects of ground shock waves and blast, a man of such luminous intelligence and charm his associates have nicknamed him 'Sage'.

From Sage, she has learned that if you look into the eye of the thing you most fear, and replace your passion with a rational curiosity, then the horror – he calls it 'funk' – goes away. So Kathleen Hosken has left the rain-swept border country of Darlington, and has boarded a train for London, the soon-to-be-devastated metropolis. This journey to the epicentre of the coming war is not just a journey of necessity – a search for employment and a place to live. It is also a test she has set herself. She believes that if she approaches her life there rationally, carefully interrogating her every assumption, then she can protect herself, even from bombs and fire storms.

The men sharing her train carriage – the crooked teeth their smiles reveal, the Players and Capstan cigarettes they offer her – are objects for observation. From Sage, she has learned something about the scientific method. This novel way of thinking requires her to suppress her emotions and to put herself at a distance from things. Besides, she does not smoke.

Some of the men on the train are in uniform. Most are not: volunteers, they have yet to be received into the service. There is a camaraderie between the two groups which marks them out from the handful of young, scrape-faced commercial travellers who also share the carriage.

'The air's sweeter over here, love.'

'There's room to stretch your feet by me.'

'I'm a Darlington man meself, dearie, come and have a chat.'

They are teasing her. She is being offish with them and she isn't pretty enough, and not nearly well dressed enough, to get away with it.

'Cat got your tongue?'

'He joined up already then, love?'

'Tore himself away, he did, from the sparkling ray-pah-tee.'

They laugh.

Kathleen takes a steadying breath. She thinks up an experiment – and smiles softly, knowingly, to appease them.

A lad with infected acne lets out a cheer. The company of friendly elders has made him boisterous. 'Knew you could do it, love!'

She notes, for future reference, the success of her strategy. She has identified, confronted and resolved a problem in her human relations. For the first time in her life, the boys have not made her cry.

She remains – for all their barracking – in the seat she has chosen for herself, riding backwards, facing west. She is looking her last at the moorland of her childhood. More than that: she is looking out, past barren scarps and low stony ridges, over long-abandoned dry-stone walls and between hawthorns stunted by the wind, for the remains of a series of sheds. Given the lie of the land, it is only by facing backwards to the direction of travel that she will be able to spot them.

That these sheds have been visible from passing trains at all is an error Sage made early on in the project, when he misread the contour lines on his Ordnance Survey map. He spotted the error while studying the map for other sites, and before the sheds were ever erected – a feat of magic which amazed Kathleen at the time. The error was tiny, however, and Solly Zuckerman, Sage's colleague and keeper of the project's top-secret experimental menagerie, persuaded him to let it go.

Kathleen remembers her first train ride with Sage. Since going to work for him, she had persisted in calling him Mr Arven, and he was teasing her, telling her that, since he was a professor, she should call him 'Professor Arven'; that he had letters after his name and, since she was so fond of honorifics, she 'ought to recite them, an' all'. Abruptly, he had broken off his jesting and took out his watch. He paused a moment – he appeared to be counting – then he glanced at the window. He took her hand and pulled her with him onto the seat opposite, facing backwards.

'I feel sick this way,' she protested. He did not reply. She wondered when he would let go of her hand. Instead, he squeezed it, painfully hard, and pointed out the window: 'Watch... watch now... There!'

Far in the distance, Kathleen glimpsed the frameworks of their oh-so-secret sheds.

Mr Zuckerman – *Professor* Zuckerman – was quite right: even as they registered on the eye, they were gone. There was no real risk of discovery.

'Feckit!' Sage exclaimed.

She smiles to think of it. The boy with the infected face comes and sits beside her. Her smile has been misinterpreted as a reply to something he has said, which she has not heard. He flicks a cigarette jauntily into his mouth but fumbles the catch, so for a moment the cigarette hangs precariously between prehensile lips. His erupted face boils over in a blush. He thrusts the cigarette pack under her nose.

'No, thank you,' Kathleen says. She turns back to the window. *Watch... Watch...*

It seems the sheds have been dismantled.

Thick clouds of tobacco smoke press white hands against the window.

School ended for Kathleen when she was fourteen. Working in her uncle's office at the abattoir was undemanding. There were clerks employed to tally the animals brought to slaughter, to calculate the number of different cuts, to calculate wastage, the company's profits, the workers' wages. There was a secretary, a long-nosed woman, no longer middle-aged, who saw to her uncle's business correspondence. For Kathleen, there were files to keep in order; 'to do' lists to type for her uncle; wages to hand to the boys who worked on the cutting floor; errands to run in town. Now she has left, Kathleen understands that her uncle employed her, above all, so that he might see her from time to time. He had played no real role in her childhood – the consequence of some nebulous rift between him and his brother, Kathleen's father.

Shortly after her father walked out for good, her uncle visited her and her mother at home. She has a vague memory of being sent upstairs by her mother; of lying on her bedroom floor and pressing her ear to a crack between the boards. If she heard what her uncle said, she has no memory of it.

She understands, now that she is leaving, that her uncle enjoyed her company, that many of the errands and tasks he set for her were made up so that the two of them might spend time together when by rights they should both have been working.

She remembers making blood puddings with him. 'We waste hundreds of gallons of blood a year, Kathleen. Well, what can we do about this? How can we turn this wastage into profit?' Whatever they were up to – visiting a neighbour's farm, experimenting in the firm's huge galley kitchen, taking drives through the country – he had a way of describing the activity so that it seemed important to his business.

'The blood'll splash my dress,' she protested.

'Nonsense.' Her uncle's dark, friendly features wobbled uncertainly towards what he thought was a 'business-like' expression. He looked as though he were sucking a boiled sweet.

He brought her an apron – a long one, it reached almost to her feet – and helped her lift the bucket. Together they strained the pig's blood through a muslin cloth into a pan, and added spices, oatmeal, fat in tiny dice. He showed her how to fill the casing, how to tie it off. Everything had to be a bravura performance with him, even the making of puddings. 'Here, you try!' She was afraid that she might mark her clothes, her shoes. What would her mother say? He could not persuade her. He shook his head, and did the job himself. She watched him, and though it was a trivial thing, she felt that she had let him down.

When the puddings were done, he lifted one from the boiling water by its string, laid it on a board, and cut it through with a knife. It was light like a soufflé. Delighted, he told her to fry some up for them. She did not know how. He showed her, dripping a knob of lard off a butter knife into a hot pan: 'You cook this at home, surely?'

Tongue-tied, she shook her head. He set places for them. He sat her down, adjusting the chair beneath her, as though she were in a hotel. She blushed.

'Eat up!'

She speared a mouthful with her fork. The black blood melted on her tongue.

*

On the bus home, and as usual, the Bridgeman boys – George and Robert, brothers, apprentice slaughtermen, who lived at the end of her street – came and sat behind her. They sniggered at her, and one of them said something disgusting about her and her uncle. She knew nothing she could say would heal their resentment of her: their boss's favourite, his poor relation.

As the bus rolled over the bridge into the village, the bigger of the boys dug about in the pocket of his trousers and produced a twist of bloody paper. He unwrapped it, leaned over and dropped a pig's eye into Kathleen's lap. Kathleen leapt out of her seat, speechless, pale with disgust. The smaller boy practically fell off his seat for laughing. 'Oh George,' he cried, and patted his brother on the arm, 'th'art a proper one!'

Her mother scolded her. 'I'll never get it out,' she snapped, scrubbing at the bloody mark on Kathleen's dress. 'I never shall. It's quite ruined.'

Kathleen mentioned the puddings and lied about how the stain was made: a splash, she said, an accident. While she talked she wrapped her arms around her body. She was cold without her dress.

'Put your hands by your sides,' her mother said.

Kathleen did as she was told.

'Stand up straight.'

The dress was a good one. The sun had set by the time the surface of the material gave way under her mother's scrubbing brush. Kathleen's mother sat at the kitchen table and cried a while, absently tearing threads from the dress she had ruined.

Kathleen stood with her hands by her sides. She did not move. She did not make a sound.

When she was done destroying the dress, Kathleen's mother began her nightly clean of the kitchen. She boiled water in a pan. She added soap flakes. She scrubbed the stove. She scrubbed the table. She swept the floor and scrubbed it. She boiled up more water in a pan. She scrubbed the pan. Knowing her daughter had handled blood, she scrubbed at Kathleen's hands till they were raw.

Kathleen's mother kept the kitchen clean. The pans and plates shone, then she put them away in deep drawers, and the drawers, too, she kept them clean. Each knife was sharp, unblemished: 'Don't touch.'

That evening, because of the dress, and the time taken to clean it, and the time taken to establish that it was altogether ruined – the time spent mourning it, in fact – there was no supper. Normally, supper consisted of tea, bread and butter.

By morning, however, her mother's mood had improved. Night-time had wrought its necessary revisions upon the events of yesterday. It was the shoddy dress at fault, that would not clean up. It was her uncle's fault, that he was careless: 'Why, you might have been *scalded!*'

Her mother's mood was so solicitous, Kathleen dared to ask her for a second slice of bread. Mother laughed. 'Little piglet,' she said. 'Greedy little piglet ears.' It was true: Kathleen was always hungry.

Rather than give her a second slice, Mother poured her a glass of milk. 'Drink up,' she said, 'it's good for you.' There was a tap in the kitchen. She ran the jug under the tap, thinning the milk out for another day. The milk was never actually bad, but the jug lent it a certain sourness.

'Drink up, love, you'll be late.'

Sometimes there would be jam. Never anything hot.

During the weeks of the experiment, John Arven – the man his friends called 'Sage' – took lunch at an isolated pub, about a mile away from the sheds. He drank weak ale and ate sandwiches: huge doorsteps of white bread crammed with thick strips of baked ham. A piece of ham, ointment pink, fell out the bottom of his sandwich onto the table. 'Pitch in, lovey,' said Arven, handing her a sandwich.

Her blush was deep and prickly like a fever.

Arven was curious-looking. His nose hung down as a continuation of his forehead, like the guard on a helmet. This arrangement gave a certain power to his eyes, which were forever laughing and always focused on you. He had dreadful bouffant hair in which he took great pride; she could smell the dressing he used from where she sat. His clothes were unpressed and he hardly ever wore a tie. He talked incessantly, his voice rising to accommodate the broad Lancashire vowels he had picked up at school.

Kathleen swallowed down slivers of crumbly, juicy ham. She forced herself to eat slowly: first her uncle's pudding, now this ham – her shrunken stomach did not know how to handle it all.

'Mr Hosken says you're good with figures.'

Kathleen folded her hands on her lap and nodded. She expected a test. She was ready.

'Do you see 'em?'

He met her blank look. 'Figures, I mean. Only when a chap is good with figures, quite often – this is my experience – he sees them. As colours, as shapes. It's not a question of thinking. It's a question of looking. The inner eye. You know?'

She shook her head, abashed. Amazing, that he should have guessed, that he should have seen so far inside her, to where her private colours lay. 'No,' she said.

'It's a bloody business,' Arven warned her, walking up the dirt track to where the sheds were now nearly complete. The sound of hammers rose on the air in weird syncopation. 'You'll be used to that, I expect.'

A van rocked past them. Arven took Kathleen's arm and drew her up onto the verge bordering the track. The van had a horse-box on tow, and the box slid and teetered in the ruts of the track.

The sheds were wooden but for one wall, made of different stuff: brick, corrugated tin, sandbags; even a patch of dry-stone wall. Some of the sheds had windows. Others did not. The windows were either left open or fitted with a test material: wire mesh, or a coarsely woven material; glass of various sorts. Some of the panes were taped with a white criss-cross. Windows fitted with ordinary window glass were shielded by curtains of different materials.

The sheds had birdcages fixed at different heights on one interior wall, and a larger, waist-high wire enclosure bolted to the floor.

Arven showed Kathleen what to do; how the sheds were numbered, and the walls too, and the cages on the walls; how to use the record sheets he had prepared.

From inside the van, Arven drew out cage after cage of pigeons. Inside cramped mesh containers, the rat-grey birds broiled over and around each other. Arven carried pigeons into the first shed and released them, one at a time, into cages mounted at different heights on the wall facing the window.

'What are you going to do?' she asked, mystified.

A truck in army livery rolled up, drowning out his answer.

The driver and his mate lifted green metal boxes from the back of the truck and carried them towards the sheds. Kathleen, under Arven's instruction, noted down the distances between the boxes and the sheds. She found it hard to concentrate. She had heard strange sounds coming from the horse-box. Professor Arven had disabused her: 'Not horses. Apes.'

She wanted to see the apes. She had never seen an ape except once in a zoo in York, and then it was sleeping, just a big deflated ball of grey-black fur.

She wondered what their eyes were like; their hands. She imagined a troop of gorillas – huge, taller than a man – scampering out of the horse-box, rolling about, playing rough-and-tumble games. But the horse-box was opened only at the last minute, and the apes were in cages, and the cages were much smaller than she had expected, and draped in coarse cream cloths.

At about four in the afternoon, they gathered behind the army lorry: the two soldiers, Arven, Kathleen and the driver of the van – a happy, snub-nosed man about Arven's age who turned out to be his colleague, Solly Zuckerman.

One of the soldiers was fiddling with a box held close to his chest. Wires trailed from the box. When she stepped out to see where the wires led, Arven pulled her back and took her hand.

The explosion tore the roof right off the shed and blew the inner wall away. The silence which followed was punctuated, first by the clatter of shattered timber, then, from inside the broken shed, by screams. They were like the cries of a child. The driver's mate strode over to the site of the explosion, to where the air had coagulated into wisps of smoke and steam. He turned and waved a flag: all clear.

Arven and Zuckerman slogged over to him. Feeling numb, Kathleen made to follow. Arven gestured her to stay where she was. She found a flattish rock to sit on and listened, with an educated ear, to the screaming. There was more humanity to it than even a pig's cry, or a lamb's. When she saw no one was watching her, she covered her ears.

Arven and Zuckerman picked morosely over the wreckage of the shed, peered inside, then beckoned the driver's mate over.

The flat slap of a pistol shot.

A grey feather fell, smouldering, onto Kathleen's dress. She leapt up and shook it away.

Arven and Zuckerman's eventual findings were to run quite counter to the impressions left on them by that first, calamitous experiment. Back at the abattoir, in a room given over by Mr Hosken to the government scientists, the zoologist Zuckerman would spend far more time studying live, undamaged animals than dead or injured ones.

Arven, meanwhile, went from shed to shed, marking the effects of blast upon different kinds of wall: this was where Kathleen's record sheets came in. Arven read out measurements; Kathleen entered the numbers into boxes.

Back at her uncle's office, Arven showed Kathleen how to move the numbers between the boxes, shifting their values as she went. She followed him. She copied what he did.

He stared at her.

She looked up at him. 'What?' she said.

When he didn't reply, she said, 'Did I do it wrong?'

He laughed, and shook his head. He drew his chair closer to hers. He showed her how to make numbers out of other numbers, making them bloom.

Afterwards – 'to celebrate,' he said – he took her by train to Darlington.

'Mother will wonder where I am,' she protested. She was so insistent that, when they got to the hotel, Arven made a call to her uncle, to see to it that her mother was reassured.

Kathleen knew there would be trouble, but weeks of working for Arven and Zuckerman on important war work had excited her to the point where she felt that she could always use this as her excuse: the deadlines they had been struggling to meet; the fact both men would be leaving the following day – Zuckerman to Oxford, Arven to London.

She had never eaten in a real restaurant before, and they were the only diners in the old-world sitting room, decorated with hunting scenes and large solemn prints of Conservative statesmen.

'We'll survive it,' Arven told her. He was excited. His eyes shone from either side of his helmet-guard nose. 'The air war. The figures that have been keeping us up nights. Whitehall's figures are calculated on the assumption that every bit of explosive that's dropped on us will find a target. It just isn't so.'

A charge has to be shaped to fit a target, or most of its energy vanishes into the air. He drew a figure on his napkin to show her. 'It doesn't matter how much explosive the Huns drop on us, only a tiny fraction of it will do us any harm.' He grew reflective. 'The big danger is fire, of course. But better the devil you know.'

While they ate, he told her how to survive an air raid. 'Wrap yourself in an eiderdown when you go out,' he said. 'It'll absorb the blast and protect your lungs. If bombs are falling, lie face down in the gutter. Gutters give good protection – blast and splinters will almost certainly fly over you. And wear a notice round your neck. Something conspicuous.'

'What for?' Kathleen laughed: it was too absurd.

'In case you do get hurt. Blast pressurizes the lungs. So if, heaven forbid, some oh-so-keen sixteen-stone air-raid warden comes across you and fancies a spot of artificial respiration—'

Kathleen blushed.

'Well, that's you done for. So your notice will say "Weak Chest. Leave Off" – or words to that effect.'

Kathleen was awed. 'Is that what people will do? Is that what you will tell them to do?'

Arven laughed. 'I can't see very many people adopting the eiderdown as evening wear, can you?'

Kathleen smiled a small smile. It made her unhappy to think that people would not adopt good advice; that habit and convention overrode even the desire to survive.

Arven shrugged. 'Just remember the gutter trick,' he told her. 'That one's a cert, and you won't have to look like a ninny until the last possible moment.' He drank off his beer. 'Not that the Germans are likely to come bumbling over this little corner.'

Later that evening, he began to speak of other things.

He said, 'I know you see the numbers.'

Kathleen blushed.

Though he was staying in Darlington that night, John Arven insisted on accompanying her home. 'There's time for me to get back. The trains run until eleven,' he said, shrugging off her protests. 'It's you or the fleshpots of Darlington, and I've made my choice.'

On the train he told her, 'This war isn't going to be a won by bombs or bullets. You've seen that yourself, haven't you? An explosion's nothing unless it's shaped. You know what I'm talking about, Kathleen. You don't think you know. You don't know how to know – not yet. But you know. I understand what you see. How easy it is for you. The numbers...' He struggled for a way to explain this to her. 'For most of the rest of them, figures are a language they have to learn. It's not like that for you. Is it?'

She said, 'I don't know what you mean.'

He knew she was lying. 'Listen, this war isn't going to be won by soldiers, or airmen, or heroes, or generals, or any of them. This war is going to be won by numbers. Numbers, and people who know what to do with numbers. Do you understand?'

She shook her head.

As they came out of her local station and left the lights behind, he said to her, 'I can't offer much. There's not very much that's in my gift. Not directly. A job in Senate House to start with. Admiralty tables, that sort of thing.' In the dusk, he caught her expression. 'Don't look so shocked, it's not a secret! Look, I can teach you. Once you have the basics under your belt, it doesn't matter a damn that you're just a slip of a girl. With a head like yours, you can write your own ticket.'

She was shocked at his language. She wondered if she ought to say something. Her mother would have said something. What should she say?

She said, 'The colours—' and stopped.

'Yes,' he said.

'They mean I'm simple.'

He stared at her. '*Of course not,*' he said. 'What blithering idiot gave you that idea?'

In a small voice: 'Aren't I?'

He tucked her arm firmly under his own. 'If you are, then I am. If you are, then Senate House is a sea of simpletons.'

Kathleen trembled all over. It was like discovering you had a brother. A family.

Outside her house, Sage kissed her. 'Kathleen. Promise me. We need people like you. Working people.'

Her mother must have been watching because as soon as they were alone together in the kitchen she struck her daughter in the face so hard – a shaped charge, every particle of force meeting its target – that Kathleen lost her footing and banged her head on the corner of the kitchen table.

Kathleen lay on the floor. Dimly, she could hear her mother's breathing. Her eyes focused. There was a crust of bread on the floor. Her mother bent down to help her up, but she must have spotted the bread crust then because her hand, which was reaching to cradle her daughter's head, changed course suddenly and snatched up the crust instead. She picked it up and carried it off to the rubbish pail.

She returned to her daughter, helped her up, made her tea, ran bluish milk in after it, and made her daughter sit down. She apologized, after her fashion. 'Look what you made me do!' she sobbed.

Kathleen, dazed, sipped her tea.

'Look what you made me do!'

Kathleen watched as her mother, still weeping, picked up the pail and carried it past her to the back door. She passed close enough that Kathleen could see into the pail. The pail shone. There was nothing in it but the crust of bread. Kathleen sipped her tea and listened to her mother's footsteps receding, up the garden path, to where the compost pile lay. Her mother returned and rinsed out the rubbish pail. She set it down. She drew water into a pan and set it on the stove to boil. She sat at the table. She pressed her hand to the side of the teapot. She got up again and picked up the teapot and poured the dregs of the tea down the sink. She rinsed out the sink. She took the lid off the teapot and washed it. She scooped leaves out of the pot and dropped them into the rubbish pail. She rinsed out the pot. She picked up the rubbish pail. While she was in the garden, the water in the pan began to boil.

From John Arven, Kathleen Hosken has learned to look the thing you most fear straight in the eye, not with passion, with a calculating curiosity.

She is going away because she understands, now, why her uncle valued her company so very much; why he took such an interest in her; and when he was approached by his MP to give a discreet hand to two young men from Whitehall, why he thought to involve his niece in their work.

She is leaving because she understands why her mother trusted him to employ her, even though she despises him. Why he is not welcome in their house. Why her father went away.

It is as John Arven said it would be: a problem that is more or less soluble to an active intellect.

Her mother came back inside and rinsed out the rubbish pail. Kathleen nursed the side of her head. She primed the fuse to her life, and lit it.

She said, 'You married the wrong one.'

2

It was October, the time of the phoney war. Indian summer in the big London parks, a false spring in Highgate and Hampstead, perfect weather for long walks by the Thames in Kew and Barnes; and all of it given poignancy by bad news from far-away places.

The dust in the streets shone. Perfect cones of sand shone in the sun. Piles of sand ready for bagging piled up in empty lots. Sunshine glinted off the buttons on the tunics of the AFS men. Their hair. Their belt buckles. Kathleen walked the parks of the unfamiliar city. She wandered its embankments and craned her neck up at its statues. She meandered in a daze. She sleep-walked through Chelsea and Richmond and dozed open-eyed on benches in Battersea. On the grassy banks of Parliament Hill she lay down and slept, the sunlight blood-red through her eyelids, the grass smelling nonsensically of spring. The sun was like a gas fire, warming only what put itself directly in its way, and to step into a shadow was to feel the chill of the true season. Kathleen stayed in the sun.

She did as John Arven had taught her. She approached everything with an aloof curiosity. She assumed nothing. She tuned her feelings out, became all eyes. She followed the advice she had been given, or most of it. Though she neither walked around the city wrapped in an eiderdown, nor strung a sign about her neck, still, she was prepared, at the first whistle of a descending bomb, to leap face-first into the nearest gutter.

Surrounded by unfamiliar streets and unapproachable people, she made what kind of life she could. She bought milk and bread. She did not know how to cook; her mother had never shown her. Once, she tried to drink milk straight from the jar. It was thick and foamy and it sickened her. She ran water in. It was better. When the bread set hard she hacked off a slice and ran it under the tap in the communal bathroom and wrung it out; then it was all right again. Sometimes she had jam.

The first bombs fell.

There was no outcry, no animosity.

At the Lyons corner house where she was training to be a waitress, as he was guiding the girls into the shelter he had made for them in the basement, the boilerman said, 'Them lads is only doing their job, after all.'

The same night, in the street below Kathleen's garret window, two drunk AFS men walked by. They looked up at the bombers thundering overhead, and waved goodbye to them. 'Goodnight!' they laughed. 'Good night, Jerry!' they cheered. 'Sleep tight!'

Kathleen jerked away from the window. They might see her. They might see her at the window and know by her face, rosy in the light from distant fires, that the window was not covered.

On her first night in this guest-house, she had drawn her bed up under the window so that she could spend her nights looking out across the city. Thanks to the blackout, the stars were often visible above the rooftops. Sometimes they winked out as she watched, and it was only by focusing on the patterns the stars made – winking off, then on again – that she made out the egg-shaped silhouettes of the barrage balloons.

Rather than cover her window, she never made a light or lit a fire. She imagined what would happen if the AFS men spotted her. The strange thing was, in her imagination, the men did not point at her. They did not shout at her. They did not accuse her of anything. In her imagination, they smiled at her: '*Sleep tight!*'

There was a knock on her door. 'Hello?' A woman's voice. Whoever it was, she wasn't going away.

Kathleen opened the door a crack.

'Hello?'

'I'm sorry,' Kathleen said.

'What you sorry for?'

'I—'

'Come on, love, let me in, it's bloody freezing out here.'

Kathleen opened her door.

The girl in the hall was short and dumpy, with a pear-shaped face and hair in a great contrived frizz. She stepped into the room quickly, so Kathleen had to take a step back. The dumpy girl felt around for the light switch. She stared past Kathleen at the uncovered window, and snapped the light off again. 'You're a caution,' she said, impressed.

Kathleen helped her with the felt-backed cardboard shutters they used here in place of blackout blinds. Once the window was covered, they put the light back on. The room was hateful now: a box, brightly lit. Kathleen sat on her hands to control her trembling.

'You need the fire on.' The visitor's name was Margaret. 'Wass the matter, love? You homesick? Blimey,' she said, flapping her arms about herself, 'you'll catch your death in here!' She lit the gas fire and came and sat beside Kathleen on the bed. She put an arm around her. 'Bloody hell, lovey, you're all skin and bone. Are you sick?'

Margaret was the eldest of six. She had time for children. In the weeks that followed, she took Kathleen in hand.

'Don't you know no one? No one at all?'

Kathleen shook her head. She had written to Professor Arven at Birkbeck College asking to meet him, asking what useful work she might do. Concerned not to appear naive or unserious, she had carefully followed every stricture and regulation regarding sensitive correspondence: at the top of the letter, the words 'Same Address'; in the body, no mention of how they had met, or what work they had done. Perhaps she had been too oblique. Perhaps he could not place her in his memory. She had never had a reply.

Margaret had five brothers. She received letters from them every week, the army censor allowing. She read them to Kathleen. She expected Kathleen to respond in kind. She was scandalized. 'No brothers or sisters? No cousins, even? What about your mother?'

Margaret was gregarious and overbearing.

'What size shoes do you take, anyway?'

'Your seams are crooked,' Margaret would say. 'Here, let me.' Her fingers pinched and tickled, as she deftly straightened Kathleen's stockings.

Kathleen, wobbling dangerously on borrowed shoes, learned to study the backs of her legs in the mirror, to check if her seams were straight. She caught herself in the glass, peeking over her shoulder: the coy picture she made. 'Where'd you get these stockings?' she asked her new friend.

'Never you worry. Here.' There was a slip to go with the stockings. 'Mind, it's just for tonight.'

Margaret fed her and dressed her. Kathleen was Margaret's project, her doll, her pet.

Kathleen worried: what could she give Margaret in return for her companionship? What amusement could she afford? She began to see that John Arven's cool curiosity had its limits, that an icy objectivity would not suffice in every situation.

She began to measure how little she knew about being alive.

Then came the awkward moment when Kathleen realized what she was: an amusement afforded Margaret by her latest dry spell. Deep down, and all the time, Margaret wanted men.

When Margaret was seeing a man, Kathleen did not see her from one day to the next.

Moments with men were the measure of Margaret's life: evenings in the cinema or at the pub; furtive whispers on the stairs; nights when she did not come home at all. Then, his furlough done, the intensity of departure: the porter tearing her hand from the handle of the carriage as the train pulled away. The smoke, the steam, the grit. These things only piqued Margaret's appetite – when the sentiment ebbed, in a week or two – for the next glance, the next night out, another arm round her waist.

She was 'no better than she ought to be', as Kathleen's mother would say. She was 'second-hand goods'. From the aloof perspectives of the scientific method, however, such strictures counted for little.

'Want to come down the Four Feathers?' said Margaret.

'Why not?' said Kathleen, with a tremor of wrongdoing.

They got ready. Margaret did Kathleen's make-up for her. Margaret's technique began and ended at the eyes. She larded her own eyes with kohl and mascara in a vain attempt to draw attention away from her discoloured teeth. She tried this look on Kathleen.

'It's lovely,' said Kathleen, captivated by the image in her glass, the Egyptian princess there.

'Oh, cobblers,' Margaret snapped. She unscrewed the lid off a jar of cold cream and ordered Kathleen to wipe it away. 'Let's try something else.'

The Four Feathers was one of those shabby commercial drinking places where scraps of lunchtime bar-shrimp litter the sawdust on the floor of the saloon bar and the sawdust is black and malty and sticks to the heel of your shoe. It was packed. Margaret led Kathleen on, head down, elbows out, a human battering ram. A cross-current parted them. Kathleen called out to her friend. Margaret, intent on reaching the counter, did not notice her. Kathleen thought she would wait where she was, but the milling crowd drove her, like a stick in a millrace, steadily towards the other side of the room. When the current changed course suddenly, she found herself pressed up against the counter. 'What's your name, love?'

The voice was only one component of the din.

A finger jabbed her upper arm. 'Hello. What's your name?'

She turned.

Back home, the timbres of Kathleen's voice spelled property. Here, she might as well be 'the lowest of the low'. Her accent was a thick and bitter Durham: sharp, flaked, a rusted gate squealing in the wind. So she spoke only when spoken to, and very softly.

'Kathleen,' she said, softly, into the widest smile she'd ever seen.

'Katherine?'

She nodded and tried to meet the man's eyes. His jaw was too distracting, so thick and pink and smooth.

The jaw offered to buy Kathleen a drink. She asked it for a pink gin; it was the only drink she could think of by name. A woman in a dress made of tiny mirrors had ordered one at a swank bar in a film she had seen with Margaret the night before.

He handed it to her and their eyes met. His eyes sparkled. They were pretty blue eyes. She liked them. Then he smiled – and her gaze fell, magnetized, back to his jaw again: the cleft chin, the muscular smoothness of it.

She turned away, blushing, as from something obscene. She sipped her drink and tried not to splutter. The drink was bitter, like hedge clippings.

'What do you do, then?'

At this time, she still nursed ambitions for the person John Arven believed she could be. She still held out hopes for the letter she had sent him. So she said: 'I'm a computer.'

'Oh yes?'

'Ask me anything,' she said. Not a lie, she told herself: an experiment in identity.

He smirked. 'What's the square root of a hundred and forty-four, then?'

'Twelve.'

He laughed. 'Very good.'

Wrinkling her nose, she drank off a good mouthful of pink gin. She tightened her throat over the burning liquor, counted to five and risked a breath.

'Ask me another,' she said.

'The square root of a hundred and forty-five?' He said it like it was the easiest calculation in the world.

It certainly wasn't hard. 'Twelve point oh-four-one-five-nine-four-five-seven-eight-eight... what?'

His smile had gone. He folded his arms.

'You're making that up.'

'How would you know?' This from Margaret, sprung from nowhere; she muscled in between them.

'Oh,' he said, coldly. He knew Margaret. 'Friend of yours, is she?' He picked up his pint and moved along the bar, away from them.

Kathleen watched him go, disappointed.

Margaret grabbed Kathleen by the arm and led her off to the other side of the central counter. She hissed in Kathleen's ear, 'Can't you tell a bloody policeman when you see one?'

Kathleen tried to maintain eye contact with the man but he had turned his back, nursing his pint. She had to take Margaret's word that he was a policeman. He could have been anything. Munitions. Railways.

Apparently policemen didn't count. 'A policeman!' Margaret railed. 'Hobnobbing with a bloody policeman!' She parked herself down beside Kathleen on a padded bench near the toilets. Two sailors came up and offered them drinks. 'What'll you have, ladies?' asked the older of the two: he had one of those permanently flushed faces you imagine might bleed if you touch it.

'A pale ale,' said Margaret, 'ta, love.' She glanced at Kathleen. The thought of pink gin made Kathleen queasy, but she didn't know any other drinks. 'Two pale ales,' Margaret said, covering for Kathleen's silence.

The younger sailor went off to the bar. He was exceptionally tall and his straw-coloured hair, though regulation short, grew out at all angles. In the buffet and slew of the crowded bar, he tottered about like a young, well-groomed scarecrow.

With a strange convulsion – a red pocketknife clipping shut – the older sailor bent forward at the hip, then fell back into his chair. 'Oof!' he said. He was short, and squat, and his limbs had no flexibility. As he got comfortable, he moved his arms with convulsive jerks, clicking them into position. His hands were red, too.

His name was Dick. Dick Jinks. A funny name for a sailor. 'What are you drinking?' Kathleen asked him, an experiment in conversation.

'Wallop,' Dick grinned, creasing his swollen red face so that it looked as if it might pop. He meant draught bitter. 'Wallop by name and nature.' He laughed, revealing large, cramped teeth. All evening he came out with these catchphrases. He laughed at them, as at a joke someone else had made.

The sailors had met during the Dunkirk evacuation, and had run into each other again by accident, a couple of nights before. They had stories about Dunkirk. The younger sailor, Donald, went first. Donald seemed nervous, unused to company. He ran his hands through his hair, which ignored him and sprang back into place. His tale began dashingly enough. He was still in civvies at the time of the evacuation. He was one of those gallant yachtsmen who had joined the flotilla out of pure patriotism and fellow feeling. He had borrowed his father's yacht. Kathleen imagined his father waving him off at the jetty. The boy was very well-spoken. Almost BBC. What was he doing in a mere rating's uniform? 'Do you know Hayling Island?' he asked them.

'"Do you know Hayling"!' The elder sailor's laughter boomed around the lounge. Heads turned. Donald blushed. He was really very young. Margaret laid her hand on his arm. 'Go on, love.' But Dick wanted his turn. 'Pissing their pants they was!' He didn't have much of a story, though his description of the strafings was vivid. 'Pissing their pants!' He laughed. Kathleen saw right down his throat.

Dick and Donald walked them home. It was impossibly dark. Kathleen staggered. The paving stones were treacherous in the shoes Margaret had lent her. Dick offered her his arm, and she hung off it, gratefully. It surprised her to notice how short he was: he was barely taller than her. His young friend dawdled, or Margaret was holding him back; she seemed to be having trouble with her heel. Kathleen and Dick got to the door of the hostel first. He took off his cap and braced himself as though for inspection. 'Maybe I can call on you. We can have a drink again sometime,' he said.

'Sometime,' she said.

'You knows what I drink,' he said, and laughed his great red booming laugh. Even his eyes were red.

'Wallop,' she said.

'That's the ticket,' he said, stepping forward, as though she had uttered a password. He took her hands in his. An odd look spread over his face. It was bloated and empty, all at once. No one had looked at Kathleen with need before. She did not understand. 'Spare us a kiss, love – a little kiss.'

The impossibility of it was suddenly, liberatingly funny. She laughed. Surprised, he let her go. She coughed to cover her laughter. 'Frog in my throat,' she said. It was as good a catchphrase as any of the sailor's, but he did not smile. An experiment: she pecked him on the corner of his mouth. He tasted of beer and cigarettes. He ran his hand around her waist, squeezed, and kissed her cheek. She experienced a moment's revulsion towards his flushed face, his too-red lips, as though the lips might leave a mark on her. Then he let go, and she found herself wanting to repeat the kiss.

'Goodnight, then,' Dick said.

That was all.

She went inside and waited for Margaret. The sitting room was empty. She slipped Margaret's shoes off her feet – they had been too big for her, and far too high.

Weary of waiting, she went up to her room in her stockinged feet, carrying Margaret's shoes. She took off Margaret's slip. She unclipped Margaret's stockings and eased them off, ever so carefully.

Margaret was still not back.

Kathleen went to bed.

She lay still, wondering what else there was. What else she did not know.

Margaret knew, but Margaret wasn't telling. She had vanished again.

A week passed, and Kathleen didn't see Margaret once.

She was not worried or put out. She was growing used to Margaret's rhythms. Margaret's men overrode the girls' friendship for only a little while. So this time, while she waited for Margaret's man to depart, Kathleen tried to shake off her loneliness. She braved the sitting room.

The other residents were stenographers from Shepherd's Bush, WAFS from Tottenham, fellow nippies from the Lyons corner houses on the Strand and Oxford Street. They intimidated Kathleen: great iconic hulks of girls. By now, though, she knew how to smile, what to say when she entered or left the room, the gestures she should make. She loved to listen to them. The girls spoke a different language, a Margaret sort of language.

'So I said to her...'

'And he said to me...'

At night, bits of their conversation swirled about her, punctuating her dreams, a sort of verbal shrapnel, highly coloured, piecemeal and surreal. Billy drops leaflets over Berlin and Becky does firemen two at a time. David wants me to do it with him. James bought me a ring.

Each evening, as they got ready for this movie, that meal, this man or that, they gathered to listen to the BBC. The strange names of the cities the Nazis had overrun lent the news an operatic quality. The fall of Norway. In Denmark, something rotten. The names erupted like fantasies through the wireless – a huge mahogany box which took pride of place in the room.

One early evening, as Kathleen sat listening to the radio, breathing in the heady acetone of the other girls' nail polish, there was a knock on the door, and it was for her.

'Remember me?' he boomed, and laughed.

There on the stoop was Dick Jinks, the powerful, squat, red-faced sailor, much older than her, who had walked her home the week before.

Kathleen blinked at him, surprised. She had imagined him in deep Atlantic, shepherding the convoys or whatever it was he did.

'Surprised to see me, baby?' His words, glib and saucy, sat ill with the anxiety in his eyes. He raised his hand towards her – a wave? a handshake? – and stopped mid-gesture. He didn't seem to know what to do with his hand. It trembled. 'Ho, ho,' he sang. 'You're the port in my storm!'

London sunsets were a marvel, since the bombing had begun in earnest: cities of vapour taking leave of a city of stone.

'Dick?'

He sang, 'Yo, ho, ho.'

'Where's your friend?'

Blood darkened Dick Jinks's face; in the sunset, his flushed face appeared polished and hard. 'That poofter? That nancy? That queen? Fuck him, darling.' He blinked. 'Ha, ha,' he added, in mitigation.

'Dick?'

'Will you take a turn with me?' The words struck his funny bone immediately. 'A turn! A turn, Ho!'

'Dick?'

'Will you? I'll stand you a Watney's.' He winked. 'Say you will.'

She looked at him. He was no more ready for a night on the town than she was. He was in uniform of a sort, but so threadbare it looked more like labourer's clothes. Lines of braid hung off the sleeves of his jacket in tatters. The material where the braid had been was crusted white. His bell-bottoms, uncreased and shapeless like a cowboy's chaps, scuffed the steps as she led him inside.

He came forward, flinging a leg out in front of him, then falling onto it. Flinging, falling. As he passed her, she smelled something clean but unappealing, like disinfectant.

She showed him into the sitting room and ran upstairs to dress. She was as quick as she could be. She was nervous of him, afraid of what he might say to the other girls. Every so often his 'Yo, ho, ho!' would shiver the floor under her feet, as though he were directly beneath her, calling to her, his red, wet mouth pressed like a sucker to the ceiling.

When she came downstairs she found him sitting in the armchair by the radio. His grin was fixed and ghastly, his lips as white as his clenched knuckles. 'Dick?' she said, in a small voice. He turned to her. His smile grew more terrible. 'Ah! Ha ha!' It was not laughter so much as a struggle for breath. He sprang open from the waist like a flick knife and rocked upright on heavy, scuffed shoes. He led her outside.

A cab passed them; Dick hailed it. 'Let's paint the town red!'

In the taxi, he tried to relax.

'Oof,' he said.

'Aah.'

'What you been up to, then, baby?' he said.

'A bomb came through Lyons' roof last week,' she told him. 'The ovens were out of action all day.'

'Ha,' he said.

The week before, walking back from the pub, when he asked her what she did for a living, Kathleen had bit her tongue against the disappointment – she had so been looking forward to meeting Sage again – and told the truth. She was training to be a waitress.

'A fireman came to defuse it, then a soldier.'

'Ho—' He opened his mouth to laugh, and there was something shapeless about the set of his lips, something ragged, like a wound.

'There was plaster dust everywhere,' she said, warming to her theme. 'We stayed open, though. We served soup...'

He began humming.

She broke off.

'What?' he said.

'You were saying?'

He shook his head vigorously. 'Ah. No. Tell me,' he said, and just as she was about to speak, 'Soup. Yes. And?'

She drew breath to speak.

'It'll be right again,' he said.

'What will?' said Kathleen.

He blinked at her. 'It will,' he said. 'I will.' He tried to smile – and if it was not quite a smile he made, at least it was not a rictus. 'Ha!' He had surprised another pun. 'I'll *right* myself!'

They turned down St Giles High Street. Dick said to the driver, 'This'll do.'

East of St Giles, the bomb damage was immense. Tall brick terraces straggled towards St Paul's, pale under a biscuit of crumbled plaster. Dick and Kathleen avoided the pavements; walls that had not yet been pulled down slanted dangerously over them. You could see the cathedral sometimes, far in the distance, down long, treeless vistas. She could not imagine where he was taking her. She began to be afraid.

The smell of wet plaster, on the contrary, seemed to give Dick a lift. He swung her hand, back and forth, as though they were walking along a promenade.

'Ow. Dick.'

He let go, grinned at her and skipped ahead.

'Dick?'

He capered in the blacked-out streets.

'Dick, where are we going?' Kathleen's ankle was sore. Her shoe was rubbing it raw. She had not worn walking shoes. Her feet hurt. 'Dick,' she called after him. 'Dick!'

She felt a hand on her arm. Startled, she struggled. There he was – right beside her. 'Easy there, now,' he crooned, stroking her arm. 'Easy!' As though it was she who had slipped ahead of him.

They turned north, then east again, then north – was it north? They could have been anywhere, going anywhere.

'Do you know where we are, Dick?'

'Easy does it,' he said. The word he had used to soothe her stuck to him like a burr. He could not shake it off.

'Easy as pie,' he said.

'Easy virtue, eh?' He laughed, and caught her up in his arms.

Kathleen hung there, looking up at him, afraid of him. There was a moon tonight. His head blocked it out. His head loomed over her, a silhouette, a blank.

'Here,' he said, 'don't cry, baby. Don't cry.'

He set her down without kissing her. He took her hand and stared up the road.

'Dick,' she said, in a small voice, 'that's the way we've just come.'

Dick shrugged. He took her hand, pulling her gently along, retracing their steps, then turned, at random, to the left.

They weren't going anywhere. She understood that now.

The fronts down one side of the street were all torn away, revealing doll's house interiors. Wallpaper shone in the moonlight.

He tightened his grip on her hand. 'Oh, that's better,' he said, 'to be moving, that's better. I feel so tight afterwards. You know? Damned tight. Feel.' He stopped suddenly, snatched her hand and pressed it to his upper arm, the muscles there, the knots. The tremors running beneath his skin.

Plaster crunched under her heel.

'After what?' she said.

'After the shocks,' he said. 'After he shocks me. My pal the trick cyclist. My pal, ha!'

'I don't know what you're talking about,' she sobbed.

'It's new,' he said.

The back of her heel felt cold and damp. It was bleeding. It was hard for her to follow his story. 'Oh, the popping!' he cried. 'The popping in my ears!' Eventually she realized that he was not describing his 'shocks' now. He was telling her about something else. Something for which the 'shocks' were a treatment.

Something terrible had happened to him.

He drew the words out painfully, as though he were drawing his fingernails across a blackboard. He had been involved in an accident at sea. An explosion. The vessel had ruptured. It had sunk. Dick had sunk. Dick was trapped with a young rating in a compartment deep in the bowels of the stricken ship. Dick went down with the ship. As he talked, she could feel the popping in her ears, the liquid iciness of the water rising around her calves, her knees. She was there with him in the compartment. She could barely breathe.

How deep was the stricken vessel by the time Dick fought free of the boy trapped there in the compartment with him? The boy had panicked. The boy was clawing at him. How deep when Dick drove the boy's head back one final time, impaling his skull upon the stanchion? How deep when he took his breath, dived, crawled and, at last, his chest on fire, kicked free of the sinking ship?

'Oh, deep, deep,' he sighed.

You have to scream, he explained. As you rise through water, the air in your lungs expands. You have to scream, otherwise your lungs will burst.

They stood alone in the street: the monochrome dark.

'Like this,' he said.

He let go her hand.

'Dick?'

He had lost the sense of her entirely now. 'Like this,' he said.

She reached up for him. She couldn't see him. She touched his face. She surprised tears.

'*Eeeeee!*'

She fell back, gasping, fingers in her ears.

He walked on, not looking at her. She followed him. She thought he had forgotten her. After a little while, he went on with his story. 'How deep?' The question fascinated him. 'Black it was. Black.' He meant the water. 'It was daylight when we drowned. But we was too deep, you see. By the time I kicked free. Too deep for daylight.'

He stopped again. They had come out into a square. A bomb had fallen in the very centre, and there were gobs of mud over the road. Leaves. They filled the gutters. The trees stood out white in the moonlight. The branches were bare. It was deep midwinter here.

'There was stuff in the sea. Bits of stuff. From the ship. Sinking, floating. A jumper, a Bible, a set of false teeth, a child's teddy-bear. Nothing had any colour. Like here. Like this. Now.' He turned a circle in the middle of the street.

It was true: there was no colour here. Not a spot of colour anywhere. No traffic light. No yellow beam from a warden's torch. They were in the world of the movies now. The world of black and white.

A park bench hung in the fork of a tree. It was quite undamaged. The brass plaque on its back winked white.

Far ahead of her Kathleen glimpsed the silhouetted bulk of St Pancras station. She knew where she was. 'Dick? Dick. Where shall we go?' His stare was vacant, without intelligence. She tried to take his hands in hers but they were fists. She took hold of his arms. 'Dick.'

He swallowed. He was done.

Was that it? She wondered. Was there really nowhere for them to go? 'Dick,' she said, in a small voice. 'Dick, do you want to kiss me?' She thought of his mouth, red like a wound, the suck of it. 'Do you? Dick?' She leaned into him. She ran her hands up his arms.

The braid on his jacket came away in her fingers.

She picked it off.

It was metal foil.

She let go of him.

It was the foil wrappers from slabs of chocolate.

The white stuff sticking it to his sleeve was cow gum. It clung in crumbs to the material of his jacket.

So.

She let go of his arms. She felt calm. Dead calm.

'Dick?' she said. 'Where are you from?'

He gave her an address in Fitzrovia: a road off Gower Street. They were practically there. Perhaps they had been headed there all along.

She asked him, 'Is this where you're taking me?'

He stared into her eyes.

'Do you want me to come with you?'

The bloated look was back: his look of need.

'Dick? Do you want me to come home with you?'

She imagined the sort of place where he might be staying. A bleak furnished room with thin walls.

She looked him in the eye, right in the eye, without passion, with a cool, calculating curiosity. She said, 'It doesn't matter, Dick. I'll come with you.'

She imagined the tightness of his muscles, the tremors coursing under his skin, the nature of the experiment to which she was now committing herself.

Limping now, she led him across Southampton Row and around Bloomsbury Square. The gardens were chained shut. They turned off Gower Street. She counted off the houses, looking for a hotel sign.

'Here we are,' he said.

It wasn't what she'd been expecting. It wasn't a boarding house. It was one of a row of smart Georgian terrace houses. Beside the door, a plaque bore the name of a distinguished-sounding philosophical society.

Dick stood beside her on the polished marble steps, shifting from one foot to another. Out of embarrassment? In anticipation? She said, 'Are you sure this is the place?'

'Aye-aye,' he said, and winked at her, as though the whole evening had been one long, terrific joke.

'Are you going to let us in?'

He sobered up.

'Dick?'

His eyes grew big with need. 'Spare us a kiss, love – a little kiss.'

Did he not understand? 'Inside,' she said. She took hold of his hands. 'Take me in with you.'

The door opened. A young woman appeared, smoking a cigarette. 'Yes?' Kathleen let go of Dick's hands.

'What do you want?' The woman was tall and gawky-looking; her white blouse, trimmed with a dark material, carried an intimidating hint of education. Smoke from the woman's cigarette wafted into Kathleen's face. It was strong and foreign-tasting, and it made Kathleen want to rub her eyes.

Dick was staring at the pavement. He was scuffing his shoes against each other like a shamed schoolboy.

'Come along inside, Mr Jinks,' said the woman, without surprise, without ceremony, grinding her spent cigarette underfoot.

Dick stepped inside the hall.

'Dick?' Kathleen reached out after him.

He did not notice. His eyes were downcast. 'Good evening, Miriam.'

His use of her Christian name made the woman bridle. 'Get along, Mr Jinks,' she said.

Suddenly, Kathleen was afraid. 'Dick!' she cried, sharp, to wake him. 'Dick! You don't have to—'

'That's enough out of you,' said the woman called Miriam.

Kathleen peered past her, looking for Dick.

She saw ornate moulded coving; a chandelier; rich red carpeting on the stairs at the hall's far end; closed doors, painted white. An umbrella stand, heavy with men's mackintoshes.

Dick had vanished.

Miriam stood, her hand on the door, her head inclined at an ironic angle, waiting for Kathleen to be done with her inspection. Kathleen tried to make out her face, but the light from the hall held her in silhouette.

'Goodnight, then.' Miriam swung the door.

'Wait!' Kathleen's words came out in a great rush. 'Is he a sailor, really, I mean, whether what he said, I mean, his uniform, but still he could be, or could have been... I want to know.'

The door was shut, and one by one, the lights in the building were going out.

Kathleen has approached her life objectively. In this way she has protected herself, even from bombs and fire storms.

But her experiments are becoming large and unwieldy. They produce results that have no meaning, or that offer up too many meanings. Her experiments keep colliding. Unfamiliar phenomena peel off and spin away, feelings which vanish the moment she stops to analyse them.

The night following her aborted night with Dick, she went with the girls of her boarding house to the Royal Opera House. The opera house hosts regular dance evenings. Shop girls spin and caper amidst gilt and sumptuous red furniture under a dome of perfect blue, like a blackbird's egg.

There was Margaret, in a red print dress, dancing with the policeman from the pub. The smile she gave Kathleen as she rocked past was all mouth; her eyes had no warmth in them.

Kathleen, seated at the edge of the dance floor, folded her hands in her lap, as unfamiliar feelings exploded and vanished inside her like fireworks. It was not that she had liked the policeman. It was not that she had thought of him since that night in the Four Feathers. It was not, precisely, that Margaret had done anything wrong, when she'd steered her new girlfriend away from him that night in the pub. It was not that Margaret had cheated her or, if she had, it was not as though the cheat was very great. It was not precisely anything. It was simply the wreckage left behind when experiments collide: experiments in men, experiments in friendship. Kathleen wondered what conclusion might be drawn from this result.

Sitting beside her she noticed Hazel, a girl from her rooming house, in a new yellow dress which lent her skin a sallow, yielding quality that men seemed to shun. Margaret wheeled by, her face in the shade of the policeman's massive chin, and Hazel yawned, 'Kath, love, you ought to watch that cheeky cow.'

More sparks! How did Hazel know that Margaret had steered her away from the policeman? What would happen if Kathleen asked Hazel what she meant, straight out?

On and on, like dominoes. The more you experimented, the less you really knew. Kathleen has been looking the world straight in the eye, without passion, as though it were a series of soluble problems. She has been living as though life were a set of coolly posed questions. She had expected answers to her questions, not feelings.

Kathleen told Hazel the story of her night with Jinks.

'Oh my God!' Hazel exclaimed. 'Weren't you frightened?'

Kathleen shook her head.

Hazel said, 'I'd have called a copper.'

This was Hazel's one stock response to things: 'I'll call a copper, I shall.' At first, people were taken aback by such threats: awkward bus conductors; inept waitresses; men who had the misfortune to bump against Hazel on the street. Then, quite quickly, they learned that she was not very bright.

3

The Blitz is in full swing. Loss is common throughout the London herd, and exhaustion is a way of life. At the same time, there is very little terror. The government's conscientious plans to deal with the collapse of civil order seem foolish now, a nanny's unnecessary bothering. The beds in hospitals from Croydon to Middlesex, readied for tens of thousands of shell-shock victims, lie empty. Come the air-raid sirens, Londoners flock to the Underground. Afterwards, they re-emerge from the deepest tunnels quite willingly, they do not shun the light, and H. G. Wells's fearsome, trogloditic Morlocks remain a thing of dreams.

The theatres and cinemas, shut up when the first bombs fell, were re-opened almost immediately. In garret rooms in Plumstead and Elstree, young screenwriters, numbed by the Blitz, stumble gormlessly through the toils of self-expression, and Senate House, kindly and oblivious, polishes their efforts bland again, reducing their screen characters to sanctioned types: broken-spirited airman; sparky shopgirl; callow hero-in-waiting; hard-bitten New York journalist with her too-high heels and racy opinions; dependable, if tipsy, artisan. So every man, passing through the censor's narrow gate, becomes an Everyman, a symbol for the mass, hardly a man at all.

Every night, after work, Kathleen finds herself watching films so similar to each other they may as well be one film: a series of civilized exchanges conducted in more-or-less interchangeable white rooms. Each room is handsomely furnished. There is always a floor-length mirror, a box of cigarettes on a coffee table and, by the window, a man and a woman, smoking.

The handsome couple have reached some sort of emotional crisis. The man opens his mouth to speak. 'Have you any idea what this involves?' Though the man and the woman are in black and white, the inside of the man's mouth is red.

'I could get myself *shot!*'

Kathleen comes awake, trying to scream.

'The cutlets, please,' says the colourless young man, the sole occupant of the table before her.

The pencil in her hand is a complex surgical instrument. She does not know how to operate it. All by themselves, as if by a ponderous magic, letters emerge from under the pencil's tip: t... l... e... t... ...l

Kathleen blinks at the colours around her with eyes still tuned to black and white. She is at work. She is standing by table three. She says, automatically, 'Anything to drink?'

'Yes. A cup of tea, please.'

She writes: T

All day, Kathleen has been falling into dreams. It is happening to them all, and so frequently, almost every conversation drifts to the subject of sleep sooner or later: how much sleep you need, what sort of sleep it is and when you take it. Jenny from the kitchens reckons peeling vegetables for the lunchtime rush gives her a good fifteen minutes of deep sleep, 'no dreams, mind'.

Kathleen envies her. Her waking hours are riddled with dreams. Whenever she closes her eyes, a dream appears. Sometimes it is impossible to distinguish between sleeping and waking. On several occasions she has breakfasted, washed, dressed, run to the station and boarded the tube train to work – only to wake up in bed, dizzy and disorientated, and utterly demoralized at the thought that she will have to go through all this morning's rigmarole again.

Recently, dreams such as these have begun to nest inside each other, so that she finds herself waking up from a dream into another dream, and from that dream into another, and another, each one a little chillier, stiffer and more realistic than the last. Who is to say when the chain of dreams ends and reality begins?

Kathleen remembers John Arven telling her to look things in the eye. Replace your horror with a cool curiosity, he said to her: then the horror goes away. She has followed his advice dutifully enough, but last night she saw something that spoiled her belief in him. It was the opening reel of a film about the agonies of a young conductor of an orchestra of refugees.

An elegant woman in a fur coat and bright heels walks the streets of a ruined city. What city? It is impossible to tell. There are no signs, no advertisements; the headlines on the shredded newspapers which bowl along the street beside her, worrying her feet, are too far away to read. All we can say is that the city is modern, its destruction accomplished only recently, by wave after wave of bombing from the air.

The elegant woman holds the collar of her coat tight around her neck, picking her way with unfeasible ease and steadiness over roads reduced to crumbled stream beds, strands of brick-shingle, dunes of plaster dust. Her heels kick motes of light across the screen...

It was, after all, only a scene from a film. But it has made Kathleen look differently at things. The smooth, calm movements of the woman on the film suggested that the character had blocked reality out altogether, preferring to live among memories of the city before it was bombed. But you could just as easily take the scene to mean the opposite: that the woman had achieved a complete psychic adjustment to the bombing.

Utter denial or total acceptance? Everywhere Kathleen turns now, the London masses are dreaming their way through the Blitz. They are not looking the Blitz in the eye at all. They are coming to a glancing, unconscious accommodation with it. They are trying to work around it, to sidestep it and integrate it into a life they try to make as ordinary as possible. Proudly displayed in every shop window she passes, a sign: 'Business as Usual'. A triumph of fantasy.

She thinks: a city is razed, but we pretend otherwise. We survive *because* we pretend.

Waitressing at Lyons is not a job that Kathleen could just turn up one day and do. They trained her. In an upstairs room, she was taught how to dress a dining table. The idea is that it should look exactly like every other dining table of that size – not just within that restaurant, but in every restaurant Lyons own. Kathleen has learned how to dress a table for two, for four, for eight. She has memorized the place of each glass, plate, fork, knife, spoon and trivet. Precision is called for, and precision is something Kathleen enjoys. The neat creases, the bright, cruel reflections of each glass, bottle, plate and cup, the mathematical creases of the tablecloths: these things have for her a nostalgic appeal. They remind her of the kitchen at home, blistering white, and of her mother.

The idea behind all this precision is that a customer, seated at a four-seater in Piccadilly, might as well be seated at a four-seater in Holborn; that a customer might forget, seated at his table, that the restaurant has an actual location. The idea is that Lyons corner houses might become for their customers a single place, a unique, unmappable location. Behind everyday appearances – this is the idea – lies a better world; the world of the Lyons corner house.

Tonight, in her room, in the dark, by the glow of distant harbour fires, she writes to Sage, Professor Arven, John, whatever it is he calls himself: '*We survive because we pretend. Life is too rich, too complex, too uncertain. Life resists method. Life will not be examined. It will not be picked up and laid down.*'

And wakes up. The beautiful cadences of her letter evaporate on the air.

Grim, determined, she gets up, turns on the light, checks the blackout and writes, for real this time:

The Weight of Numbers

'Dear Prof. Arven, I have yet to receive a reply to my letter of 3rd inst.'

The following evening after work, Kathleen finds the buses have been badly disrupted. She does not have money enough for the cinema tonight, so she decides to walk home. She walks along shattered streets, past twisted bicycles and ziggurats of shattered masonry, walls made of sandbags and windows criss-crossed with paper tape. The air, though dry, smells wet, a trick of the plaster dust that already reddens the sky as the day slides towards evening. As she goes, a magnificent sunset builds around her, reviving the city's spirits: green and rose and deepest carmine, indigo and lemon; towers and vistas, cloudy bridges, dusty promenades. A city of spirit hangs over this city of stone.

She passes her neighbourhood library – a handsome Edwardian building – and sees that a bomb has been dropped on it.

The explosion has knocked the roof aside as though it were a lid, and the upper storey has come crashing down over the public rooms. The whole frontage has fallen away. Dislodged joists lie up against the remaining walls like pencils in a jar, confusing the geometry of the once orderly rooms. The walls are lined with books. The bomb has done them no harm, though the upper storey has crushed and buried the centre stacks completely.

Kathleen is surprised to see six or seven men inside the ruined library, browsing the shelves. They are like her: ordinary people returning home from work. They wear hats and coats. They carry satchels and leather bags. They move past each other, abstracted, intent on the titles before them. Business as usual.

A short, ill-favoured old man in a sort of quilted smoking jacket – something that went out of fashion long before she was born – opens his satchel and takes out a book. He surveys the stack. He locates the spot he was after, and slots his book back into its rightful place on the shelf.

She says, 'We survive because we pretend.'

She is among them. She has joined them. She is browsing the books, tilting her head to read titles in the fading light. She is picking her way over loose boards, easing past strangers, murmuring 'excuse me' and 'thank you'. Plaster crumbles underfoot. Index cards stir and flap at her ankles as she edges sideways along the shelves with slow, muted movements. Three tall, book-lined walls surround her, shielding her from too much reality, and slowly the fantasy, the browsers' brave 'as if', takes hold.

She reads: *'Apart from its mode of projection, the construction of the space vessel offers little difficulty since it is essentially the same problem as that of the submarine. Naturally the first space vessels will be extremely cramped and uncomfortable, but they will be manned only by enthusiasts.'*

It is from the entry for the biologist J. B. S. Haldane, in an encyclopaedia of philosophy so large it has been published in two volumes: 'A to K' and 'L to Z'. She glances back at the flyleaf and receives a shock. The editors' names are printed there. J. B. Priestley is one, and underneath his name, in smaller type: J. D. Arven.

A hand settles upon her back. There is someone beside her. She steps forward a little, to let him by, and the pressure on her back is lifted. However, the man does not move by. She senses him there, to her left, not reading, looking at her. She pretends to ignore him. The light is failing. Words swim about, tadpoles in the reticular grey pool of the page.

One by one, visitors are leaving the ruined library. She listens to them: shoe leather against stone and brick; a coat-tail brushed over planks; something dislodged; a hollow, confused sound from within the teepee of broken joists, charred linoleum and ceiling lathe which fills the room.

The hand settles on her back once more. Her heart races. She does not step away.

The man has a scent. It is mild and pleasant. It is the scent of tar soap and aftershave, and sherry after lunch. It is smoky and adult. It is the smell of her uncle, who was so friendly to her, and who, she has guessed, is her real father.

The hand moves down her back, over her rear, to the vent in her coat. The hand moves inside, then out again.

She had said to her mother, 'You married the wrong one,' and after that, there was no going back. Her mother did not even come to the station to wish her well. This was all the confirmation she needed that it was true.

She waits for the hand to settle on her back a third time. Browsing the stack opposite theirs, where the light is still strong enough to read, one or two men still linger. The man – her 'uncle', her real father, her fantasy taking root in the shelter of three tall, book-lined walls – waits, not touching her, but standing close beside her, so she can smell him. The scent of the cigars her uncle smoked behind the wheel of his low-slung car. Their famous 'business trips', so urgent, so important, ending always in a picnic in some pleasant spot, and him so kind and smiling, making conversation. Kathleen eating everything in sight. Falling in love with him.

'Dear Father' she had written: a letter she would never send.

'Dear Uncle': that, too, went in the bin.

Did he know by now, that she had found out who he really was? Did he even know, himself? Had her mother told him? Or, once Kathleen had failed to turn up at the abattoir, had he worked it out?

Has he come after her?

Is it him?

In the shadow of three ruined walls, the fantasy blossoms.

They wait to be alone. The man bends forward and takes a book from the shelf. She turns aside. She does not want to see his face. She does not want to know who he really is – some civil servant, bank clerk, inspector of drains. She does not want to know the truth. She does not need the truth. She needs the dream.

By chance, he has picked up the companion volume to her encyclopaedia. He opens it: 'L to Z'.

He leans in to her.

He runs the edge of his volume against hers, back and forth. She studies his thumb. A clean, square-cut nail. Strong. A tiny scar above the knuckle. It might be her uncle's hand.

Yes, she decides. It is his hand.

It has become too dark to read. Her uncle turns, making sure they are alone.

They are alone.

He closes 'L to Z', steps forward and slips the volume back into its place. Kathleen lets 'A to K' fall into the rubble at her feet. What does it matter?

The man sighs. He bends down. She cannot help but look at him. When she sees that he is wearing a hat, she sighs with relief. He can still be her uncle. She has not seen him. He can still be who she wants him to be.

He slides the volume into the stack, beside its mate. He turns to her. She turns away.

He takes her arm, turning her to face him.

She pulls away, keeping her back to him.

He takes her arm again.

Again, she pulls away.

She feels his breath, fogging the back of her neck. He takes hold of her again – not her arm this time, her shoulder. His hand is heavy. It squeezes. It knows what she wants, now. It drives her forward, over the rubble, to an open doorway.

It used to be the door to a reading room. The reading room is gone. There is a cluttered nothing beyond the door, a waist-high maze of shattered masonry and scorched timber. He pushes her and pushes her. She staggers, her ankle twists and she loses her balance. She falls to her knees. She stops there, on her knees, swallowing the pain. She gets up. Her knees are bleeding. Her stockings are torn. One of her shoes is missing.

Hands reach around her and draw her coat from her shoulders. Her arms hang loose by her sides. She shivers. She waits. One hand at the back of her neck, one hand in the small of her back, he bends her over. She clasps her legs just above her grazed knees. He reaches up under her dress and pulls.

Her knickers will not tear, however hard he tugs. He curses, lets her go. She stands up. It might all be over now. Dreadful. Mortifying. What if the moment is lost? She hoists up her skirts, hoping to keep him. She runs her hands in and down, pulling her knickers to her ankles with a fluid motion. She kicks off her remaining shoe. She steps out of her underwear. She waits.

He lifts up her dress, higher, higher, around her waist, up over her breasts. He runs his fingers down her back, to the crack of her bottom, and in.

She steps forward, surprised, away from him. There is a piece of wall in front of her. Brick, with something painted on it: letters from an advertisement. She leans against it. It shifts sickeningly under her hands, and she is afraid she will fall. She readjusts her weight. The surface holds under her hands. She spreads her legs.

His fingers run lightly down between her buttocks. He cups her cunt with one hand, runs light fingers over her back with the other.

He parts her lips with fingers that are already wet. He runs a finger between her lips, and finds the weak point, enters, curls. She sobs. He moves forward. The wings of his coat tickle the backs of her calves.

He enters her quickly. It is like he is stubbing out a cigar inside her. She cries out. He leans forward, over her, and his free hand covers her mouth. She smells sherry and cigars and soap, closes her eyes and licks the palm of his hand as he snaps her head back.

She thinks of her mother doing this. Bent over. Bent back. Filled. She tries to imagine her mother, given up to this dream. It is impossible. The mother she knows is a woman who looks things in the eye with a terrible dispassion. A woman who looks beyond every pretty dream to the inevitable rot. Beneath the skin, always the skull. Beyond the dress, a pile of rags.

This, she decides, moaning against the restraining hand, is why Sage's method is not enough. Not *wrong* – but nowhere near enough. Because, after all, there's appetite, the human itch. No method can accommodate it. 'Look what you made me do,' her mother used to say to her. Perhaps, when he was spent, she said it to him, too – her real father.

'*Look what you made me do!*'

The image is so ludicrous, Kathleen laughs out loud.

And wakes up.

The man's hand is gone from her mouth.

How much time has she lost?

She nearly forgets her purpose. She nearly turns around.

The man's hand falls on her just in time, firm across her buttocks, holding her to her intention. This dream she is having. Her daddy inside her. His fingers feeling for the other way in.

He sucks his thumb and presses it between her buttocks, wetting her. He licks it again and brings it back to her bottom again. His thumb stirs the muscle there. His breathing becomes laboured. He withdraws from her cunt, then tugs at her hips, repositions himself, and presses his erection against the rose of her anus. He gasps. There is a wetness coming out of him. He presses harder against the muscle of her bottom, the wet lubricating him, so that he begins to penetrate her there. His thrusts are irregular and wet. Another kind of fire runs through her, and her body fights him, fights him, then suddenly, without her meaning to, surrenders, and his erection splits her.

He holds her very still until she has stopped crying. She feels him inside her. She squeezes him, feeling him there. Little by little, savouring it, she squeezes it out like a turd.

She stands upright. She looks for her shoes. The man's hand curls around her arm.

Shuddering, repulsed, she pulls away.

'All right?' he says.

This is her fantasy, not his. She will not share.

'Shall we have a cup of tea somewhere?'

She needs to shut him up. She needs to get rid of him. Fast. She wishes there was a sign around her neck: 'Keep Off'. She will have to speak to him. What should she say?

She remembers the sailor Dick Jinks, the night he turned up at the guest-house door. What he said about Donald, his friend.

'Poofter,' she says.

She hears the breath catch in the stranger's throat.

'Nancy!'

The electricity between them is palpable. Behind her eyes, she sees his fists begin to curl, the knuckles whitening...

'Queen.'

She screws up her eyes, tight shut, anticipating the blow. She is afraid. What if his fists aren't enough? What if he picks up a brick? It is too late now.

'Fuck you,' she says.

She counts to ten.

She opens her eyes.

She feels that he is gone.

Her coat is lying at her feet. She picks it up and slips it round her shoulders.

Her shoes are nearby. Her knickers. She puts them on.

Dizzy, disorientated, it takes her a moment to recognize the sound of the sirens. How much time has she lost? Where is she? Is she alone?

She turns around.

She sees the bomb. She actually sees it falling, the great mass of it, the unlikely speed, as though it has toppled out of the sky by accident. Surely this is not something anyone could ever mean to happen. The whistle at its nose glints in the moonlight as it bursts through the

outstretched branches of a tree and the whistle is a terrible, familiar
'*Eeeee!*' as it fists the earth.

Kathleen rises. Idly, she backstrokes the air. Something showers her.
She is expecting plaster dust, but no, it is a rain of shredded leaves.
Bright birds spin around and around the stripped trees. The birds are
very bright. Their wings are on fire.

Kathleen lies back and watches the burning birds.

And wakes up.

She is alone. The street smokes and crackles. She sits up. Ahead of
her there is a great crater. She looks down at herself. She is covered with
earth. She gets up, and the earth falls away from her, and as above, the
burning birds wheel with a great scream towards the moon and vanish
in its glare, so below, inside her belly, the stranger's sperm, one flagellant
stray, finds its mark.

WHITE MAN'S MAGIC

1

It is 1952 and early in the year: already dark by five.

'So dark out there!' Kathleen wails. She is stood before the rain-beaded lounge window, framed by orange-and-brown geometrically patterned curtains. Her shoulders are hunched and rounded under a shiny blue nylon housecoat.

She and I are the only ones home.

'Saul! What are we going to do?'

William, my father, is late home from work. Driving back from Fratton, it is not unusual for him to run into heavy traffic, especially in bad weather. You might think that the more there are of these unexpected late homecomings, the less frightened my mother would be. You might think that the more often William returns home unscathed, cursing the traffic, the less likely Kathleen is, on the next occasion, to assume the worst: the skid, the collision, the closed coffin. But Kathleen lives in a dangerous world, in which every act is a game of Russian roulette, and William's safe homecomings are as the empty chambers in a pistol barrel which, turning, can only draw the fatal bullet, chamber by chamber, closer to the pin.

Home – since she left London with her husband on one arm and me in the crook of the other – has been this new-build bungalow on a residential street running parallel to the London–Portsmouth trunk road. It is small and snug, though the gardens, front and rear, are huge and wild, as though they belonged to a much grander property. Kathleen reckons that I will have a lovely safe time here as I grow up, playing about in these gardens. I am such a happy, lively child! I am sure to have many friends!

Beside the bungalow is a garage big enough for two cars. A second car is an unimaginable luxury, especially since Kathleen has no desire to learn to drive. More likely they will one day buy a caravan; when not in use they can keep it on the patch of hard-standing, screened by conifers, which William has already prepared. He is so practical. So very organized.

Where will they go in their caravan? The Isle of Wight. The Lake District. Up to Darlington, even; Kathleen would like to visit the North again one day, and show me the landscapes of her childhood.

Kathleen has painted every room of the house white. It is the colour of the starched tablecloths in the Lyons corner houses where she used to work. Also, it is the colour of her mother's kitchen. Neither association is a wholly happy one, but associations, memories, the past – these are not the point. The effect of so much whiteness is clean and bright and aspirational. It is the décor of becoming, not of being. This is what her life is: a crisp new blouse, fresh from the wrapper.

William insists that Kathleen need not go out to work. She is a mother. He, meantime, has a job in Fratton, introducing new breeds of calculating machine to the offices of the Southern Electricity Board. (In 1939, flat feet and childhood rickets saw to it that William waddled, ignominiously rejected, out of the Hackney volunteer station. Soon after, he had stumbled into one of the duller reserved occupations, doing sums for the electricity board. He has been in that line of work ever since.)

In vain, Kathleen tries to talk to her husband about his job, the machines and the calculations they perform. In vain, she tries to engage. 'It is very complicated, Kathleen,' he says. He is tired, after a long day at the office and such a long commute. 'It is too complicated for me to explain.'

In idle moments during the day, while Saul naps or plays in the garden, Kathleen may take one of William's books down from the shelf in the lounge. Flashes of colour light the backs of her eyes as she reads, ragged remains of her synaesthetic gifts.

Binary notation.

Boolean algebra.

Algorithms.

Regret is cheap, she knows that. She has much to be thankful for: a handsome, happy child, a generous and handy husband, a clean new home to treasure. But she is not so much of a Pollyanna that she cannot see the opportunities that have passed her by. The strange gift detected in her at the very beginning of the war – her easiness with numbers, her vivid understanding of them, almost a sixth sense – this gift has never found any outlet, for all the professor's encouragement, for all the hopes he stirred up in her, for all the letters she sent him.

She had wanted to be a computer, back in the days when a computer was still a person. A trained and respected computer, perhaps with her own office. How strange her hopes sound now, as though, with the change in the meaning of one word, some part of history has been erased. These days her wasted talents are worth nothing. Any adding machine can perform as well as she ever could, if not better. Even William could best her, armed with one of his precious machines. ('It really is very complicated, Kathleen,' he says, with an exasperating little smile. She finds herself hating him.)

So it is not good for her to look back. She must look forward. She must always be looking forward, to the bright white future of her Second Chance as Wife and Mother.

By day, the limitations of their new life mean less to Kathleen than her own project of improvements. Every year she repaints the bungalow's interior with paint that, every year, promises an even more intense whiteness, a whiter-than-white whiteness, a whiteness that is (according to the changing fashions of the advertising industry) Chemically, Biologically, even Optically White. She longs for surfaces like shells, for the opalescent shimmer of mother-of-pearl. Surfaces from which would issue, on demand, a kind glow. An early convert to the pleasures of indirect lighting, she has asked William to fit dimmer switches in every room. William grumbles that with the lights turned so low, he cannot see to eat.

As the daylight fades, so the colours of the street begin to leach away, and the bungalows to either side of them – early experiments in prefabrication – seem to flatten themselves out against the grey ground of the evening. The whole street becomes a shoddy simulacrum, and the bright white emptiness of Kathleen's future closes around her like the cold enamel walls of a bath.

'So dark, Saul!' Kathleen wails.

'The traffic is so heavy,' she says, gazing across her road, and up, over the earth embankment and through its screen of trees, to the fleeting red-and-white tracer fire that marks the trunk road proper.

'If only the traffic wasn't so heavy.'

And: 'Please let him be careful in the heavy traffic.'

There is panic in her use of the same image, over and over again, and there is poetry, too. *Heavy traffic.* While trying to find the words to express her fear, she has found that it is best expressed, not by the right word, the apt phrase – which, once uttered, can only leave her dumb – but by the wrong word, the trite phrase, repeated to the point where it acquires the ecstatic mumbo-jumbo of an incantation.

'Why is there so much heavy traffic?'

'This heavy traffic isn't necessary.'

'The traffic's getting even heavier.'

Reason cannot comprehend reality, and fantasy cannot manipulate it. This is the lesson Kathleen has drawn from life. Reason and fantasy are two sides of the same bent key. They unlock nothing. They reveal nothing. Step into the world expecting magic; cause and effect will crush your every expectation. Look at the world objectively, and everything before you turns fantastical and absurd. You only have to look at this place. Our address mentions the village of Horndean, but Horndean, pretty as it sounds, is not a village so much as a line of ribbon development, straggling pointlessly by the side of the trunk road as it carves its way through the South Downs. You drive for miles by lawns of tall dead grass and glimpse, now and again, far away down crazy-paving drives, houses of peeling green pressboard and untreated corrugated iron, sheds on concrete stilts surrounded by fences of rusted chicken wire; sometimes knee-high walls, their bricks Post Office red with a thick poisonous resin, the mortar white, a kitsch criss-cross. Hand-painted. Madness.

Whatever strategy Kathleen picks and puts her trust in, it lets her down. There is no compass in this life, no way to measure latitude or longitude. There is no certainty in Life but Death. She knows this now. So the cold white walls of her Second Chance have risen around her. Within them, imprisoned by them, Kathleen has become bullet-proof. She will never be fooled again.

'Look how heavy the traffic is!'

'Why is the traffic so heavy tonight?'

'I've never seen the traffic so heavy!'

Kathleen stands before the window, chanting. Powerless. She is beginning to frighten even herself. This is what she wants: to be frightened by something other than life, that wellspring of escalating terrors. If she can only frighten herself, then it will be like being frightened by a friend; in other words, hardly frightened at all.

Heavy traffic.

'So many accidents, Saul!'

Heavy traffic.

Evoked by her panic, an image forms behind my eyes. William, my father, sat in his Hillman Minx, jostled from side to side by great juggernauts and tankers. He squeezes his elbows in and straightens his back, as though proper posture might save him. He keeps to his lane and maintains his speed, but this pathetic assertion of will only makes a collision more likely.

I would like to give my mother some comfort – for my sake, as much as hers. God forbid she gets any worse. Her panic is an emotional flash-flood that leaves me winded and trembling. 'Dad will be all right,' I assure her, with all the hard-won authority of my nine years, and – painfully aware of my insufficiency – I hug her waist.

Kathleen's imagination is contagious. I can see, behind my mother's eyes – clearly, as though it were a painted miniature – my father torn to shreds, strung between steering column and door pillar in a cat's cradle of bleeding ribbons in the rain, somewhere outside Cosham, or Waterlooville, or Cowplain – all these wet barnyard names.

Misery loves company. 'What are we going to do?' Kathleen cries.

Ten years later: 1962.

'Everybody makes mistakes,' says William Cogan, the day he takes his final leave of the Southern Electricity Board. Today is the first day of the rest of his life – it says so on his card.

To William Cogan: 'The very best of luck'; 'Be missing you'. No one has had the faintest idea what to write.

A radio, tuned to an easy-listening station, snags the air the way a torn fingernail catches on clothing. The air is hot and chlorinated. A cake. A glass of warm white. For a leaving present, a crystal decanter.

'Everyone makes mistakes,' William says, towards the end of his thank you speech, as though excusing his colleagues for their shoddy performance today.

Acutely aware, in this moment, of the possibility of making one of those inevitable mistakes.

His eyes fixate on a point a few inches above his small, shuffling, distracted audience. 'Everyone makes mistakes. The thing is—' He swallows. 'The thing is, to make as few mistakes as possible.'

Saul, his son, gives a sober nod. Ah, my boy!

The truth is, I'm finding something stirring and tragic about my dad today. Not much thought of by his workmates. Misunderstood ('Relax! Have fun! Travel the world!'). Unacknowledged master of the straight line and sharpened pencil, amidst these messy office girls. ('Look who he's had to work with!' Kathleen sighs in my ear: her sucked-lemon face.)

In a couple of months I'll be leaving home for Trinity College, Cambridge, where I will be studying Russian literature. Product of a sheltered upbringing, denied bicycles and sleepovers and childhood friendships, I have not the remotest conception of the world that is about to hit me.

'Machines will take over what I did there,' William says, with not one hint of regret, when we are home. Machines reduce the world to black and white. To zeros and to ones. Everything is either one thing or the other. Something or nothing. Such a system cannot make mistakes. 'Machines will do this now.' For another few years his pianola chest will labour, gears turning: his hands moving automatically across the paper, drafting a mill, a turbine, the plan of a granary. (To fill his retirement, he has joined a local society set up to encourage an interest in such things. He goes on trips to mills and goods yards and derelict factories to measure and draw for the little pamphlets the society prepares, two or three times a year. His drawings are professional, accurate, useful. Art without mistakes is art reduced to the techniques of draughtsmanship.)

He says: 'I have to get this done.' He says, 'They want me to do this.' And: 'This has to be finished by…' I understand that these are expressions of happiness.

William's retirement means that there is little by which one day might be distinguished from another. Shopping day follows washing day. Gardening follows cleaning follows decorating follows gardening. In such an atmosphere, change becomes synonymous with accident, and novelty brings with it a tremor of fear.

Kathleen, however, finds she cannot heighten her experience of life with the usual anxieties. She no longer has any reason to stand at the living-room window, looking out at the rain, dreaming up accidents.

Now she says, 'Do you have to leave all this everywhere?' She says, 'Do you have to do that at the table?' She says, 'Do you have to have it on so loud?'

Come winter, returning home, after my first term at Trinity, I find my father fixing strawberry netting over the garden pond.

'Why are you doing that?' I ask him.

'Your mother is afraid the hedgehogs will drown.'

'Why?'

'We have hedgehogs,' William says. 'They can't swim.'

'Of course they can swim.'

'The netting will keep them away from the water.'

'Everything can swim.'

'If they want a drink they can use the bird bath.'

'You just need to prop something up in the water so they can crawl out. There's nothing in there for them to crawl out on.'

'She has it all arranged.'

'A bit of wood or something.'

'She has it how she likes it.'

'They'll still drown.'

'This is good netting.'

'They'll still drown. They'll still find a way in and then the netting will trap them and they'll drown.'

'I'm fixing this properly,' he says.

'It won't make any difference.'

'It will if I do it properly,' he says.

'No,' I tell him, 'it won't.'

'What's the matter?' Kathleen calls out from the kitchen. 'Saul? What have you done?'

Even now that I have left home, it will be a while before I acquire much mature coloration. I remain, in my dress and manners, that gifted, shy, nineteen-year-old schoolboy. My interests are broadly the interests I had as a child and I make a point, during the vacation, of visiting our neighbour – Mrs Wilson, an old woman, long widowed – so that I can thump about on her bizarre, oversize piano.

'What are the pedals for?' I remember asking her, many years before, confronted by the instrument for the first time.

Mrs Wilson, a diabetic and double amputee, had her little legs on that day: stubby metal legs without joints, paddles in place of feet. They helped keep her upright in her chair. They were pretty useless for walking unless you were simply heaving yourself over from one piece of furniture to another. 'Pedals?' said Mrs Wilson, blinking at her paddles, where they dangled over the edge of her Cintique chair. 'These?'

'No! In there. The piano pedals.'

'Ah,' she said, and smiled. 'The *pedals*.'

'Yes.'

'Well, Saul, as I'm sure you've noticed, they make the piano softer or louder.' Playing a little game with me.

'Not *those* pedals. The *others*.'

'Ah,' said Mrs Wilson.

It was a pianola. Mrs Wilson, perched precariously on the piano stool, directed operations: 'Now turn that catch. There. Yes. Now let it down. Gently, Saul, gently.'

The belly of the instrument lay revealed: a handsome gutwork of rollers and spindles, needles and hammers.

'See over there? In that basket? Get a roll.'

I fetched a roll of paper from the basket. It was heavy, the paper thick like parchment. Mrs Wilson showed me how to string the punched paper roll between the sprockets. 'There. Help me down now,' she said.

'Take a seat,' she said, exhausted, balanced on her little legs. 'You pump them. Those pedals. Like riding a bicycle. Do it hard, they'll be very stiff.'

I sat down before the pianola. I pretty much had to slide off the stool to reach the pedals. I began to pump, hard and heavy, on the wide rails set to either side of the usual *piano* and *forte* pedals.

Within the belly of the pianola, something stirred.

The thing played itself.

Bar after bar, line after line and unfailingly, the pianola realizes its self-idea. As I stood in the Fratton office, sipping Blue Nun with his co-workers, I imagined spoked drums turning in my father's chest. His narrow perfection.

2

'Must enjoy filing,' it said on the card – and a Bloomsbury address. The library of a private society, requiring temporary assistance.

I imagined the place, its pre-war interiors given over to elegant decrepitude. I pictured hallways lined with glass-fronted cabinets, and books and manuscripts in teetering piles. Portraits and small Byronic landscapes, steeped in a thick brown lacquer, lined the faded, silk-panelled walls; and were I to negotiate my way through the complicated, dust-smothered window-dressing in the first-floor drawing room, I would come at last, through the age-rippled glass of a sash window, upon a view of a secret garden contained by high walls, swathed in thick ivy of the deepest green. At first glance, the garden would appear deserted. Then, at the last moment, through the straggling knitwork of budleia and rhododendron, there would come a suggestion of movement, a figure. A young woman in a white dress. Were I to wind up my courage and raise the matter with my shadowy employers, of course they would deny her existence.

'Six shillings an hour,' my temp agent told me. Poodle perm; miniskirt; smooth, sallow thighs; thick ankles; large, unlikely breasts. Whenever she stood over me during my typing training, they hung over my head like a threat.

On Monday morning I climbed the stairs and pressed the buzzer. The door honked angrily. I tested it with my hand. It gave smoothly, and I walked in.

Fluorescent light robbed the hall of shadows. The sand in the fire bucket by the door was littered with fag-ends, all of the same make: the banded white filter of Gauloises Disque Bleu cigarettes.

I moved towards the only open door, at the far end of the corridor. From it issued the sound of an old typewriter, as loud and loose-actioned as a steam loom. It stuttered, clack following clack at a rhythm just slower than a heart's beating. The music of depression.

Her name was Miriam Miller. She was tall and bird-like, her greying hair folded softly into a shapeless bun; fastidiously groomed but with a face so lined, dry-cured in French tobacco, it could not help but look dirty. A white blouse trimmed with navy blue.

'Your attention to specifics is very important.' Miriam's gnomic turn of phrase was less distracting to me than her strangely impeded speech. It sounded as though a tape were stretching inside her, shifting everything vowel-wards. 'S's shushed like waves lapsing on a gravel shore.

What was this place? I wondered. What did it do?

'We service an international clientele,' Miriam said. She made the place sound like a high-class knocking shop.

'We concern ourselves with preservation,' she said.

I supposed at first she was talking about herself.

'We foster Research.'

What kind of research?

The Society's library resembled less an academic collection, more the well-worn core of an underfunded public library. What coherence could there be in a collection that rubbed the nasty blue-edged pages of Robert Heinlein's *Revolt in 2100* against six volumes of rambling theosophist autobiography entitled *Old Diary Leaves*?

'Researchers' came and went: men with unkempt beards and unreliable trouser zips; one or two utter derelicts (baffling hints of public library again); well-groomed women of a certain age. The more flirtatious of them would sometimes ask me, 'What's a handsome young man like you doing here?'

In 1965, my last year at Cambridge, my father suffered his first stroke. Because my mother needed my help, the college authorities agreed to defer my final few semesters. This saved me the trouble and embarrassment of dropping out. It also entailed going home – something I had solemnly sworn never to do.

In the featureless shell Mum had made of our home, Dad's cerebral accident took on a terrible rightness: as though he, too, had been integrated into her vision of interchangeable white walls and wipe-clean surfaces.

Mercifully, the repugnant fact of my father's condition – the obscenity of adult helplessness – took my mind off home's other horrors, at least for a while. His infantile walk, his arms extended, hands interlocked to straighten his paretic arm. The way he slumped in his chair, as though unstrung. The keening sounds he made when my mother and I forced his arm and shoulder through their exercises. The ridiculous bright ruler he used when he read the *Express*, so that his eyes would remember to travel to the left to start a new line.

'He doesn't even try!' Mum cried.

She brandished the word the way a maniac brandishes a blunt instrument.

'Why don't you try?'

'You've got to try.'

'Just try a little.'

'Try just once!'

Sadly, in this instance, she had a point. He did not fight back. He did not speak. He did not walk. Now and again – and according to the nurse this should have come under his control long since – he shat his pants.

The truly grotesque element in all this was the degree to which none of it was novel. It was more like the physical manifestation of a psychological state with which Mum and I were already familiar.

Throughout my childhood, he had depended entirely upon my mother for every bite of food, every drop of drink, every clean sock, every fresh towel; at the same time, he seemed entirely self-sufficient. Our affection left him indifferent, and so did our anger. He could take anything the world threw at him. How do you wound a ghost? How do you make a ghost stay? It was only his own inertia which kept him here with us. Had he had a fraction of the energy of other men, I am certain he would have found a way to leave us; and I would have run across him eventually, pursuing some solitary happiness.

As it was, my father had done little for years but sit in his chair in the corner of the living room, watching the football results. When he rose from his chair, which was rarely, he moved from room to room with an air of muted dissatisfaction, like a commercial traveller, forever delayed, who has decided to eat just one more passable meal with the same reliable but overbearing landlady. Not forgetting her son.

So though I trusted him, and even admired him, as children do, my father had never given me any reason to feel that I was related to him. Year after year we had observed each other through the thick glass of our mutual reserve.

When Dad suffered his first stroke, I found myself bursting with such energy, I couldn't sit still, I had to walk up and down the carriages of the train. By the time I was jogging up the hill out of Guildford towards the big new county hospital – I hadn't the patience to wait for a bus – I could no longer pretend to myself that these feelings were normal. I was excited, but not anxious. I was happy to think of my father gone out of control at last. I wanted to hear him say 'Gah' and 'Wonk'. I wanted to see him dribble.

The fact was, I wanted him to be someone different.

I remember when I got to the hospital, the nurses had only just found him a bed, so for a while we had to wait outside the ward. My mother's face was white as though dusted. She was full of that queer, nervous energy I had dreaded to see in her: an overwound toy, exhausting and useless.

'What have I done!' she wailed. (Six hours into my father's stroke and she had already cast herself in the lead.)

They let us in to see him.

Half his face was missing. Where the left-hand side of his face should have been, there was only a greyish bag of loose skin. Where his eye should have been, there was a slit in the skin, and a black marble swimming inside it. His lips were bleary and thick and very pink. There was something grotesquely sexual about the smear his mouth made.

Home again, and in her gleaming kitchen – impossible to imagine these surfaces have ever been contaminated by food – my mother weaves her web of unenticing possibilities: tea or apple juice, or there's some orange barley water in the pantry; Jaffa Cakes or homemade scones. There are some chocolate biscuits somewhere, only she can't find them, she's been looking everywhere. You bite into a scone and she says, 'Or there's some cake.' You stir your tea and she says, 'Or would you rather have coffee?' You tip strawberry jam onto an edge of a scone and she says: 'Would you rather have honey?' You take a bite of scone, raw flour coats the inside of your mouth and she says, 'Ooh! There's some quiche!'

In the middle of the night, a scream.

'Saul!'

'Saul!' she wailed, and entered my room, my old room, this room she had kept for me, and painted white for me, and which I had sworn never to sleep in.

'Saul, he was such a good man!'

Mum wanted to get her elegy in early.

'He took me in, Saul! He took me in!'

'Go to bed, Mother. Try to get some sleep.'

'No one else would touch me. No one.'

'Is there anything in the bathroom cabinet that would help you sleep?'

'Saul, you don't understand.'

'Some hot milk?' I was baiting her. It was irresistible. I was so tired.

'He's been like a father to you. Hasn't he? Hasn't he been like a father to you? He's given you everything, hasn't he?'

'Yes,' I said. Biting my tongue. Crossing my fingers. 'Yes, of course he has.'

'Not every man would do that, Saul.'

She was calming down now. She was Delivering a Lesson.

'I know that, Mum. He's been a great dad.'

She burst into tears.

I laid my hand on hers.

She clutched it.

'He did know, Saul. I didn't trick him. He knew before we were married. I did tell him.'

'Tell him what?'

She blinked at me. 'That I was pregnant,' she said.

'That you were *what*?'

She tried to get into bed with me.

I eased past her and out of the room, touching her as little as possible.

'What have I done!'

'Kathleen,' I said, from the kitchen, 'shut up.' I filled the kettle. My hands were shaking with excitement. I was filled with a sense of sudden and unexpected freedom.

As soon as my mother had learned how to handle things, so that the spotlight of her anxiety shifted naturally onto me:

'Have you done your university work?'

'Have you got much university work to do today?'

'Don't forget your university work.'

'Leave this – go and do some university work.'

('*Wonk,*' my father added. '*Gah.*')

– then I got the hell out of there. I couldn't face going back to my studies and, without my college grant, I had no money. So I did the only thing left to me. Yet another thing I had sworn never to do. I got a job.

The Society hosted speakers. There were talks on Wednesday evenings, sometimes illustrated by means of slides or an overhead projector. P. J. Mills of Surrey University presented 'Teaching Systems, Present and Future – a Multiple Image Tape/Slide Presentation'. There were poetry readings.

When I first began working here I used to wonder how on earth the Society – this dowdy old maid off Gower Street – survived the modern world. It should surely have perished of its own anachronisms years ago. So much for the arrogance of youth. As I began to understand the Society's past, I began also to understand its strength.

The Society had accreted around the writings of the Polish-born American linguist Alfred Korzybski. In the early 1930s Korzybski had developed a theory of relations that did away with the notion of cause and effect. (He was, like all his generation, besotted with Albert Einstein's recently published General Theory of Relativity, and his misreading of it made him the first and greatest of the century's many quantum quacks.) Korzybski declared that everything exists, not because it acts, not even because it thinks (which is, after all, only another kind of acting), but because it is already related to everything else. Cause and effect are merely special manifestations of a relation that already exists.

But if everything is connected to everything else, then the dimensions that separate things from each other – the three spatial dimensions that place things at a distance, and a fourth dimension, time, which makes that distance meaningful – these have no absolute reality. They are, in fact, contingent upon this higher relation of universal connectedness. That being so (the Society's earliest pamphlets argued) might we not use dimensions to our own advantage? They might not turn out to be barriers at all, but doors...

So the spirit of the times drew the Society away from a dry study of Korzybski, and into a frequently confused relation with the many other societies trying, with varying degrees of rigour, neurosis and faith, to come to terms with the scientific ideas of the time. Madame Blavatsky and Colonel Olcott spoke here, and for a while the Society toyed with the principles of theosophism. Bequests from leading spiritualists sustained the Society during the war years, and after the war, science fiction had a major impact on the Society: files of correspondence with A. E. Van Vogt and Robert Heinlein – both at one time or another devotees of Korzybski – were treasured between sheets of acid-free tissue in a fire-proof safe.

The Society had been gorging itself on the new ever since. The second week into my job, I nearly passed out to discover that John Lennon topped Miriam's wishlist of future speakers. (He never came.)

Sat at the back of the Society's puzzling library with my card indexes, my sharpened pencils and my plastic loose-leaf binder detailing the Society's bizarre scherzo on the Dewey system, I was cut off from anything resembling a lived life. Three years went by while I sleep-walked among the stacks.

In March 1968, I woke to discover I had become one of the Society's less vital internal organs.

A spleen.

A gland.

Something unspecialized as yet. Something barely aware that it served a greater metabolism, that discerned only dimly that it lived in a body at all. Something which, if you excised it and grafted it elsewhere, would survive; and not only survive, but adapt, adopting over time the structure and function of the part to which it was newly joined. ('*Saul, do the books*', '*Saul, introduce our speaker*', '*Saul, type a letter*'.) The outside world had been coming through to me so thoroughly digested, so strongly flavoured by the Society's guts, I was hardly aware what strange times these were.

It was Noah Hayden who woke me. We ran into each other on the street, one evening at the beginning of March.

'Saul!'

I didn't recognize him at first. An honours student at St John's, the latest in a long line of academics and political players, my old room-mate had exhibited, all the time I had known him, the careless charm and casual irony of a privileged caste. Darling of the left-wing, founder of the New Left Reading Group; wits had it that Noah Hayden put the champagne into socialism. It had never occured to me that he would turn native. Bumping into him three years later on the corner of Frith Street and Old Compton Street, confronted with his beard, cravat and velvet coat, I stepped backwards and practically fell into the road.

We went for coffee to Bar Italia – a brightly lit utilitarian café so long and narrow it was more a sort of corridor. We perched on stools beside a chrome shelf which ran the length of the room. Everything glittered: tiles, mirrors, crockery. The broiling reflections in that place were an open invitation to schizophrenia.

'So what are you doing now?' Hayden asked me.

What was I doing? His lack of self-consciousness amazed me. In that get-up – he looked like a demonic ring-master fallen on hard times – it was surely Noah who owed me the explanation.

I opened my mouth to tell him about the Society, the library – and no words came. This was the moment it dawned on me that maybe three years was a long time to spend treading water. Maybe it was too long. I made some noises eventually, using my father's condition as an excuse for my lack of news. Noah Hayden reached over and squeezed my arm in sympathy, and I felt like a shit.

At college, Hayden's inherited self-confidence had made him class-blind. He would drink himself under the table with a party of hoorays one evening, all political differences suspended for the sake of good companionship; the next day he'd be talking protest tactics with the sons of Jarrow marchers in a little diner in the Backs, stuffing his greenish, hungover jowls with cheap waffles.

I was the petty-bourgeois dullard in the corner, the one who belonged in neither camp, and I was as solemn as an owl. Though the first in the family to go to university, I could hardly pretend to be working class, what with my piano lessons and my Penguin Classics paperbacks for Christmas.

If I had kept to myself, it wouldn't have mattered; no one would have stopped me living an anonymous life. But I had discovered, dragged along to meetings by my room-mate, that politics offered a different sort of anonymity: identification with a tribe.

While student revolt gathered pace in Paris and London and Madrid, in the New Left Reading Group we contented ourselves with organizing sit-ins to protest the college curfews. The rest of the time we spent living up to our name: we read. Because I had the knack of languages, I proved useful to Noah Hayden and his precocious Group when it came to unpicking the gnomic pronouncements of Guy Debord, founder of the Situationist International in Paris. It is possible that I was Debord's first English translator. This was, for my money, a much better thing to be than what I truly was: the passive beneficiary of my parents' graft and saving; the grammar-school-educated child of parents who had had to buy their own education late in life, in church halls and schoolrooms after hours, who believed it was a right and good thing to aspire, to amass everything they could in order to invest it, all of it, in their child.

My parents believed, as no generation since has been able to believe, in the overwhelming moral power of financial generosity. Having lavished so much on me, they took my gratitude as a done deal. Their psychological incompetence was extraordinary. At the end of my first term at university my father sent me a cheque, bailing me out of a debt I'd run up at Heffers bookshop. He signed his accompanying letter, 'Yours sincerely, your Father.'

'Why's he writing "yours sincerely"?' Noah Hayden asked me, when I showed this letter to him. 'That cap "F" is very good, by the way.'

'Because I am known to him,' I replied. 'If I was not known to him he would have written "Yours faithfully".'

I had to tell someone. I had to turn it into a joke. I didn't think I could bear it otherwise. For these first, difficult months Noah Hayden was my lifeline, and he never let on that he knew.

'And what about you?'

He told me the New Left Reading Group had fallen apart not long after I dropped out, stifled by its own inertia. Hayden took his finals, but claimed not to know whether he had even got his degree. 'I'm not bloody going back there again,' he said. His scowl was extraordinary. It was ludicrous. It was pasted on – the worst sort of bad acting.

'St John's?' I said, not really understanding him. 'Cambridge?'

He waved his hand, dismissively. 'Any of that shit.'

For all the fierceness of his political rhetoric and his increasing obsession with the situationists, I had never had Hayden down for a drop-out. But how else was I to interpret his words? Or his clothes? The longer we talked, the more it seemed that Hayden had fallen out the bottom of his political convictions into some hyper-theatrical space of his own.

'Are you coming on the march?' he asked me.

There was a big demonstration planned in Grosvenor Square the next day, a Saturday, to protest the war in Vietnam.

'We'll show those Trot bastards a demo!' he exclaimed, rubbing his hands.

It was a different language he was speaking: a puerile rhetoric of cheap aggression. Vietnam was a distant blur on his radar: he was more interested in the other marchers and how misguided they were.

They weren't his own words, of course. They were something he had learned over three years of drifting and unemployment – what he called 'action'. This was a good time for Svengalis, and just as I had fallen under Hayden's spell at university, Hayden – unexpectedly daunted by the world outside St John's – had found himself someone to believe in.

The real story, such as it was, came out in asides and gestures. It was all 'Josh went to Strasbourg in sixty-six.' 'Did you read Josh's piece in *IT*?' 'Josh is planning this freak-out happening in Selfridges.' (Even his syntax had been torn down and rebuilt in his master's image.) It was all 'Josh's barmy army' and 'Josh's knit-your-own revolution'. Scathing and intimate, Noah's off-hand comments revealed his infatuation.

I don't remember much about the march itself. I only went along to meet up with Hayden, and in the press of people we somehow missed each other. From the Society's top floor, I had got not a hint of how strange the world had become. Now I was in the thick of it, trapped by the press of marchers up against a party of German students, row after row of them, running on the spot, then performing lusty squat thrusts, as though they belonged to some sort of youth movement. There were even a handful of *bona fide* clowns and jugglers. A welter of languages I'd not heard before outside the classroom dissolved, as we paraded along Oxford Street, into one long monotonous chant: 'Ho! Ho! Ho Chi Minh!'

Three men in gorilla suits and straw boaters passed me, howling in reply: 'Hot Chocolate! Drinking Chocolate!' One of them took off his head to grin at me. It was Noah Hayden. The next second, he was gone.

I don't remember much else.

I remember Grosvenor Park; the darkening of the day; the sealing of the exits.

I remember the sky filled with clods of earth, and from this I know I must have been near the embassy, right near the front of the line, because the clods were raining down on us, and they hurt.

I remember someone screaming, and the hooves of the police horses and the sound they made, that non-sound, so unthreatening, like a thousand packets of soft butter falling onto a wooden floor. A great turbulence swept through us, the whole crowd knocked off-balance, and I remember, in that crowd, it felt as though the world itself were dipping and swinging like a passenger plane hitting a pocket of dead air. I remember the crowd scattered, and a white horse reared, and I remember a man with a stick, and the stick coming down.

I remember the taste of earth, and hands under my shoulders, testing my weight. And a gorilla's head, seconds before a boot stoved it in, and another boot, scissoring, kicked it away.

I woke up on a mattress on the floor of a big, tatty room in a house I didn't know. The trees outside the window were orange, and the sky was black. It was night-time. Beside the bed there was a bedside lamp, and a scarf over the bulb, and a smell of scorched linen. I pulled the scarf away. The light lanced my eyes. I groaned and turned away, and found myself facing a door. It was ajar. Beyond the door, a chair dragged; there were footsteps.

A teenage girl with blond hair shorn close to her scalp came in and knelt down beside me. She laid her hand on me: my brow, my hand, my shoulder. Her eyes glittered oddly in the light coming from the lamp. She went out again and came back with a bowl of tinned tomato soup and a cup of tea. While I ate I heard other footsteps; a loud, laughing conversation, curtailed suddenly by the careless slam of a door. Comforted, I slept a while more.

I had a crashing headache when I woke up again, and the room was full of people. I sat up.

My shoulder was red raw: there would be a bruise the size of a plate there tomorrow. But it moved OK. I wondered who had undressed me.

'Hey there,' said the girl, noticing me from where she sat, propped up against the opposite wall. She wasn't much more than a child. The rest of them were hardly older. A boy came in with a bundle of something wrapped up in newspaper. I assumed it was chips, but I couldn't smell them.

'Where's Noah?' the boy asked, glancing round.

'Still in the Rio trying to get served, I'd guess.'

The boy knelt down and unrolled the newspaper, revealing a bundle of cannabis.

There were books propped up on the window ledge. I could tell I was coming to, because the spines began popping into focus. (Colin Wilson. John Braine. No wonder the revolution failed.)

'Hey there.'

It was easier to interrogate the books than the people. I couldn't maintain eye contact with anyone for more than a couple of seconds before their faces began to distort, as though their eyes were little gravity wells.

'Hey.'

The air was spiced suddenly; someone was holding a joint under my nose.

The girl who'd fed me soup went out and came in with a wicker sewing basket under one arm and a bundle of black fur trailing across the carpet behind her.

It was a gorilla suit.

She dropped without ceremony onto the middle of the floor and began unpicking the threads at the gorilla's sides. Without thinking, I took a drag of the joint and handed it over to her.

'How you doing?' she asked me.

'The gorilla suits.'

'That's right.'

'You're urban gorillas.'

She smiled. 'Yes.'

'I don't get it.'

'You just got it.'

'I did?'

'Yes.'

'What's to get?'

'That,' she said, nodding at the gorilla fur spread over her lap.

'The pun?'

'The deconstruction.'

'The what?'

She was really very young, maybe sixteen or so, and wanted to be taken for someone older. I thought about Noah Hayden and his extraordinary transfiguration from political player to anarchist clown.

Was everyone here playing a part?

She pushed the suit aside, crawled over and hunkered down beside me on the mattress. '"The Spectacle is a slave society's nightmare, merely expressing its wish for sleep."'

Guy Debord again: a more elegant rendering of his famous line than any I had ever come up with. 'What's your name?' I asked her.

'Deb,' she said. 'Debbie. Deborah.' She seemed unsure.

Another handful of people walked in and Debbie nudged me over, making room on the mattress. It was then, glancing at her, that I noticed, through her fuzz of blond hair, that her skull had a perfect dent in it, the size of a half-crown. Her brutal hairstyle suddenly took on a new and disturbing meaning for me. What if it wasn't some sort of statement? What if it were something to do with that frightening dent?

About an hour later, Noah came in. He was still in full Jerry Cornelius get-up. Debbie got up and went over to him and kissed him on the mouth. Noah had a black eye and news from Vine Street, where two of their number were spending a night in the cells. 'You know Josh is still bound over?'

'Fuck.'

'That's right.'

'Josh is *fucked*.'

News of Josh's fuckedness rattled around the room like a bean in a can. Underneath their anger, people seemed secretly delighted, as though, of all of them, Josh had made it to the next round.

'Yeah, but what about Saul?' said Noah, when the commotion died down. 'Saul took on a horse.' He gestured broadly, conjuring a beast of great size, and his arms, emerging from the capacious flared cuffs of his Paisley shirt, were as white and shapeless as roots. 'He pulled a pig from his horse.'

'No, I didn't.'

'The nasty fucker had his truncheon drawn. Saul ran straight up to him.'

'No, I didn't.'

'Saul is our hero.'

The whole room cheered me. A fresh joint slipped itself between my fingers; a box of matches.

It was a good-natured joke. They were making me feel welcome. I managed a grin. A tin of beer found its way to me.

When people went off to bed, it was all at once, as though someone had blown a secret whistle. The joint was back with me again; I stubbed it out on the nearest ashtray: Guinnless isn't good for you. Noah and the girl remained in the room. It was their room. They were sleeping in the bed, opposite mine.

'Place is stuffed to the gills tonight,' Debbie explained.

'You OK there?' said Noah.

'Yes,' I said. 'If you're sure—'

'OK, then,' he said, cutting me off. 'Good. Good to have you here.' He hunkered down and gave me a hug. His hair was long and unkempt, but it smelled sweet. Before I could figure out whether to hug him back he was halfway to the light switch.

I had never been hugged by a man before.

I lay back in the dark and listened to them undress.

I woke the next day with an even more painful headache to find the house was already virtually empty. After much stumbling around I found the kitchen. Noah was in there eating toast. 'How're you doing?' he greeted me.

'Where the fuck am I?'

Noah and his friends had manhandled my bloody, semi-conscious form onto a number twelve bus, bearing me like a trophy all the way to Holland Park.

'Great,' I said. 'Thanks.' Now all I had to do was work out where Holland Park was.

'If you've a shilling for the meter I've got eggs for an omelette.'

I fished about in my pockets and came up with a coin.
He took it and pointed to the chair next to me.
'Try that on.'
Lying on the chair was a ball of black fun-fur – a gorilla costume.
'What's this for?'
'Try it on for size. We're going gardening.'
'We're what?'
'Gardening.'
'Where?'
'A garden.'
'What?'
'Parsley? In your omelette. Cheese?'
'OK,' I said.

I liked the Society. I liked its location, five minutes from the British Museum and its eclectic, down-at-heel satellites – a comic shop, a science fiction bookshop, several showrooms of Middle Eastern antiques, a dealer in defunct stringed instruments. To the east, Senate House resembled nothing so much as an outsize version of those Victorian obelisks you find in cemeteries. I liked the regularity of the architecture, the neat terraces, the sober bulk of the institutional buildings, the absence of bustle. Never did I imagine that I would one day be wandering these streets armed with a pair of bolt cutters, let alone a gorilla costume strapped across an old duffel bag stuffed with balloons.

The gardens of some of the smaller squares here were privately owned. Just over the road in King's Cross there were whole housing estates with nowhere for kids to play. Josh, our leader *in absentia* – he was serving a month in Brixton – had a lively idea of what redistribution ought really to be about. The idea – fleshed out and agreed upon well before the VSC march and Josh's arrest – involved bolt-cutters, balloons, a van full of sand and a great deal of sweat.

Noah drove the van; the rest of us had to cart our gear to Tavistock Square on the Underground. This was risky – people were starting to hear about Josh's 'urban gorillas', and were cottoning on – but we arrived at the square with no one following, no whistles blown, untroubled, as yet, by what Josh liked to call, in his understated way, 'uniformed support'.

They expected me to use the bolt-cutters on the gate.

'We could just climb over,' I protested.

'We could, stupid,' said Noah, 'but what about the kids? You expect mums with pushchairs to scale the bloody fence?'

Josh's plan gave us twenty minutes to turn a private ornamental garden into a public play area before the pigs turned up. Frantically, we dug and dug, while another of our number, a dwarvish girl with pigtails and a cut-glass Rodean accent called Nova (a corruption of Veronica), tied balloons to the busted-in gate, the oh-so-private trees, and nearby lamposts. Noah plucked the Do Not signs out of the lawns and beds and ran off with them hidden in a carrier-bag.

When the hole for the sandpit was ready, we laid a scrap of tarpaulin down as a crude liner and ran to the van to fetch the sand. The efficiency of the operation surprised and impressed me, and I could barely lift the sacks Noah carted about so nonchalantly on his shoulder. By the time the sand-pit was half full, the girls were into their gorilla costumes, and little kids who were passing, snared by the sight of balloons, were dragging their mothers over to see what was up.

Nova shouted for help with the swing we'd planned to sling over the park's one serviceable tree-branch. 'I wish Debbie was here,' she said, when we were done. 'She'd love this.'

'Where is she, anyway?'

Nova shrugged. 'Gone.'

'Gone?'

'She and Noah – it's kind of stormy.'

I thought of Debbie, her glittery eyes and damaged head. I thought of her feeding me soup, and the way she had scrambled up to hug Noah when he came in the room, and Noah, in his loud shirt and threadbare velvet jacket, bending down to kiss this child on the mouth. The two of them undressing in the dark. 'She's very young,' I said.

Nova thought I was being critical. 'Hey, you, she's, like, dead sound,' she scowled.

I didn't even know what this meant.

'Where's your head?'

'What?'

'Put your head on.'

'What? Oh.'

Kids were streaming into our freshly liberated park; kids from the Brunswick estate; kids from the expensive terraces round Coram's Fields; kids out shopping with their mothers; latch-key kids, their fingers black with engine oil.

I put on my gorilla head.

'Come play with the kids. Come on. The uniformed support'll be here in a minute.' She let out a couple of comedy pig grunts and ran cheerfully ahead of me to welcome the children.

I handed in my notice at the Society and served out my week as conscientiously as I was able. Then I went to live at Josh's squat in Holland Park.

The house was an anomalous survivor of clearances for the new Westway. The terrace it belonged to had been bulldozed away long since, and the Edwardian building, its weak side-wall supported on a timber frame like a man on crutches, stood in a complicated geographical relationship with the feedlanes and towers of the half-built motorway.

Josh and his friends occupied all but the basement. That remained inviolate: the lair of Mr Sadberk, formerly of Istanbul, the autocratic ruler of his little kingdom. He did not own the house, and he had no special relationship with the company that did, but he was as territorial as any other imprisoned beast, and his intermittent rages, his savage bangs and kicks upon the front door, his haranguing us from the pavement whenever he caught a glimpse of a sign of life, these things kicked up clouds of anxiety in the house, like dust, a pain between the eyes.

For as long as the moonscape beyond the front door promised the advent of something futuristic and exciting, Josh and his band rode easily above the locals' occasional hostility; but it was, after all, only a road, rising to block out the light, and, as work progressed, the mundanity of the future it represented began to bite. The scene Josh knew was moving inexorably East. The *International Times* was put together in Covent Garden now; *Oz* came to replace it, to be a voice for the area, and although many of us wrote for it, it seemed weak by comparison. Experiments in community learning and action foundered on the apathy of the straights. Mr Sadberk continued to live up to the weak jokes we made of his name.

In a big unheated front room cleared of furniture, piled with cushions, we overstated these problems to each other, warming ourselves on the idea of embattlement. We were young and frightened. Rather than occupy the future, we preferred to enshrine the past, and hanker for the good old days of last year, last month, last week. Each one of Josh's friends told me, at one time or another, that I should have moved in earlier; that it was a shame that I had missed this happening, that march; that had I moved in *then*, or *then*, then I would truly know what Josh was all about.

Even in 1968, the sixties was a time we looked back on dreamily: the Past.

Debbie was back with Noah by the time I moved in to the squat. Then she vanished again. Then she was back. I asked Noah where she went when she disappeared. He just shrugged.

'You must have some idea.'

'She's a free agent,' Noah replied.

Everyone here seemed very keen on defending Debbie's freedoms. I wondered if anyone had ever thought to defend Debbie. Noah and Debbie's 'stormy' relationship seemed to consist of Noah not giving a shit and Debbie walking out on him – only to return, three or four days later, invariably famished, and with eyes that were even more glittery than normal. The next day they spent in bed – never a sound from the room, though, not the remotest sigh or stir. After that the whole cycle would repeat.

'What happened to her head?'

'Why don't you ask her?'

'She isn't here.'

'She'll be back.'

'Until she isn't.'

Hayden held my look. 'Meaning what?'

'Where does she go, Noah?'

'How should I know?'

'Where does she go once you've fucked her off?'

Christmas 1968, and in Selfridges department store, eight unsanctioned Santas are working the queue for the grotto, handing out presents, spreading good cheer, and all for free. The parents – Kensington mothers in the main – stand by, nonplussed. They know something is off, but they can't pin it down. The event's not falling into any category. And of course, the kids are enjoying themselves.

From shelves and from boxes, from tissue-wrapping and brown paper: free Christmas gifts for everyone. Dolls, cars and fluffy toys. Bears, tanks, footballs, packets of transfers. Model aeroplanes. Angel costumes. Glitter. We sweat up a storm in our rented Santa outfits: everything must go. A crowd is gathering. Some sort of psychic force is drawing in kids from all over the store, from every floor, tugging reluctant mums and dads into the toy department.

Ladybird and Palitoy, Pedigree and Galt and Waddingtons, everything must go. Meccano, whose mind is pure machinery! Monopoly, whose blood is running money! Action Man, whose fingers are ten armies! Sindy, whose breast is a cannibal dynamo!

'Ho! Ho! Ho!' the Santas cry. 'Ho! Ho! Ho Chi Minh!'

How long have we got? Not long. The pigs are on their way, they must be by now, surely, and what began as children's theatre acquires an air of adult desperation: 'Take it! Take it!'

Blindly we thrust free stuff at whoever will accept it. Mistakes are made. A six-year-old girl brandishes a Roy Rogers pistol thoughtfully in front of her parents. Two boys, brothers in the misery of corduroy, wrestle blindly for possession of a My First Make-Up Kit.

'Take it! Merry Christmas!'

'Do you work here?'

'Take it! Here!'

'Excuse me...'

'Merry Christmas!'

Now that the shop's security staff are bundling in, the kids are not so certain about this giveaway. They are not so eager for the gifts we press into their hands. Parental eyes are narrowing. In prams and pushchairs the youngest children sense a change in the air and fear – without a thing to fear, and in the midst of plenty – rips through everyone.

A baby starts to cry. Then another, then another: gentlemen, our work here is done.

So back to Notting Hill, a quick drink in the Rio and out the back, our grass done up in newspaper like chips.

'What happened to your head?'

Drink has made me forward with my questions. Besides, we are alone in her room. Noah has gone out to stuff his face with toast again; everybody else has gone to bed.

Debbie passes me the joint and touches the side of her head, where the dent is. 'When I was a kid,' she says, 'I was in an accident.'

'What sort of accident?'

'A car accident.'

She is lying.

'What do your parents think of you being here?'

She looks at me, incredulous. 'What have they got to do with anything?'

'It's just a question. It's not like I'm saying you're not a free agent or anything.' (Clumsily, I am adopting the tortured rhetoric of this place.)

'Anyway,' she says, 'Mum's dead.'

'What about Dad?' I say, straight off, refusing to be sidelined by this invitation to pity.

She shakes her head.

'What about him?'

She stands up, running her fingers through her close-cropped hair. 'You know, Saul, you're really doing my head in.'

An unfortunate turn of phrase. I am gripped by sudden inspiration: 'Did he do that?'

'What?'

'Your head. Did your dad – *hit* you or something?'

'For Christ's sake!' Her yell is so loud it brings Noah in from the kitchen. '*Of course not*, you stupid bastard.'

All that night I lay awake in the next-door room, listening to Noah and Debbie argue their way up to their next bust-up. Debbie was furious with me and wanted me thrown out of the squat for being 'an arsehole'. Noah defended me.

I listened as the row built and built. When I couldn't bear it any more, I got dressed.

When the argument finally boiled dry, this is what it reduced to: her or me. Either I went, or she went.

Noah, more exhausted than angry, told her to fuck off, then.

I stood there, forehead pressed to my bedroom door, listening while Debbie got dressed. I heard her leave the room she shared with Noah.

She was crying. I heard her clatter down the hall. The front door opened, and slammed shut again.

I grabbed my jacket and went after her.

We put ourselves on the housing list, Debbie faked a doctor's letter, and we moved out of the squat and got the keys to a big, cold flat in a council block not far from the canal above King's Cross.

Hayden insisted on helping us move in, turning up at half-past seven in the morning in a brand-new white rental van which bore the unnerving legend 'Impact Hire'. He had been up all night scavenging from skips. 'You can make bookshelves with these bricks I nicked.'

'Thanks, Noah.'

Because we were so much taller than she was, Hayden and I stayed out on the road while Debbie lowered things down to us from the back of the van. One moment it was, 'Come on, let me have it! Let go!' The next it was, 'Debbie, love, can you not just drop things? Jesus.'

Then Hayden had to leave and Debbie helped me carry my gear up the communal stairwell and into the flat. She insisted on lifting heavy weights and kept having to set things down on the stairs so I couldn't get past. There was a passive-aggressive quality about Debbie's helpfulness that had me guessing about her motives. 'Debbie, stop – my hand is pinned. Deborah!'

We lived together for about three months. We rubbed along pretty well. We washed up. We cooked. We rowed. We scoured skips for more second-hand furniture. We shared the bathwater and the bed. We were as intimate as it is possible to get without actually having any sex.

Her lack of enthusiasm took me by surprise. I thought at first she just needed time. But the longer we spent together, the more remote the possibility seemed. I was disappointed, but I was also relieved. She was very young.

We hugged and kissed. But the slightest suggestion of sexual interest, intended or not, had her turning away from me and the tremor of her tightly wound body would keep me awake for hours; it was like lying beside an unexploded bomb.

She wanted, none the less, to be part of my life. Her insistence was so great she eventually wore me down enough that I took her by train to Rowland's Castle to meet my parents.

Mum expressed her excitement at the prospect of meeting Debbie in a way uniquely hers, by making a chore of everything. 'What does she eat?' she asked me when I made my weekly phone call.

'Grass, mother. She eats grass.'

'I can defrost a chicken pie.'

'Congratulations.'

'Oh, but it's very small.'

Hours and hours of this.

'How will you get from the station?'

'We'll walk.'

'If you get a taxi I can give you the money.'

'You don't have to give me any money, Mum, I've got money.'

'Oh, but there are never any taxis there!'

'No. That's true.'

'What will you do?'

'We'll walk.'

'You can't walk.'

'Then we'll crawl.'

'She won't want to walk all that way.'

'Then I shall bear her through the burning stubble fields on my back like Anchises.' I was twenty-five years old, and still I was punishing her for my grammar-school education.

Dad was sleeping in the garden when we arrived. Hi, said Debbie, walking up to him. He straightened himself in his deckchair. Debbie was so little, her tits were about level with his face. 'Unh,' he said, greeting them.

Debbie and my mother circled round each other all afternoon. It was impossible to imagine they had anything in common: Debbie, all kohl and bangles and barrow-boy haircut; Mum in her slacks. Debbie was by far the more nervous of the two. She had everything an iconoclast needs except for imagination; this is what I supplied. Every few minutes I heard one of my own sardonic *bon mots* spill, lumpen, from her uncomprehending mouth.

Mum, non plussed, chuntered happily on, partly to herself, partly to me, partly to a young lady of her own invention. As the day wore on she grew more confident. She squeezed Debbie into the mould she had dreamed up in the days prior to our visit. Debbie could no more resist the cascade of my mother's logic than a terminal patient can resist the blandishments of an aggressive oncologist, and by two that afternoon, there was Mum snapping away merrily with her Instamatic camera, and there was Debbie, tottering about the garden in one of Mum's old summer frocks.

'Saul, get in the picture!'

Mum sent me one of these photographs a couple of weeks later. Debbie is standing in our back garden wearing a sleeveless summer dress smothered with brown and yellow flowers. She is trying to show willing and flounce for the camera; as a consequence, one of her legs looks shorter than the other. She is looking down and away, hiving herself off from the world. Sealing herself up. You imagine her staggering away from a car accident. Debbie's combination of shorn hair and this old John Lewis summer dress, at least two sizes too big, makes her look even more like a doll hurled out of a pram.

It amused me, that afternoon, to see Mum's quiet egomania carrying the field. On the train back to London, I fed Debbie the story she needed: how kind and patient she had been, and what a good sport. 'Those bloody dresses!'

Debbie had been made to choose one for herself as a present. As we rattled through Godalming, alone in the second-class carriage, she fished it out of its polythene bag: Mum's gift.

'Jesus,' I said.

Debbie laughed, and spread it out on her lap for me to see.

I covered my eyes. 'Take this abomination away.'

'If I slip it on,' she said, 'will you kiss me?'

With an Oedipal howl, I tore the dress out of her hands, pulled open the window and stuffed the dress through.

And that was the end of that: one more moderately disheartening return to the place of my birth. I remember Debbie looking out of the window, as the orange suburbs of London coagulated around us: Croydon to Clapham, Wandsworth to Waterloo. The flatness of her mood. The empty polythene bag, scrunched up in her hands.

Afterwards, whenever the subject came up, she would talk about our 'ghastly' visit. That 'ghastly' day we had. 'Ooh, do you remember that ghastly dress!' But whatever she might say afterwards, whatever she might tell herself, my taking her home with me that day had represented something. All she had to show for meeting my parents was that dress; and I had thrown it away.

It seems so obvious, this long after the event, the damage I was doing to her. I was leading her on. I was making it possible for her to believe in this calamitous idea she had of herself since moving to the squat in Holland Park: Debbie the contrarian, the under-age radical; Debbie the teenage iconoclast.

She was none of these things. She was, like most children, hungry for life, full of energy, desperate for validation.

'What about your dad?' I was still trying to unpick this – still trying to solve the twin mysteries of her injury and aloneness.

'What about him?'

'What's he like?'

It wasn't his cruelty she had run away from. It was his care. 'He thinks he could have stopped the accident,' she told me, in bed one night. 'He thinks he should have prevented it. He's always trying to make it up to me. The accident – I was eight years old when it happened. Ever since he's been... surrounding me.'

The image of herself she had conjured – a child running away from her father's terrible need – should have been enough for me. I had never been as honest about myself. But like a fool, I took this as my cue to ask her again about the accident.

'Leave me alone,' she said.

She liked the idea of independence. For her, solitude and freedom were the same thing. This made for a frustrating sort of companionship. All I could do was inflate her self-confidence or tear it to rags in front of her eyes. Either, or. There was no middle ground with her. Those who were not with her were against her.

It was astonishing the degree to which even the brute stuff of the domestic world resisted her. The vacuum cleaner didn't need emptying so often, she said; eventually it burst into flames on her. You just need a dash of water in this, she said, preparing the pressure cooker; it took a whole day for the smell of burnt beans to clear.

She was one of those people who never follows a recipe and claims to be able to do things with vegetables and pasta. She made us a cauliflower cheese once, only she reached into the wrong cupboard and ended up using laundry starch instead of cornflour. 'It's the same stuff,' she said, swilling the paste from her teeth. She was sick the next morning, and every morning for a week after that.

She took her push-bike to a shop to have new brakes fitted. When she got home she told me the shop had adjusted them all wrong. She spent the rest of the day tinkering with them, and every so often she would start crying: strange little yelping sounds like a puppy caught in a trap. The next day she rode her bike slap into the back of a number twelve bus.

When I phoned him, Debbie's father thought I was a private detective. He had paid two separate agencies to track down his runaway daughter. He thanked me for calling. When he turned up at the hospital, knowing who I was, the atmosphere was different. He seemed as afraid of me as I was of him; seeing the size of his hands, I was heartily thankful.

Debbie's fits were under control by then: one grand mal seizure every twenty-four hours or so. No one could explain why her messy but hardly life-threatening accident with the bus should have triggered epileptic seizures. I wasn't family.

Then, of course, what with one test and another, they found out she was pregnant. Harold wanted his daughter to have an abortion. One of the few things he actually said to me, that he made very clear, standing with his face just a couple of inches from mine, the air between us thick with his Old Spice aftershave, was how much he wanted his daughter to have an abortion. This had nothing to do with me. But since trying to convince him of this would have been an impossible task, I didn't even try. And when Debbie insisted on keeping the child, I steeled myself for a disappearing act of my own. One of the things that had kept me going throughout my miserable three-month charade with Debbie was the thought that Noah Hayden hadn't got to fuck her either. Discovering otherwise was galling enough; there was no way anyone was going to strong-arm me into fathering his bloody kid.

Nothing happened. No one phoned. No one beat at the door. When I visited the hospital a couple of days later, Debbie was gone. Her father had collected her and driven her away.

There was something fairy-tale about Debbie's abrupt disappearance – her clothes and few belongings abandoned in the flat we had shared. (My flat, I would have to learn to say.) She had broken through into the outside world only to be spirited away again. It was as though she had never existed.

I rang up Miriam at the Society, and I went back to work.

3

'My mother was a passionate believer in education. After my father died, she said to me, "You must learn the white man's magic!"'

General laughter.

That's right. Keep it light. Remember: last week this same audience of well-intentioned whites was over at the Africa Centre in Covent Garden, learning how to make traditional costumes with Sally Mugabe.

White man's magic!

White man's 'lore', he might have said. White man's 'skill'. White man's 'culture'. But he has learned, when addressing Western audiences, not to be too po-faced. When he tells the tale they want him to tell – 'When I was but a simple goatherd, my mammy said to me' – he uses the word 'magic', even if it does make it sound like he crawled out from under a mushroom.

It is Tuesday, 4 March 1969, and in the library of a distinguished philosophical society in a leafy offshoot of Gower Street in central London, Jorge Katalayo, president of FRELIMO, is speaking about Mozambique, the country of his birth, about the revolution he is fomenting there, and about the serious threat that he and his comrades – educated revolutionaries – pose to their own cause.

Under colonialism, he says, bureaucracy is the only career open to the educated black man. Paper-shuffling is the only thing at which he is permitted to excel.

(He has a complex, assymetrical face, kept this side of ugliness by its smile. He is wearing a cheap, neat polyester suit. He looks, ironically enough, like a bureaucrat.)

'When the Europeans have gone, we lift it as a shibboleth: this power, not even of the pen, so much as of the carbon copy. This is why we so often find ourselves – to our consternation, yes, but also to our considerable personal profit – colonial rulers in our own land.'

Even at the back of the room, by a draughty window where his every other word is snatched away by the street, Jorge Katalayo's oratory prickles the back of my neck.

When, on my return to work, I discovered that the Society had developed a curiosity about the politics of anticolonialism, I was pleasantly surprised; no more. The Society was insatiable, and it had the stomach of an ox. It had long since learned how to cram down every crumb of novelty, lick every smear of fat off the New and, furthermore, how to render this stuff, however intractable – the Black Panther movement, *Nova* magazine, Free Love – into a rich and easy stew on which even its most elderly members might feed.

Mornings, I shuffled paper in the Society's library or typed up little articles for its stream of newsletters. Afternoons, I yawned my way around the arrivals hall of Heathrow airport, holding one sign or another to my chest: Lewis Nkosi; Dennis Brutus.

I was the Society's runner and factotum. I showed our guests the sights of the city. I took them to cafés and paid for their tea with petty cash. I reminded them of their schedules. I got them to the meeting room on time.

Invariably, as we climbed the smart white steps up to the front door, our speaker would pause before that discreet brass plaque, and frown. How the Society managed to attract its speakers mystified me. Not one of them, entering the magnolia-painted hallway, seemed happy to be here. What had they been promised? They followed me up the stairs to the meeting rooms, speechless and staring, as though waking from a spell.

Joshua Nkomo; Agostinho Neto; the ANC leader Oliver Tambo. Holden Roberto cancelled at the last minute. A bout of the flu meant I missed Benedicto Kiwanuka. (Years later, Idi Amin would have him killed for not finding the right people guilty.) Amilcar Cabral, the leader of Guinea-Bissau, spoke so softly that I could not hear him from my place at the back of the room.

Would-be presidents and statesmen-in-exile in sober Methodist ties, the Society's speakers were demonstrably adult in a way Josh and his followers were not.

Katalayo tells his audience that when he was twenty-five, and barely out of elementary school, Swedish missionaries arranged a scholarship, plucking the frustrated student from his obscure province and depositing him in the Douglas Laing Smith Secondary School in Lemana, northern Transvaal. It was here that Katalayo came across a book larger and more impressive than any book he had ever seen before, other than the Bible. It was so big, it came in two volumes – 'A to K' and 'L to Z'.

'I remember learning to read English from this book.'

The English language, from a dictionary of philosophy. Was this possible?

Anarchists are not supposed to be interested in politics. These deadly serious Africans and their wars appalled my Holland Park friends. What possible revolution in human relations could mere politicians bring about, with their antediluvian baggage of ideologies and inter-changeable figureheads? In vain, Josh, Holland Park's *eminence gris*, dispatched Noah to guide me back to the path of righteousness: 'What are our actions, our trespasses, our performances, our carefully staged "situations", if not attacks upon the dialectic between property and privacy, that narcotizing dialectic from which the State itself emerges?' These were the kind of rhetorical sticks he beat me with.

Noah and I both knew time was passing, that dressing up in Santa costumes and causing havoc in Selfridges' toy department would accomplish nothing, that the squat was slowly but steadily falling apart.

Seeing it was hopeless, Noah admitted to me that my shacking up with Deborah had sent a number of long-running residents scurrying to the bathroom mirror for a long, hard look at themselves.

When I asked him why he remained, Noah's windy lecture deflated like a wet bag. 'Change is hard,' he said. 'So we go out in scary clown costumes and we sow a little bit of unease – so what? It just makes the straights even more grateful for their old comforts.'

He was finding a way out of the squat's rhetoric. The buzzwords were still in place but the old debating society grammar was knitting itself round them like a vine. It was good to hear Noah sounding like himself again. At the same time, I knew that our friendship could never be what it was. He had been too much someone else's eager fetcher-and-carrier. I could not look up to him any more and, without that, I couldn't see that there was much else left. Deborah had begged me not to tell Hayden about his baby, and I didn't find it hard to grant her plea. I was only doing the right thing; her wishes had to come first.

Later, of course – too late – even I could see the real motive behind my silence. I had been given a certain power over Noah Hayden, and this enabled me to release myself from his influence. So I deliberately let him down.

Red with embarrassment, Noah Hayden confessed that he was in the process of smartening himself up. Once he had paid off his library fines, the authorities at St John's would be more than happy to hand him his forgotten first-class degree. After that, there was an opening for him in public service. His family had probably had a hand in this, but I reckon he was bright enough to fulfil whatever promises had been made on his behalf. I wished him luck with his mission.

'What?'

'Your secret project to change the system from within,' I explained, with a smile.

Hayden bridled. 'And what about you?' he said. He thought I was being sarcastic. This was a shame; given his talents and background,

Hayden's course of action seemed eminently sound to me. 'Back to that ridiculous drop-in centre, I suppose?'

'That's not fair,' I said.

'Why can't you go to work for somebody sensible, for Christ's sake?'

How was I supposed to answer?

'I mean,' said Hayden, waving his hands about in exasperation, 'what does your outfit actually *do*?'

In order to fund its latest hobby horse – *Africa: a Way Forward?* – the Society had embarked on an operation to 'realize its assets'. This was Miriam's important description for the jumble sales she ran, every month or so, in the building's basement. A small, forbidding sign tied to the railing the week before ('Bring Your Own Bag') was her sole advertisement, but she need hardly have bothered. The same dowdy regulars attended these sales as religiously as they attended the Society's talks, seminars and 'tape/slide presentations'.

The first jumbles were ambitious ('Sale & Auction' the sign announced). There was an old Underwood typewriter. A couple of card-index cabinets from the library – fine examples of the sort of eccentric, looks-useful-but-isn't cabinet-work that these days crawls away to Portobello Market to die. A kilim with a pale-brown stain on it – dried blood? An adjustable couch with brass handles and a smell of horse hair under the perished leather – less like a seat, more like a deluxe operating table.

By the second sale, we were reduced to recycling our waste paper. At the absurdly inflated prices Maureen wanted to charge, the Society's past publications were slow to shift, even among the regulars. There were boxes of old programmes: Dr J. R. Rees lectures on the work of Ugo Cerletti and Lucio Bini for the Drill Hall Open Programme on Mental Infirmity and the Arts. Sir Richard Gregory speaks on 'Science and World Order'. There were little pamphlets on the semantics of Korzybski, the poetry of Mayakovsky, the paintings of Kazemir

Malevich. There was a box, never opened, sealed with tape so brittle it crackled to pieces when you tried to pull it, which turned out to contain mint copies of a wartime spiritualist self-help book called *You Can Speak With Your Dead*.

Miriam's third sale was advertised with a justified baldness: 'Clearance'. The first box I unpacked promised much: a set of padded leather straps and a rubber gat carrying unmistakable bite marks. This was a dimension of the Society's business I had not suspected: I imagined Kinseyite sexual experimentations.

The second box contained framed photographs of a European city between the wars. Looking closer, I saw the shop signs were spelled out in a language I did not recognize: not Vienna, then, as I had at first thought, but a place long since swallowed up into Soviet anonymity.

These were the highlights of the sale; the rest amounted to no more than some bizarre bric-à-brac: a leather hat box; a foot-long stuffed alligator; an able seaman's uniform.

The rest of my time I spent watching as modern Africa invented itself, scribbling itself out on paper napkins in cafeterias all over London. I remember sitting in a greasy spoon on Gray's Inn Road, among squeezy ketchup bottles and mugs of half-drunk orange tea, with Tariq Ali and Vanessa Redgrave. With Joseph Nyrere. Kenneth Kaunda getting drunk with Margaret Feeny in a guest-house kitchen in Gower Street. It sounds strange to recall now, I know. The libretto of a comic opera by Doris Lessing. The future of a free Africa, drawn up on a napkin. These good men, with their fragile dreams: all the ironies of their educated, depatriated condition.

And there, in the corner, trading literary recommendations with Sally's husband Robert, a bald little man in a grey suit – the Soviet negotiant.

You had to admire the man's bulldog determination, the weeks and months he spent making friendly overtures and warm promises to the future masters of Mozambique. But Jorge Katalayo and the FRELIMO council had agreed upon a trenchant policy of non-alignment. This policy, put into action in the cafés of east London, gave Katalayo ample opportunities for mischief. Witness the conversation he started, the day following a party at the Chinese embassy.

'Weren't you invited?'

'No,' replies the Soviet purseholder, sulking already.

'The Chinese ambassador congratulated FRELIMO on its self-reliant approach.'

Guarded: 'Yes?'

'He praised our belief in the people's capacity for autonomous change.'

Big eyes now: 'Really?'

Katalayo smiles his trademark smile.

Sweating now: have his paymasters been gazumped? 'What did you tell him?'

'I told him where to stick it. Much as I keep telling you.'

We laughed.

No one took him seriously.

Miriam's sales had by now taken on a life of their own. No room was spared, no cupboard, no shelf. The atmosphere – the desire to shrive – achieved a Lutheran intensity. Chandeliers vanished from under dusty ceiling roses. The cork message board disappeared from the entrance hall, leaving a bright magnolia square on the tobacco-stained wall. At last, Miriam's Lenten ritual drew near to the Society's holy-of-holies – its library.

Towards the end of every afternoon, Miriam and a couple of elderly regulars combed the shelves of the library for volumes to discard. They were like people eating mussels, who start by picking out the choicest shells and end up consuming the lot. The philosophy behind the Society was itself so smudged by the passage of years that even these old hands had trouble deciding which volumes were necessary to the collection and which were not. If *Winged Love* and *Wellington Wendy* had no place here, what case was there for retaining an incomplete set of John Lehmann's *New Writing*? What did the poetry of Keith Douglas have that the short stories of James Hanley did not? If illustrated catalogues of Henry Moore deserved shelf space, who was Graham Sutherland that he should be excluded? And what kind of philosophical society was it that gave shelf space to Arthur Koestler, while expelling J. B. Priestley and J. D. Arven?

I stopped what I was doing. I took the volumes out of the box again and laid them side by side on the table.

'A to K' and 'L to Z'.

A dictionary of philosophy, in two parts.

By then, Jorge Katalayo had left London for Tanzania. He had given me a forwarding address. I wrote to him on the flyleaf of the first volume: 'You actually learned English from this tosh?'

I posted the dictionary off the same day, and forgot all about it.

Jorge Chivambo Katalayo: former goatherd, former UN researcher, freedom fighter, doctor of anthropology. I never saw him again.

My abiding memory is of the afternoon before his speech at the Women's Institute. We spent it in a greasy spoon on the Roman Road, cramming doughnuts into our faces, hoping that the sugar might substitute for inspiration.

'Before we do anything,' Jorge declaims, 'we have to get our own people working with us.' Ring, jam, chocolate icing: it's all one to him. 'Fragmentation is our biggest problem,' he says. 'At the moment, one village barely knows another.'

I say to him, 'Your audience won't understand that. That won't mean anything to them. How can neighbours not be aware of each other? Roads are like trees to us. Like grass. The idea you have to build a road before you know what's at the end of it – it's not in the Home Counties vocabulary.'

'Home Counties?'

'I mean it won't play to the women of the W.I.'

He makes a note.

'We cannot begin to build' – he tries again – 'while our men and women live in hate and fear of each other.'

'Meaning what?'

'Meaning, on any ordinary day under the Portuguese system, two cattle trucks might pull up in the middle of a work village – an *aldeamento*. The men are told to board one truck, the women are told board the other. The men are driven off to work the fields. The women are going to mend the roads. These men and women, from the same village, married, some of them, sweethearts, brother and sister – they may never see each other again. It's not a deliberate policy, exactly. It's just the soldiers lose track of where they've been. It's a big country. Everybody looks alike. The soldiers don't speak Chichewa and the authorities have made damned certain the locals don't learn Portuguese. So the soldiers can't keep track. In the evening, they drive you to the nearest *aldeamento* and dump you there. Where's your wife? Where's your girlfriend? No one knows. No one cares.'

He looks at me.

'Well?'

I nod.

'What does that mean?'

'Yes.'

He lifts his gaze to the ceiling. 'Help me with this, Saul.'

'I just don't think they're going to believe you,' I tell him. 'They grew up with Kipling. They think law and order is a European invention. Whatever else the Portuguese visited on the black man, they've surely been making the trains run on time.'

Sometimes, when Jorge Katalayo is out of inspiration, when he has drunk too much coffee, and eaten too much sugar, and especially when he is nervous, all you can do is make him angry; see if a spark will catch.

He shouts at me: 'You think we have some sort of enlightened master–servant bond? Mozambique isn't the Raj. Even the Raj wasn't the Raj, but let that go…'

He has an idea: 'In the forties there were only about three thousand whites in Mozambique. Now there's two hundred thousand of these idiots dragging their knuckles across our country, thinking they're better than we are because of the colour of their skin. Which, I might add, is like diarrhoea.'

'Jesus, don't say that.'

'The point is, the junta's bankrupted a generation and robbed them of an education. If it leaves them at home, they will topple the government. So it exports them. It sends them to lord it over us.'

He drains his coffee. He looks pleased.

'I thought this speech was supposed to be about the role of women?'

He shoots me a sour look. Silence while he sluices the dregs of his coffee round his cup. 'Better the devil you know, I suppose,' he sighs. 'When my father died, my mother said to me—'

'That's not about women. That's about you.'

I have pushed him about as far as he will be pushed. 'No,' he says, 'it isn't. Listen. Our educated men do not know what women are. They barely know their own mothers. Like me, they had to leave home to go to school – and I really mean leave, journeying for miles, departing for other countries even, just to get some schooling.'

'Meaning what? For the women?'

Katalayo holds my gaze. In a soft voice: 'Meaning we hate them.'

'God, you're not going to say that, are you? They'll tear out your liver with their teeth. Those that still have them.'

'Why shouldn't I say it? It's true. We hate our women. We blame them. They are our scapegoat. They represent what we would have become, had we not got away. Do you know I have a girlfriend, Saul? A white American girlfriend? Why do you think I have a white American girlfriend, Saul? I know. She knows. We're not stupid. We know what this is.'

'So do I – and it's still about you.'

'For the ones who don't get away,' he goes on, ignoring my interruption, 'what of them? What's the point of falling in love, in trying to start a family, in making any real human connection across the sexual divide, if any given day the trucks can pull up and make your mother, your wife, your daughter, disappear? It's the same for the women, too. Men and women are learning to have nothing to do with each other. We are being taught this. Our children are growing up with this. This is what slavery does. This is what slavery is.'

Finally, we are getting somewhere.

It is not the greatest speech of his career, but from the back of the meeting hall I can feel the audience responding to him.

'The future of our country rests with its women,' he says. The girls of Lourenço Marques, for instance. They have a reputation that runs up and down the entire eastern seaboard of the continent. Now, though, they are running away. Every day, another woman flees into the liberated provinces, through minefields, every once in a while a pretty foot blown off at the ankle. 'We're building them their own barracks,' he says. 'We're putting them to work in the fields. We are teaching them to read.'

I am so proud of him.

The day after his speech at the W.I., very early in the morning, Jorge Katalayo hammers on the door of this little flat I have got for myself over a chip shop near Regent's Canal.

He says the walls of his guest-house in Bloomsbury are so thin you can hear everything that goes on in the neighbouring rooms, every whisper, the sweet and the not-so-sweet, every tear of foil, every condom snap. 'I just need a sit-down,' he says, having walked all the way through Fitzrovia, past King's Cross. 'Can I have a cup of tea?'

I know there is more to this visit than meets the eye, and when he mentions the letter he has received from FRELIMO's Paris office, I figure this is it. Katalayo hands me the letter over the crumb-littered breakfast table. I am teaching myself Portuguese. I have a knack for languages.

Portuguese soldiers have ransacked a mission near Beira which they suspected of harbouring FRELIMO soldiers. They stumbled into an arithmetics class. The pupils were teenagers and young men. The soldiers marched them down the beach and into the sea. They ordered the students to clap their hands. When the students clapped their hands, the soldiers shot them.

Katalayo reminds me that atrocities like these are the last acts of a dying regime. Young conscript officers are returning home to Portugal, broken by what they have seen. You find them in the bars of Lisbon and Porto fomenting revolution under the very noses of the PIDE. The Portuguese army wants out of Africa. The generals saw the writing on the wall back in 1961 when India seized Goa. Dr Salazar didn't listen to them then, and now their poor bloody infantry are paying the price in costly colonial wars in Mozambique and Angola.

Katalayo refuses to be intimidated by force of Portuguese arms. The scourge of colonial might is a theme he leaves to others. He has learned how to turn the brute material of his harassment, imprisonment, and even his torture, upon itself. Each arrest, beating and midnight visitation adds one more blackly hilarious episode to his repertoire of amusing autobiographical tales. He is the David Niven of black power.

This morning, for instance, he tells me about the time a protest by Swedish missionaries got him out of a PIDE gaol in Nampula. By the time he got to South Africa, he tells me, the security forces were waiting for him. The men parked outside his apartment building got so sick of him coming over to bum cigarettes from them, they started dropping full packets into his mail slot each evening.

It was during this strange moment of unlicensed *rapprochement* that a bunch of drunken PIDE men in black-face had burst into his home, gang-raped his wife, surprised his ten-year-old daughter as she returned home and pressed a loaded pistol into her hands.

'"You don't have to kill her," they said, "just aim at her knees."'

I am making toast under the grill when he tells me this. I have my back to him. I am afraid to turn round. 'What happened?'

'After an hour or two of that sort of thing, they persuaded her to put a bullet through Memory's head.'

Memory was his wife.

'My daughter's in Tanzania. She must be nineteen now. Twenty.'

I turn to look at him. He is wearing an expression I have never seen before. He looks utterly helpless.

'She disappeared,' he says. 'She ran away. Now she has come back. She says she wants to see me.' There are tears in his eyes and I know, in that moment, that I am not, and never can be, what I most want to be: Jorge Katalayo's son.

I come to the airport to see him off. 'It will not be long,' he tells me. He means the war of liberation. He wants me to join him, when the time is right. FRELIMO needs educated men. The party has such ambitious plans.

All summer long over plates of doughnuts, over pots of tea, over mugs of instant coffee, Jorge Katalayo, FRELIMO's first president, has been sketching out for me his plans for the future of Mozambique – a colour-blind, gender-blind, ideologically fluid Utopia. A land without hate. A land of total literacy and high levels of general education.

It has not escaped my notice that he has been describing Sweden.

'I'll see you in Maputo!' he says, at the gate.

Maputo is the local name for the capital, Lourenço Marques. In 1968 it is still a Portuguese stronghold.

'Write to me,' he says, and I promise I will. He has given me his daughter's address in Dar es Salaam—

*

'His daughter's address?'

They sat up. They looked at each other. Suddenly the polite, buttoned-down young men of the Mozambican consulate were taking notice of me.

The one nearest me put down his tea mug. 'His *daughter*, did you say?'

On 21 July 1969, details of Apollo Eleven's successful moon landing pushed Jorge Katalayo's assassination deep into the bowels of *The Times*. The half-page article devoted to his killing was short on political analysis, but rich in forensic detail. The explosives used were 'characteristically Japanese', whatever that means. The brown paper wrapper in which the bomb arrived had originated in London. The bomb itself was secreted in a hollow cut into a large reference work.

Someone had intercepted my gift of encyclopaedias.

A to K and L to Z.

Someone had knifed out the knowledge and laid death in its place.

ANNIHILATION THERAPY

1

It is 10.30 a.m. local time in Lourenço Marques, the capital city of colonial Mozambique, and so far this is a morning like any other. The street-sellers are setting out their wares: pyramids of peppers and potatoes, expired medicines and Chinese prints. It is Sunday, 20 July 1969. Today, a man prepares to set foot on the moon, another will have his head blown off by a bomb.

Three floors above the street, in the tiny offices of a cash-strapped educational charity, project director Gregor Dimitryvich is startled by the arrival of his sole remaining employee.

Indeed, Anthony Burden's arrival has so surprised him, Gregor Dimitryvich jumps up from behind the table. Now there is a cloth spread over this table – a fancy, frilly Portuguese lace tablecloth – and on it are arranged a bizarre and evocative assortment of batteries, wires, clock parts and scribbled notes. Gregor has tucked an end of the tablecloth into his trousers, presumably to catch stray parts of the watch mechanism he's dissecting. When he jumps, a spool of wire falls to the floor; a clock, and a pencil. A hand magnifying glass follows, shattering on the bare boards of the room. A notebook slides after; a soldering iron; a spool of solder. Another pencil.

Had he burst into the office brandishing a gun, Anthony Burden could not have made a stronger impression.

'Get in!' Gregor barks.

Anthony closes the door, deposits his walking stick in the antique umbrella bucket and lowers himself gingerly into his customary seat, opposite his employer.

Gregor remains standing with the tablecloth spilling from his trousers like a long, white tongue. 'I am expecting a package. A man will deliver this package. A sailor. When the sailor arrives you can wait in the next room.'

This is the name Gregor gives the toilet. The Institute has no other rooms.

'Or I could simply go,' Anthony offers. 'If it's inconvenient—'

'This would not be best.'

'Oh?'

'Please. Sit down.'

Anthony shrugs – he is already seated. The gesture makes him wince: his back is bad today.

'I mean stay seating. I mean...' Sighing, Gregor gives up his attempt to correct his mangled English, and releases himself from the tablecloth.

All of which is disturbing enough, but not at all surprising.

The moment he hobbled off the plane in Lourenço Marques, Anthony Burden guessed that this 'institute' he was supposed to be working for was nothing more than the cover for yet another moribund KGB field station. There should have been a driver waiting for him at the gate, holding up a cardboard sign with his name on it. But the teenage factotum sent to collect him felt so under-used, he instead approached Burden, *sotto voce*, by the newspaper kiosk, slipping a hand under his arm as he did so.

When, rather angrily, Anthony Burden shook him off, the boy responded as if electrocuted, every muscle tensed for action, his hand already inside his coat. 'You are the teacher, yes? You teach the little nigger kiddies?'

Lubyanka's finest.

Pathetic.

Since 1951, when he left the Migdal Tikvah kibbutz, mathematician and communications expert Anthony Burden has been working within the nascent aid industry. With a CV like his, and omitting mention of his treatments for manic depression, a fifty-two-year-old ex-academic of Anthony's stripe should have been able to carve out for himself a small but profitable niche in a top-flight Western NGO. Instead, Anthony has trodden a steeper, stonier path. In reaction to his unhappy years in Israel – the gulf that opened up between his own socialism and his wife's Zionism; their eventual separation; the company he kept in Haifa; the trouble it got him into; finally, his ignominious expulsion – Anthony's political leanings have slid ever leftwards, condemning him, since the Cold War became truly global, to a life of straitened living and unsatisfying piece-work. The latest of the many half-hearted, left-leaning 'friendly institutions' to have employed Anthony Burden is this Soviet-sponsored and practically penniless 'Institute of Field and Distance Learning'. No doubt his old friend John 'Sage' Arven – wartime scientific guru to Whitehall and a lifelong communist – would appreciate the irony of his situation.

He does not expect to be stuck here much longer. Given the wobbly state of the junta in Lisbon, it is a wonder the police have not closed them down already.

Meanwhile, outside the urban strongholds, the forces of black liberation are gaining strength and reputation. From friendly Tanzania, FRELIMO guerrillas are conducting a successful military campaign against Portugal's conscript forces. Their behaviour towards the imperialists – if you believe the pirate radio stations – is positively ethical. On the front line, revenge attacks are forbidden. Soldiers killing white civilians are trucked back to Tanzania for political re-education. Portuguese land-holdings are not targeted. The soldiers of the liberation are not permitted to confiscate food, and so they eat what the peasants eat – millet, a crop in which the Portuguese have no economic stake.

Unsure how much of this to believe, Anthony turned – not unreasonably, he thought – to his colleagues. But all they cared about were the women who walked the promenades above Maputo Bay. The gaudiest fabrics Macao could supply found their way around the waists of those girls. To Anthony's enthusiastic enquiries about the new socialist independent state, surely just around the corner now, the staffers – deadbeats and fumblers, mice-men with grey flannel trousers and myopic, light-frightened eyes, 'the intelligence community' – well, they simply sneered.

Peeved, he started quoting the pirate broadcasts at them: 'There won't be girls on the bluff much longer.' This caught their interest. 'They're running through the minefields to get to the FRELIMO line. FRELIMO are building them their own barracks. They are putting them to work in the fields.' Acidly: 'They are teaching them to read.'

'What do they need to read for?'

'"Ensure all air is expelled from the teat. Do not re-use."'

The men were too bored and demoralized even to laugh at their own jokes.

Oafs, thought Anthony, steering carefully around the idea that he was like them, one of them, another Comintern discard.

He'd known he was in for a rough ride when he discovered that the office of this 'distance learning institute' had no short-wave radio. There was a telephone, but it rarely worked – the area exchange kept 'borrowing' the line. There was a very limited stock of paper, and when Anthony set to work drawing up some of his ideas for discussion, he was told, in no uncertain terms, to obtain his own supply. His enthusiastic descriptions of distance learning techniques; his suggestion that short-wave radio communications might cast 'nets of political mentorship' across the disadvantaged communities of this huge and empty country: these things were greeted with humourless incomprehension.

So he has sat, day after day, nursing the knot in his ruined back, at this big, heavy antique table, covered with a smutted, ink-stained linen cloth; to his left, a heavy German-Gothic sideboard; to his right, a grandfather clock that would not have looked out of place in a railway station ticket hall; behind him, a wrought-iron safe in which all official papers are kept, and to which he has no access. Such furniture might, in another context, generate a pleasant atmosphere for a gentleman's study. Alas, since the room itself is a featureless concrete cube on the top floor of a recently finished towerblock, these wonderfully heavy, lustrous objects have taken on a dejected aspect, like old lags in a cell.

Talking of which.

'He is a British sailor,' Gregor confides to Anthony, around half-past one. There are bags under his eyes. He hasn't shaved for days.

The men sit facing each other across the table.

They wait.

Silence.

2

'Please don't. I'll be all right.' The words grate and quiver in Anthony Burden's schoolboy throat. At the back of his tongue, the taste of silver foil. 'I promise I won't do it again.'

It is 10 p.m., Valentine's Day 1930, and in the gymnasium of Stonegrove College, a cash-strapped Derbyshire grammar school, twelve-year-old Anthony Burden is struggling to explain away the belt around his throat and his trousers round his ankles.

John Arven, fourteen years old, captain of Anthony's dorm, nurses the side of his head where the younger boy's legs, flailing spastically against the wall bars, delivered their inadvertent kick. 'Who did this to you?'

Choking and blubbering on the floor of Stonegrove College gymnasium, his throat on fire, his thighs wet with piss, how is Anthony Burden to explain that he did this to himself? How is he to put into words that this is what he wants, however much his drab, ungainly boy's body fought to keep him living in this world? Even more daunting: how is he to explain that it is not despair that drives him, but hope?

'Who was it? Tell me. Don't be afraid.'

Little Anthony Burden bursts into tears.

Anthony Burden has a secret. Every few months or so come days of bubbling energy and nervous agitation, days when nothing seems impossible and everything takes too long. Then, with a burst of exhilaration indistinguishable from terror, Anthony receives a vision of Paradise.

Paradise is a city. A municipal fantasia of great public works: fine temples, massive aqueducts, embankments, statuary, formal gardens, parklands, bandstands, amphitheatres and parades. A sunlit urban masterpiece, glittering and fine. In the very centre of the city there is a wooded glade, criss-crossed by geometric paths, where deer graze beneath tall, mathematically perfect trees. A girl in a shimmering cotton pinafore dress plucks flowers. A gardener in a wide-brimmed straw hat, his shears in his hand and a little dog at his feet, stands beside a dark lake whose fountain sends a crystal jet into the air like a glittering whip, spreading coolness all around. Above the treetops rises the ornamental outline of a magnificent castle.

How often has Anthony wished that he could carry his physical body into this land! Alas, since that one farcical schoolboy attempt, Anthony has had to content himself with visiting his Heaven disembodied, a soul *sans* flesh.

Anthony's body, meanwhile, clings to the clay of life with dirty fingernails. It longs to wallow unchecked in the stew of life.

Nine years later, at 6.30 a.m., on 10 July 1939 Anthony Burden, King's scholar, twenty-two years old, wakes up in an unfamiliar room – sheets that are too hot, too damp – and in the presence – close, naked and erect – of Cambridge mathematician Alan Turing.

Anthony lets out a scream and tumbles from the bed. Whimpering, he half runs, half crawls, for the nearest door. He finds himself in a bathroom. He slams the door shut behind him and fumbles with the bolt.

'Anthony?' says Alan.

Anthony Burden presses his back against the bathroom door and sinks to the floor, eyes tight shut. Anthony knows who it is, all right. Alan Turing's lectures have been the highlight of his week since they started: 'The Foundations of Mathematics'. But how on earth—?

'Anthony, sweetheart, what the devil's got into you?'

Anthony covers his face with his hands. If he is very quiet, if he is very small, maybe everything can go back to how it was.

*

Two months later. September 1939. Anthony Burden takes a deep breath and wills the tension out of his tight-wound limbs. How dreadful, that he should be rehearsing these shameful episodes, even as he turns over a new leaf and journeys to a new city!

No possible way he could continue his studies after the Incident, of course. How could he trust himself? It is as his Blessed Mother tearfully predicted. The stresses and strains of the academic life have proved too much for him. He must find some other occupation.

This war could not have come at a better time for him. It is time for Anthony Burden to do something practical for his country, something that might, he hopes, deep in his Fabian soul, improve the lot of the Common Man. His school-friend John Arven has persuaded him not to enlist. 'There is so much you can do on the Home Front,' John insisted, bright bird eyes transfixing him, the day Anthony told him of his decision to quit academia. To prove his point, Sage has arranged for Anthony to be interviewed, later today, by the board of the Post Office Research Station at Dollis Hill.

Visions of paradise have accompanied Anthony Burden ever since puberty. They have shaped his life, his interests and his inventions. They do not frighten him any more. He accepts that they are a gift, like perfect pitch, or a precocious talent with brush and pencil. He sees that they have something to do with his aptitude for mathematics. But he does not understand them, and he is troubled by his own ignorance.

Once he is settled in his London digs, Anthony seeks out the distinguished-sounding philosophical society with rooms off Gower Street, and there, in its curious and ramshackle library, he reads everything that might shed light on his condition, from Mme Blavatsky's accounts of spirit travel to the personal diaries of blind introspectionist T. C. Cutsforth. Nothing he reads undercuts the magic of his visions. The visions themselves are the primary Fact.

Arven, meanwhile, encourages Anthony to spread his wings, now that he is living in the capital. He cannot understand why Anthony won't agree to come and lecture to his students at Birkbeck College. He cannot see why Anthony is so determined to shun academia. 'There is so much you have to offer,' he says, flattering the younger man.

Strange, the bond of care between the two old boys, persisting after all these years.

Twelve-year-old Anthony, sprawled choking and half-naked on the floor of the school gymnasium, did not imagine for a second, fervently as he begged, that his dorm captain would keep his suicide attempt a secret. What had happened, that night, that John had stuck by his side, helped him clean himself up and never said anything to anyone, ever, about that night? What, on passing the gymnasium for an illicit smoke, had the older boy seen? What about Anthony's condition, if anything, did he understand?

For years, Anthony has been too afraid to ask. Because if John Arven saw that night what Anthony saw, and continues to see, every few months – the towers, the parades, the fountain – then...

Why, then, the vision must be true!

And why should we go on living, if it was? If the door to Paradise was always open? If the Way was clear?

'Dear Prof. Arven, I have yet to receive a reply to my letter of 3rd inst.'

Well yes, dear little Kathleen, it is true. I have not replied to you. I have not made good my promises. Consequently, I would lay money that wherever you are, and however you make your living, your talents are being belittled or ignored and your potential value to the nation is going entirely to waste. No, I have not written: a misfortune for you, and a tragedy for the country. Or should that be the other way about? In any event, I have not replied. I have not invited you for any interview or examination. How can I? Perhaps next time you write, instead of heading your letter 'Same Address', you could just tell me *where the bloody hell you are.*

Irritated, Professor John Arven – Whitehall guru and the star of Mountbatten's 'Department of Wild Talents' – screws up Kathleen's letter and drops it neatly into the ashtray.

London. October 1940.

What else is there? Arven glances through the rest of the day's meticulously time-stamped correspondence: letters typed and handwritten; a couple of facsimiles from the War Office; a fuzzy transatlantic telephotograph. Most of this material is not supposed to leave his office, but his workload has forced him to play fast and loose with the regulations. Every couple of seconds a paperclip *pings* and falls to the floor, just out of reach. You could eek out a smallish engine component from the paperclips his secretary gets through in a week.

Another mouthful of beer. At this rate he'll be on his second before Anthony arrives. Every time someone comes labouring up the carpeted stairs, John expects to see his old schoolfriend Anthony Burden. They have agreed to meet in the upper bar of the Wheatsheaf in Fitzrovia for a drink after work. John's already got in a pint of the ghastly porter Anthony prefers, and that was twenty minutes ago. Not that it will make any difference to that muck.

John Arven's lifelong friendship with Anthony Burden has recently become a source of mild but persistent annoyance. Anthony is like an unintelligible relation for whom John is always having to find excuses. Take, as a case in point, this paper he has written. John digs it out of his bag.

'What, after all, is a machine?' Anthony asks, with his trademark demotic flourish. *'Where does the operator stop and the machine begin?'*

Anthony has been urging Arven, in his role as a Birkbeck professor, to referee this paper and advise on the possibilities of publication. This is a rather sad business, John feels. When Anthony quit Cambridge, declaring his intent 'to do something for the Common Man', John was intrigued. He awaited developments with anticipation. What would his old friend become? The last thing he expected or wanted was that Anthony should drift into some nebulous reserved occupation, while at the same time plying him with page after page of amateurish philosophy. Anthony is so obviously wedded to the life of the mind, his ambitions for the fruits of his intellectual labours are so painfully nursed, why the devil did he ever leave the purlieus of King's?

'Take a bus driver, for instance. A bus driver operates a bus.' Anthony maintains this irritating *faux naif* style throughout. *'But in what sense is he an "operator"?'* John correctly identifies the central theme of Anthony's paper. It is a tango. Some rather weakly analysed sentiments regarding free will on the one hand; Bertrand Russell's set theory on the other. *'Certainly he is not a free agent. He cannot freely choose his route and schedule. Not if he wants to keep his job.'* John Arven skims Anthony's folksy phrases with a great weariness, all the way to the end. There. Promise kept. Now all he has to do is think of something to say.

Ever since school, Anthony has exhibited an unfortunate talent for frittering away his gifts on wild goose-chases. John still recalls, with some bitterness, their last summer together at Stonegrove – two halcyon months they might have spent walking, sailing; they might even have visited Europe together, and caught a last glimpse of a way of life now gone for ever, crushed beneath the jack-boot of the Reich.

At the last minute, Anthony had scotched all their plans, for all the world as though their friendship meant nothing. In order to do what, exactly? Why, in order to collect fir-cones from the woods behind his parents' house! All because of that obscure, second-hand book he had picked up, linking maths and nature. Twenty years old, written by a naturalist no one had ever heard of. By the summer's end, poor Anthony still had nothing to show for his obsession. No special insight into the relationship between numbers, birds and bees. No, not even a mathematical bauble to dangle in front of the editors of *Eureka*.

It is not that Anthony Burden is without talent. God knows, John has rarely met his equal. At school, Anthony demonstrated an instinctive grasp of mathematical operations. More recently, he was filling his letters from Cambridge with some really quite extraordinary flights of number theory. It's not his talent that's in question.

It is his common sense. The way he allows himself to be borne away on this hobby-horse or that. His insistence that simple operations, repeated endlessly, mechanically, perhaps using some sort of switching system like a telegraph, will revolutionize the practice of mathematics.

'I would argue that the bus driver is a functional "unit" inside a larger machine, more distributed but no less mechanical – namely, the bus route or system...'

John Arven shuffles the sheets back together and stows them away in his bag. He checks the clock above the bar. Really this is insufferable, where the devil has Anthony got to? John contemplates his own irritation, feeding it until it swells into anger. He does this out of choice, and diligently. He has to. If John doesn't work up some anger now, then all he'll be left with by the end of the evening will be fear, for what might have happened to his friend.

In years past, John has felt an intense duty of care towards Anthony Burden. He has lain awake fearing for his friend. But their friendship is past its best, their destinies have come decoupled, and he does not want these feelings any more. The apprehension and fear and dragging sense of responsibility. It is surely time, John tells himself, that he release himself from memories of that overwhelming evening of their first acquaintance: how Anthony, blubbing, extracted from him an oath of secrecy so solemn and profound that it forged an iron bond between them, a bond which John may regret but which, up to now, he has never been able to break.

All afternoon the streets of Fitzrovia have roiled drunk with every type of London life. Free French have rubbed shoulders with displaced African dignitaries, soldiers on furlough have pursued working girls through crowds of muttering black-clad Jewry. Negro poets from Paris have been flashing their gold-capped teeth at all the pretty computers clipping in, figure-dizzy, from the toils of Senate House. From his vantage point in the shadows, Anthony marvels. It is impossible to tell whether these people are masters of their surroundings or unwitting captives. How can they live, dreaming as they do?

As the daytime noises fade, so the people of the street acquire a cool grey uniform of sameness, and Anthony Burden remarks how self-absorbed everyone has grown. Strange, he thinks, that the day should end like this. Why, he wonders, do we not connect with each other constantly in this extremity of war?

Anthony is on fire tonight, with that occasional energy he exhibits prior to a crisis. It is the manic fervour he displayed the week before he fell into bed with Alan Turing. It is the same fire that lit his eyes, back when he was simply 'A. Burden' (much humour in the quad over that), the new boy at Stonegrove, days before John Arven discovered him.

Anthony has, as a consequence, clean forgotten his evening's arrangement with John Arven. He is, instead, on his way through Soho towards the National Gallery. There is a concert tonight, for the benefit of some refugee group or other, and though the programme is not his usual fare, in the Blitz he has learned to seize what shreds of cultural life he can. The only other entertainment tonight is *The Lion Has Wings* with Merle Oberon, playing at the Haymarket, and Anthony has seen that twice already.

He has paused in a shop doorway, feeling in his pocket for his cigarettes.

'Excuse me, sir,' he calls out to a passer-by, 'have you got a light?'

The man bridles. 'I certainly have not,' he snaps, in a thick, East European accent. 'Goodnight.'

Anthony is confused at first, then blushes, mortified. He didn't mean...

Or did he? What did he want, stood here in the dark? Not a light. More than a light.

Here are the matches, in his hand.

He finds it so hard to understand himself at times. He lights his cigarette with trembling fingers and heads south.

It takes him no time at all to see why the foreign gentleman reacted so badly to his innocent hello. At this provocative hour of the evening, pansies line the streets. Pansies leer at him from first- and second-floor windows. From high windows, rouged pansies lean, leer and whistle. They loiter at street corners, inflaming his imagination with their narrow ties and narrow suits with narrow trousers and pointy shoes.

Sill blushing, Anthony stares straight ahead and clips smartly along, closed off to every imagined disturbance, spiralling deeper into purblind fantasy. One by one the colours vanish from the scene. Soon all is black and white. Buses, robbed of their red, slink past along Shaftesbury Avenue. Furled umbrellas spasm like jellyfish. In Trafalgar Square the lions are pacing. Nelson on his column teeters and hesitates; is there really no way down from here? The National Gallery steps trill and tinkle like piano keys when Anthony treads on them and threaten to buck him into the street below.

He enters the gallery and follows the attendants' directions. The walls of the great galleries are bare. According to *The Times*, their treasures have been borne off for safe-keeping to a disused slate quarry somewhere in North Wales. In each room he passes knots of calm grey figures. Is it his imagination, or are they studying the walls? Are they adopting these contemplative poses out of long habit, or are things hung there that he cannot see?

In the basement room the audience is gathering, grey and silent, everyone exactly like everyone else. Above them, the low ceiling bulges, foams at the corners and rises suddenly to make a vault. The audience make no sign of having seen their surroundings transformed. Are they used to miracles, or blind to them?

Anthony's heart thunders in his chest. He'd hug every man and woman to his bosom if he could. At times like these the Truth peeks through appearances, illuminating everything. How everyone is exactly alike.

The audience is given very little time to settle before the Budapest Municipal Orchestra enters and launches into its premiere. With the first swoop and tremble of strings, Anthony Burden knows this isn't going to be his sort of music.

In the days of his mania, as Paradise trundles closer and closer, music fills the space behind Anthony's eyes with images. Different musics build differently: Benny Goodman and Count Basie string bridges between his ears; Bach and Handel erect Venetian palazzi. From the mushy romanticism and mangled folk idiom of this sorry *Budapest Concerto*, however, Anthony manages to construct very little: a blasted heath, a couple of tumble-down cottages; a pond; a mill. He is, without thinking about it, constructing a kind of pastiche or portmanteau Constable to put in place of the paintings missing from the walls upstairs. The sight of those bare walls shakes Anthony. He imagines the art of the nation turning troglodyte, as Londoners themselves might, were the Underground left open during air-raids. Hiding there for safety, going mad, refusing to surface.

What will the art be like when it re-emerges? Anthony wonders. If it emerges. He thinks of the mine, so dry, so secure: D. G. Rossetti and John Martin pressed promiscuously up against Turner, Gainsborough, Dadd. What sort of Morlock art will it be when we drag it from the comfortable Celtic twilight of the mine?

Will we even find it?

He is deliberately scaring himself now.

Will it *hide*?

A delicious shudder...

Applause wakes him – and what on earth is going on? The audience is going wild. The audience is cheering. The audience is leaping to its feet. He folds his arms and keeps his seat, wishing neither to be one of the herd, nor to let his musical standards drop so far. Only then it dawns on him, poor unworldly technician, that he is surrounded by refugees. He looks at them anew. The calm grey figures surrounding him flicker and snap, thick ham hands a-tremble; the glint of tears.

Shamed, Anthony struggles to his feet and joins in their applause, if not for the music, then for the effort, the extraordinary and brave effort of the plucky Jewish people – and a bowler hat, tossed with more energy than circumspection by a jubilant concert-goer, cracks him on the nose.

Several hours earlier, that same evening – and in the Lyons corner house on the Strand, Rachel Causley sips delicately at her hot chocolate, looks at her watch and says: 'I can't be long, Mummy will be waiting for me. Is it done or not?'

Her Major would pull his hair, if he had any. He beats his skull instead – muted little punches to the frontal lobes. 'Have you any idea,' he says, 'what this involves?'

Rachel sits in silence. They both know the answer to this question. Twenty years old, Rachel already knows her business.

'I could get myself *shot*!' the Major declares in a non-too-subtle stage whisper. Rachel glances to their left, to the gawky, pretty waitress standing there – but she is like the rest of them, asleep on her feet. She has not overheard.

The Major waits for a response. Rachel says nothing. Her eyes drill into him. She is waiting for her answer. God, but the bitch is beautiful! He fumbles a cigarette into his mouth. How wise she is, in return for his services, to offer what she offers without love. The unaffectionate kiss. The indolent and bored caress. He knows that at the slightest show of affection from her he would ruin everything: his marriage, his son at Sandhurst, his dear sister, his savings, the whole petty, cherished edifice of his life. She is wise, his Rachel, his blackout girl, to show no chink of light.

'*Is it done?*'

He stubs out his cigarette, bites his lip, irritated, and snaps at the waitress, standing gormlessly there: 'Please may we have a clean ashtray?'

'Of course,' says the waitress, shaking herself free of her waking dream. 'I won't be a moment.'

He watches her go.

'I've diverted the shipment through Alexandria,' he says. 'I can't do anything about the ammunition, it's already been dispatched, you'll have to look elsewhere for that. Much good may it do you. Do you really think your people... Where are you going?'

Rachel Causley – Clausen as was, in her family's way-back-when – uses a napkin to wipe the chocolate from her lips. She is a creature of extreme times, party to great plans and terrible intelligence, balanced on a knife-edge between promises of promised land and rumours of extermination, emptied of hope, wired with determination, but when the city's cocoa supply runs out – next week or the week after – she will take to her bed and cry like a baby.

She gives the Major what he wants – Tomorrow? Very well – and gets out of there as quickly as she can.

Tomorrow.

The truth is, the Major frightens her. He is one of those well-meaning bumblers whose frustration with life has never found its proper outlet. Tomorrow in that little rented room, alone with her, an unexploded bomb. In his bluster and abjection she has diagnosed a sentimentalist who, given the right sort of encouragement, might just break a bottle in her face.

She wishes that she did not have this power that is not even hers, but belongs to her body so that, as she steers her way to advantage through the infantile expectations of this or that fellow traveller – *Oh, Princess! Let me kiss it! Oh, go on! Let me hold 'em!* – she is no more in control of the process of seduction than if she were put behind the wheel of a racing car. Sometimes, in her darker moments, she even wonders whether the politics in which she has become embroiled is not a sand-trap or thicket into which she has instinctively swerved in order to slow her body's uncontrollable sexual career.

There is something puritan growing within her; it will not leave her sex alone, but must always be pressing the roses in her cheeks into service for the common good. The truth is, Rachel Causley – Clausen as she will be again, entering Zion – is not the Mata Hari she imagines herself to be. She puts herself in the way of these helpful War Office types – communists, closet and not-so-closet; men whose parentage or upbringing enables them to identify, or at least sympathize, with the Zionist cause. Still, the favours she bestows are not much. Every kiss she blows, every glimpse of knee, every button on her blouse, earns the cause another gun; she herself remains unmoved. Undiminished, unenlightened, she still imagines that love – true love – is something unconnected with erotica, something cuddly and vaguely parental. When she imagines her future husband, she imagines a creature not unlike Flopsy, the rabbit she had as a child and petted through a long and terminal illness.

On the steps of the National Gallery, her mother is waiting for her. This benefit is her doing, her bit for a cause of whose deep dark criminality she is merrily unaware. 'My dear! You are so late!'

There is nothing in her mother's appearance to betray the cruel exigencies this war has put her to. She wears the family's recent internment lightly, as though it were a joke at her captors' expense. Neither is there any sign of the punishing hours she keeps now, fire-watching in the dead of night. Tonight she is dashing as ever in a borrowed evening gown and paste jewels. Though bankrupted at home, yet she walks this foreign soil full of happy expectation. Face to face with her, Rachel feels none of the contempt towards the older generation felt by the other members of her cell. It seems cheap to her, to sneer at her parents' lives. It is not hard for her to imagine why her father, awarded the Iron Cross First Class in the last war, should view the idea of Palestine with incredulity. It is not difficult to see why her mother, with her childhood memories of Johann Strauss and concerts in the Vienna Volksgarten, should treasure the culture of Schiller and Schopenhauer above the socialist experiments of the East.

Come the revolution, it will be up to the young to re-educate their parents.

Rachel takes her mother's arm and walks her back inside. She is overcome with affection for her poor parents; the pride they take, even now, in their assimilation; their innocent reverence for *Bildung*. When the revolution comes, she will be able to make everything clear to them. With humour and compassion, she will show them, step by step, why she is right and they are wrong.

The stiff hat-brim cracks Anthony's nose and somewhere behind his eyes, a tap turns. His nose will not stop bleeding. Blood gathers in his moustache as though it were a sponge. His handkerchief is sodden. He is going to faint.

Through his dizziness he feels sympathetic hands upon him, propelling him across the hall, through a door and along an unlit corridor, to where the musicians of the Budapest Municipal Orchestra have retired to smoke, talk and loosen their ties.

'Come over here to the sink.'

He did not expect a woman here among these heavy, sweaty men. He receives a muddled impression that she is familiar to them. Is she a theatrical agent? She is wearing a pale, figure-hugging dress, the colour indeterminate under the weak light. Her skin is the colour of Greek honey. She beckons him. Her arm is like a polished branch.

His heart tilts. *O my America*. He shies away, afraid that he might bloody her clothing.

'Come on.'

She sits him down by a small china sink and tilts his head back. She pinches his septum. Her fingers are strong and capable. Her hand at his temple reminds him of his mother. He closes his eyes. 'What's your name?' he says. He could hug the whole world.

'Rachel,' she says – and seeing something in him she misses, some childhood thing she has lost – strokes him absent-mindedly behind his ears.

They wake just before dawn the next day, naked, spooned under a blanket of leaves in a hollow hidden by thick undergrowth in a little-frequented corner of Regent's Park.

Rachel shimmies against Anthony's warmth. His arms are curled about her. She takes hold of them, tightening his embrace.

Bliss.

She closes her eyes against the colours of the waking world, trying to hold on to last night's vivid dream. Boulevards and squares, great houses, courtyards – all built of space and light.

The city Anthony showed her as they walked had form but no colour. There was a cloistered air to it, as though every street and channel and staircase, followed far enough, would lead inexorably back into itself. Even the distinction between day and night seemed to be a function of perspective. And all the while, slowly, confidently, his hand was stealing across her back to clinch her waist.

They kissed. His moustache tickled her. She ran her hands through his hair, his widow's peak which made him appear so devilish somehow, his rough cheeks, his slim, hard body. He led her on…

Anthony stirs. He wakes. With a little cry, he lets go of her. He sits up.

Rachel, exposed, wraps her arms around herself and shivers.

'What?' says Anthony.

She turns over, chilled through. Still, in one languorous corner of her mind, she is enjoying the feel and rustle of mould and leaf. She smiles up at her seducer, delivers a chipper 'good morning'.

'Where—?' says Anthony.

He smells of leaf and mushroom, of earth and sweat. She lies back into his lap, braving the morning cold to stretch, lifting her little breasts for him. 'Mmmm,' she says.

Anthony casts around. 'Where are our clothes?'

She gazes round their dell, eyes lazy, slitted with sleep. 'Dunno.'

With anxious, mincing gestures, Anthony slides out from under Rachel. He kneels, hunted, like a dog. 'I can't see our clothes anywhere.'

The urgency in his voice wakes her more fully than the cold has done. She sits up. 'They must be somewhere,' she says, unhelpfully.

Together they explore their grotto. Through the dense undergrowth, Rachel sees a park gardener already hard at work with his sheers. He is tidying the edges of a path. Clip by clip, he moves towards them.

'Ah!' Anthony sighs. Rachel turns to shush him.

He has found her dress and her purse.

'Is that all?'

He nods.

'What shall we do?'

Anthony bites his lip. His penis is hard with fear. She wants to hold it. But the moment is gone. 'Help me on with your dress.'

She blinks at him.

'Come on.'

'Why can't I—?'

'I wouldn't dream of it,' he says, gallantly. He holds up her purse. 'May I borrow halfpence for the phone?'

He looks funny in the dress. He elbows his way through the undergrowth and onto the path. Lightly he runs, bare hairy feet a blur. Rachel lies down and covers herself with leaves.

The ground is not so comfortable now. There are twigs and thorns and crawling things.

She wonders who he is going to call, and how long he will be.

3

Even through the lenticular grey warp of his mania, Anthony Burden sees that, of all the women he has ever been introduced to – a slew of sex rabbits, neurotic amateur poets and surrogate mamas thrust upon him by 'understanding' friends – Rachel alone might serve to draw him into a life that is more keenly felt. Wandering the streets of Paradise with her, he has been struck by her social skill, her appetite for adventures. Waking with her in Regent's Park, aghast at their animalism, he has expected everything to go sour – but who would not be charmed by her perky 'good morning'? It gives him the unaccustomed courage, breathless as he is from the sprint from undergrowth to phone box and back again, and half out of his mind with panic, to ask to see her again. And then and there, stood there in their dell, a bare-chested Rosalind, she says yes.

Against all odds, Anthony's erotic encounter with Rachel leads to another, and another. An understanding blossoms. There is even talk of marriage. When the time comes for Anthony to seek the blessing of Rachel's parents, Rachel takes him home to St John's Wood. There is her father's Iron Cross, framed and hung above a bureau designed by Ernst Freud. Beside it hangs the childhood portrait of Rachel painted by Kurt Schwitters. They have arrived to find Rachel's mother playing four-hand piano with the world-renowned violinist Max Rostal. The polite, strained conversation that ensues is gritted with the names of everyone who is anyone in European music. Lili Kraus, Szymon Goldberg: thanks to Hitler, there's not one of them lives more than half a mile from Lili Montagu's new synagogue in Swiss Cottage. For Anthony, this is a different world, impassioned, fiercely intellectual: he longs to be a part of it.

When, alone with her, Anthony speaks of his intentions, Rachel's mother becomes flustered. She is all too aware, this once, of being in a foreign land, her old rules and niceties swept away. Her first response is to demur to her husband – and this is a complicated business, as Mr Causley – his value to the war effort recognized, at last – has been billetted in some out-of-the-way corner of the West Country, monitoring Nazi broadcasts for the BBC.

Together, Rachel and Anthony board a train for Evesham. There, and greatly to Anthony's surprise, Rachel's father responds to news of the match with an enthusiasm that borders on the unseemly.

The men's conversation, conducted on the lawn of a guest-house in the sleepy hamlet of Wood Norton, is one of the more surreal exchanges thrown up by a surreal time. The business of the wedding quickly packed away, Rachel's father wants to pick Anthony's brains. 'I'd like to know all about matrices,' he says. 'Tensors,' he adds, out of the blue. 'Projective geometry.' He has not wasted his internment, his holiday on the Isle of Man. There are some very clever people sitting on their hands in those camps, and giving and attending lectures – on everything from Byzantine art to marine biology – helps them while away the time. 'So what about this "group theory", then?' The breadth, if not the depth, of the man's recently acquired mathematical knowledge is astounding. Anthony half wonders how he can get interned himself.

It is only as the wedding nears that Anthony learns why Rachel's father is so relieved to have him for a son-in-law.

Rachel is young. She was born the year Versailles was signed; she was fourteen the evening her father returned to their Berlin apartment, ashen and shaking, to report the first of many book burnings; she was with her mother in the audience of the Dresden Opera when Fritz Busch was booed for his Jewish violins; three years later, in the stands of the Olympic Stadium, her father gripped her hand, nails digging in, so she would remember not to cheer so loud when Jesse Owens won.

To meet these betrayals, Rachel says, a new, muscular, socialist Jewry is needed; a self-aware Jewry organized into a modern state, defended with modern weapons! Statements like these, screamed across the breakfast table of the family's genteel, cash-strapped exile in St John's Wood, thoroughly unnerved Rachel's parents long before Anthony came on the scene.

This is why the old man is relieved: his dangerous-minded daughter has settled for a middle-of-the-road Fabian, after all. He has concluded from this that his daughter's revolutionary fervour has been just a phase. On the night of their wedding, Anthony, in a mischievous spirit, points this out to his wife.

Rachel laughs as she mounts her new husband. 'Dad said the same about Hitler,' she says.

May 1942. It is several months since Rachel and Anthony were married, yet this is the first opportunity they have had for a honeymoon.

From Fort William, the Road to the Isles follows the crinkled Highland coastline. It is a road of steep inclines, blind summits and sharp, muddy bends; a road for farm wagons, tractors and clapped-out cars. After a couple of hours' steady driving, confusion is assured. It is virtually impossible for a stranger to read this landscape, where every feature feathers into every other feature, so that to distinguish between a channel and a loch, between mainland and island – between land and sea, even – becomes little more than a game of language. The light here turns seawater gold as furze, and rock to an ocean green. Their minds slide off the landscape constantly.

At moments of dizziness like these, Rachel seizes Anthony's knee. Anthony slows the car. Sometimes, he stops. Whenever they stop, they kiss.

It excites Anthony that he has married a Jew. If every new wife is an unexplored territory, then Rachel is a mysterious land indeed: a heady mix of the cosmopolitan and the exotic; the glass and steel of new money seen through the dust and yellow light of an ancient civilization. At night, if Rachel's sex fails to arouse him (and who, in strict honesty, achieves such direct responses, straight away? After all, thinks Anthony, we are not dogs) then her exoticism serves.

Naturally, he says none of this out loud. Rachel's parents are Austrian aesthetes, Goethe's children; for them, their Jewishness is little more than the stick Hitler and his thugs chose to beat them with, once they decided to expropriate the family's bank. As for Rachel, Anthony has been left in no doubt where she stands. He has gone to public meetings and has sat, squirming with embarrassment, as Rachel makes perfectly clear her abhorrence of what she calls 'the argument from blood'. It is the Jewish faith itself – its aloofness and its quietism – which has failed her people, and the desert realm she dreams of and conspires towards is robustly secular.

Anthony Burden drives them over hills of bare rock, rippled and layered by the ages like old wax, and pulls up at last at the village their RAC map promised them.

The place is a figment. There is nothing here but a pond, reflecting the ruins of a castle. A handful of dairy cattle sit by the pond, chewing the cud. A ramshackle gate hangs open on one hinge, and a fence, all but ruined, leads from the pond to a nearby farm. Beyond the castle lies a wide, calm estuary.

The newlyweds climb from the car. A cobblestone jetty stretches a tentative finger into the water. Lobster pots are stacked high along its left-hand side. Rachel pulls gently from Anthony's embrace – he is nothing if not uxorious – and walks the length of the jetty. He pauses a moment before he follows. She is magnificent, he decides, abandoning himself to the unfamiliar heat of sensual observation. Her buttocks are really very narrow for a girl. He surprises a desire to smack them very hard. To pull. To part. She is his wife, after all.

His nerve fails him, or the smell of the lobster pots cuts through his lust, and by the time he is standing beside her again, his mind has turned to safer, more familiar subjects. He says, looking out across the coast, 'One could write the maths for this.'

He is thinking of the Fibonacci series: one plus one equals two, one plus two equals three, two plus three equals five, each term the sum of the previous two, expanding forever into the arrangements of leaves, the patterns of flowers, the arrangements of fir-cones. D'Arcy Thompson wrote this up in 1917 – how nature is underpinned by mathematics. Nobody since has taken a blind bit of notice. It is only by chance that Anthony stumbled on Thompson's book, the year his friend John left Stonegrove. The field – the mathematics of creation – lies wide open. It spreads out before him. A new-found land, there for the taking.

'With one formula,' he says, trying for an unaccustomed clarity, 'you could generate a billion different valleys.'

She looks up at him with beautiful, big, dark eyes. 'What of?' she asks him.

'What?' Anthony thumbs the wedding band on his finger, turning it around and around.

'What would you build them of? These billion valleys.'

Rachel is a practical woman. Hers is a solid, material world. She wants to know what things are made of. She wants to know what things are for. Rachel is just the sort of companion Anthony needs, for he has spent too much of his life among abstract thoughts. *What of?* Her enquiring smile is a bracing challenge, and he confronts the question as a yachtsman turns his face into the wind.

He would build valleys of light. He would build valleys of numbers. 'It would be like watching a picture show,' he tells his new wife. 'But one where the film has been shot at every angle, from every point in space. As you move your eyes across the screen, as you shift about in your theatre chair, the image adapts to your movements, giving you the sense that you are moving through a real place.'

Rachel says, 'There isn't film stock enough in the world for a film like that.'

But the seamlessness and completeness of the world is an illusion. In fact, the film is short, and composed only of the shots you yourself see. Only your view of the world exists: the rest is darkness. In Anthony's fantastical world of numbers, a tree falling in the quad with no one to witness it would make no sound.

'The time it would take,' she continues. 'The time you would need to make such a film – you would never be able to keep up with your audience.'

This is true. This film needs to be composed, painted and shot, even as it is being watched. This film cannot therefore *be* a film, in the conventional sense, but a series of still images presented at speed enough to trick the eye – fifty-six frames per second or not much less – by some other yet-to-be-invented apparatus: a machine closer in kind to the facsimile machine.

'What's it got to do with telephones?' she asks him.

'Telephones carry pictures, as well as sound,' he says.

You could draw up a place, draft it the way an architect sketches a building. You could send its geometries down phone-lines to people all over the world. 'People all over the world could visit this place from the comfort of their armchairs!'

'Don't call them places,' she says.

There is silence between them. She says, 'If you can't be buried in it, it's not a place.'

And a moment later: 'Don't tell a Jew what a place is.'

He walks back along the cobblestone pier to the car. He gets in and slams the door. It is the old challenge again, the one he loves her for, the mental habit that has drawn him to her – but since they set out together this morning she has been wielding her lack of imagination like a club.

She gets in the car beside him.

'All set?' he says.

'What?'

'What?'

'What's the matter?' she says, as though she had not attacked him.

'Nothing,' he says, as though he is not hurt.

In Anthony's land of light and mathematics, there are no conflicts, because there is an imaginary abundance of everything: sunshine, shelter, space. Space above all. There is space enough in Anthony's land for everyone to be alone. In his land, this is how everyone wants to live.

It is a sort of three-dimensional cartoon, rendered in fine line-work by an army of mechanical draughtsmen. The inhabitants move about its infinite coves and inlets with a calm, myopic tread. In Anthony's imagination, there is a mathematical formula for people, too.

Home again, and sequestered in his study, Anthony thinks and writes, filling red school exercise books with exquisite diagrams, drawings, formulae and commentaries. He uses up every square inch of paper – a habit drummed into him at Stonegrove – and on every fourth or fifth day, he reaches for a fresh exercise book. Each book is tied to its neighbour by trains of thought and even sometimes by single sentences, begun in one book, finished in the next.

Since moving to London, Anthony has formalized his working methods to the point of ritual: always the same brand of exercise book and pencil. The same chair, made stable on the study's uneven, uncarpeted floor with a back-copy of *Eureka*. The sounds of familiar streets through a window opened just so. Rachel knocks before she enters. It is a rule with him.

When Anthony first told her about what he did, it sounded to Rachel as though it would change everything; that it was a tool with which to build a new kind of society, a more open, egalitarian way of being. She has spoken up for Anthony's work among her comrades. She has described in glowing terms his brave new world of teleprinters, television scanning and automatic exchange connections, his new model society, linked by wire and radio-wave. But Stalin's behaviour during the war and his anti-Semitism have thrown Zionism's left flank into chaos.

The Party has too many problems of its own to listen to yet another visionary, or sit patiently through descriptions of glittering tomorrows.

Rachel looks in the mirror, sees her mother, and wonders what has happened to her fire. She remembers Anthony, the night she met him, his nose streaming blood, his smile swallowing the world.

She wonders where he went, the man with whom she fell in love.

A bright Tuesday morning in the summer of 1943.

'Sage, thank you.'

John Arven is not listening. 'Get in the car.'

'You really have done enough—'

John Arven is not interested. 'Will you get in?'

'I'm most terribly sorry to put you to—'

John is blisteringly angry, to the point of spitting and blaspheming, and if Anthony bloody Burden doesn't— 'Anthony! Get in the buggering car!'

Anthony Burden gets in.

It is still only half past nine. It feels like two in the afternoon. John Arven is exhausted. Anthony has had neither the patience nor the good sense to wait till a civilized hour before making his one phone call. He shook his friend out of sleep at half past four this morning. John hasn't been able to sleep a wink since. He's been up most of the night, drinking some ghastly burnt-tasting stuff that stands in place of coffee these days, trying to work out what he can say to the duty officer that will have him drop all charges. However much he racked his brains, the 'war work' card was the only one worth playing. A dangerous ploy. If Anthony's work at the Post Office is so vital to the war effort, surely his employers have a right to know that he has been caught wandering Mayfair without his trousers? After four lengthy phone calls and an appearance in person at the police station in his best suit, John hopes he has managed to flannel the affair to a satisfactory conclusion. If Anthony arrives at work on Monday morning to a stiff note and an awkward meeting with the board – well, it is his own look-out.

Anthony directs John along the southern edge of Regent's Park and into a series of dull, unforgiving streets.

They park up at the entrance to a road closed off by sawhorses. 'Is this it?'

Anthony Burden's whole head is blushing. 'I – I think so.'

'Well, is it the place or not?' John fairly shouts at him – and immediately regrets it. There is no point baiting the man. What's done is done. He is here, as usual, to contain the damage Anthony Burden has done himself. Shouting isn't going to help. 'Come on,' he says. He takes Anthony by the arm in a grip he means to be friendly, but which is probably too tight, and leads him through the ruined street. 'Now, do you remember where you took them off?'

His kindness and patience do what his bad temper couldn't, and Anthony Burden bursts into tears. They sit together, companionably enough, on a stub of wall, and John offers Anthony his handkerchief. 'Why don't you phone Rachel?'

Anthony shakes his head.

'She was out of her mind with worry when I phoned her from the station.'

Anthony looks up at John, aghast. 'You did say I was in a hospital, didn't you? Not a...' He cannot say the words.

'A police station, Anthony.' Acidulated tones break through John's veneer of patience. 'You have spent the night in a police station. Yes, I lied for you. But I want you to understand something.'

Anthony looks up at him, puppy-eyed.

'I am never going to lie for you again, especially not to your wife.'

Anthony is suitably humble. 'Yes, Sage. I quite understand.'

'If I were you I would tell Rachel everything. Everything. Things are bad enough without you acting a lie to the one person who is supposed to stick by you.'

'Well,' says Anthony, without conviction, 'I will try...'

'There is another thing.'

'Yes, Sage?'

'I want you to see a psychiatrist.'

Anthony dares a little laugh. 'Oh, now, Sage—'

'Find one yourself this week, or I will find one for you. I promise you, Anthony, I will walk you into the nearest hospital if you do not agree to this.'

Anthony swallows against a fresh flood of tears. 'All right, Sage,' he says, in a little voice. 'I don't really know about such matters but I suppose I can make some enquiries.'

'You do that.'

'Though in days like these—'

'There are plenty of good medical men sitting on their hands, Anthony. I want you to find one, this week – or it's off to the Maudsley with you.'

The air here is yellow with dust and, though dry, the plaster shivered off all the ruined buildings has given it an odour of mould and rot. John thinks: he might have got up to anything in a place like this. Anything. Afraid of what he might find, John draws Anthony to his feet, and together they set about combing the ruins.

'They are a kind of twill,' Anthony tells him, trying to be helpful.

'How many pairs of trousers are we expecting to find?' says John. The joke's on him: there are whole wardrobes strewn across the rubble, scattered by multiple blasts.

'Are these them?'

Anthony peers. 'I don't think so. No. No, I'm afraid not.'

Well, won't they do? John wonders, irritated. What can be so special about a pair of trousers? In fact, why are we hunting for them at all? If Anthony wants to spin a lie about last night to his wife, all he has to do is invent the sort of accident that would damage a pair of trousers. He could fake a sprained ankle and say that the nurses, fearing to disturb bones that might be broken, cut the damn things off his leg.

Come to think of it, what story does he have it in mind to spin? Does he even have the guile to act a lie?

'I say, Sage,' says Anthony, a little later, as they teeter on the edge of a pile of masonry – any moment now a policeman is going to spot them and blow his whistle – 'you know, I am terribly grateful for these things you've lent me.'

As well he might be. John is all out of rags now. These trousers Anthony's wearing are the bottoms to a perfectly serviceable suit. 'I want them back,' John says, brusquely. He is not in the mood to mend fences – not today and not tomorrow.

'Of course,' says Anthony.

'*Pressed*.'

Silence.

'There is one thing,' says Anthony.

John clenches his fists and drives them into the pockets of his trousers. 'Yes?'

'About Rachel…'

'Yes?'

Anthony lays a hand delicately on John's arm. 'Today, before I go home. Do you think…? I mean, could you…'

'You mean, could I go round there first and smooth the waters?'

'Yes.'

'Make some excuses for you.'

'Well, ye—'

'Tell her that she must not question you too closely. That you remember very little. That you have had a nasty shock.'

'Why, yes!'

It is hopeless. Simply hopeless. Anthony hasn't listened to a single word he's said.

This, it turns out, is not strictly true.

The following week, Anthony calls in sick and retires to the little philosophical society he frequents whenever he is passing Gower Street. There, in the library, he falls into conversation with one of that strange breed of somatic therapist who have taken up lodgings in the society's rooms. This way, Anthony can keep his promise to his dear friend John Arven, without at the same time having to admit that anything is actually wrong. John wants him to see a psychiatrist? Well then, he will see a psychiatrist. They will have a pleasant little chat about philosophy. Anthony's promise will be discharged. And that will be that.

He has not counted upon the zeal and perspicacity of Dr Loránt Pál.

Two years earlier: 15 June 1940.

The British Expeditionary Force is being evacuated from France, and in the foc'sle of the cruiser *Arethusa*, tied up at the mouth of the Gironde, Dr Loránt Pál tunes a borrowed fiddle.

Its owner, first violinist and *prima* of the Budapest Municipal Orchestra, lights a Turkish cigar and lies back on his pallet. 'Come along, then.'

Pál plucks and frowns, frowns and plucks. Shaving off that sharp high E does nothing for the pounding in his head, but he is determined to prove his mettle among his countrymen.

Dr Loránt Pál, psychiatrist and medical pioneer, is coming to Britain at the invitation of a small, well-connected philosophical society, to practise a new form of somatic therapy: a treatment for melancholia and schizophrenia that involves the careful application of electricity. Undaunted by the worsening international situation, Pál has managed to finesse his way across Axis Europe with a medicine bag full of apricot brandy. But who would have thought – after running the gamut of so many greasy *fascisti* – that his heaviest binge and his hardest persuasion would be expended trying to get a berth on this miserable tub? The quartermaster shielding the British Naval Attaché had insides of lead and a brain of pure tin.

'Read the *letter*,' Pál demanded, exasperated. 'The letter, it *says*—'

'What's this?' The quartermaster held the paper at arm's length and squinted. 'Ah, now, you see, here's your problem, this isn't a *chit*. It isn't any use if it isn't a *chit*. (Ooh, ta, don't mind if I do.)'

The final irony came when Pál, several bottles the poorer, was finally able to present his *chit* to the guards officer and climb on board. He couldn't believe his eyes, seeing who had got here before him. How often, blinking from the cheaper seats of the Pesti Vigadó, has he yawned away through evenings of their Mahler? Or, in the early hours, tripped over their sprawled, sausage-stuffed corpses in the Fészek Club or the Café Japan? The Budapest Municipal Orchestra! It really is too rich, a cosmic joke, that he should be entering Britain on this boat full of musical Jews!

Cue a rollicking *csarda* that has even the fussily intellectual *prima* puffing syncopations upon his cigar. What gypsy folk memory must Pál be drawing from that he stirs, electrifies and finally breaks this violin's humble heart? A favourite encampment among wooded hills? Dark tresses in the night-time? Tracing the cool gold chain around a hot fourteen-year-old Romany ankle? A reading of grubby cards, with their intimations of fortune and tragedy?

No, just professional annoyance. Pál, in talking about his work and his plans, has once again allowed himself to be eaten up by the knowledge that the bloody Italians got there first.

Electricity.

Of course.

Why did von Meduna never pursue electricity? Ladislas von Meduna, Hungarian innovator and Pál's first and best teacher, is the true father of convulsive therapy, but a really reliable means of triggering seizures eluded him. Why did he waste so many years casting about for something chemical? Strychnine, caffeine, nikethamide. Even wormwood. (The *csarda* collapses, swooping, outrageous, atonal, as Pál recalls how the great von Meduna returned unexpectedly one night from the *kávéház*, soaked to the skin, a bottle of absinthe under his arm and a dangerous light in his eyes.)

Still, does it really matter that it was the Italians who put the 'e' in ECT? Using electricity to induce the seizures is, when all is said and done, an operational detail. No matter what the trigger, it's the seizure that's the thing: the brain stem's primal *I Am*, ringing through the addled cortex like a bell, setting everything in harmony again.

Speaking of which...

Loránt Pál works his bow across the strings as though he were weaving a rug. Smoke curls appreciatively from the *prima*'s cigar. Racial purists like Kodaly and Bartók can brandish staves all they want at this 'restaurant music'. Authenticity be damned; in a time of crisis and with a sea-crossing only hours away, Pál's gypsy fiddling is as poignant a taste of home as a plate of sausages and *lángosh*.

It is morning, and after a night spent at anchor, the ship is under way. Unescorted, painfully vulnerable to U-boat attack, the SS *Arethusa* zig-zags its way towards Devonport where the WVS are waiting with tea urns.

The hours pass.

Past noon: from her room in her parents' Edwardian terrace in Maida Vale – a room little changed from the one she played in as a child so that her feet dangle from the end of the bed at nights – Miriam Miller, Girton graduate, bluestocking factotum of a small philosophical society off Gower Street, looks up at a sky full of dirty air and ties a perfect blue bow at the neck of her starched white blouse.

The hours pass.

Evening: in a Devonport dock shed echoing with the ghosts of donkeymen and trimmers, Miriam Miller meets Hungarian medical genius Loránt Pál. 'Extend every assistance' the telegram has instructed her.

Pál, true to form, ruins everything, slumping down the gangplank drunk, his clothes drenched in the miasma of apricots, and his mind, what there is of it, stuck like a gramophone needle halfway through a story both incomprehensible and vulgar, something about electric shocks; about how he was gypped by a couple of Italian quacks, and how they 'made a complete balls of everything'. Miriam leads the boy – he seems hardly old enough to drive, let alone offer medical treatment to another human being – to her borrowed car, brushes his hand angrily off her lap and starts the engine.

Miriam is a good driver. Had the Society not acquired an unexpected usefulness to the war effort, she might have spent the war travelling. (Pál is sawing his arms now as though he were playing a fiddle. He starts to sing.) Were it not for the Society, she might be seeing the world from behind the windscreen of a bullet-riddled ambulance. She might be undressing in a room with a bed long enough for her chaste, lanky body, watching a sunset unbloodied by Battersea smoke.

Pál, oblivious to her little tears, accompanies her: dreadful, cod-Verdi recicative, as he lovingly rehearses his Italian competitors' initial, unsuccessful trials...

'Feerst, we feed theese wy-eer intoo thee *mawth*,

'Then wee feed theese wy-eer intoo thee *arsehewl*,

'Then wee FRY-UH THEE *HAART!*'

One year later: 1941. In a pleasant upstairs room belonging to the Society, émigré medical practitioner Dr Loránt Pál assembles his new couch.

It is a robust, extremely heavy piece of engineering. Poor little Miss Miriam Miller: when she opened the door to all those delivery boys, the eyes nearly started out of her head. *More* equipment? *More* noise? *More* interruption? Is it not enough that the lights gutter whenever that nasty little Svengali charges up his self-built therapy unit?

Pál lays out the pieces of the couch over the Persian rug in the centre of the room. The daylight is fading fast. He enjoys the green-brown penumbra of evening – the way the shadows of trees dapple the dark, scratched wood of his desk, and seem to animate the photographs he has hung about the room; photographs he brought with him, stuffed and crumpled in his doctor's bag, all the way from Budapest. Daimlers and horse-drawn *fiacres*. Society women with their little dogs. French and English nannies pushing their sailor-suited charges. Seeing these pictures dapple and shift in the light of evening, Pál fancies he can almost hear the hooves of a *fiacre*'s tired horse on the soaked wooden boards of the pavements below the Corso; the obsequious whisper of the barrel-bellied *Fö-úr*, leading him to his table at the Fészek Club.

Pál shakes off his reverie and tears the brown paper from off a shaped headrest. Oh, but this is splendid. He moulds the handsome red leather block in his hands, and appreciates the neat, discreet stitching: acme of the farrier's art. He can't help a mischievous smile as he recalls poor little Miriam, stood there at the foot of the stairs while the delivery boys paraded up and down. Opening and closing her mouth like a fish. What did she imagine these parcels contained? *Exhibits*?

Eyes straining against the dying light – he hates, and will hold off as long as possible, the yellow claustrophobia of electric light and blackout blinds – Pál slots and bolts the couch together. The piece has been manufactured precisely according to his instructions. How delightful it is, to have his idea come to life like this in his hands. He turns a brass wheel. The back of the couch rises. Another wheel: the pads supporting the legs articulate smoothly downwards; the headrest inches forward. Another: the pads supporting the torso part and curve to accommodate the larger patient. Pál sighs. Bliss. He casts around for the canvas bag containing the restraints.

Though he went along to that mews house in Notting Hill armed with several original ideas regarding the immobilization of his clients, in the end he left these details pretty much to the craftsman's discretion. The chap was astonishingly expert in these matters. In his bright, chilly studio, on high stools beside an angled drafting table, the two men contemplated the design in silence. Pinned to the table, the shape of

Pál's couch-to-be seemed to hover in front of the paper. It had been rendered in an exploded orthographic projection which suggested something sleeker and more streamlined than a mere piece of furniture. A space plane, perhaps, from the *Flash Gordon* serial.

'A sheepskin lining will provide security and comfort,' the craftsman opined. He was a big, liquid man with a big, liquid face.

Pál wasn't sure what to say.

The man bit his lips, then let go; the lips emerged, wet and red, and – has he got this right? – did the man actually *wink* at him?

'Compression fractures of the spine are my biggest concern,' Pál explained, confused.

The man closed his eyes and trembled. 'Yes. Yes.'

'Then there is the matter of the gat.'

The man's eyes sprang open. 'The what?'

'The gat. Or something, normally it is a gat – is this the right word? Excuse me. A rubber piece to bite on. To stop from swallowing the tongue.'

'Oh. Oh, yes. Yes.'

Another silence.

'Why—?' More biting of his lips. 'May I ask what will, ah, *occasion* the, ah—'

'The application of electricity.'

The man's enthusiasm for Pál's work was very gratifying. 'Oh, yes! Yes!'

Pál takes the straps out of the bag and reads the accompanying notes. Eccentric as he was, that strange jelly of a man has done an excellent job. It is no laughing matter, this business of immobilization: there's precious little point to Pál's therapy if his every other client ends up in a wheelchair.

Pál threads a braided calico tape experimentally through metal loops on either side of the headrest. Won't this strap interfere with the placement of the electrodes? Ah, no, he understands now, this part crosses *that*, comes *over* the skull to this attachment point here...

Pál, shaking his head, succumbs to a little light melancholy. Here he is, pioneering the most exciting advance in psychiatry this century, and all he can think about is how to lace these silly straps. How can a mere *couch* excite him, he who has the secrets of the human psyche to explore?

Life is like this, he has found. Petty details moss over and obscure the dramatic features of one's life. Pál puts down the bag – it really is too dark to work now – and climbs on board the couch. It is firm, cool and comfortable. Good. So now, perhaps, it is time to think about other things.

Closing his eyes, he wills himself back to the moment that ought to define him, and which, in dark moments, he replays behind his eyes, reminding himself of who and what he wants to be.

He remembers the morning von Meduna first administered camphor to a human patient.

For four years the man had barely moved. A catatonic stupor had rendered him little better than a vegetable. Extreme measures seemed justified, if not positively welcome: anything to break the tension. The man's mother, ashen-faced, had gravely bestowed her consent.

Pál recalls the forty interminable minutes while they waited for the seizure. The terrible tension in von Meduna's face.

It came, at last, with a terrible violence.

Steadily, von Meduna tested the patient's reflexes, he examined the pupils of his eyes, he spoke as steadily as he could. No one was fooled. Meduna's sweat spattered everyone and everything.

Pál remembers von Meduna's achievement chiefly through the look on the great man's face as the seizure took hold: a look that stared the world straight in the eye and would not look away – no, never – not until the world itself was changed.

As for the patient – what does Pál remember of the patient?

Very little. Only one little memory survives. But such a one! Pál chuckles to recall the chap's friendly little wave, a few days later, as he trotted, fully recovered, down the steps of the hospital in his borrowed clothes and into the arms of his mother.

At the open door of Pál's consulting room, a stifled cry.

Pál sits up.

Another, sharply indrawn breath.

Miriam stands in the doorway. 'I—' she begins, fighting for breath, 'I thought no one...' She is blinking against the last of the daylight. The sun is very low now, it is shining in her eyes.

'Hello, Miriam.' Pál slides smoothly from the couch. Miriam, he has decided, is a good-looking woman, if only she would learn to relax a little. He tries his warmest smile.

Miriam raises her hands to cover the blue bow at her neck. From where she is standing, Pál's smile is invisible. He is reduced to a silhouette. His solid shadow rises and straightens against the blood-red window, the rust-red room. His form is as distinct and mobile as a spillage of ink on a metal plate. Pál indicates the couch. 'Miriam, dear Miriam, would you care to experience my device?'

With a scream she barely bothers to stifle, Miriam runs back to her office and slams the door.

'"Poofter! Nancy! Queen!"'

Mr Anthony Burden shrinks in his chair as he recalls his shame.

A year has passed. It is the summer of 1943, and Pál finds himself engaged in work far different from the sort he expected from his London practice. Arriving in England, he had imagined wards of raving lunatics, bomb neurotics, crazed suicides and padded rooms. The mass panic the authorities expected has never come to pass. The people of London, through a combination of denial and habituation, have turned their backs on the Blitz: 'Business as usual'. Such stray neurotics as pass Pál's way are usually referred to him by interested sponsors at University College Hospital, down the road, and he has an uneasy sense that he is their circus dog; they want to see what tricks he can perform.

At least this chap has referred himself. Still, Pál wonders, who exactly is this Anthony Burden? Does he really want to be expending his professional energies on the sort of frayed intellectual that haunts the Society's library?

From Mr Burden's own account it is impossible to understand why he was never called up. He says that he 'tinkers'. That he is 'a tinkerer'. Eventually the words Dollis Hill crop up in conversation. Pál, a stranger here with no great appetite for general knowledge, does not understand their significance at first. Later, following some phoned enquiries, he establishes that his client works at the Post Office Research Station. So Burden is no mere 'tinkerer'.

'Oh, you know, I have these schemes, good enough that I can flannel my way through meetings. They never get me anywhere, they're not important.' Melancholics churn out this self-abnegating rubbish by the yard. In truth, Burden is an expert in telecommunications, in wireless telegraphy, in switching systems. This is why his occupation is reserved.

Loránt Pál records his enthusiasm in his notes: *'The man is an ASSET.'*

For Pál, no shirker, the treatment of Anthony Burden now acquires a special urgency. Yes, he would like to see more of him. Yes, he will be happy to arrange further appointments. For this will be no mere 'treatment'. This, at long last, will be war work!

Pál writes in his journal:

AB presents the classic symptoms of melancholia. He is agitated. He is underweight. He cannot smile. Already there are manifest signs of the patient's lack of personal care. His appearance is dishevelled beyond even the generous norms of English eccentricity. His face is a mass of razor cuts (first hints of hesitation marks?). His fingernails are black. The hands, sooted, unwashed, tremble in his lap.

Anthony Burden gulps and sobs – a little boy's stereotypical boo-hoo. Impossible to gauge what actual emotions underlie such a display. 'She *knew*!' Really it is very embarrassing. 'She never even saw my face, she never even cared to see my face, and still she *knew*!'

Thrown out of gear by the astonishing lewdness of Mr Burden's tale, the youthful therapist instinctively tries to make it less than it is. 'Perhaps she meant it as a joke,' he offers. A friendly act, and of absolutely no therapeutic use to his client whatsoever. *Concentrate!* Pál admonishes himself. *Concentrate. You are new here. Every client is a test. Even this one.*

'A joke?' Anthony Burden echoes, doubtfully.

'Yes. A joke. Maybe she was teasing you. I mean—' Pál can only plough on, with false jocularity. 'You did in the end decide to try and take her up the, ah, *passage...*' He feels a blush spread across his cheeks, hot enough to prickle. He wishes he felt better prepared for this. It's not as though he wasn't forewarned. When a previously buttoned-down civil servant blunders raving into an ARP patrol in the middle of the night without his trousers...

In a small, intense voice: 'This makes me a faggot, doesn't it?'

Pál weaves his hands about in front of his chest like an Anglican priest explaining the Trinity. 'Um,' he says. He knows next to nothing about the invert personality, and cares even less. 'Ah,' he says.

In fact, Pál feels a great deal of sympathy for Anthony Burden. The man's sexual indiscretion was unpardonable, of course, but to have your co-respondent turn around afterwards and look into your heart's deepest, darkest place! To have her drag that repressed Thing, pallid and blinking, into the harsh light of day: *'Poofter! Nancy! Queen!'*

If only the woman had had the good sense to keep her mouth shut. Then Mr Burden might even have had his little peccadillo with nothing worse to follow. It was a strange time, after all, in a city made stranger by bombing. He could have put his sordid little knee-trembler behind him – or found a more conventional way to satisfy his taste for anonymous encounters. The red-lit room. The sink in the corner. Money on the table. As things stand…

These are wild times for electroconvulsive therapy. It has only just wrestled free, strongest of the litter, from out of that slew of somatic therapies – malarial fever therapy, prolonged sleep therapy, insulin coma therapy – whose false dawns brightened many a psychiatrist's breakfast-table reading during the twenties and thirties. ECT works, but no one knows why. The relative therapeutic benefits of electrical dosage and strength of convulsion have yet to be established. The philosophical foundation is missing.

In this atmosphere, it is inevitable that Pál, though he has no great respect for the work of Lucio Bini, will be influenced by that pioneer's theories. What other resources has he? Following the precedent set by the Italian's 1942 'theory of annihilation', Loránt Pál considers himself a sort of mental hygienist, using electricity as a loofah to slough from the grey enamelled brain the scum of past mistakes and long-held misapprehensions.

It is clear to him, after a few preliminary consultations, that Anthony Burden is a sexual invert. A homosexual, in other words. It takes no *a priori* assumption on Pál's part to establish that this affliction lies at the heart of Burden's spiralling melancholy.

Now ECT's efficacy as a treatment for melancholy is beyond question. Six to eight treatments have, in Pál's experience, always sufficed to bring about an improvement. The sixth session's unclouding effect can be positively miraculous.

Some patients, however, require many more treatments before any improvement is seen. In addition, at the back of Pál's mind there is always the daring possibility that their sessions might eventually root out, by the annihilation method, the inversion that lies at the root of Mr Burden's despair.

Besides, the patient approves. He *encourages*. This is the first time in Pál's career that therapy has taken on the quality of a collaboration, and the doctor is flattered as well as enthused. It is as though the two men have embarked upon an adventure together, at this pioneering and dangerous time, into the mysteries of the sexually deviant personality.

Pál does not think to question his client's enthusiasm. Why should he? Who is he to stand in Mr Burden's way when he begs, tears pouring down his face, that everything – from his first, moist, prep-school fumblings in his best friend's Y-fronts to the close relationship he enjoyed with his mother, from his navy father's frequent absences to the precise sensual recall he has achieved, with the professor's help, of his wife's anus at the moment of penetration ('Does it tighten? Does it suck? Tell me your impressions, Mr Burden, leave out nothing. Does it welcome like a mouth or repel like a tightened fist?') – that everything, the lot of it, the very meat and veg of sex, and everything to do with spit and spew, should go?

Beyond the Society's front door, a sumptuous fitted red carpet lies like a spillage of fur over the entrance hall floor, and a wide staircase leads, with barely a creak, to the upper rooms. The industrious clatter of Miriam Miller at her typewriter rises, greatly muffled, through the rugs lain across the first-floor waiting area.

There, on the landing, a handsome carved mahogany bookcase with glass doors sums up in little the Society's pre-occupations: *Science and Sanity* by Alfred Korzybski; a slim pocket hardback called *You Can Speak With Your Dad*.

Anthony Burden, intrigued, goes to fetch this book – only to discover, with a chuckle, that he has misread the title. This misprision of his is something he might mention to the doctor, a revealing 'Freudian slip' which may afford them a minute or two of entertainment, and perhaps an insight or two, before the paddles are applied.

Dr Loránt Pál is not a psychoanalyst, but in the year he spent in Vienna studying brain-behaviour relationships, he learned a trick or two. Take, for example, his consulting room. Pál has transformed his modest upstairs space at the Society into something which resembles the retreat of an elderly gnostic: antique rugs, shelves crammed with cryptic *objets*; framed photographs of a middle-European city.

The machineries of his therapy, by contrast, are wonderfully explicit. Turning the brass wheels underneath a narrow table, padded with horse hair and upholstered in red leather, adjusts the height and angle of the pads on which Anthony lies down, ready for his seizure. Anthony, seeing this table for the first time, imagines a rack. This impression is not lessened by the rasping tightness of the leather straps with which he is bound, the chill kiss of paddles at his temples – metal paddles, with small wooden handles, like library stamps – and the unforgettable taste of the rubber gat that keeps him from swallowing his tongue.

The spasms he endures exhaust him. Several days, sometimes, may pass before he can move without discomfort. Of course, Rachel is worried.

Sighing, John Arven agrees to do his part, as a friend of the family, to put her mind at rest. 'But for goodness' sake, Anthony, what are you doing to yourself? I never expected – I mean, is all this still necessary? Why do you keep putting yourself through this mill?'

Anthony, sprawled blear-eyed and exhausted across his couch, blinks up at his faithful old friend as, from the very bottom of a surprisingly comfortable warm well, one might blink up at the shaft's daylit opening. 'What mill?' The tiredness brought on by his treatments feels positively healthful. After his spasms it is as if – having never knowingly taken a day's exercise in his life – he has run a heroic distance. He could take any amount of this physical 'punishment'.

He is fascinated by the way Dr Loránt's machine dims certain memories; even, in some happy cases, erasing them. His mind is losing its tackiness. It is losing its purchase on the pure everyday. It is becoming more and more polished, more glossy, more adamantine.

Of course, Dr Loránt's 'massage of his diencephalic centres' doesn't come without its sacrifices. The music Anthony loves is losing its power now. Palaces no longer ascend in handsome etched volutes up to the ceilings of his mind. At the resolution of a particularly difficult modulation, no Brunelleschi dome sphincters at nipple's point. All is flat, a grey landscape, a Friesen island of the mind, where fallow fields dribble off in gorse and dunes towards a spit of sand that slides, with aching slowness, beneath a shallow sea.

Dr Loránt is delighted. 'Our enemy,' he tells Anthony, 'is *evasion*. I see this clearly now. You are *evading* your *inversion*. You are trying to turn it into something that you can control. This is not the solution. Tell me, Mr Burden, do you dance?'

Anthony, fascinated, shakes his head. 'Never could stand it,' he concedes.

'You see?' the doctor laughs. 'You are afraid that if you dance to music, you will take the woman's part. So you turn music into architecture – into something you can control! These gifts of yours are veils, behind which you protect yourself from direct experience. I will go further (I think you are ready for this): I believe your *inversion* is itself an *evasion*! But what is it that you are evading? What are you running from, that the anus makes for you a hiding place? This is what we must discover!'

So Anthony, drunk on an orgy of self-annihilation, waves himself goodbye. His work means nothing to him now. He cannot understand it. He boxes up his exercise books and is carrying them out to the bin when he remembers the Society where Pál has his consulting rooms. The irony of it tickles him. He will donate his books to the Society. Cataloguing them will give Miriam Miller something to do during these long, lonely winter nights.

That same evening, when he returns home, Anthony embraces Rachel and bursts into tears.

All evening he stumbles over what he has to say. That he longs to participate in the muscular future of her people, with its hardships and setbacks. 'Our future lies in Palestine,' he says. 'You have been right all along, my darling. Any life worth living belongs to the land. Land you can grow things in. Land you can be buried in.'

Rachel, dumbfounded, stares down at him, sprawled exhausted on their couch. 'Has this something to do with your accident?'

He opens his mouth, but there are no words.

'Why do you shut me out?' she says.

He can only shake his head.

'Tell me,' she says. 'I will understand.'

Of that he has no doubt. Oh, it is hopeless, hopeless... 'My love,' he sobs, and tells her everything.

Afterwards he closes his eyes, spent, content, and waits for his world to end.

Of course, it does not.

He opens his eyes.

Rachel, her brown eyes full of a terrible love, bends over him and strokes him behind his ears.

Now they have a project to work towards, hand in hand, Anthony and Rachel are able to behave more freely towards each other. The air between them is clear. Rachel does not have to value Anthony's work. Anthony no longer pretends to find Rachel attractive.

Their marriage is empty, and therefore powerful: Anthony's honesty has created a vacuum which the future rushes to fill.

As the war in Europe ends, Rachel's friends are making their way to the Protectorate. They send the couple literature from the United Workers' Party. They send photographs of themselves brandishing guns from the Scda Arms Works in Czechoslovakia.

Anthony says they should go. It is exactly what he needs and wants. 'You see, I used to think we were all just bits of some greater whole, a sort of Leviathan. Maybe that's true. I realize now, though, it is up to each man, how he lives. We each decide what we are a part of, and what we stand apart from. For the first time in my life, I feel ready to make that choice. I feel ready to let go, and live my life at a human scale at last. To dig. To hoe. Think of it! To breed...'

'Once you are better, my love,' Rachel promises, still not quite able to understand him. 'As soon as you're quite, quite well.'

4

In 1950, the Migdal Tikvah kibbutz, founded by the Kibbutz Artzi movement in 1930, consists of two long accommodation buildings, an armoury, a school and a canteen. There are no roads, just gaps between the buildings, tracks of beaten earth, and here and there a puddle of concrete to plug a pot-hole. The concrete is all broken up, making stones which the children kick about, viciously, as though they were harrying small animals.

The kibbutz is built on a hillside some way above the tree-line. There is no natural shade to speak of – only the mathematical trapezoids of darkness cast by the squat buildings. Anthony Burden's dazzled eyes cannot adapt to the darkness of these dangerous metallic shadows. He is afraid to approach them. He imagines children in them, watching him with wide, unblinking eyes made dull by dust.

In the machinery store, the muscular men of the kibbutz work in silence. The middle-aged ones made Aliyah here in the 1920s. The youths, barely pubescent, are their children. An intermediate generation fled here as teenagers during the world war. Anthony imagines the stirring letter he will write this evening to Sage:

… They come from Bucharest, from Krakow, from Berlin and from Pécs. They speak Yiddish, German, Hebrew, whatever tongue will serve. They communicate with each other by means of strong, muscular gestures, miming the actions at which they are habitually engaged: ploughing, hoeing, planting, digging, driving, wrestling, shooting. They are miming out a new life for themselves, all the while expecting Soviet forces to roll in from the north, to help them realize their final vision.

Anthony raises a hand to these sons of toil.

They do not respond.

He gives them an ameliorating little wave.

Nothing.

He will write: '*Give my love to Rachel.*'

He comes to the lip of the ledge on which the kibbutz is built. Fields edge up the lower slopes of the hill opposite in a half-hearted, experimental manner. There is nothing cooling or vegetable about those squares of malarial green. They look more like swatches, trial colours for a better creation. Here and there the earth is reddish orange, in other places it is yellowish-orange. Mostly it is greyish-orange.

He misses his wife.

Oranges are the kibbutz's speciality. The oranges of the Migdal Tikvah kibbutz grow from green pips to rock-hard little fruit the size and weight of limes. Unspeaking and unsmiling, the kibbutzim teach Anthony Burden how to prune and how to tend.

The oranges swell. Ditches are dug, cisterns are cast, sacks of concrete and buckets of sand are lined up ready for mixing. Lorries arrive bearing lengths of clay pipe to feed the new cisterns, and pumps that never work, so that the old men spend the day deep in the metallic shadows, stripping the pumps, while Anthony and men younger than him work under the blazing sun among the parched trees.

Looking around him as he works, Anthony sees that the young kibbutzim tend the trees with the same unsmiling seriousness with which they fire their guns at targets set among the rocks. The faces of his comrades look as though they have been carved out of thorn. They looked oiled, no, *resined*. They look as if the sun might set them alight. Burning, they might crack open like seed-pods revealing new, even more brightly burnished faces. He can no more look at the faces around him than he can look into the sun reflected off a polished metal mask.

At first Anthony supposed that these young, fit, handsome men must resent the sweaty hours they have to spend among the trees – that they would sooner be at target practice. He was wrong about this. When the muscular young men take up their guns and fire at the rocks, they have it in mind to prune the very stone, to tend it with a savage love into the shapes they require, until no stone is left unshaped, and the whole land has the even solidity of the bunkhouses in which they sleep.

He cannot speak to them. His rusty schoolboy German barely allows him to ask directions, never mind converse. On their arrival it was left to Rachel, his wife, the conscientious student who had already picked up the rudiments of Hebrew from night classes in London, to teach the ancient tongue to her husband. Her sudden decision to return to England has left him deaf and mute.

In his infrequent letters to friends, he puts on a brave face.

... In this deserted land the people of Migdal Tikvah are shaping a socialist Eden. Soon the Czechoslovakians will be here themselves, in arms with their comrades the Russians, to realize this latest outpost of edenic Soviet futurity, here in ancient Palestine. For now they send guns and promises, and the muscular young kibbutzim of the Migdal Tikvah kibbutz practise among the orange groves, shooting at targets crudely stencilled on the rocks.

The inclusiveness of this vision – the rallying call to a common cause – is illusory. These are not and never were his politics. It is just that he has learned to ape his wife's opinions. This is not his battle; it is hers – or was.

Bad enough that she should have abandoned her dreams; did she really have to leave him trapped in their wreckage?

Since Rachel left him, Anthony has learned to resent this nation. He resents the rocks over which he stumbles, and the sunlight which swells and reddens his skin, so that he looks ever more like a sunburnt child. However hard he works, he has a dilettante's face. A soft, exquisite face: he probes and prods its schoolboy redness and hopes in vain for it to acquire a metallic sheen.

He resents, finally and overwhelmingly, the orange trees themselves. This is their first commercially viable fruiting, and the elder settlers, entering the groves, weep to see this sweet fraction of their dreams realized. As he labours and stirs the cement for new cisterns, Anthony wants to dash the men's tears from their eyes with his fists.

Now it is time for the kibbutzim to harvest the oranges; crate them; transport them; worst of all, eat them. For the next month, at the Migdal Tikvah kibbutz, oranges will be the only fruit. Glasses of the corrosive syrup are served at every grainy, garlicky meal. Migdal Tikvah's orange juice eats into Anthony's gums like battery acid. It drills a line of tiny holes across the tip of his tongue and plants a row of ulcers there. It bloats him like a toxin. At night, it bubbles through the lining of his stomach, eating holes in him that he can locate precisely, that he can count. Its colour, drunk out of a tin mug, is as brilliantly artificial as car paint, and it discolours the tin, leaving little black patches that no amount of scrubbing will remove.

Each morning, Anthony rolls his bloated stomach out of the dormitory pallet, the stomach that does not seem to belong to him any more. It has become something apart from him, some unit of production intimately connected with the economy of oranges. He enters the canteen and there, beside every bowl of gruel, sits a plate heaped with oranges. Then he shambles, with the strange crab-like gait he has developed since his therapy, down the hill to the terraces marked with huge boulders that the original settlers, now old men, have spent their youth moving aside – by main force, they would have you believe, by donkey and hemp rope and pulley and finally with their bare hands. He pauses a moment, looking over the rough, rusty land beyond the hill, imagining that every square foot is covered in discarded orange peel, peel gone rusty, peel bleached in the sun and soft and rotten in shadow, so that flecks of green here and there are a thin penicillin-like mould growing over the discarded peel covering the earth. Then, hearing the tractor, he comes away from the edge and goes and takes a corner of tarpaulin and helps spread it over the ground, and then the young men take their hooks and scissors and ladders and they harvest the oranges, which fall to the ground with a soft, complacent thump. These are the poorest of the crop, the bruised runts that he will eat this afternoon, because the kibbutzim, drunk on oranges, these emblems of their success, have stopped the midday bread-making in order to make room for more delicious oranges.

When they are done with the runts, the young men and women take up panniers and climb the trees and snip off fat, shiny, healthy oranges, one by one. Anthony considers this a sign of the kibbutzniks' lack of imagination, that they do not keep the best for themselves, that they prefer to gorge on runts and let the choicest fruits be shipped away.

For lunch he eats an orange, facing away from the others so they will not see the grimaces the acid forces him to pull as it eats his face away from the inside. The others eat oranges as though they were soft rolls. They are monsters of consumption, and he is afraid of them.

In deference to his injured back he spends afternoons helping the women in the packing plant. Packing the oranges means laying them in straw, in crates stamped with the name of the kibbutz in dark, blood-like ink. The time he spends bent over box after box, hardly moving, does his back no good at all. It is only with the greatest pain and difficulty that he is able to sit down to his evening meal, rounded off, as always, with a sharp, pippy orange.

The next morning, the orange crates are driven by truck to the market in Haifa, Red Haifa, where the leaders of the United Workers' Party crowd the cafés and talk of revolution and, looking north, anticipate the day when Soviet tanks will lumber into town, bringing to fulfilment the socialist paradise towards which they work so very hard. The men of Haifa imagine laying palm leaves before the tanks. The women of Haifa dream of throwing garlands of orange blossom up to the boys on the tanks. This constant expectation occasions an atmosphere of permanent festival in Haifa. It is the hysteria of a community living always on the brink of millennium.

Something of this telegraphs itself even to the impassive kibbutzniks of Migdal Tikvah, on the day the lorries leave for Haifa. Women run from the terraces with covered baskets and lift them, smiling, up into the hands of the drivers sitting high up in the cabs of their lorries. Under chequered cloths lies a rich abundance of oranges for the drivers and their mates to eat as they go on their way, the juice spitting and spurting over their rough woollen jumpers, the seats, the dashboard, the windscreen and down their sunburnt cheeks. All the way to Haifa, roadside wasps, launch themselves in desperate dives through cracks in the truck windows, and even through the air vents, to get at the oranges within.

Anthony looks forward to these runs to Haifa, in spite of the market, the tiers of crated oranges, the littorals and dunes of loose oranges, the clouds of wasps.

He looks forward to the cafés most of all: sweet coffee and cakes to soothe his burned and bitten mouth. There is, in spite of the sight of so many muscular sun-loving Jews, an atmosphere, or at any rate a saving shred, of *luxe* about the cafés of Haifa. A feeling conducive to conversation, even to thought.

Anthony remembers thought, what it felt like. He recollects how anxious he was, once, to stop thinking, how treacherous thought had proved. He is beginning to wonder whether his decision to stop thinking was entirely wise.

As a man who has been on vacation too long – a man whose languor has begun to turn to a ponderousness that he cannot enjoy – Anthony, sat outside his favourite café overlooking the market square in Haifa, begins to toy with the idea of ideas.

He writes: *'I used to think the individual was redundant. Groups of people, working in concert, were the future. Together, people knew more, and this made them wiser; this is what I believed. And when at last everyone was joined to everyone else by a length of telegraph wire, on that day, everything would be known by everyone.'*

He wonders for whom he is writing.

'I thought this would be a good thing. A coming together. A final wordless reconciliation between people and their world. An end to Others, and to the messy business of living.'

Yes, this is true. He is aware now of his limitations. If nothing else, Pál's treatments have levelled his moods and cleared his head. He may not have very much to say any more. Few dreams, and fewer hopes. What little he has to say, he can say it now. Now that it is too late.

The fag-end of the war and its aftermath are a grey sea of disconnected memories.

His back kept giving out, again and again.

He remembers lying in a hospital bed, quite crippled.

He remembers begging his old schoolfriend, John Arven, to take a compassionate interest in his wife.

He remembers – this must have been in 1948 – waking up after a delicate operation to correct his fused spine. John Arven was in the recovery room when he woke from the anaesthetic. He was so sore and stiff he couldn't show any expression, which was lucky, as there was no expression he especially wanted to show.

'Shall I pull the blinds?' John asked, already moving to the window.

'God, no,' Anthony croaked.

John looked around him at the curtains, the flowers, the machinery that kept Anthony's back in torsion. 'Up in no time!' he cried, desperately. 'Back on your feet!'

As though, by these efforts, he might conceal the fact that Rachel was not there.

The recollection makes Anthony shudder. A breeze is picking up around the market square. He smoothes out the paper and writes:

The Weight of Numbers

The War fascinated me. The movements of money and machines and people, the strategies, the shifts in the global balance of power. Of course, the longer the war went on, the more innovative it became, the more scientific, the more apparent it was that no one was in charge; that the war would have to play itself out across the world in its own way; that even Churchill was dwarfed by events, no more, by then, than just another cog in a vast economic 'metabolism'.

The coldness of these sentiments makes him shiver. He imagines what Rachel would make of these easy, inadequate abstractions. What any passing Jew would make of them. Any girl from Terezen with a number on her wrist.

He puts down his pen and watches the business of the town. The oranges. A sudden gust blows his paper away. He tries to leap up, to follow the paper, and his back sings with pain. He falls back into his seat, gasping. Everything he has written vanishes.

A second later, another breeze blows a paper liner past him – the sort used to cover orange crates. It wraps itself around a table leg. Gingerly, Anthony bends down and picks it up. The printed side shows a smiling buxom girl in a headscarf, plucking big juicy oranges from a tree. Anthony shudders and turns the paper over. The other side is blank.

Strange, the give and take of the world.

He spreads the paper across his table. He picks up his pen, and finishes his thought: no matter that the start of it is lost. What does it signify, after all? Having the idea is what counts.

He writes: *'My life has changed since the war, and I no longer enjoy the luxury of distance.'*

It is harder, and for that reason more admirable, to think of things at a human scale. It is difficult to be honest.

He begins: *'In Palestine I have buried my marriage, and I have uncovered my heart.'*

220

One of many long letters he is writing to a man he can no longer call his friend.

He remembers the lengths to which John Arven went to explain Rachel's absence. How Rachel had moved to the country, in order to create a separation between herself and her London circle: 'She knows that moving to Palestine will effect a very great change in the pace of her life.'

Such casuistry. Anthony, bedridden, reached inside himself for a sympathetic word or two. He found nothing but bile: 'It seems she has chosen to emigrate by degrees.'

'What she is doing,' Arven said, annoyed at his friend's flippancy, 'is waiting for you.'

Why hadn't she come to see him? Why did she not write?

'Just bite the bullet,' John Arven insisted. 'It's time for you to take up the reins of your marriage again. I'll be there with you, if it helps.'

So he was, standing there on the station platform to meet the London train, scruffy as usual, his shirt-sleeves rolled up to his elbows. He drove them to the cottage – with a nice care, and very slowly – in Rachel's car.

There were rhododendrons in the front garden. The lawn was new, a slightly sickly yellow-green in the weak, overcast light. The house, by contrast, was big and hunched in on itself with honeysuckle over the door and old roses, with wicked thorns. Next door to the cottage stood a hideous, white concrete shell of a garage. There was a lawnmower out, a pair of shears, a fork stuck in the earth with an old tweed jacket draped over the back of it. As they walked up the path, Arven stepped casually over, rescued the jacket, and slipped it on over his shirt.

Anthony could not have said what it was about that moment. Was there something casual or proprietorial about John's action? He did not know. But he sensed it contained a meaning which excluded him.

John led the way through the back door into the kitchen.

Rachel was kneading dough in a large china bowl. Her arms were dusted in flour up to her elbows. She looked up. There was a streak of flour, like war paint, under her right eye. Everything about her had a sheen. She had grown out her hair. Anthony had never seen her looking more beautiful. He couldn't say anything. He couldn't move.

She smiled, seeing John enter the room.

Then she saw Anthony.

'Oh,' she said.

She had not been expecting him. John had not told her.

'So you're here, then,' she said.

Remembering all this, he writes: *'I miss you, Sage, my darling. I hope with all my heart that you have found happiness together. I do not blame you for making love to Rachel. But how I wish you had fallen in love with me!'*

5

It is 20 July 1969, and evening in Lourenço Marques, colonial capital of Mozambique. The street-sellers are packing their wares into suitcases: batteries, handbags and carved hardwood boxes. Toy cars made of cans, random pharmaceuticals, fried cakes, combs, cheap make-up from Hong Kong. Pictures of saints. Pictures of Elvis Presley.

Anthony sees none of this. He is still sat opposite Gregor in the offices of the Institute of Distance and Field Education, and he still has no clue why he is being kept here. Plus, the knot in his back feels like a hot coal wedged in his bones.

The tension in the room has been building up all week. Strangeness has followed strangeness. Anthony has arrived at the office to find the place locked up, while silent figures moved behind the frosted glass door panel, ignoring him and the rap of his stick against the frame. Other times, Gregor has welcomed Anthony into the room with the sort of smothering friendliness a murderer in a stage farce might adopt, desperate to draw attention away from the body in the corner.

On these occasions, Gregor has kept Anthony talking after office hours, long into the night, regaling him with stories drawn from his wartime experiences. Gregor is an explosives expert by training, skilled in defusing enemy ordnance. Earnestly, and at great length, he has described to Anthony how various trigger devices succumbed, one by one, to his craft.

At 3 p.m., with the tension at breaking point, Gregor, trembling, turns on the little Bush radio he keeps on the sill of the window. Slumped, his back turned, he resembles the deputy headmaster of an unsuccessful public school.

As the Junta's power has seeped away, so the station's staffers, one by one, have drifted off. Gregor, by contrast, is a man whose keenness for everything borders on the abject. He has assumed the role of caretaker for the defunct office with the punctilious enthusiasm with which he approaches everything: a piece of paperwork, a telephone call. Why has Gregor remained? Can his energy not be harnessed to more useful work? Perhaps now the mystery will be solved.

The radio is tuned to the local government station but the news, as ever, is focused on a glorified tin can, 240,000 miles away. Anthony struggles to hear the American English of Houston's mission controller over the garbled real-time Portuguese translation:

'... *You might be interested in knowing, since you are already on the way, that a Houston astrologer, Ruby Graham, says that all the signs are right for your trip to the moon. She says that Neil is clever; Mike has good judgement and Buzz can work out intricate problems. She also says that Neil tends to see the world through rose-coloured glasses but he is always ready to help the afflicted or distressed.*'

At twenty minutes past five, a newsflash interrupts the broadcast. 'International black fanatic' Jorge Katalayo has died in an explosion at a 'suspected terrorist cell' on the outskirts of Lourenço Marques.

Gregor makes a sound deep in his throat.

Anthony, annoyed by the announcer's boorish interruption, assumes Gregor is voicing a like frustration. He is about to make some bland remark about the radio station when Gregor falls to his knees.

Anthony's next thought is that Gregor is having a heart attack. When he hurries over and sees that Gregor, far from falling at random, has flung himself down before the institute's fire safe, he is momentarily reassured. Has Gregor remembered something? Something urgent? What? 'Gregor?'

Gregor claws at the safe; his fingers tremble as he rattles through the secret combination.

So many of Gregor's recent actions have left Anthony nonplussed, he hardly sees the importance of this one. It is only as Gregor swings open the great steel door and begins pulling out documents in great handfuls, that Anthony wonders whether his employer's actions might not be connected to the recent newsflash.

As Gregor rifles through the papers, Anthony takes advantage of his absorption, stealing forward to study the institute's secrets.

From a sea of bills, receipts and final demands, Gregor plucks a slim white envelope. He tears it open, and unfolds the contents within. He hands a sheet to Anthony, stuffs another in his trouser pocket, crumples up the remainder and the envelope and throws them back into the safe.

He says, without looking at Anthony, 'Do exactly what it says. Don't ask questions. Don't wait here. Don't go home.'

Anthony scans the paper. Typed on a faded ribbon are the details of an escape route. The name of a shipping company. A telephone number. The accompanying instructions are so infantile, they can only be a kind of code:

> *If time allows, be sure to obtain a sufficiency of warm clothing.*
> *Do not under any circumstances accept rides from strangers.*
> *Discard your house keys.*
> *Avoid intercourse.*
> *Stout shoes must be worn.*

Once the papers are back in the safe, Gregor bends awkwardly, reaches into the top right corner of the safe, and pulls out a metal pineapple.

Anthony blinks.

It is a grenade.

Gregor pulls the pin, tosses the grenade into the safe and heaves the door shut.

The door is heavy. It takes a second to close. In that second, the grenade rolls off the papers piled willy-nilly inside the safe, and falls onto the floor. Anthony gasps. Gregor heaves the door open again on smooth, silent hinges, plucks up the grenade as though it is hot, and places it on the papers, all the while pushing at the door to close it again.

The door slams shut.

The grenade goes off. The safe is well built, and the explosion makes no more impact than if someone had rapped it with a spanner.

Far louder is Gregor's wail as he spins up and away. The stub of his amputated forefinger drizzles blood across the floor, the table, Gregor's trousers, his shoes, Anthony's shoes, the door and the door-handle, leaving a trail for Anthony to follow, as Gregor makes his getaway.

Anthony, mystified, follows Gregor out of the building, only to lose his trail across a busy junction. He wonders where to go. He pulls out his paper and reads: *'If time allows, be sure to obtain a sufficiency of warm clothing... Stout shoes must be worn.'*

He wonders if he shouldn't just go home. He wonders what is going on, and what it has to do with him. Of course he should go home.

And tomorrow?

What should he do tomorrow? Should he come into work? What will he find? Will Gregor be there, his hand in bandages, full of apologies and explanations? Or will the place be locked up, secured by the police, surrounded by military vehicles and PIDE men in dark ill-fitting suits?

Or will the room be empty, unlocked, just as they left it, a chaos of imported newspapers and out-of-date gazetteers? If it is, should he sit down? Should he wait for the phone to ring?

Utterly at sea, Anthony thrusts the mysterious paper into his trouser pocket and sets off at random through the town.

In his rush to follow Gregor, Anthony has forgotten his stick. He wants to go back for it. He wants to return and sit down with a cup of tea and listen some more to the little Bush radio on the office window sill; to hear again the miraculous conversation, conducted over a distance of some quarter of a million miles, with the men who will soon be setting foot on the moon. But he is afraid: Gregor's panic and the strange, minatory instructions in his pocket have taken hold of his imagination. There is no way he can go back.

In the yard beside a rundown hotel two old women stand beneath a fig tree, pounding maize for *nsima*. In the street opposite, another woman stirs a pot of *caril de amendoim* – he can smell it from here. The cook's face is covered with the garish white pan-stick make-up you see women use in Tete, against the sun.

He comes to the bluff overlooking the bay. A woman calls to him from a doorway. He knows that if he looks at her, her smile will break his heart.

There is nothing from which he has to run away. There is no need for him to flee. Flee what? Yet he keeps on walking.

'Do not under any circumstances accept rides from strangers.'

Well, really.

He looks around him. This is not the way home. This is not the way back to the office. It is not that he is consciously walking *away* from these places, exactly. On the contrary, when he analyses what few feelings he can muster in response to these bizarre events, it seems to him that he is walking *towards...*

Towards what he doesn't know: whatever shadowy existence is implied by the strange paper in his hand.

'Christ,' he says aloud, reading his instructions over for the third or fourth time. He is not sure whether to be disgusted or amused; it has just dawned on him that this list could just as well double as an account of his life: *'Discard your house keys... Avoid intercourse.'*

The shipping office occupies the first floor of an old Portuguese villa to the north of the port. The room's shelves are lined with old fabric-bound ledgers, and its heavy furniture swims in a dark, resinous light. Near the window, a white girl pecks at a typewriter. She glances at him, then returns to study the keys before her. Her tongue edges between her lips and glistens in the nicotinic light.

He hands over his paper. The girl's tongue withdraws, leaving a wet trail upon her lower lip. Idly, she waves at a connecting door, lays the paper down on her desk and goes back to her typing. Anthony reaches over for the paper. The girl's hand shoots out and slaps the paper, keeping it from him. He meets the girl's belligerent eyes, but lets his gaze slide away. Asking her a question will force her to speak, and he is afraid of what her voice will sound like.

He opens the connecting door.

The room beyond is lighter, busier, more modern. Fluorescent lights hang from a ceiling stained with damp. The uneven floor is covered with a thin carpet of an indeterminate colour. A big, unhealthy man waves him to a desk. There is a radio playing, tuned to an international station. The voice of Mission Control comes through uncluttered by translation: *'We have loss of signal as Apollo Eleven goes behind the moon. Velocity 7,664 feet per second, weight 96,012 pounds. We're seven minutes and forty-five seconds away from lunar orbit insertion.'*

Seven minutes and forty-five seconds later, the means and timing of Anthony Burden's departure from Lourenço Marques have all been dealt with, quickly and without fuss. The false name on his documents sounds the only unorthodox note. Otherwise he might be any other independent traveller signing aboard a tramp steamer.

'Apollo Eleven, Apollo Eleven, this is Houston, can you read me?'

'The captain will hand you your new passport shortly before your arrival.' The man's patter could only have been acquired by his dealing with a dozen similar requests a day. Burden imagines this stream of men who enter the shipping office, more or less desperate, more or less confused, only to emerge, a few minutes later, rebranded.

He knows of no reason why he should run, much less why he should abandon Mozambique, or why he should make his getaway in so uncomfortable a mode of transport, and under a false name at that. At the same time, he is finding it increasingly difficult to think up reasons why he should stay. Everything about his life here is evaporating like the toils of a dream a minute after waking.

How can he go home? He cannot even remember the name of his road.

Neil Armstrong says: *'We're going over the Messier series of craters right at this time, looking vertically down on them and, hey, we can see good-sized blocks in the bottom of the crater. I don't know what our altitude is now but those are pretty good-sized blocks.'*

Anthony walks reluctantly out of range of the radio, out of the room and the building, and into the eyeblink-short tropical evening, boarding papers crumpled in his hand, and with the dizzying sensation of having been flushed through a gap no wider than a clerk's anonymous smile into a new world.

Back in the office, Buzz Aldrin sighs: *'When a star sets up here, there's just no doubt about it. One instant it's there and the next instant it's just completely gone.'*

PQRD

1

Summer 1944.

Dick Jinks – a merchant seaman long since invalided out of the service – takes apart his customer's starter motor and spreads the pieces across his work table, its surface scarred by years of plier-work, chisel-work, horse-chains mended, bridles restitched, saddles restuffed and invisibly repaired. The table's legs are raised on bricks so that Dick can work standing up. Sitting down, alas, is a fond and ever-dimming memory for him, whose red-faced 'oofs!' and 'aahs!' have given way this past year to more clenched forms of suffering. Dick picks up a piece of the dinky little motor, studies it – what will they think of next? – and pops it into his mouth as though it were a plum. He swills it around his mouth until it is clean, spits it out onto a cleanish rag, dries it and picks up the next.

Alice, Dick's wife of eleven years, threads her way into the covered yard, their new baby in her arms, and tries not to muss up her cotton frock on the gear piled all around: farrier's irons in a rusty tin drum, heavy rubber tyres, some of them inflatable, most the solid sort, huge wooden horse collars, an anvil; a broken tractor wheel, higher than a man. Sunlight shines into Dick's dark nook through her frock, silhouetting thighs grown thick from child-bearing, calves still shapely, and knees – well, knees, as ever, too small; fragile knots of bone. Dick Jinks harbours a secret, wincing fear for her knees.

Their first child, the trigger for their shotgun marriage and young Dick's precipitate flight to sea in 1934, would have been eleven now, had she not died within hours of her birth, leaving Alice, fresh sea-widow, heartbroken and alone. For his part, Dick was none the wiser for the longest while, for he was already out in mid-Atlantic and, at the moment of his baby girl's death, only hours away from the engine room explosion and the defining cataclysm of his own life.

So this new arrival, apple of his mother's eye, this little Nicky Jinks, represents an unexpected second chance (cafeteria sign still faced 'Open', gingham-curtained door unlocked, a memorably swift, stiff violation against the serving counter, the only copulatory position of which Dick, her poor spinelocked darling, is now capable).

From 1934 to now, in the interval between their dead child and their live one, between Dick Jinks's running off to sea and his return, what has his life been?

He cannot remember.

Dim impressions of a horsehair couch, leather, like an operating table. Pictures on a wall, a foreign city, nowhere he knew or could imagine. The echo of a name, Pál, as in, 'me and my pal', the pun as hollow as a skull's grin. The taste of rubber.

Nothing coheres.

'*Come along, Mr Jinks.*'

Instructions. Admonitions. Corridors of pale green or mustard yellow. Doors with numbers. Hoses. Beds.

'*Where are we?*' says a voice inside his head. A woman's voice.

He looks around him for an answer. This grotto, filmed with oil. These things – tat for farmers' horses, tyre irons, lifting tackle, all the stuff of a modern blacksmith's trade. It should be colourful in here. Yellow paper wrappers round the tins of engine grease. Wheel jack a cheery red enamel. Saddle leathers tan and butterscotch. The colours here have been first muted, then swallowed up utterly by dust, grit, the sump impurities of his trade.

This is no grotto.

He knows what this is.

This place of black and white.

Fighting for breath, Dick drools the motor part out of his mouth onto the table. It glistens there, grey, like a spent tooth.

Alice, babe-besotted, does not see the panic in her husband's eyes, the hollow tremor of his diaphragm as he fights for air. She says, 'A nice day out. The plums are ready for picking. You can hold the ladder for me when you're done in here.'

Even as he draws breath for his terrible *Eeeee!*, the normal, friendly strains of his wife's voice avert catastrophe. They sever the red wire, disarming the terrible thing inside him, and he is back in the present. He lets go a ragged breath and covers, as he always does, with a big piratical 'Yo! Ho!'

One thing is certain: whatever the other details of his history, Dick, like a pocket-knife rusted open, has seized up to the point where he can be of no imaginable wartime use. So he is cast up here – after many strange and shadowy excursions – like a timber shivered from a wreck. He has much to be grateful for. This blacksmithing business for a start, pride and joy of his lowering father-in-law. And his wife, of course. Above all things, this wife he had practically forgotten. Not for a second had he imagined – returning, like a wounded animal, back to his starting point – that he would find her still living here and, if not exactly waiting for him, still amenable enough to his seaman's bluster, his rough re-wooing and finally, his cap-in-hand suggestion that they take up where they had left off, a dozen years before.

He remembers the ripe eighteen-year-old who'd straddled him in 1933, child that he was, for want of older suitors. This girl he'd had to marry. He remembers feeling proud and ashamed at once of such necessity, afraid of his bride, and at the same time unable to believe his luck, his hair plastered down for the ceremony with a redolent dressing he half-suspects, knowing his mother's humour, was plain lard.

This girl, after such an interval, is grown even more buxom now, and she's not at all the bitter shrew she might have become, the jealous termagant of every sailor's fears.

'Take little Nicky, Father,' says Alice, bending forward over him, cleavage branding a holy Y into each confused eye. 'We've customers.'

235

The business: this smithy, sliding seamlessly to garage now horse-power has had its day; a clean dirt forecourt with two hand-operated petrol pumps; a tea-house for the haulage trade; round the back of the house, an orchard of plum trees.

Gently, Alice lowers their infant son into Dick's arms. Dick would protest, only the space under his tongue is a tray of grit. Of their own accord his brawny arms, built for furnaces and fisticuffs, arrange themselves into a cradle for twelve pounds of alien life.

Already, Mother is vanished, her frock catching for an oily split-second on a pile of articulated metal plates, once a tractor's treads, now – the tractor done for – bound for the foundry, so that the base metal might be granted a brand-new and deadly incarnation at the hands of de Havilland, Browning, Marconi.

Dick cannot imagine achieving greater happiness than this: he has a new trade, and his old wife; he even has a son. But present pleasures, he has found, do not content the past. The happier his present, the more furiously Dick's past bangs on the gates for his attention. Perhaps this is what happens as you grow old. Or maybe that infernal Professor Pál played one too many shocking tricks. In any event, the slightest thing can set him reeling through time. One careless turn of thought, and he is back there. The explosion. The sick tilt of the deck. Seawater bursting chamber after chamber of their ship, as solid-sounding as a hammer swung by a maniac, scampering from compartment to compartment. The struggle to escape. The things in his way. The young able seaman he killed. The look in the boy's eyes as the metal stanchion oyster-knifed the back of his skull.

Sat there in the monochrome gloom, father and son share a look of mutual horror: for Little Nick Jinks, at four months old, is unmistakably the boy Dick killed, reborn, returned and bent on who knows what subtle revenge.

Dick has said nothing to Alice. It is too absurd. But just look at that nose. Those little eyes, so close together.

That rosebud mouth.

2

Sixteen years later: 1960, a weekend in late March.

It is a dank, chilly, febrile sort of spring. The sky is overcast, with bands of cloud staining the eastern sky. They are sitting in the garden of the local pub. It is a Saturday. Dad is drinking his pint. Deborah is sucking her lemon-and-lime up through a straw. It is so much nicer than Coke, so much sharper. It is what her mother used to drink.

'For over nine hundred years people have been drawn to visit and admire one of this country's finest towns...'

Deborah Conroy unpicks what she can from the Tourist Board pamphlet. Her father Harry, a retired wrestling promoter, helps her over the few difficult words. They are reading about their home, about the windmill that launched Deborah's first word, 'Win-will!' About the church in whose grounds her mother is buried.

Deborah is eight years old. She opted out of her school trip – her class's wild week away on the Suffolk coast. She feigned an illness, and though Harry saw through her in an instant, he did not say anything. It is a guilty secret they share: since her mother's death, neither one can bear to be parted from the other.

At school, for the handful of children who did not go on the trip – those whose parents could not afford to send them, or whose behaviour was atrocious enough to disqualify them – there is another project. 'Penance' might be a more apt term. While their gadabout friends are exploring the creeks and quicksands of the River Alde and the River Ore, Deborah and the rest of them – the poor, the wicked and the lame – are meant to be exploring 'this place right here'. This is just one of many formulations which, like a fixed grin of embarrassment, convince no one:

'this place we call home'; 'this exciting place we walk past every day'; 'this place we think we know, but we don't'. Thaxted: the English country village as it never was. Such a solid, bumptious place. Until the rain comes. In the rain, the whole place looks hollowed out. Only the frontages on the high road stay solid. Everything else hangs in a weird, contingent relationship with the planes of the rain, the twist of the branches of the few trees, the line of a wall here, a roof angle there, as if in a second it might all screw itself up and tumble away in the wind.

Deborah is thinking a lot about the rain. She is doing 'The Geography of Thaxted' this week. She is writing about rainfall. About weather. Dad is trying to be helpful, he got hold of this pamphlet for her, but he isn't keeping up. History was last week. This week is geography.

The weather improves in time for Easter.

The Saffron Waldon District Children's Biblical Weekend is a big outdoor event: an extravaganza of egg-and-spoon races, jolly Bible songs, competitions and prizes for everyone. It's growing year on year. There are four tents in the field this year – four 'houses' – though how the organizers choose which 'house' a child belongs to is a mystery. They are: Panda House, Penguin House, Pony House and Pigeon House. Nobody wants to be in Pigeon House. Even 'pony' is a bit of a kludge. The boys cavil: 'Father Peter, a pony is only a kind of horse!' But the girls are besotted; they surrender unquestioning to the animal's aura of leather and rhythm, obedience and hot breath.

Of course, a panda is only a kind of shrew, but you don't hear Panda House complaining. Pandas are *endangered*. The kids in Panda House have drunk deep from this particular well. Ennobled by visions of mortality, they have been religiously tattooing bear-outlines into each other's upper arms with sharpened pencils.

Here they were, the organizers of this year's Saffron Walden District Biblical Weekend, looking for neutral house names – names picked purposely so as not to put off the more anti-clerical parents – and now these kids are bootstrapping their own theologies around ponies and pandas, a system of personal ethics around penguins. Pigeon House is the only manageable group of the four, because the name has left everybody feeling uniformly dispirited.

The bald fact is, some animals are religious, and some are not. It is easy to imagine the existence, somewhere, of a Horse Cult, even a Pony Cult. But whoever heard of a Pigeon Cult? Some *things* are religious, and some are not. The Divine pervades precisely half of everything.

In the afternoon of the second day, Sunday, the Lord's Day, Father Peter (Saffron Walden), Father Gerry (Thaxted), Father Richard (Great Chesterford) and Father Neil (Linden) erect a bright white marquee in the centre of their camp. They call this the Big House. Deborah Conroy, eight years old, is filled with quiet certainty: she is going in this year, whatever the flutters in her belly.

It is the final event. Ponies, pandas, pigeons and penguins sit cross-legged and higgledy-piggledy facing the bright, pure white marquee. Their parents perch on tiny tubular school seats at the back, and children and parents alike squirm and shudder. The Big House!

Because God slips in without invitation. God in motley, capering.

Which of you is brave enough to step into the Big House?

Eight-year-old Deborah Conroy rises.

Beside her, another child stands, turns and follows her. And another. Then a great rush of children. They are pressing past Deborah now. They are overtaking her, stepping on her toes. The priests are beside themselves. Hard-shelled old tortoises. Something has wormed its way into them: a gift of tongues. 'Are you ready? Ready! Steady! Are you ready? Ready, steady, go!'

This isn't the way Deborah imagined it. It isn't a solemn procession. It is something rough, a great herding, Jesus's flock mounting the metal ramp into the cramped stink of His lorry.

She nears the great white wall of the house of the Lord, and she sees how it flaps in the wind like a sail. This House does not stay still. If she enters, it will bear her away for ever. Everything will change. She is afraid suddenly. She wants to enter, but even if she changed her mind, she would not be able to evade that great wide rent.

So Deborah lets the crowd bear her towards the bellowing House of the Lord; there, she is filled with a joy so all-consuming, it blasts her awareness clean of everything except itself.

Dick Jinks is dead.

Nick, his surviving son, prises the bedsheet from his frozen grip and pulls it up to cover him. The sheet settles over Dick's face and smoothly idealizes its shape. A hollow forms over the mouth, the jaw dropped open as if to scream.

Nick draws up the room's only chair and waits. There will be no more *Eeeee!* in the night. No more of his father's tongue, weaving molten in the air. Silently Nick sits, scratching absently at his oil-stained corduroys, and plumbs the depths of his relief.

Crossing to the dressing table, Nick leans forward and studies himself in the fly-spotted mirror. Even now, at the narcissistic height of his adolescence, Nick accepts he is no oil painting. His head is too small for his body; his features are too small for his head. But what is there about him to make anyone so afraid?

There is no doubt in Nick's mind that his father died of fear; that over the years fear ate through his guts, caustic as an acid. Nick tried to reassure his father and win his trust, never with much success.

Nick wipes away a tear and turns back into the room. He knows his father loved him. Even as he stumbled away from him, or backed into his room's corner, even as he drooled and shook, there was love.

They had learned to live together, to love each other as father and son, by indirect means: in the empty morning kitchen, a bowl of warm porridge; clean clothes outside the bedroom door; shoes cleaned for the next day, and occasionally polished; a little money on the table and a list made out in one hand (milk, bread, bog roll), that by day's end, unfailingly, was ticked off by the other. So they looked after each other, cooked each other's food, cleaned each other's clothes. They were not happy, they were not friends and they hardly knew each other, but they did love each other.

Nick Jinks walks with heavy tread over to the room's only window – a rattly sash that looks out over the rear of the property.

Their life had not always been like this. Nick can remember a time in his childhood when he and his father were still able to speak together. It is from these dimly remembered, yet dearly cherished conversations that Nick knows of an even more distant time, before memory, when his mother was still alive. From his father's stuttering descriptions, Nick knows that Alice was a beauty. There are snapshots, too, though in the absence of memories pictures can never convey much. The truth is, Nick cannot really envisage her, but thinking of her brings a scent to mind, which he concocts from all Dick's talk of what she did: the cakes she'd bake, the fruit she'd pick, the jams she'd stew, the plum trees she would walk among, tending them, eating the fruit, so that the crimson juice would run down her chin onto her apron – 'Always sinkin' her teeth into a plum!'

Nick shudders to recall his father's story, told and retold to the point where it has become a sort of memory: the ladder's fatal toppling, the way his mother, clinging grimly to the top rung, acquired all the lever's deadly momentum. The tree-trunk and her head in spectacular dry collision. Her mouth a mess of blood and fruit pulp. Soon, leaking from her ears, not blood but something clear. Aqua vitae. It drained away into the orchard earth, leaving her brain parched, her spine hollow. Her seizure. Her shoe coming off, kicked off. In that magic instant, death.

Nick presses his head against the cold window pane, hard, harder.

The pane snaps.

Nick pulls back, surprised. He raises a hand to his forehead. No blood. He focuses on the crack in the glass, a crude Y, then beyond the crack, down, to the ruined lot.

The times have not been kind to businesses like these. Highways have funnelled off all trade, stranding the old trunk roads as surely as a river cuts its coils free, leaving them beached, strange shingle hieroglyphs. Still the faithful tanker comes, once in a blue moon, to top up their reservoir with four-star. The pumps are so old they can barely suck, but there is no money for a refit. The tea-house that was his mother's pride is long gone, the country measled now with Little Chef. As for the smithy, its subtle craftwork, that is all forgotten, leaving nothing for Nick to inherit.

To that extent, the whole is doomed, but the lot at the back of the house where the plum orchard once stood – here a deeper, darker curse is lodged.

A curse is a sequence of operations, each one of which will stand the light of day and reason. A curse never shows its hand. Of course the orchard came to grief, once Nick's mother died; how could it not? She knew these trees and loved them. She had tended them all her life. She knew how to bring them on. They flowered and fruited for her. Naturally, under Dick's uncertain management, they would not perform so well.

Then there was Dick: the man the trees had widowed, whose late happiness they had destroyed. He did his best by them. He pruned. He plucked. He cut away dead branches with a dull and rusty saw. Sickness spread. He snapped and tore. He bared green timber to the filthy air, beneath hot summer's eye.

The seasons cycled. The fruits of his first year's husbandry emerged: hard pips, crisp and healthy. All seemed well. They grew. Dick waited impatiently for them to take on their mature coloration, their dark bloom. For a few, strange, happy days, he forgot what the trees had done to his wife; he remembered only how his wife had taken care of the trees. He watched the fruit, and was proud.

The plums swelled to the size of apricots; then, to the size of pears. Their greenish-yellow skins burst, but if he tried to pluck one, it would resist his fingers, the branch would dip and toss, then the skin would give way, revealing a thready, whitish pulp that smelled of nothing. He did not dare taste it.

His son mewling in his brawny arms, Dick watched the trees, dumbfounded and afraid. Their delicate branches began to sag, dragged down to snapping by the mutant fruit. The skins of the plums split and dropped of their own accord, leaving balls of pulp to drip-dry in the autumn air. The pulp was not white now, but the brownish yellow of diarrhoea, and it was not tasteless; it had the corrupt sweetness of spoiled meat. Wasps gorged on the useless fruit. They smothered each soft dung-ball with a broiling, black-orange carapace. Then, as evening approached, drunk and dying from the season's cold, they would crawl away into the house. A moment's inattention, and they would fill your shoe, your slipper, a fold of your sock. Objects had to be examined from all sides before one dared take hold of them. Dressing of a morning, Dick would shake each piece of his and his son's clothing from his window and Nick, listening carefully, heard the husks of the stricken wasps bursting on the flagstones of the path.

Abortive nests hung from the corners of each room as the wasps, confused and desperate, sought sanctuary from the strange poisons which even now were liquefying them.

Come winter, Dick subjected the trees to a thorough and savage pruning.

The following year, the plums hardly grew at all. They shrivelled to a sort of leathery pouch, lobed like a walnut. Inside, the plum stone was ordinary enough except for its colour, which was white. This year the infection attacked the leaves, too. The leaves grew galls, and the air around the trees that autumn was thick with big hairless flies with pendulous brown bellies. They blundered carelessly about, indifferent to heat or cold or time of day. One could only suppose they were a kind of horsefly, because where they bit a boil would rise, much like a horsefly bite. They were something between a cockroach and a wasp and they never slept. Until well into November Nick spent sleepless nights trying to calculate, from their flatulent buzzing, how many flies had managed to penetrate his bedcovers.

Once its first exuberance was past, the curse grew less inventive. Consistently, the plums would shrivel; every year, piles of the abnormal flies built up in the corners of each bedroom window sill. Every spring for eight years, hardly a day went by when little Nicky did not hear, from the desolate depths of the covered yard, a deep, satisfying rumble of the grinding wheel, followed, now and again, by the abrasive swish as a metal edge came into contact with the spinning stone. He knew, or guessed, from the sheer volume of bright hard sounds, that this was no mere knife his dad was grinding. Dick's pale silence, whenever Nick asked him what he was up to, added to his son's conviction that a special blade was being readied for a primal act.

When his father's fear of him began to escalate, around his eleventh birthday, Nick had nightmares that this axe was being made ready for him.

The Act, whatever it was to be, seemed forever delayed. The axe, which surely had an edge to cut a single hair by now, never saw daylight. Until one day in early summer, Nick, then in his twelfth year, woke early and heard the sizzing of the stone.

He cannot now recall in what way the sound was different that day. What it was about the air, or the light. He got out of bed and went to his window. With fresh eyes, he saw the knobbly branches, amputated by so many prunings, their ends, clubbed like fists, sporting twigs like insect hairs, and from the tip of every hair a leaf, or what he took to be a leaf, but which, to his freshened eye, revealed more gall than leaf, each leaf a greyish sac.

He put on his clothes and left the house by the back door. At ground level the trees looked even stranger, more bone than bark. It came to him that the trees were no longer trees; that something new was growing in their place, which, while it was young, had used the coloration and form of trees to conceal itself. It was older now, and strong. It was shedding its camouflage.

Nick met his dad coming the other way along the path that skirted the old house. Dick was carrying an axe. The sight of it made Nick feel sick, because it seemed to have suffered much the same fate as the trees. It was, after so many years against the wheel, hardly an axe at all any more. The metal head was ground down to a sort of truncated sickle blade. With sightless eyes, Dick strode past his son and in among the trees.

Blindly, stiff-legged, he swung.

The axe blade sank without effort into the flesh of the first tree. Dick paused, his glued back a little bent, the axe still buried in the tree. Uneasy, afraid of frightening his father, Nick stepped forward. He wanted to help. His father was struggling to release the blade. 'Dad?'

Dick, startled, stood upright, yanking at the axe. The tree-trunk crumbled. Man and boy stood by, dumbfounded, as the tree fell and shattered. Two big branches shivered free of the trunk, puffing sawdust as they fell. There was no moisture in the thing, no strength. Silently, Dick dropped his axe and walked up to the next tree. He pushed. The trunk snapped with a soft crack, like a biscuit. The tree toppled. Nick came forward and studied the stump. The wood was pale and crumbly. There did not appear to be anything living in the wood, but Nick was afraid to touch it. Dick must have felt a similar revulsion, because he went and fetched two pairs of work gloves. Then, together – and with the axe quite forgotten, lying there in the long grass – father and son went around the orchard, pushing over trees.

Their victory over the curse seemed suspicious. They waited for a plague of flies. It never came. They watched the trees. The galls, in time, dropped off their little twigs and vanished into the lank grass. The grass grew around the trees. The grass was green.

They did not burn the wood. They were afraid of what it would release. Come winter it simply crumbled and blew away, leaving only the shapes of trees in reddish dust. Rains drove the dust into the earth. The grass fed on the earth. The grass was green, and it grew.

Afraid of what might grow there if they planted something new, Dick let the lot go. He did his best to keep the garage business alive. The work was hard. He was not an old man, exactly, but his back was growing stiffer and more painful as he aged. Though Nick was willing enough to help, Dick's fear of him kept him at bay.

So, inevitably, the space where the orchard had been filled with the waste products of the garage trade. Old tyres. The sagging panels of defunct caravans. Wheel-less farm machinery. Empty cans. Things Dick had not the strength to deal with on his own.

When the rats came, Dick and Nick had no one to blame but themselves. What did they imagine would happen, once they had made the old orchard into such a weather-proof warren of abandoned tarpaulin and machinery? After all, the rats were only rats. Bigger than your average rat, perhaps, but only rats. If they were exactly the colour of the galls which had vanished into the long grass two years before, the coincidence was hardly remarkable: what colour should rats be, if not a pewter grey?

Dick, enfeebled, unable any longer to fight his own battles, was forced to turn to Nick for help. For the boy's fourteenth birthday, he dusted off the ancient farmer's shotgun that had belonged to his wife and passed it over, tight-lipped and trembling. Nick also received a puppy, which Dick had rescued from a nearby ditch: a sly, dead-eyed mongrel Nick never named, thinking of her, always and only, as the Rat Catcher. Nick felt that with the gifts of gun and dog, a bond was now established between him and his father, a circuitous trust that dared not speak its name, or look itself in the eye, but which was tangible enough. It was, for Nick, a happy time. He had acquired a purpose: to defend hearth and home.

Nick turns from the window to his father's bed. He has raised the sheet to cover his father's face, and in so doing he has uncovered his father's feet.

Three toes on the left foot are missing.

There is no blood: the rats waited until he was dead.

Nick's little mouth puckers, and he squints through close-set eyes. This, in Nick's ill-favoured face, is what passes for fury. 'Girl!' he cries.

The Rat Catcher hurls herself up the stairs and lands bodily against the door. She never barks. Nick opens the door. The dog, having made her presence known, is already heading down the stairs. There is no time to waste. She knows what this is. Battle is joined.

Nick goes into the cellar, fetching gun and ammunition. He stuffs his pockets, and wipes the last tears from his eyes.

There will be no such display from the Rat Catcher. No keening or scratching at the door as she pines for her old master. Already she is worrying at the edges of the rubbish heap. There is nothing hang-dog about this dog.

The Rat Catcher is a professional.

Harry Conroy watches with amused pride as Deborah leads the children into the big white marquee.

After a little while – no more than ten minutes by Harry's watch – the children come out again. Whatever went on in the Big House, it has contented, rather than transfigured them. They are quiet, with an inner glow. They are smiling, as though they have each been given a small piece of good-quality milk chocolate.

Harry waits patiently by the mouth of the tent. He recognizes some of the children. One or two say hello to him. Deborah's best friend walks straight past him and does not notice him, even when he waves. Then, when they have all come out, and Deborah has still not emerged, Harry walks around the tent, thinking there may be two exits.

There aren't.

He enters the tent. There is no cross. Bunting decks the fabric walls of the marquee. In the middle of the marquee is a folding table covered in a white tablecloth. The table is bare. The marquee is empty.

*

George Bridgeman's preparations have been meticulous, circumspect and expensive. His plans have been written down, then memorized, and all documentation carefully destroyed. The old concrete air-raid shelter, abandoned since the last war, and swamped long since beneath a cloud of savagely spiked blackthorn – a barrier only George knows how to circumvent – has been damp-proofed and sound-proofed, tamper-proofed and child-proofed throughout.

The moment he brings the padded hammer neatly down upon the little girl's head, George expects everything to go to hell. When it doesn't is when George's problems start.

He drops the hammer, catches the little girl up in his arms as she crumples, and checks the pulse in her neck. Alive enough. Who would have thought it would be so easy? The little kitten walking past him, all alone, oblivious to everything, drunk on everything, 'off with the fairies'...

Life isn't like that. It is very important to him that over the next few days, or weeks, or however long it takes, he shows this little lamb what life is really like. That he rubs her face in it. That he reams her clean of all personality, and shows to her the beast she really is. Because people are so stupid. People pretend so much when really they are no better than beasts. Someone has to show them what they really are. Someone, damn it, has to stand up for the truth.

Among the trees, hidden from the tents, his hands moisten against her thin white dress. He picks her up and bears her to his Ford Consul. A peach. So why is he shaking?

The truth of it is, George Bridgeman does not know how to win. His life to this point has been a series of small, spiteful victories secured in the teeth of universal indifference. If the little moppet had struggled, screamed, kicked him in the balls and run away, or if, after his twenty-odd years in an abattoir, George had failed to judge his blow correctly, and splattered her brains over his shoes – then he could have found a comfort in the way the world had turned reliably against him yet again.

As it is, things have gone swimmingly. He slips her into the boot of his car. She fits the space perfectly. Not too big. Not too small. Pale and pretty. He wonders what she looks like naked. He'll know soon enough. He checks her over. Both shoes still on her feet. Hair clip still in place. He glances back the way he has come. No dropped hanky. No trail of bloody spots. Perfection. He gets in the car, turns the key in the ignition, and–

The car rumbles into life.

He jounces down the rough track, out of the copse and into the little lane which runs so near, yet does not meet, the main road. Any second now a hummock in the track will ground the Ford's chassis, or twist a wheel out of true...

It does not happen.

The world absolutely refuses to slap him down. The only way things can go wrong now is if he messes them up himself. George feels a childish need to pee, and a spot of unusual tenderness at the tip of his penis. His palms upon the steering wheel are wet. It's up to him now. It's up to him.

I must have missed her, Harry Conroy says to himself. He goes in search of Deborah. He bumps into the parents of Sarah, Deborah's best friend. They reassure him, and speak to their daughter. Dumb, wide-eyed, Sarah shakes her head; she has not seen her friend all day. So they lead Harry to another, smaller tent, where the organizers are gathered. Father Peter, Father Neil and Father Gerry sit Harry down. One by one, they join in the search for his daughter. Harry is alone.

Harry waits in the small tent...

... for about half a minute. Then he gets up, goes out, joins the search. There are no parents now, no children. The people running around are people he has never seen before. The sun is brighter than ever, but in the opposite corner of the sky, there is a black line on the horizon – a heavy charcoal smudge.

It is about now that Harry starts shouting. It's an incoherent sound – there aren't even any words. Something is working his mouth with strings. Even if Deborah hears him – even if his daughter is near enough to hear – Harry doubts very much whether she will recognize his cry.

The act of reloading the heavy gun is a balletic blur. After two years of practice Nick no longer has to aim the barrel to score a bloody hit, and his arms and shoulders are strong enough to dampen the gun's most awkward recoil. The Rat Catcher has grown into a machine for covering distance, her jaws scissor unstoppably and her spittle, whipped away like foam from a wave, scorches whatever it lands upon. Where her mouth cannot penetrate, the Rat Catcher reaches into cover with powerful forelimbs, killing rats with single blows, like a cat.

Their revenge for Old Father Jinks's mutilation is swift and thorough. Whole rat families have perished this morning, whole gobshite dynasties. The rats, completely demoralized, are pushing their young out in front of them now, a kind of rattish shield. Nick Jinks and the Rat Catcher will not be blackmailed; blind, mewling infants, dismembered by shot, their innards liquefied by hydrostatic shock, plaster their coward parents' pelts with bright, unmissable blood. Deep within the warren, meanwhile, the old and the infirm, the ones with cracked teeth and lame forepaws, gather in bunkers of rusted wire and perished rubber. One, driven mad with despair, sinks her teeth into the belly of her mate, filling her mouth with foamy yellow fat. A third, infuriated by the squeals of the victim, garrottes himself with a transmission wire. All through the nest, young, lithe, healthy rats lie trembling, shell-shocked, beneath blankets of cardboard, while their doughty mothers, deafened long since to the gun's monotonous and terrible blast, hurl themselves out of the nest and through the lank grass towards the house – a suicidal tactic of diversion.

Straining, cursing, Nick pulls the rubbish heap apart. Slavering and silent, the Rat Catcher watches for movement within. Little by little, the nest is crumbling. Rats pause, quivering, before their transformed surroundings, uncertain where to run. Their familiar warrens are being erased, and new and deadly vistas spread before them. The bright white light of day expunges the warren's old chiaroscuro, turns everything shoddy and contingent, demoralizing the rats still further. So they head down, deep down, into the loamy tunnels beneath the rubbish pile, there to encounter a lost tribe of terrible red-eyed sub-rats who have never seen the sun.

Escaping them, his ear torn to cauliflower shreds, his left hind paw stabbed through, his right eye bleared and bleeding, one rat, a sorry sight, stumbles up into the upper air: a deadly mistake.

The rat hurtles pell-mell between Nick Jinks's legs, heading for the corner of the house. Nick Jinks, startled, cries out. The dog makes no sound. The rat powers on. It rounds the corner of the house. The gun goes off. Brick explodes in a red cloud as the rat, unscathed, hurls itself towards the road. Behind it come the heavy, clumping footfalls of the boy; beneath it the faster, softer, deadlier scratchings of the dog's paws, scrabbling on the flags of the path, building up speed.

The rat reaches the road. The ditch is in sight. Safety beckons. Death comes so suddenly, the rat does not even hear the discharge of the gun. A bundle of unwitting, mangled joy, the rat tumbles, propelled by the shot, into the ditch on the far side of the road.

The Rat Catcher, her blood up, ignores her master's call and pursues the dead rat over the road.

George Bridgeman has driven the route to his magical wartime shelter countless times in preparation for today. He does not need a map as he tacks smoothly from lane to lane, east toward the fens. He does not need to consult, or even navigate in any conscious sense. He knows the way.

All hell inside him now. Time to think means time for doubt. Time in which George can measure his loneliness, and feel the weight of responsibility: only he can mess this up now. It's up to him.

He stops the car. A quiet spot. He gets out, walks round to the boot, opens it up. She's still out cold. He touches her. If she wakes up, if she screams, then he can panic, run back to the glove compartment, take out the hammer and spoil everything.

She does not wake up.

The world absolutely refuses to give him an 'out'. It's up to you now, George. It's up to *you*.

He lifts up the girl's skirt, drags it up, up past her white cotton knickers. He sticks a finger into the band of her knickers and pulls. Her hairlessness there gives him an immediate erection, and it frightens him, this fierce bodily response. Of course he is planning to rape her. He has a room full of objects carefully selected over the years, common household objects, tools purloined from the abattoir, a handful of china souvenirs – 'A Gift From Bridport' – to rape her with. But this sudden – well, what would you call it? Lust?

He pulls her roughly over, so one leg falls free of the boot and dangles, shoe half-off, toes tickling the long grass of the verge. She slumps onto her front, her bottom upraised over the sill of the boot.

He checks her pulse. It ticks back against his finger, slow and strong.

He pulls her knickers down and off – much struggling and slapstick here – and crams them into her mouth.

Now what?

He listens for approaching traffic.

He waits.

Nothing comes.

By now thoroughly demoralized, tremble-kneed, George shoves the girl's leg back in the boot, slams the lid shut, climbs back in the car and drives.

George's mission is, he believes, essentially spiritual. Even his earliest experiments lean in this direction. Since the day he flensed out a lamb's eye and dropped it, still warm, into the lap of that stuck-up neighbour girl, that Hosken girl – what was her name? Katherine?

Kathleen? – it has been his mission to awaken his fellow man to his contingent and temporary nature: his equivalence, in other words, to beasts. In better circumstances, and with a better gene-pool to draw from, Bridgeman might have made small, gloomy contributions to moral philosophy. As it is, he is something more imbecile, more direct. He plans to expunge the little girl's spirit, drag her down into his animal reality. Marry her in darkness on all fours and no more words ever again. An end to meaning, sequence, rule. Only cries, a flash of teeth, the bliss of living without thought, his own pet lamb to warm him in the night. But how does he think he can scrape the girl out of that little animal body? How?

It comes to him that his plans do not extend beyond the first couple of days of the child's suffering. What if a couple of days are not enough? He has this image of her, a few days in, tattered beyond further violation, exhausted – and *still* not an animal.

The tools he has amassed. They'll mortify her flesh, but who's to say they will not leave her girlishness intact? What to do?

In need of comfort now, unnerved by his success, George Bridgeman takes one hand off the steering wheel to knead his groin. Ejaculation is a great comfort. Always has been. He imagined, in his twenties, that this endless, importunate tossing would wear itself out, but here he is, balding, hands chewed to red rags by years of handling raw ice-cold meat, sharp slivers of bone, knives slippy with blood and fat, and still he cannot leave his John Thomas alone. It is his only friend.

The car leaps out from a wooded hollow, jerky and undependable as a foal, as George Bridgeman wrestles with his fly. There is a house ahead, an old garage, hand pumps in the yard. By now, crushed by his own success, Bridgeman has retreated into the sort of thinking a child might employ. He tells himself that if he ejaculates before he reaches the garage, he will persevere with his plan, he will smuggle the little rabbit into his theatre of horrors, he will operate upon her, he will do his very best. If orgasm eludes him, however, the game is up.

George's right foot responds, pressing hard against the accelerator, so all his scary, too-ambitious plans might come to nought. No, no way he will be able to toss himself off in time. Oh well. What a shame. He will just have to dump her somewhere.

He thinks about this.

Of course, he'll have to kill her.

He thinks about this.

Just in case.

Very stiff now.

With the hammer.

He thinks about this.

Glans wet and slippery.

The long, cool, polished shaft of the hammer.

He thinks about this.

A black dog runs across the street ahead of him.

Her beautiful white bottom.

He thinks about her buttocks.

Semen leaps acrobatically to splash the decal of his steering wheel, silver 'Ford' inscribed on shiny black enamel.

The dog runs back across the road, something in its teeth.

George Bridgeman is captivated by the sight of his semen, the F of Ford flecked shut to make a P, the o tailed to a q – Pqrd. As if by magic he is driving a Pqrd.

Before him, unregarded, the dog hunkers down in the surety of death, and its head, impacted at high speed by the car's nearside wheel, absorbs all the forces of the collision, shaping them like a bell, so that the wheel, vulnerable at the point of contact, conducts the energy of the crash back into itself and twists itself out of true. As soon as it is back in contact with the tarmac, the car wobbles like a drunk all over the road, squealing horribly, tyres smoking, before it settles softly, as if relieved, into a ditch, barely fifty yards beyond the dirt forecourt of the garage.

*

Nick Jinks is reloading his weapon when the car runs over his dog. Stunned, he walks over to the body. There is no question that the Rat Catcher is dead. Her head is a rubbery smear.

George Bridgeman raises his head from the steering wheel. He touches his hand to it. The top of his head explodes, like a knife has sliced the cap off his skull. When he can bring himself to look at his fingers, George is surprised to find no blood.

Nick, numb and cold, looks up the road. The car has come to grief in a ditch, just beyond the forecourt. Is the driver all right? Nick drags himself away from the ruined body of his companion.

Something moves in the rear-view mirror. It hurts when George moves his eyes. He moves his whole head instead, and freezes, abject, at the sight that greets him: a man with a gun. What if the girl wakes up now? What if the accident has woken her? He has to do something. He has to take control. He reaches for the door. His spermy fingers slip off the catch, reminding him to fasten his fly. He yanks up the zip.

The man inside the car lets out a scream. How badly is he injured? Will Nick know what to do? Daunted yet determined, Nick hurries towards the car to see how he can help.

Gingerly and gasping, George Bridgeman attempts to ease folds of his foreskin from between the teeth of his trouser fly. The pain is too great. Sobbing, sick, he abandons the attempt. Perhaps the youth will help him. It is a garage, after all. There will be tools. Pliers. Cutters. Saws. He looks up into the rear-view, seeking succour.

Oh my God, the youth is running towards the car. George has killed his dog and now the youth is going to kill him. George stares helpless into the mirror. The gun is getting bigger. There is nothing he can do.

It's all falling apart around him, as he surely knew it would. He's just going to have to make a run for it. He fumbles his door open. Every slightest movement threatens to split him. Keening horribly between gritted teeth, he edges his way out of the car.

The car door opens, and from the cabin comes a terrible squeal. Of their own accord, Nick Jinks's hands perform their ballet, snapping the gun breach shut.

George Bridgeman hobbles into the road, His white, sweating face stretched in an O of agony, arms spread for balance, bloody swollen penis dangling like a fruit. Terrified and helpless, he cannot run; he shuffles round to face his nemesis.

With an efficiency born of long practice, Nick Jinks's eyes rake the scene, hunting out the squealing thing. Astounded, his gaze settles upon the stranger's groin. Never has his enemy been so savagely inventive! The rat dangles there by its teeth, spattered with blood.

A split-second later, and Nick will see things differently. His senses are acute. His powers of reasoning are adequate. It will take him no time at all to shake off his rat obsession and see the man's plight for what it actually is. The whole process of revision will happen so blindingly fast, and unthinkingly, that Nick will not even remember why he fired the gun.

None the less, the gun has gone off.

George Bridgeman sprawls in the road, his groin a bloody mess. A piece of shot has shredded an artery in his thigh. Death is coming very quickly now. It towers over him. George Bridgeman sees that his youthful attacker is Death, and that Death is an angel. It has a small, pursed mouth and a smooth, rounded, cherubic head. It might be any angel, were it not for the eyes. Eyes that bore into him, pitiless and strange. As his consciousness falters, so the eyes seem to move closer and closer together...

Nick Jinks stands above the stranger, helpless. What to do? A chill creeps over him. Was this what his poor dead father feared? Was this something of which he knew his son was capable? Blood pools at his feet. Nick begins to tremble all over. Why did he fire the gun? He has not the remotest idea.

The stranger's eyes glass over. Nick crosses to the car. The garage has a phone, but it has been disconnected. Nick has a confused idea that he will drive the car to the nearest village in order to summon help.

The ditch into which the car has been driven is not deep, and the rear wheels are still in contact with the road, more or less. Nick, at fourteen, has grown up among cars and knows how to drive. Besides, he has his father's confidence with machinery. He wrestles the car back onto the road, shifts into first and wobbles away.

He passes through the first village bolt upright in his seat, buttocks clenched to raise him that vital extra half-inch, afraid someone will notice that a child is driving. He passes through the second village, more confident this time: he is getting away with it. By the time he reaches Ipswich and the first breath of sea air, he can no longer pretend that he is going to be making a clean breast of this appalling incident to the authorities. How can he? He cannot even explain why he pulled the trigger. Perhaps he is a killer, after all.

As he drives he comprehends for the first time just how big the world really is. He can count on his fingers the number of times he has set foot outside the county of his birth. Apart from occasional, lacklustre visits to zoos and seasides – journeys buried so far back in his childhood, he can barely remember them – Nick Jinks has never known another landscape. His whole upbringing has been morbidly inturned.

As Nick cruises the streets of Felixstowe, and sees the port cranes towering over the roofs of the drab terraces, it occurs to him that he is truly free for the first time in his life. Liberty has been thrust upon him. He not only has the opportunity to run away, he has a positive obligation, as fast and as far as he can.

He finds his way to the harbour, parks the car and climbs out. The salt air fills his lungs with energy and hope.

Why not?

The ships, the jetties, the very buildings seem to thrum with unfamiliar and purposeful life.

Why not?

It will only take the slightest nudge, and Nick Jinks's destiny will be set.

It comes.

The faintest scratching. The faintest squealing.

Nick Jinks stiffens where he stands.

The old curse has pursued him. Somewhere in the toils of the motor car, that old grey curse sits, preening – but it has overreached itself. It has become separated from its source. It has no power now. It is just one miserable rat, trapped in the belly of a greasy old car.

One more movement, and Nick will be free of the curse for ever.

He steps away from the car. As he goes he smiles, to hear the curse calling him, a thready squeal, desperate, weak, as piteous in its defeat and final extremity as the pleas of a child.

3

It is 10.30 a.m. on Sunday, 20 July 1969. One man is preparing to set foot on the moon; another is going to die, assassinated by a bomb. For now, though, it's like any other mid-morning in Lourenço Marques, and the street-sellers are setting out their wares. There are toy cars made of cans, random pharmaceuticals and pictures of Elvis Presley. Along the promenade, girls are selling themselves.

Nick Jinks passes by, pondering the choice on offer. The girl he settles on finally is not a typical street-walker. For a start she is a good ten years older than the others. Nick assumes this must be the reason why the competition have gathered around them, hissing. Really hissing: from two dozen rouged and milktoothed Mozambican mouths comes a great long *sssssssss!*

Nick leads the girl into the doorway of a Sunday-closing barbershop. That he has already forgotten her name is hardly his fault. They all have such nutty names round here. The two he bought before her were called Majesty and Hope...

His line of thought is broken as he feels her hands moving to the straps of his wartime canvas satchel, a satchel he has promised his masters not to remove. This inevitably triggers the first of many minor *contretemps* with which encounters like this are inevitably gritted ('Don't kiss my mouth' – 'Don't touch my feet' – 'You'll put my arm to sleep') so that the satchel remains strapped, as per instructions, to his back, no way he is going to let go of it until he is safely in off the street. He pushes her hands away; they purse instead around his groin like a codpiece while, shoulders drawn back manly by the weight of his burden – what the fuck is *in* this bloody thing? – he cops his feel of her between the folds of her *capulana*: a line of sweat beneath each little tit, a line of fur up her tight tum, from thick-pubed mons, her bush V-d to a clit-bound arrow. Some stubble there, and he thinks about offering to tidy up her topiary with his fancy new Gillette, ask her nicely, say please, winning smile. It is an arrow that might Braille the most insensate fingers, the burned and calloused pads of firemen and dockers, to their mark. Finding it for himself, pressing it cruelly so she squeals, Nick Jinks laughs a hearty seaman's 'Yo ho!' and swells into her hands.

Back home, every once in a while, an ambitious young detective will open the file on Nick Jinks: wanted for murder, wanted for the abduction of a child. Nothing is ever resolved. There is next to no information on the suspect – not even a photograph – and besides, the circumstances of both crimes are so confused, it is hard to see how a prosecution would get past a sceptical judge.

Nick, for his part, keeps a weather-eye on the British press, concerned for the child as well as himself. The story of the little girl's abduction, widely reported at the time, is as horrifying as it is baffling. What child? Was there a child? And how on earth did this story get caught up with his own? The grotesque details trouble him nearly as much as the risk of false accusation.

Eight years have passed since Nick took to the high seas. There is little about him now to remind one of the taciturn rat catcher of his youth. In the time he has been at sea, Nick has grown hardier and happier. He knows something about the world and this has made him less afraid of himself. He knows what stone-cold killers look like, from brawls in Singapore and from one dangerous, ridiculous feud on a container run from Japan to San Francisco. He knows he is not one of them. Knowing this he has begun, over the years, to put the accident behind him. He calls himself Jiggins now, Nick Jiggins, and with the new name comes a sunnier outlook on life.

His father's fear of him was his own affair. No use picking at it now. Loyal as Nick tries to be to his father's memory, he's come to understand the limits of Dick's philosophy. 'Not worth the candle,' Dick Jinks had said of the seaman's life. God knows it was a brutish kind of existence, but who could say it was not worthwhile? If it had been up to his dad, and had it not been for the accident, Nick might never have left the fenland of his birth. Then what would he know of anything? He imagines himself sometimes – when nostalgia and weariness threaten to rain on his parade – crouched in his father's room, loaded shotgun across his lap, listening to the rats scuttling behind the wainscots. Picturing this, his appetite for the sea comes rushing back to him.

Rats, the sound of them paddling in the bilges, the sight of them at dusk, playing tag along the chains and hawsers; rats alone have the power to taint Nick Jinks's happy-go-lucky present. He stays as far away from them as he can. Not for him the flop-house floor, the budget brothel, the knee-shaker in the alley. An inadvertent consequence of this is that Nick has acquired a reputation as a man who conducts his shore leaves with a certain amount of panache. Take, for instance, this woman's well-appointed theatre of delectable operations.

(Her hands move across his tired back, hot and slick and warm from the coconut oil she is working into his skin. He turns his head, sees the old army satchel lying at the foot of the bed, the satchel he must deliver, the brown-wrapped package inside, yes, it is there. What can possibly go wrong?)

This upmarket taste of his requires funding additional to his meagre seaman's wage. Nick's courier work has been relatively smalltime up to now, but his inventiveness and discretion have not gone unremarked. The years he spent with his dad – concealing signs of his presence, so as to minimize the old man's terror of him – have made Nick an unobtrusive operator.

This most recent courier job represents the high-water mark of his career. Afterwards, he intends to lay low for a while. Frankly, the whole business has unnerved him.

To start with, the men he went to see refused to come out of their basement. Then, when he had been persuaded to join them in their cellar, he found himself in the middle of some bizarre musical number. At least, this is the only way he has to interpret what he saw. He's never confronted black-face outside *The Black and White Minstrel Show*, let alone seen it used as a disguise. Impossible to tell even the race of these men under such fairground slap. The ointment smell of the local sunscreen – a crackly white porridge – mingled sickly with the smell of black shoe polish, as he slipped their satchel round his back.

'Item: if you look inside the package, we will know. Item: if you take the satchel from your back in a public place, we will know. Item: if you discuss our arrangement with a third party, we will know. Item: if you fail to deliver the package to the correct address, we will know.'

Overkill enough to make the young seaman grin through his sweat – a rictus of fear to answer their painted white grins. Afterwards, he wrote the address he was meant to memorize ('Item: do not write down or share this address with anyone') in big crayon letters all over the packet, just to make doubly sure he couldn't fuck this up.

He balks at the memory, muscles tensing. Bad enough that he should have been led under the ground, let alone that he should be confronted with this. Fatigues without insignia. Guns. Somewhere in that cellar, unmistakable, the scurry and scratch of rats.

'Shhh,' the prostitute soothes, hot hands working him.

It is not the tension of the moment that will spoil his first day's shore leave here, in infamous Lourenço Marques. Nor even the anxiety he feels about the delivery he must make, a couple of hours from now. What scuppers him is, oddly enough, the tale he decides to tell, his favourite ice-breaker, a tale of derring do on the high seas.

'It's proppant,' he says, his voice muffled by the pillow. '*Proppant*. I'm telling you.'

It's little china beads with a coating, a resin, they use it in drilling, in the offshore industry, on drilling rigs, and he is getting dizzy, all the ways there are to explain this thing, this material, which is frankly the least of his story.

'Not "propellant". I'm telling you. What's *propellant*? What kind of *propellant* do you know comes in *sacks*?'

'Proppant.' The girl tries it on her tongue. Her fingers dig his shoulders, like there are gold coins between his muscles, dubloons between the muscle and the bone, and she is rifling these secret pockets in his flesh, not so much a back rub, more an intimate mugging. The trouble with asking for a massage is you occasionally end up with a real masseuse, whatever else she is, with frightening thumbs, really strong, like her day job is screwing on the lids of jars you can't undo.

'Proppant,' she says, 'OK,' in that tone of voice, how do women do that? Letting him know in four syllables that nothing he says now is she possibly going to take seriously. Discouraged, he recalls that at some point in his story he is going to have to use the word 'phenolic'. Though he hardly looks the part, Nick is wedded to an ethic of accurate *reportage*. Words should fit closely the events and situations they describe. Because the world is big, he needs many words, the more accurately to render the truths around him. Word-power is his unlikely passion. So that the third mate, rigging a vacuum line for their second loading attempt, and still white-faced and shaky-fingered from the explosion, couldn't have been more startled when Nick rose up on his ladder out of the silo – where, anyway, he had no place being – a stained rag held close to his mouth and saying: 'What kind of dust, d'you say? Fen-something? How d'ya spell that, then?' The third mate was unable to take his eyes off the Stanley knife tattooed on Nick's arm, an eye where the shank screw should be and shark teeth for a blade. You could tell it was a Stanley knife because the word 'Stanley' was picked out along the thing in the red of venereal rashes. Without it, it might have been anything. A razor shell. A baby eel. A banana.

'Mmm,' the woman says, over him, behind him, and something brushes him, an unmistakable tantalizing point of rubbery contact that is definitely not a finger and this ought to excite him, only that...

263

The Weight of Numbers

The thing is, he's pretty sure her *capulana* was secure before she started this – he expecting her to strip at his word and she instead wanting to tantalize, oh, very European – and both her hands are on him now, either side of his hips, working the handles there. So assuming this *is* a nipple – well, not that he's ungrateful or anything but O! the mysterious toils of this world – if both her hands have been working the flab above his hips all this time, *how in Hell did she get her tits out?*

And here's its twin, tracking through the oil spread like engine lubricant over his back. He arches his back, kitty-friendly, feels the nipple snub and turn, the half-moon of her tit against him. 'Lie down, now.' She pulls away, then tracks again, with both tits now, no hands, just the nipples against his back, angled perfectly like something mechanical come to read his skin. She must be angling them with her hands to maintain such precise and even contact and then it comes to him, a great wave of mystery and unknowing: *how come she doesn't fall over?* Leaning over him all that way, her tits in her hands, how is she able to balance? Maybe, he thinks, she has climbed up onto the table. Maybe she has hooked her feet around the end of the table. He has lost track of her nipples now, he has completely dropped out the bottom of the whole experience, he is off in the land of levers, the land of weights and measures and GOD DAMN WOMAN WATCH WHERE THE JESUS YOU ARE PUTTING THAT THING – but her hand is deep in the crevice of his freshly washed, sweet-smelling buttocks by now – when in hell did that happen? – fingers questing for his BALLS NOT MY BALLS NOT – AHHHHHHHHHHHH and she's PULLING THEM now, she is LIFTING HIM OFF THE TABLE BY HIS BALLS and he is kneeling and he thinks, if I hook my feet to the edge of the table I wouldn't need my hands to balance, and really, it is enough to make him despair sometimes how his mind goes wandering off without him and this is really too fucking homosexual she is actually tonguing his balls and where the hell is her nose all this time? Oh CHRIST, there it is, her lips grazing the hair of his balls as her hand reaches round to his prick and she mumbles,

'Proppant, then, come on,' and she is milking him like a cow so he goes on with his story because this is what you do when some mad bitch has your testicles between her teeth you do *exactly what she says.*

The sunlight that morning was of a sort that has resisted his every subsequent attempt to describe it. The low, even white cloud, far from barring the sunlight, trapped the light and pressed it against the sea's surface, so that everything appeared incredibly bright and reflective and the sea was turned to liquid chrome.

The lensing effect of the clouds extended even to sounds, magnifying them and at the same time stripping them of all reverberation, so that every sound seemed to come from inside the ear. In the early-morning quiet, when they were still a nautical mile off the harbour, Nick swears he could hear the footfalls of the crane man, dawdling on the quay. A car starting on the hill above the harbour. A conversation between two elderly men, one out walking his dogs, the other leaning on his gate.

A Navy helicopter hammered by, rotors clipping the clouds. Even this racket was transformed, each element sounding pure, precise, as intimate as the flob of Antonio Carlos Jobim's spittle on 'The Girl from Ipanema'.

It was a strange sort of landfall. No town, no din of machinery. Just a couple of houses – and the quay itself was an untenanted, industrial thing, thrown up as a handy transfer point for the tons of aggregates and chemicals that would one day be consumed by the rigs.

No real town for twenty miles. No pub. A tea shack for the men. One public telephone on a piece of hard-standing that, for sheer size, dwarfed the quay itself: big enough to land a SeaKing on. Why was the phone-box set slap bang in the middle like that? What use was it meant to serve?

'Houses,' said the second mate. 'It's foundations for houses.' He broke into a weird country-and-western drawl: 'Boom town a'comin'.'

'Fuck that.'

The proppant was waiting for them in sacks, paletted on the quayside. They had spent a day, about six weeks ago, vacuuming the material out of the hold, bagging it for later use. Now, coming to collect it, they had the whole job to do again in reverse. They used a mobile crane – the key, as usual, chewing-gummed to the inside of a wheel rim – to lift a smallish hopper, about a ton weight, over the aft silo. Nick guided the hopper into position over the mouth of the silo, thumbed off the karabiners and waved the crane away.

The operator swung the arm back over the quay to the first sack. Men clipped extra chains to the crane arm and hooked it up. The engine laboured, the whole body of the crane shifted, as the operator raised the sack off the quay and began slowly to swing it over to the hopper.

Nick gawped, for all the world as if this operation had nothing to do with him. It was only as the arm came to rest, the sack swinging with dreadful, pregnant force over the mouth of the hopper, that he remembered what he was supposed to be doing.

He reached into his back pocket for his knife.

It wasn't there.

Cursing, he hurried back to his bunk. It was hidden beneath his tiny pillow, nestled in its own, permanent dent in the cheap foam pallet. Not that Nick expected trouble, this trip or any other, but simply because it had become his talisman: slippy cold body, more like stone than steel, wicked lino-cutter blade. He ran his thumb crosswise over the scimitar edge – ah, a tell-tale roughness there. He dug about in his bag of books – Carpentier, Asturias and Marquez, his passion – and fished out his dad's old tin box. From the box he pulled out a stubby screwdriver. Lovingly he loosened the screw in the knife handle. Gingerly he lifted out the blunted blade and reversed it. He did up the screw again and ran his thumb over the unused edge. There was something thrilling about a razor-sharp blade – how it could cut you and you'd not feel a thing, just a wet burn as you first put pressure on the cut, sliding one surface of the slice against the other, revealing damage slowly, by stages: the sick inevitability of it. Like the cartoon coyote, who falls only *after* he finds he's hanging in mid-air.

By the time Nick had recovered enough of himself to pull himself out of this latest excursion through his own head, the first sack of proppant had already stopped swinging, it was in position, suspended over the hopper, ready for emptying.

'I'm there!' Nick shouted, waving the Stanley knife over his head. 'I'm there!' – flinging and flapping his way across the deck.

Anxious not to lose the highlight of his day to another, he threw himself on the sack as though it were a lover. The bright sliver of Sheffield steel slipped neatly through the coarse plastic weave. With a smooth downward motion, Nick disembowelled the sack and the proppant spilled through the hopper into the silo. The air filled with a dust that was, in its frenzy and iodine smell, a distillation of thunderstorms. The air crackled in his nostrils and laid a sourness on his tongue. Nick danced about by the side of the silo hatch, impatient, his blood up, while men fastened the second sack to the crane.

He slashed the second sack back-handed and casual, as he saw his heroes slash their way to victory in the movies he preferred. 'Thank *you*, Mr Jiggins,' the second mate announced, dryly. A few private smiles among the ratings, quickly hidden, as Nick, brandishing his father's doughty Stanley, frowned them away.

So Nick stood, arms folded, Horatio on the bridge, waiting for more sacks. The crane lifted a third sack over the hopper. Nick, catching the second mate's eye, cut the sack carefully, a five-inch gash, letting the proppant out in a steady stream. He stepped away, patient, waiting for the sack to empty. He rubbed his thumb over the blade and felt already, through long practice, a little dullness there.

Black dust lapped the edge of the silo, busy, a midge-cloud, and fell back again. The sack sagged, the flow of proppant eased. Nick stepped forward.

The explosion blew the hopper right off the top of the silo.

The hopper's dented sill missed Nick's nose by inches.

He felt the air on his face.

He watched the hopper rise.

It tumbled through the air.

He felt a chill as its shadow crossed him.

He was aware, for the first time, of the sound of the blast, the great blunt fact of it, ringing in his ears.

The hopper rose and toppled. He watched it curve through the grey china air.

He saw the crane operator throw up his hands in front of his face.

The hopper hit the quay a yard or so in front of the crane, bounced, bounded along the quay, checked itself, ran off in a new direction, stopped, turned over, and rang – the sounds running always a fraction of a second behind the visuals, as though his brain were experiencing the world too fast to put everything in its proper order. The channels falling out of whack, the sound un-synching, and a mutter from the cheap seats: 'Fuck' and 'Christ'; from the English captain, a 'Christmas Day'.

In his lungs, the taste of the forge.

Nick knew that taste, was sent back twenty years by it. The rotting cars. The carcasses of caravans, their plastic and fibreboard walls leant in upon each other like a ruined house of cards. The rats...

'The cause of the explosion,' says Nick, to the head bobbing at his lap (things, at his insistence, taking a more orthodox course now: his hand firm on the back of her head, directing the action), 'was probably a combination of electrostatic charge built up during the loading operation and the volume of phenolic dust free in the silo.'

There is a loud – and in tactile terms, not unpleasant – sputtering, followed by a monosyllable expressive of female incredulity.

'Phenolic,' he insists, succinctly, and his erection softens like a toffee between her teeth. He frowns. *'Phenolic.* What? I am telling you this.'

She shrugs, climbs back on the bed and falls back, lifting her knees to her shoulders. 'Whatever,' she says.

He fucks her once, hard, for her insolence. Twice, for the fun of it. A third time, intensely and with feeling, for romance. A fourth time, all

wet eyes and slithering tongue and 'I never knew my mammy' –
– and drifts pathetically to sleep.

He dreams:

The hopper, rising.

He sees it rise, he feels the air stroke his face as the lip of the hopper leans over, as though to touch him, as though to kiss him goodbye.

Up it goes, into the silver sky, and its shadow comes over him then, the hopper a gigantic black hexagon in the sky, rising, rising. The bright sky silhouettes it now, backing it like the satin cushion for a piece of jet. The sky is purest white.

Nick Jinks has always wanted to see a rocket launch. This is what he has most wanted to see, ever since he was a child. And today – the very day a man sets foot for the first time on the Moon – at this moment, in this dream, it occurs to him: the accident he witnessed, and maybe even caused, *was a launch*. A detonation. Dead weight, hurled into the air by gigantic unseen forces. (The men on the quay reported a large blue flame shooting out of the silo; Jinks saw nothing like that.)

So, when he wakes, and without quite being able to work out why, Jinks feels an extraordinary sense of fulfilment. Waves of contentment will continue to wash over him at regular intervals, driving him and sustaining him throughout his peril once he discovers, the moment he sits up, shivering in wet sheets, that

(1) he is alone here

and

(2) his satchel is gone.

4

Apollo Eleven's lunar module lands at 3.17 p.m., Eastern Standard Time, and once it is confirmed that astronauts Armstrong and Aldrin are safely settled on the surface of the Moon, Mo Chavez snaps off his dad's little black-and-white TV.

'Moisés!'

'It's time to go, Papa.' Mo opens the curtains to the blinding Miami sun.

'But men are walking on the Moon, Moisés!'

Mo brushes the cookie crumbs off his father's best shirt and adjusts his tie. The men hardly know each other; there is a nine-year separation dividing them. They connect best in the dumb-show of gesture, the grammer of touch and nudge.

'Come along, Papa, you want to look your best for the St Patrick crowd,' says Moisés, hustling him out of his rundown Collins Avenue apartment. Mo wanted to do better by his father than to install him in this semi-derelict thirties hotel, but Anastasio is happy here. He can walk down the street and smell the ocean and the garbage and drink rum and eat roast pork sandwiches. He picks up a little pin money writing numbers for *bolito*, and around here no cop would ever dream of pressing charges. This place, in all its growing squalor, is a kind of Havana for the old man, now that the original is lost.

'St Patrick's?' Old Anastasio is scandalized. '*St Patrick's?*'

'It's the only church on the Beach, papa. We don't want to go far now.'

It was his father's idea that Man's first steps on the Moon – an event that commands a TV audience of one-fifth of the world's population – might be conveniently combined with an exposition of the Holy

Eucharist. Anastasio's regretting his decision now, of course, in thrall to the mission and its enormity, but he can't be seen to ignore the call of the Holy Hour, not in front of his tearaway American son. He spent nine years battling the revolutionary authorities over his freedom to worship. So, muttering, he follows Mo into the unreliable old Deco lift. 'How long have I waited to receive benediction among my countrymen, and now my son takes me to an *Irish…*'

Mo glances at his father, amused, as they cross the dusty lobby. Heaven only knows where this objection has sprung from. Another piece of Yankee folklore his father has somehow misconstrued. Anastasio only got out of Cuba eight months ago, and his desire to acquire the local US colouring has something desperate about it. A strong man growing old, Anastasio expresses his vigour in anxious, opinionated outbursts. He hasn't the patience to soak up America, no, he must forage for it, he must stitch it out of scraps like a naked Adam covering himself with leaves.

What he ends up with – a motley of overheard conversation, misdirected sentiment and poorly comprehended talk-radio – says less about the old man's American present than about his Cuban past: the way Castro's UMAP labour camps stripped his ordinary human dignity away. When people look at Mo's father, they see what Mo sees: a powerful old man, bullish, a survivor. The camps taught Anastasio to see past all that – past his personality, history and character – to some bare, grub-like, essential man. They taught him to be ashamed of himself, so now he is free, he is trying to be someone different. He is trying to be an American.

'Welcome to Florida, Father,' says Mo, baiting the old man a little. 'The melting pot.' This front of easy sarcasm is Mo's antidote to the pity and anger which would otherwise overwhelm him, thinking of his father, for years shackled to the worst dregs of Havana's lowlife, the winos and the queers. For nine years, in prison and out of it, since the day in 1960 he put his fourteen-year-old son on the boat to freedom,

Anastasio has paid the price for his treason. Mo can never let him know how seriously he honours this debt.

Father and son leave the shadow of the dilapidated Greystone Hotel. Mo's automobile is at the kerb, a Thunderbird with brilliant ice-cream bodywork that contrasts obscenely with its cherry-red leather interior. God forbid his father ever catches wind of its nickname among the blades of the *corporaçion*.

The old man makes a big production of how difficult it is to climb into a car so sporty, so low-slung, *tan desrazonable*, and he is messing with the radio before Mo can get to the ignition. Valuable minutes are wasted while Mo hunts for the station, and they are past Lummus Park and its ocean views before the familiar voice of NASA's public affairs officer returns to the air.

'You see?' says Mo. 'Everything'll be fine.'

The two astronauts are still sat in their Eagle, doing whatever it is spacemen do once they have landed on a new world. All month the TV and the radio have been talking about how much rehearsal has gone into this. There have been talk shows, cinema newsreels, pull-out souvenirs in the magazines. But there must be some element of chance, there has to be, a part of the mission the astronauts make up as they go along. Or why would they bother to volunteer?

Mo and his father are headed for Garden Avenue, a stone's throw from the 195 causeway anchoring Miami Beach to the mainland metropolis. The traffic, normally so heavy, has vanished. Mo takes advantage, and the Thunderbird trembles, roars and (eventually) accelerates.

Anastasio glances at his watch. Exasperated: 'Moisés, we are early. We are much too early. Why didn't we wait? Moisés—'

But Neil Armstrong has come on air:

'It's pretty much without colour,' he says. *'It's grey and it's a very white chalk-grey as you look into the zero phase line, and it's considerably darker grey, more like ashen grey as you look up ninety degrees to the sun.'*

It is the Moon, seen from the surface of the Moon, and it is grey.

'Moisés, we are missing it!'

'Papa, it's fine, it's under control, enjoy the radio, there won't be any TV pictures until they leave the rocket.'

St Patrick's occupies the whole block between West 39th and West 40th Street. There is a church, a rectory, a convent, a school, such an excess of space and ambition that, when Anastasio climbs (grumbling) from the car and sees it all, an actual *mall* of Catholicism, he struggles, unsure what attitude to strike. 'Well, it doesn't *look* Irish,' he allows, as they climb the broad white steps to the door. Mo, in a brief, dissociated moment, wonders just what idea of Irishness a Cuban dissident entertains.

A small, malevolent-looking man in a broad suit is standing by the porch, a portable radio in one hand, listening intently.

'Some of the surface rocks in close here that have been fractured or disturbed by the rocket engine are coated with this light grey on the outside, but when they've been broken they display a dark, very dark grey interior…'

You heard it here first, thinks Mo: the Moon is grey.

Mo isn't too sure where this sarcastic inner voice has sprung from. He wants to lose himself in the poetry and majesty of the day, but this voice keeps tripping him up. This bleak voice reminds him, every time the public affairs officer comes on, that this is the Voice of official America, reporting the Daring Deeds of America, Land of Promises and promises and more promises, a superpower whose reach extends to the very stars, but a power so idle it is unable even to sweep a tin-pot dictator from an island not a hundred miles from its own seaboard. Maybe things will get better now that Nixon is in charge – Dickie Nixon who worked so hard and with such passion to make the Bay of Pigs invasion a working reality – but he is not holding his breath. Neither is the *corporaçion*. Even its CIA handlers – Dick's men all, and veterans with Cuba in their blood – have been muttering mutinously into their shot glasses.

He knows today's Moon landing should outweigh these matters. On a planetary scale his can only be local troubles. But it doesn't. It doesn't mean anything more than this: that three crew-cut middle-class boys are putting their lives on the line for the sake of an extraordinary adventure. And good for them, their bravery and dedication and undoubted skill. He salutes the adventure, Hell, yes. It's the national symbolism that sticks in his throat. In 1961, at fifteen, he was too young to join the Brigade. He missed the sorry hash American planning and intelligence made of the Bay of Pigs landings. He was not martyred, as so many fathers of so many friends were that day in April, on the altar of expedience and deniability.

The astronauts, too, have put their lives in the hands of America, and Mo knows, with some bitterness, how risky this must be for them. He wants to see them walk on the Moon, and when he leads his dad into church, he'll be as glad of the little surprise he's been saving as, hopefully, his dad will be. Because there's a television – the biggest you can rent, booked weeks ago from the biggest rental store in the city – hooked up to an aerial in the church tower. The priest is a rocket nut and plans to slip the Holy Hour into whatever dead space becalms the coverage.

There is another reason Mo chose this church.

A baptism party emerges from the portico. They are a miscellaneous bunch: the men tense, overmuscled; the women young, overdressed and at the same time underconcealed, more likely girlfriends than wives. The little man with the radio goes to join them.

'I told you we were early,' Anastasio grumbles, but Mo isn't listening. Mo is shooting his cuffs, he is running his fingers through his hair. The party passes.

'Señor Conroy!'

The mother, striking but pale under her garish white cake decoration – more of a bridal gown than an outfit for baptism – is walking arm in arm with a balding, heavy-set man, who tenses visibly as Mo calls out his name.

This Conroy was a strong man in his day, old Anastasio sees that. A strong man who has applied his strength against other men: the signature of combat is written indelibly in his poise, his hand reluctantly extended to brush Mo's.

The girl blushes and smiles. 'Very many congratulations, Deborah,' Mo says, and bends to coo over her baby. Anastasio is not so old that he does not notice Mo's attention shift fleetingly to the girl's breasts.

'Mr Conroy is a sports promoter, Papa, he holds cards in all the big venues, the Auditorium, the Convention Center. Mr Conroy, I'd like you to meet my father.' Mo's solicitations are so proper they border on parody. This is obvious to everyone, and Anastasio feels shame on his son's behalf.

Conroy waits patiently, holding Anastasio's hand, until the old man looks at him. When he speaks, his accent is soft, not American – Irish? 'Your son tells me you enjoy Jackie Gleason.'

Anastasio shrugs.

'Come to next Wednesday's match and I'll introduce you.'

Gleason works out of the Auditorium. Anastasio saw him coming out of there once, beaming blindly into the sun, hand half-raised to greet a crowd, or fend it off. Expecting a public that, for that brief anomalous moment, had vanished, the street and sidewalk empty. Gleason dropped his hand, noticed Anastasio looking at him from across the street and mugged up an act for him: a big shrug and a disappointed shamble down the street.

'The Great Malenko versus Wahoo McDaniel,' says Mo.

'What?'

'The match. At the Auditorium next Wednesday. Right, Dad?'

This from the girl, Deborah, and straight away the alarm bells are ringing in Anastasio's head. Because if this is her father, and this bundle in her arms is her baby, then where, in the name of decency, is her husband?

*

Hours pass. It is twenty to ten before Armstrong begins his moonwalk, and Harry is drinking in his usual bar down by Woffard Park. The bar is packed and silent, everyone transfixed before the screen on its shelf above the optics. They are wrapped in an atmosphere more profound and deep-felt than church and his own granddaughter's christening.

Harry raises the beer glass to his lips but forgets to drink.

'Neil, you're lined up nicely... toward me a little bit...'

The restricted environment of the lunar module means that Armstrong will enter the history books arse-first, the way his granddaughter Stacey entered the world.

'OK, down...'

Everyone is moved in some way. Harry feels his jaw tighten, but there are men around him weeping into their beer. The wonder of it is, these are his people, men whose profession it is to beat the living shit out of each other. These Mexican hardcases have so little left to prove they can afford to let themselves be children when the occasion suits. Harry has learned to admire their easy sentiment – but from a distance, Belfast still strong in him. Tears can never be Harry's way, brought up as he was under a strict Falls Road ethic, the rod thrust firmly – as his late wife once so delicately put it – up his Fenian backside.

'Roll to the left... put your left foot to the right a little bit... you're doing fine.'

Still no live picture yet.

Beside Harry, below him – he is only five feet six to Harry's six-two – Benjamin Donoso is making the sign of the cross repeatedly across his chest. Donoso is a former ice-house navvy Harry discovered moonlighting on the Guadalajara circuit. This was just a few weeks after Harry arrived in Mexico, wrestling's new El Dorado, Deborah big-bellied on his arm and the pair of them out to start their lives again as far away as possible from 'swinging London'.

The second time they met, Donoso handed Deborah a charm against the devil, a sugar-and-straw trinket Harry didn't understand and, more than that, suspected. Only the sadness in the little Mexican's eyes prevented him from ramming the little juju thing down his neck.

Over time, Harry has come to understand that Benjamin Donoso's superstitions are real to him, turning his every performance in the wrestling ring into a Mystery he could, if he was put to it, explain to any priest. Every Wednesday Donoso puts on a black cloak, white face-paint and a cardboard half-mask painted like a skull, and climbs into the ring with men a foot and a half taller than he is.

Back in 1969, before Donoso came on board to explain it to him, this sort of caper was a closed book to Harry Conroy. Arriving in Mexico, he'd been dismayed to discover that the wrestling scene there was a circus. Literally: there were costumes. Masks. Capes. There were props. In Tijuana the fights were, if possible, even more brutal than those he remembered from Belfast, but here there was an added grace to every bout, and a kind of fairy-tale logic Harry despaired of ever understanding.

With Donoso's encouragement and Deborah's medical bills to pay, Harry finally cracked it. He gathered together the best wrestlers Donoso knew of and showed them the kind of wrestling *he* knew: the sea-sick rhythms of Submission, the brutal groundworks of Collar-and-Elbow. The Mexican fighters watched, and grew pale.

What can we do with this? This was Harry's question: no angle, no pitch, no promises. What can we do? Can we do anything? Is there anything here?

There was. When they were ready, Harry arranged a tour Stateside, and from the very first night, it was a rout, a massacre, an event to change the sport of wrestling for ever.

Harry's outfit settled finally in Florida, integrating uneasily with the already strong promotion there. There were tensions between the natives and the newcomers, and by persuading both sides to let him exploit these tensions in closely scripted angles, Harry made every match he promoted part of a larger epic – a statewide grudge war with instalments every week in an auditorium or school hall near you. It was the birth of modern wrestling, with its storylines, its flawed heroes and irresistible villians, its catastrophic injuries and superhuman returns from the dead. It was pure gold.

Donoso is the most exciting heel on the Florida circuit and certainly the most unlikely. Whoever heard of a heel who was shorter than his opponent? Who, before Donoso, ever imagined that a crowd could be persuaded to bay for the blood of the little guy? Donoso has a way of lending true terror to his litheness, his odd, asymmetric moves and especially his short stature. He is everyone's childhood nightmare of a puppet come to life. He makes even Harry shudder sometimes, even though Harry writes all the angles and keeps him supplied with rubber teeth.

Donoso the Vampyre, at five feet six the undisputed master of the figure four leg-lock, lays his hand on Harry's arm. 'The boy's a blade,' he murmurs as they wait for pictures, any second now: Armstrong's first steps. 'When Castro gets his joke-shop cigar from Uncle Sam, this boy wants to be there with the lighter.'

Christ. 'What else?' Harry asks. He has been turning cartwheels trying to keep his lovely daughter out of the shit, but the evidence is pretty bloody clear by now, Deborah has an unerring instinct for trouble. He had hopes for Mo, too. 'What does he use his boat for?'

Donoso shrugs.

'Weed? Is he shipping weed?'

'I don't think so.'

Every son of every Cuban martyr plies the coast of Cuba in a borrowed boat. It is like a rite of manhood. They are looking for something to tell their handlers back on shore, men they imagine belong to the Agency. They don't even know what it is they are looking for. They missed their moment in history, too young to get butchered with the 2506, so now they wander the Florida Straits like derelicts foraging for scraps. Six months later the ones who don't manage to drown themselves are tacking into the Keys with packets of emeralds and holds full of marijuana.

Still, this Moisés kid is doing a damn good impression of being smitten, and who else is going to look at Deborah now she has Stacey to look after? He's persistent, too. Harry has made sure of that. He's not given the kid the easiest of rides.

'Thanks, Ben,' he says. Benjamin Donoso shrugs, because thanks are nothing to him, he loves Harry fiercely.

Harry wonders what he has done to deserve such friendship. Without Donoso he would surely be down and out in Tijuana still, and Deborah, poor damaged Deborah, this child, the image of her mother, whose precious life he tries to save, but which pours through his fingers like water–

The balance in the room changes. He feels it, a shift of energies.

Above them, on the television, Armstrong's boot appears.

At the same moment, across town, Moisés Chavez has taken advantage of Harry's absence to steal a couple of hours with his love.

'Careful,' Deborah gasps, 'careful.'

Mo lifts his body higher above her, teasing her, his cock inside her but only a little way.

'Mo.'

His quick, shallow thrusts grow deeper, longer, he lowers himself over her, flicks at her lips with his tongue, and she begins to come.

They are still in the flush of things, still new to each other. Next to them, sleeping in her cot, Deborah's baby Stacey stirs in her sleep, comforted by smells and sounds of human need.

The TV is on but the sound is down. Mo wheeled it in from the sitting room so that they could enjoy the bed together and still not miss the moment: man's first steps on the Moon. Plus if Harry her dad comes home early, being in here rather than the sitting room gives Mo precious seconds in which to leap out the window into the shrubbery.

Mo closes his hand around Deborah's throat, playful but firm, choking her softly to her climax.

He turns her over then, or she turns over for him – they are developing a rhythm now, a mutuality of response, impossible to say who gives, who takes – when events overtake them: on the TV, the news studio has been replaced by grainy grey static.

'Shit.' Mo slides out of her.

'Mo.'

'I need the john,' he says. 'Sorry. Shit.' He scampers out the room and across the hall.

'Hurry,' she calls after him, needlessly.

On the TV, Armstrong's boot appears, feeling for the rung of the ladder...

And Deborah Conroy wakes from her evening with Mo into a blast of pain, trapped in the hollow metal dark with the certainty of having been touched.

She is eight years old and she is seventeen years old and she knows exactly what is happening to her.

Beyond the confines of her hot coffin, the scream of gulls. And Mo's voice from the toilet, telling her some joke or other, something from the day, about his dad.

The uselessness of her limbs; paralysed, she cannot even lift her hands to beat against the tight metal lid, inches above her face. And at the same time, the press of pillows at her back, and the draught of the air-con unit.

The taste of Mo's cigarettes; and in the self-same moment, her mouth is stuffed with her own underwear.

Opening her mouth to scream, eight-year-old Deborah discovers what her seventeen-year-old self knows already from memory and regular repetition: that all her consonants have disappeared, that she can make only idiot sounds so unlike the sounds of distress, neither of her selves will be heard. Mo does not hear her, though he is zipping up his fly only feet away; and it is dark and freezing cold before passers-by, a tow-truck driver and his mate, twig to the truth and pop the boot to reveal eight-year-old abductee Deborah, shivering and spasming in Felixstowe's night air.

Even as Neil Armstrong's boot settles into the lunar dust, she is falling.

Mo enters the bedroom, zipping up his fly, in time to see Deborah topple off the side of the bed, headfirst into her baby's cot. Mo's funny story dies on his lips. The baby, pinned beneath her mother, is silent, little hands spinning as she struggles to inhale. Even the TV is silent, in the split-second before Neil Armstrong delivers his famous line. Yet the room is full of sound. Later, sat with Harry in the emergency room, their ritual hostilities suspended while the doctors fight to reinflate little Stacey's lung, Mo presses his hands to his ears against the memory of that sound: the idiot gurgle in his lover's throat; the spastic thump-thump-thump of her head against the floor.

It is the summer of 1974.

They set sail from the Keys last night, around 9 p.m.: Mo, Deborah, little Stacey; Mo's new business partner is alternating watch. Also onboard is Father Turi, a priest Mo's father knew, himself an escapee from the old country and game for a voyage as charged as this one: dropping old Anastasio's urn into the warm waters of his commandeered home.

It is not a usual thing: to burn a body once washed in baptism, anointed with the oil of salvation, and fed with the bread of life. It is not – the first priest Mo approached made this obnoxiously clear – a practice approved of by the Church. But better old Anastasio returns home as ash than he keeps his flesh to moulder in a foreign grave.

So he is ash now, and free to return home. Here is the water, and Father Turi says, 'Lord God, by the power of your Word you stilled the chaos of the primaeval seas, you made the raging waters of the Flood subside and calmed the storm on the sea of Galilee.'

It is five years since Mo Chavez married Deborah and took baby Stacey for his own. A good and happy time, but also a painful one, because his father naturally did not understand why his son, so full of life and wit and blood, should saddle himself with another man's bastard child. Never mind that the girl he was marrying was sick in the head.

This last objection melted over time as Deborah's seizures tailed away, vanishing as mysteriously as they appeared. But it wasn't until little Stacey started to talk that Anastasio allowed the possibility that he might be charmed. Then, of course, he saw what Mo had seen all along: that there is something wonderful in the electric field humming between mother and daughter that overrides the imperatives of pride and blood.

The last two years of Anastasio's life were good ones, reconciling father and son; bringing a new family into being. Though he never spoke of his own deterioration, perhaps Anastasio knew there was no time left for him to nurse his disapproval, only a headlong rush into a future that would not contain him. Accepting this, how could he not accept the love and games of a little child?

Stacey loves her grandfather. 'Grandpa's an angel now,' Mo told Stacey, the day he came to the hotel and found his father dead, the TV on, and Jackie Gleason cracking weak jokes into his open eyes. Stacey blinked. 'Funny,' she said.

The terrible iconoclasm of children.

'How funny?'

'Funny he didn't say anything,' she said. The abruptness meant more to her than the death. 'Where is he, then?' Looking around.

Ill-health barely grazed Anastasio's final months. Whatever was the matter with his heart erupted, decisive and muscular as the man it killed.

'As we commit the earthly remains of our brother Anastasio to the deep, grant him peace and tranquillity until that day when he and all who believe in you will be raised to the glory of new life promised in the waters of baptism.'

Deborah squeezes Mo's hand. Stacey leans in to him. Mo's business partner appreciates that this is a family occasion and has made himself scarce during the committal. Mo is dimly aware of him straddling the bowsprit, book in hand, as Father Turi draws to a close.

'We ask this through Christ our Lord. Amen.'

Mo steps forward and drops the urn containing his father's ashes into Cuban water.

It was a risky thing to do perhaps, to sail into these waters in broad daylight; with his wife and kid, too, a real provocation to fate. But he owed the old man, and he could not have borne the day without Deborah beside him and five-year-old Stacey hugging his knee. (She is trying to look solemn, but she really doesn't know how; she keeps scowling and wrinkling up her nose. Grandpa's an angel now, and because she believes this, she cannot feel grief.)

Afterwards, hands trembling, the urn still sensate in his fingertips, he takes the wheel and pulls them out of there as quickly as he can, breezing up the Santaren Channel like any other clueless Bahamian tourist, taking the long way home. Deborah sweetens the priest's delay with glasses of home-squeezed guayabana juice and Stacey goes below, playing a private game. His business partner joins him by the wheel, tosses his book – Fuentes, *Cambio de Piel* – onto the wheel housing and, after a little rigmarole of handshakes and commiserations, distracts Mo, as he knows Mo likes to be distracted, with tales of April 1961.

'Seaweed! Some fuckwit Yank pilot looked out the window of his U2 and saw *seaweed...*'

Wednesday, 7 August 1974: for five years Mo has been running his boat charter, running ulcer-making surveillance in the teeth of Castro's shore batteries and trying to believe, against all evidence and logic, that another Bay of Pigs is possible. Now, as of today, he is on his own, the very last shreds of Operation Mongoose thrown away, the *corporaçion* disbanded, its handlers gone without goodbye, exiled to desk-jobs in Langley or to moribund research libraries on the Washington outskirts.

Some are retired; some plain thrown out. Mo sees them mumbling their way along Collins Avenue, big men with wet, disappointed eyes.

Two days ago Nixon released three of the transcripts and admitted he had tried to halt the FBI's inquiry into the Watergate break-in. Is this really the same Dick Nixon Mo cheered at the Republican Nomination, all those years ago? The news is full of conspiracy and cover-up but Mo Chavez, blooded in the hot disorder of Little Havana with its three hundred front companies, its six hundred veterans' groups, knows a cheap fantastist when he sees one. There's no conspiracy here: just Dickie leaving others to wipe his drool off the furniture. He will surely not outlast the week.

This is old news. The real damage occurred when it turned out the campaign office burglars were Cubans. This news has hurt Miami past all hope of healing. Five years Mo has spent in the Agency's service, paying back in effort and in peril the debt he owed his father. There will be no second invasion, no bigger, better Bay of Pigs. It has all been for nothing.

Or if not for nothing then – this is the bitterest pill – merely for this lumbering money-pit of a boat. This little perk by way of the Agency's pursuit of plausible denial. (If he'd been running a print shop, they would have given him the shop.) This boat bought for him by the Melmar Corporation, the CIA's Miami front. This boat which is now his, to do with as he likes.

What does he want with a boat? Where will he sail to, now Fidel has been left to lord it over his home?

'We never stood a fucking chance,' the business partner sighs, in conclusion, and lights up a cigar.

Mo's gut responds as always to the old and much-repeated tale. This first-hand account of the Bay of Pigs fiasco makes a hollow space within him for a cocktail of conflicting emotions: regret, envy, incredulity, admiration. There are just two years between them, but this man fought on the beaches; Mo did not. This man served twenty-two months in La

Cabaña, within earshot of daily executions, 'and Gagarin laughed and told me, "You too wear the Order of Playa Girón!"'

Mo has the boat, but he has no idea what to do with it. An image looms: season after season spent helping lobster-faced tourists fish marlin; not a life so much as an afterlife.

This man knows what to do with his boat. They met two years ago, a Thursday in December, the night the last Apollo rose, plangent, a broken promise, through the star-white skies of Cocoa Beach. They reeled together, drunk, along the boardwalks and watched the lift-off, watched as this little bubble of broken hope became another star. Seventeen. The last men on the moon.

'I thought I'd missed them all,' Nick sighed as they wove from one side of the beach to the other through quiet, manicured streets, from the Banana River to the ocean and back again. Nick was newly arrived from east Africa, an experienced merchant marine. 'I dreamed of seeing this.'

When the rocket had vanished from sight they went and found a bar, but even here, in this resort town where old NASA men come to die in the sun, the patrons were glued to a sports channel.

They threw beer tins into the quay and talked about Apollo, what of it they had seen; they played where-were-you-when. They talked Kennedy and Nixon, about history and the way things end and what if anything comes next.

They talked about the Straits of Florida.

Mo has the seamanship, the CIA training and the boat; Jessup has the contacts and the experience. Watergate has laid waste to Miami, and Jessup knows what comes next. Jessup knows what to do with his boat.

Nick Jessup. This is what he calls himself.

Mo understands, of course, that this is not his real name.

RENAMO MOTO

1

It was towards the end of 1984, the aftermath of Mozambique's droughts, and I was leaving Maputo and heading north to the town of Goliata on the Mozambique–Malawi border.

Were God in His heaven, Mozambique, a thousand-mile-long beach state on the eastern seaboard of southern Africa, would be a paradise. Instead the country has laboured for five hundred years under whimsical Portuguese 'government'. Finally, in 1969, even as they mourned Jorge Katalayo, their assassinated leader, and just in time to tweak everyone's Cold War paranoias, Mozambique's socialist liberators, the Frente de Libertaçao de Moçambique or FRELIMO, declared their country's independence. The sovereign state of Mozambique, they said, would align itself neither with the Warsaw Pact nor with the West.

In choosing this difficult and perilous path, FRELIMO's leaders also chose to disregard certain glaring realities. For instance, the fact that they had land borders with Rhodesia and apartheid South Africa. Or that the sea corridors that passed through their territory were crucial to the economies of their landlocked (and, for that reason, increasingly paranoid) neighbours. If I could see the seeds of disaster in all this, why didn't they? In 1969 I was still in London, far from the action, reading newspapers behind the library counter of my dear little philosophical society. How could they have missed what was so obvious to people like me?

The staff of FRELIMO were, like their fallen comrades, all honourable Western-educated blacks who had spent their formative years in countries like America and Sweden. They imagined post-colonial Africa would submit to the rules of fair play. And they were wrong: retribution

289

for their daring stab at self-government was long and terrible. In 1977, Apartheid-backed RENAMO contras launched a war of terror against the civilian population of Mozambique. The campaign lasted fifteen years, aided first by Rhodesia, then South Africa, then by the two severest droughts in living memory.

When I heard the army had wrested Goliata back from the contras, I thought: Now at least I can get there by plane. But RENAMO still controlled the surrounding countryside and the airstrip was too badly damaged to risk a landing. 'Goliata is free,' a well-meaning apparatchik in the ministry of education told me, 'only that you cannot go in or out.'

I thought about travelling steerage on a cacao boat as far as Beira, taking pot luck after that – only RENAMO's piracy had reached a pitch where anything moving outside Beira's mothballed harbour, regardless of flag, ran a risk of being shelled by nervous government batteries scattered along the shore.

All the big roads in Mozambique were built by the Portuguese to speed up their looting, and they all ran east–west, connecting the coast to the interior. Naively I traced out a course which mazed laboriously northward over dirt tracks and seasonal roads. When I showed it to the officer in charge of the car pool, he nearly fell off his chair laughing. Had I not heard of land mines?

A week or so later, a team of Italian engineers managed to hand-wave their way past the border checkpoint on the Malawian side of the Shire river. They mended the airstrip, and finally I was able to piggy-back a government charter.

The only other passenger – Joseph Lichenya, the new district administrator – met me an hour before dawn on a military airstrip just outside Maputo's city limits, by the tailplane of the ancient pre-war Dakota.

Clean-shaven and in his thirties, wearing sunglasses even in the pre-dawn dark, Captain Lichenya was typical of the careful young men the socialist FRELIMO government turned out of Maputo these days. A few years ago he would have been overseeing Operation Production – the government's catastrophic experiment in collectivized agriculture. These days it was all that men like him could do to gather Mozambique's scattered rural population into temporary villages, safe from RENAMO's predations and in reach of the international aid agencies. The irony, that these safe havens were often built on the foundations of *aldeamentos* – Portuguese work-camps – escaped no one.

I asked Lichenya where he hailed from.

'Oh,' he said, shrugging. 'That's a difficult question. I'm from all over.'

Ah, a man of mystery. I elected to dislike him.

The pilot and his mate – two boisterous Soviet airforcemen – turned up to inspect our aircraft with incredulous fascination, as though it were some sort of exhibit. After some persuasion, the engines turned. There were no seats in the Dakota. The captain and I settled opposite each other on sacks of pinto beans.

'Sit on two sacks,' Lichenya said.

'I'm fine.' At forty-two I was older than him by at least fifteen years, and an experienced traveller. I didn't need him to nanny me.

He turned his hand into a make-believe pistol and pointed it into the air; he pulled the trigger. 'Two sacks will stop a bullet.'

I moved to higher ground. This put me closer to the doorway than I wanted, given the plane had no doors.

We swung a lazy arc over Beira's harbour. The curl prolonged itself, turned full-circle, repeated... The pilots were wasting fuel, and it was not hard to see why. At the horizon the sea was a vivid bluish green, as distant waves caught and refracted light from a sun that had yet to rise. The green spread as though a lush prairie were unfolding itself across the ocean. A couple of seconds later, as the sun's first arc came into view, the prairie burst into flames of red and gold.

Nice to know that even Russian pilots have the souls of poets. Content, they changed course and hurled us inland and up, out of range of RENAMO's heat-seeking missiles, and into the strange, marble world of thunderheads and cloud columns that awaited us, five thousand feet above my adopted country.

Jorge Katalayo's assassination had not fractured the liberation movement, nor did it delay the colonists' inevitable defeat. Victory over the colonial power had been achieved by 1974 – much sooner than expected – when a coup in Lisbon cut the Portuguese imperial project off at the root.

So FRELIMO had found itself in the disconcerting position of a dog that's been chasing after a speeding car: once it's caught it, what on earth is it supposed to do with it?

With tiny resources, few personnel and next to no education, FRELIMO found itself with a country to run. Worse, a *Portuguese* country. Even then, the situation might have been saved, had it not been for the exodus.

Boats arrived from Lisbon and carried whole harvests away. What the settlers couldn't carry, they destroyed. These were acts of pure spite. Tractors were driven into the sea. Job-loads of concrete were poured down the lift-shafts of half-finished beachfront hotels.

Once these moral pygmies had returned to the motherland, burped and bedded, their tummies swollen with home-stewed *bacalhau*, the Africans they had so laughably 'governed' for five hundred years took stock. In the words of Yelena Mlokote, *née* Katalayo, bereaved daughter of FRELIMO's first president:

> We have nothing to learn, because there is no one left here to teach us. We have nothing to buy because there is no one here left to sell us anything. We have nothing to do because there is no one who can pay us for our labour. We have nowhere to go because no one here knows how to drive a train. Very soon we shall have nothing to wear. Already in the country you find people weaving jerkins and skirts out of tree bark.

This comes from a standard letter Yelena sent me in the summer of 1975. Well, it was her signature printed on the bottom. How many hundreds of these things must they have posted to contacts and friends in Britain, Sweden, America? In it, she invited me ('dear friend', 'valued colleague') to assist the struggling administration:

> For as long as anyone can remember, bureaucracy has been the black man's only route to preferment. No one here knows how to operate a seed drill; no one here can afford to buy a seed drill; but everyone with a primary education knows what the requisition form would look like. At the moment of liberation, we have the skills required to operate a tin-pot fascist backwater. These skills, and no others. God protect us from our strengths.

It didn't take much exegesis to discover, behind her words, the writings of her father. Did she read his speeches now? Did she search out his words in the back numbers of obscure Marxist periodicals? In foreign newspapers, microfiched at the SOAS library in London? In correspondence with helpful, if bemused, journalists from Sweden and Japan?

Though I kept her letter, as you might keep a wisdom tooth or a gall-stone, I figured there was nothing to be gained by replying to her. Then, a couple of weeks later, on a whim, I bought a postcard of a Beefeater and scribbled this on the back: *'A to K or L to Z?'*

It was the most compact, brutal way I could think of to tell her what I knew about her father's assassination. What FRELIMO's serious young men had told me, visiting my flat that day in 1969.

About a month later, a second letter arrived. It was very different from the first: much shorter and entirely personal. Yelena is changing bed-pans in a clinic in Lourenço Marques ('We call it Maputo now'). She spends her nights studying in a rented room by the light of a paraffin lamp: *'My father understood that the greatest threat to black power in*

*post-colonial Africa is the educated black. Home rule that side-steps
revolution – he appreciated that threat far better than I did. I realize
that now.'*

She was trying to locate herself in history. To present her acts in the
light of the complex circumstances. *'It was a mistaken path,'* she wrote.
(She had acquired the rhetoric of her father's generation: the road; the
path; the long march.) She wrote: *'I believe I took a wrong turning.'*

I took this to be her confession.

*'By day, I perform menial duties at the hospital. I dress cuts and
bruises. I hand out aspirins, when we have any, to the chronic cases. I
empty bed-pans in the fever ward. I study at night.'*

She wanted every mistake she had made to yield a valuable life
lesson.

'Come to Maputo,' she wrote.

The cold shook Captain Lichenya out of his sleep. He'd looked so
vulnerable, curled up on his sacks, that I had laid a blanket across him.
Some sort of a blanket, sewn together from burlap relief sacks. He
pulled it up around himself and blinked. 'Christ,' he said – the *lingua
franca* of blasphemy – and added, in English: 'I hate flying.'

Holding the blanket around himself, he climbed off the sacks and
began pacing stiffly back and forth along the hold.

'Do you know Goliata?' I asked him.

'I know Goliata.'

I let the silence – or what passed for silence in a doorless prop
aeroplane – drag on for as long as I could stand. 'I'm the new teacher
there,' I said.

'I know who you are.'

The view out of the open doorway seemed to mesmerize him: storm
clouds over the purple carpet of the earth. He stopped to stare, for all
the world as if he were surveying the view from the balcony of a hotel.
'Where have you been working?' he shouted back at me.

'Maputo,' I told him. 'Tete. Beira, a few times.'

I had been doing this kind of work for nearly ten years now: arithmetic, literacy, hygiene, a smattering of *Marxismo-Leninismo*. I was a valuable commodity: an educated foreign worker allied to FRELIMO's socialist administration. A *cooperante*.

'Nampula?'

'No. It's odd.' Nampula was Mozambique's northern capital. 'I've never been.'

'A pity.'

'Yes?'

Engine noise filled the hold, and there was a worrying smell of petrol.

'You've never worked in the countryside before?'

'No.'

He nodded. He had guessed as much.

'Is it safe?' The words were out of my mouth before I could stop them.

The captain turned back to the open doorway, the world of strange currents and inversions giving way now, as we dropped towards cloudbase, to a clearer view of the land.

Looking down, I scoured the landscape for its human component. A smallholding, a field of rice or cassava, a stand of cashew trees: the eye leapt to one, then to another, as to a major landmark. Most of the time, there were no tracks in view and no villages worth the name. Rocky bluffs and acacia trees jumbled the landscape like a deliberate camouflage: an outrageous sculptural scatter-painting in purple, white and yellow-green. People lived here, but this was not an ordinary human landscape. It was not carved out, the way the land in other countries is carved and parcelled, cleared and divided. The human parts of the landscape had not agglomerated, the way they had elsewhere, into the ribbons and clumps – villages, roads – which humans usually make on their nation's petri dish. Down there (we had reached the district of Zambezia) it was as though the humans had been scattered evenly over the land in a fine drizzle, and had made do wherever they landed.

The Weight of Numbers

Many of the people didn't even know that their country was called Mozambique. The RENAMO contras were just bandits to them – *matsangas*. Socialism was another word they couldn't spell. If they had heard of South Africa at all, it was as a distant place of fabulous wealth. They tilled their land. They wanted to be left alone. They left each other alone. This was the problem: it was virtually impossible for men like Lichenya to defend them.

Of course it wasn't safe.

2

The T-shirt was frayed. It had been washed many times. Across the front of the blouse, glass and concrete towers reached into a sky that must have been blue once, but time and frequent washes had bleached it to pale green. In front of the towers, a beach stretched away in naive perspective: a distant headland, a bikini-clad sunbather, a parasol, a long iced drink in a glass beaded with sweat. Splashed across the sky in big pink letters: Sunny Beirut.

The sunbather's midriff stretched and tore, the glass broke: the T-shirt's wearer inhaled. 'They burned the school, stole the books and used the children to carry the furniture over the border.' Goliata's FRELIMO administrator was a big woman. It was in her face that the hardships of the two-year drought were written: it was shrunken and bruised-looking, like a fruit that has been left out in the sun too long.

Beirut? The top was older than the children I was here to teach.

'Then they sliced off the boys' noses and fed them to the girls.'

Entering this room, I had feared the worst: 'RENAMO MOTO' smeared on the walls in sump oil. 'Moto' meaning fire. But even as we talked, a boy came in silently, unacknowledged, and began pasting frayed posters of FRELIMO President Chissano over the slogan. (The glue smelled foul – his own concoction?)

'One of the girls, she was eight years old, refused to eat her brother's nose. The captain wanted to make an example out of her so he tried to rape her.'

This was Naphiri Calange's office. Naphiri herself stood facing me across a desk knocked together out of crates. We didn't sit down; there were no chairs. Above our heads, the room's central light was missing, along with the fitment, and a jagged tear in the ceiling plaster, from the middle of the room to just over the door, marked the path of the electrical wire: this too had been torn out. The floor of the room was a crumbling skein of cement.

'She was too small for him, so he widened her with his machete.'

The windows had neither glass, nor the cheaper, more common and practical mesh grilles. More ominous still, the windows had no sills or frames, for these too had been ripped away. Their regular shape distinguished them from the artillery holes which had otherwise colandered the town.

'Welcome to Goliata.'

There were two windows. Naphiri stood with her back to one. The other was to her right. Through the window behind her, no building stood tall enough to look me in the eye. Most had been reduced to stubs and slopes of dusty scree, bound already by weeds and creepers. The ones that remained standing – either roofless, or sporting a recent, disreputable-looking greenish thatch – had fared little better.

I asked, 'What happened to all the roofs?'

'Stolen,' Naphiri replied. She told me how RENAMO had kidnapped villagers to carry zinc roofing sheets out of Goliata, across empty cattle pens and through the bush, to the border crossing with Malawi, where the metal was bartered for motorcycle spares, radio batteries, oil, sugar, salt.

Through the other window, bright afternoon light came into the room dappled and scented by shade trees – flame, jacaranda – which grew in the grounds of the old Portuguese church. These were the last trees in Goliata. The RENAMO guerrillas had not touched the church. It was completely undamaged. To stand with a view of both windows was to see in tableau the recent history of the town: the before and the after.

'Come.' She motioned me over to the window overlooking the ruins.

From this distance it was impossible to tell what building was useable, what was a ruin. She pointed down the street towards what must once have been the pretty end of town. The shops – they must at one time have been shops – still sported pillared arcades, shading their frontages from the sun.

'The new school.'

I wondered whether to thank her.

'If you find any cases of gin hiding there, let me know,' she said. 'It used to be the tea-planters' club-house.'

Naphiri wasn't giving me the whole building, just the veranda – at least, the half of it that had survived RENAMO's occupation. I glanced over the collapsed part. It had not been hit by artillery, as I had thought at first. It had been chopped up by hand, and to such a fineness, only a psychopath would have had the patience.

'Well?'

I quickly adjusted. The location made sense. There was shade; we were separated a little way from the street; we could see who was coming. Elsewhere, the grass grew to the levels of the walls. 'Thank you,' I said.

What could be taken away, RENAMO had taken away: roofing sheets, copper wiring, furniture, vehicles. Even the street signs were gone. What could not be carried had been smashed. Vehicles waiting for repair had been set on fire. Water and drainage pipes had been dug out of the earth and broken open with a hammer. A decorative pavement ran under the frontage of an old barber's shop; every tiny tile had been methodically splintered.

More seriously, every generator and water pump serving the town had been hammered to scrap, set on fire, then laid into with axes: bright flecks showed where metal had met metal.

'All this will be cleared!' Naphiri declared, leading me through the town.

And after the clearance – what? Everyone was calling it an occupation, but the truth was RENAMO had razed the town. There were no pipes to lay in place of the ones that were smashed, no bails of electrical wire to restring the unstrung town. Even the shade trees that had once lined the *avenidas* of the elegant quarter had been cut down and burned.

'All this will be cleared!' Naphiri insisted, with something like desperation. 'With the earth-mover, we will sweep the street. Many streets are cleared now. It is a good vehicle.'

'It's still here?' It was my understanding that the Italians had left the area as soon as they'd finished repairing the airstrip.

Naphiri sucked on her lower lip. 'It broke down,' she said. 'It was most unfortunate.' She caught my eye and smiled. 'Our friends had to leave it behind.'

Every couple of weeks, and at great risk, a truck driver ran the gamut of National Highway Number One to bring fuel to Goliata.

We had little enough use for it. The town blacksmith was still working away at his replacement generator, gathering parts from spoil heaps and burnt-out vehicles; bartering for motorcycle spares across the Malawian border; whittling a flywheel out of wood. So most of the fuel ended up in the belly of the Italians' earth-mover.

It could never have broken down. Had it ground to a halt, who here would have had the resources to fix it? By the little hints she kept dropping – 'Most unfortunate. The damnedest thing. The day they were leaving' – Naphiri let me in on her chicanery. How she had got this valuable item all to herself. She was pleased with her cleverness. It was at this point – with Naphiri revealed as a thief and a cheat – that I began to like her.

I had been suspicious at first, and particularly of the feasts Naphiri held every few evenings by firelight, between reed fences, in Goliata's 'cane town'. Everyone was expected to bring something to the meal: a chicken; a flat basket piled with tomatoes or chard; a woman dressed in a rough red shawl arrived with skewers of what looked like satay, but turned out to be roast field mice. It wasn't the food that disturbed me; it was the money. Naphiri saw to it that everyone, no matter how poor, dropped a donation into her old aluminium paint-can.

My neighbour at the feast was a comparatively old man – I guessed mid-forties – whose lips had been cut off by the RENAMO rebels during the occupation. In halting Chichewa, I asked him what the collection was for. 'For FRELIMO,' he replied, as best he could, sucking the spittle back through his teeth. 'A donation to the party.'

What was Naphiri doing, shaking the tin under the noses of people who had nothing?

The man next to me passed me the pot, and I looked inside. It wasn't Mozambican currency. It was Malawian. 'Why *kwacha*?' I asked him, indicating the pot. 'Why foreign money?'

He shrugged. 'You can buy things in Malawi.' He tilted his head back to swallow, so the food would not fall out of his destroyed mouth. 'There are shops in Malawi.'

Naphiri sat with her arms folded, glowering at me. It occurred to me I had not made a donation. I had some hard currency in a bill-fold. I dropped a ten-dollar bill into the pot, slowly enough that people could see.

Ten dollars was an unimaginable amount of money. Nobody reacted. Nobody cared. Even my neighbour seemed not to notice.

I sensed that, with their circumstances this reduced, money had ceased to mean very much to the people here. The food they had brought to the feast had more value to them than currency they could not spend.

Naphiri jumped to her feet. 'Where is Samuel?' she cried.

Silence fell across the feast.

'Where is he?'

All around me, people were exchanging awkward glances.

'This is our banquet.' Naphiri stretched her arms wide, measuring her magnanimity. 'Why is my brother not eating with us?'

The villagers stared into their dinners. We were using leaves as plates; big and leathery and so practical for the purpose, I had barely registered the oddness of it until now.

'Has he somewhere better to be?'

My Chichewa wasn't nearly good enough to follow this performance.

Happily, my neighbour knew a few scraps of Portuguese and – probably as a way of sidestepping the row that was brewing – he muddled up a translation for me.

'Sam is gone.'

This much I had gathered.

'Sam is gone to the graveyard.'

'Why would anyone be going to a graveyard at this time of night?' I asked.

'Because he is eating with the *matsangas*,' my neighbour replied, and pulled the rough reddish jerkin around his matchstick chest, as against a chill.

We were overheard. Around us, the conversation turned to vampires. Only ghouls and the undead, it was agreed, would break bread in a graveyard.

It was my prissiness that had prevented me from understanding Naphiri. Once that wore off, I even began to admire her. Without Naphiri, there would be no Goliata. Naphiri was the only employer in town. Whatever money you dropped in her paint can one evening, you earned it back the next day, scrubbing RENAMO's slogans from the walls, thatching roofs, lifting rubble into the bucket of the earth-mover. When it wasn't being used to clear the cement town, the Italians' abandoned vehicle was dragging gimcrack ploughs through new fields to the west of the cane town. As far as I could see, Naphiri didn't charge for these services.

She was Goliata's inescapable first principal. She was more than our 'administrator'. She was our chief, our *régulo*.

So, imagine Samuel's feelings.

Imagine Sam, former *régulo* of Goliata under the Portuguese colonial administration. A headman deposed by his own sister.

I grilled my neighbour for information. 'So FRELIMO put Naphiri in charge, in her brother's place?'

He unskewered a field-mouse, necked it and wiped his ruined mouth. 'Why not?' he said, sucking spittle back through his teeth. 'Naphiri can read.'

True, Sam's education at the hands of the Portuguese must have been pitiful, in comparison with the education Naphiri had received from FRELIMO in Dar. Sam had no official status any more, and he didn't know much about *Marxismo-Leninismo*.

What he had, in abundance, was an instinct for small-town life. Ever since I'd got here, he and his cronies had been haunting Goliata like a bad smell. The town's old power-brokers had returned from obscurity: a couple of popular *curandeiros*, a former local agent for the Ford motor company, a local landowner who had made his fortune in the mines of Johannesburg. They were shaking hands, they were building bridges. With a casual cynicism, they stirred the rumour mill against Naphiri and the party: FRELIMO has banned private ownership! FRELIMO is demolishing monuments in the cemeteries!

Had I known nothing of this, the way Sam first approached me would still have got my back up: all glad-hands and pat-heads for the kids I was in the middle of teaching, and a patter of twisted subordinate clauses and long loan-words for me.

'Tell me, sir, what is your specialism?'

It was a slick performance, and the level of polish probably counted for a lot in this land without books, where oratory is everything. It had exactly the opposite effect on me. I replied in my dreadful Chichewa, keeping my distance, letting him know my dislike.

'Why don't you come eat with us tonight?' he asked me, coming straight down to business. No prizes for guessing who 'we' were. RENAMO contras still controlled much of the surrounding countryside. Yet he had delivered his invitation in elegant Portuguese as though offering me supper at the Ritz.

I thought about Goliata's spacious new cemetery, and declined Sam's invitation with a shudder. Sam shrugged. It was all one to him. He had felt the wheel turn beneath him. He knew it was only a matter of time before he wore cotton again.

Sam was not the lean, hungry creature I had been expecting. Though they shared a mother only, the family resemblance between Sam and Naphiri was striking. Sam's face was a more evolved version of Naphiri's; his frame lankier and less clumsy. His eyes, far from burning with a wicked flame, crinkled charmingly with every smile. Should he ever be handed back his old mantle as head-man of the town, I could imagine his response: the modest amusement with which he would rehearse all the twists and turns that had brought him back to power: 'Well I never!'

He lingered on the steps of the veranda, listening to me teach. I made a point of ignoring him, so every couple of minutes he grunted his approval, making sure I knew he was there, a sympathetic presence. How long did he intend to keep this up?

Just then, the earth-mover rounded a corner into the main street. It rattled towards us, wreathed in eddies of smoke. The children leapt up cheering and rushed to the balustrade.

Any minute now they would jump into the street and mob the vehicle and tease the driver – Redson, a man who'd driven machines bigger than this in the mines of South Africa. And Redson, obedient to the rules of their cheerful game, would brake sharply, start off again with a jolt, throw gears, brake, start forward and brake again, shaking kids from the scoop as fast as they could clamber on.

Sam Calange just laughed.

'Have you ever seen such a ridiculous contraption?' he said, appealing to me, tears of mirth in his eyes. He was using Chichewa now, so the children would understand. 'Listen to it! The old rust-bucket! I give it another week.'

The children, mortified, turned to me, awaiting their teacher's spirited defence of the village's earth-mover.

Sam pressed home his attack: 'Still, my sister, she is only a woman.

How can we expect her to know what engine oil is for?'

I stared at the vehicle, lumbering smokily up the road, and hunted furiously for an adequate retort. True enough, it was not the most impressive machine of its sort: a tractor with a detachable scoop bolted onto the front, and the scoop was already badly buckled – but I had been here long enough that it had begun to make an impression on me: a valuable mascot of the party.

'Listen to that engine! It's tearing its guts out! Look!' Sam pointed. 'If someone doesn't align that wheel soon...' Gripping an imaginary steering wheel, he mimed the earth-mover's drunken progress. The kids whooped and applauded as Sam wove across the veranda, his face twisted in comical terror: man on runaway machine. When it came to working an audience, there was no competing with Sam Calange. He leapt from the balcony and capered about in the street, running up to the earth-mover; shying away. Redson had to swerve to avoid him, which only made Sam caper the more.

How the children laughed. Even the ones without noses.

The worst thing was, I couldn't stop him. Sam had succeeded in wrenching me back to a place behind my eyes where I could see the earth-mover for what it was: a dinky little plaything with a life of approximately one more month – if we were lucky – before it seized up for good. That, in its turn, was what made Sam's performance so purely cruel. He wasn't saying, 'I will oil your tractor.' He wasn't saying, 'My friends in the bush can get you spares for that buckled axle.' He wasn't offering us anything. He was simply belittling what he didn't control.

'Redson!'

Redson looked up, harried and red-faced, from the wheel of the earth-mover. Sam's ridiculous ballet had brought his vehicle to a stand-still.

'Redson,' I shouted, at the top of my lungs, seized by a sudden inspiration, *'run him over!'*

The children gasped.

Redson frowned.

'Run him over!' I yelled, scenting an advantage. 'Come on!' I rallied my students. 'Man versus machine: *let's see who wins*!'

Redson was a serious man. Clowning was not his style. Scowling, he climbed down from the tractor and tried to remonstrate with Sam. Naturally, it only took a few seconds before Sam had managed to charm him. What could I do but stand there, powerless, while Redson, arm in arm with Sam, the Old Boss, laughed along with his jokes?

The kids, disappointed and uneasy, sat back down. I did my best to smother the seeds of their doubt. *Amo amas ama; c* is 'kuh' before *a, o, u;* 'sss' before *e* or *i. Eu nasci em mil e novecentos e cinquenta e cinco.* Pay attention in the corner.

And all the while I could feel Samuel's smile boring into the back of my neck.

No one was meant to win this war. It existed for one purpose only: to turn a sovereign nation into a no man's land of burnt schoolhouses and decapitated nurses, mine-littered roads and unharvested crops. In line with the Total Strategy coming out of RENAMO's paymasters in the Transvaal, nothing was to replace what had been destroyed. And just as South Africa had no real intention of letting RENAMO take over Mozambique, so RENAMO's bandits had no intention of handing Goliata over to Samuel Calange.

A couple of weeks before a regrouped RENAMO launched their second big offensive in the region, it dawned on Sam – much, much too late – just who he had been breaking bread with.

'Please come with me to the feast,' he said to me, not for the first time. This time, however, his invitation was not a piece of public show. He had knocked on my door in private, and after dark. 'Please.'

I had been issued a freshly thatched brick blockhouse, more or less intact after hurried repairs, right on the border between the cane town and the cement town. It was a prime location, so Naphiri had given me an AK-47 for protection. The rifle hung off one arm, my lantern swung from the other, as I swaggered back into the living room, leading Sam inside. If he could play-act, so could I.

I was surprised that Sam was moving around the village after sundown. Apart from the obvious risk of attack or a mugging, it was too easy to trip and break your neck on an overcast night like this. Though we were in the middle of the village, no light showed. Even the household fires you'd normally expect to burn on after supper-time were snuffed out early, in case the unwelcome dinner guests hiding out in the bush got ideas. Myself, I kept the windows shuttered tight. To be walking around at night, Sam had to be feeling very desperate.

'Please,' he said.

It was the usual deal. You turn up to the meal with a contribution of food, clothing, money: tribute, in other words.

'No,' I told him. I knew I had him over a barrel. The rebels were relying on him and his friends to bring influential villagers over to their side. The price of failure was likely to be high. I set the lantern down in the middle of the floor and sat myself down in the room's only cane chair – I had been over the Malawi border and bought it for myself – with my AK-47 across my knees.

There was a lot of bluster to begin with. Sam's appeal to nostalgia – to the imaginary 'good old days' before FRELIMO's uppity socialists took over – had served him in good stead in the past, and old habits die hard.

'I think it is important – and I feel sure that an educated man like yourself will agree with me – that we should have the ear of the rebels, if only to barter for our own safety.' All week, stories had been flying around town: how the bandits were increasing in numbers; how they had hammered their way into Yelena Mlokote's house, brazenly, without fear of resistance; that they had taken everything of value away with them: goats, clothes, batteries, even a mirror in a metal frame.

'Stop,' I said. He had become almost painful to watch. 'Whose house, did you say?'

'What?'

I couldn't conceal my irritation. 'The goats and the mirror. Whose house?'

Sam blinked. 'Yelena Mlokote's. What? Do you know her?'

'I thought you said someone else,' I said, waving the matter away. I strung him on a while longer – *Tomorrow night, did you say? What should I bring? What should I wear?* – before kicking him out of my house.

3

The next day I borrowed Naphiri's bicycle and cycled out past parched fields of cassava and pineapples and neglected, overgrown shacks to Yelena Mlokote's house.

By local standards, it was a mansion: a brick house surrounded by cashew trees and mangoes; a paved path lined with herbs. It was isolated, though; much further from town than I had expected. There were other houses nearby, sprawled under the shade of the jacaranda trees, but most had been boarded up. Her neighbours had left, she told me, afraid of what RENAMO might do to them if they stayed. They were sleeping rough now, under the few surviving porticoes of Goliata's cement town.

'And you?'

Yelena shrugged.

We were sitting in her kitchen. Walls of wood and iron sheeting; a cement sink for washing clothes – 'only that I still go to the bathing pool to wash my clothes, so that I meet people.' The weird, finicky rhythms of her Chichewa disguised, for a moment, the fact that she had not answered my question.

She didn't bear much resemblance to her father. Until we got talking, I couldn't be sure it was her. She was attractive, in an ironed-out sort of way. She was pushing forty by then, and the recent famine had taken its toll.

She was damned if she was going to be kicked out of her home.

'They took my radio,' she said. 'I had three goats, they took the goats.'

'For God's sake,' I said.

'They went away,' she shrugged.

'They'll be back.'

'Samuel Calange is talking to them. The *curandeiros* are with them now, treating their injured. They are hungry, out in the bush.'

'What are you saying?'

She was doing the only thing she could do. She was trying to come to terms.

'Look,' I said. 'There's room in my house for you. There's room with me.'

The clumsy fixes of white men: she shook her head and smiled.

It was wash-day, so we walked together to the stream that had once fed Goliata's municipal bathing pool.

While Yelena slapped the screwed whip of a *capulana* against a rock, to agitate it clean, and her baby boy Mateu, indifferent to us both, lay on his rush mat, waving his arms about as though conducting something difficult and modern, I sat dangling my legs over the edge of the old bathing pool, thinking through the chances that had led me to this place and moment. This opportunity.

The pool was dry. The pipe supplying it with stream-water had been smashed, and the pool's every decorative blue tile – fish, shellfish, seaweed, sailing boats, windmills – had been cracked. The bandits had demolished the changing blocks, too, which had once preserved the modesty of the planter and his children, the hairdresser and his family, the driving instructor and his wife: the petty white elite of a bygone Goliata. So that now, sitting here, we had a clear view down the hill, past the stubs of the changing blocks, right across Goliata, to the brown scar of the airstrip – and further yet, the air was so clean and clear today, over the Malawian border to the Mulanje plateau.

I watched Yelena wrap up her son in the *capulana*, which was quite dry now, from the fierce sun of that morning, and seeing her tie her son to her, I noticed the trembling of her hands. She gave Mateu a look of hopeless yearning.

'What is it?'

She shrugged. 'I am remembering a friend of mine,' she said.

I waited for more.

'Come with me,' she said. 'We will visit her grave. I like to visit her, to talk to her.'

She led me down the hill to the cemetery. By day there was nothing to fear. In one part of the cemetery there were stones raised for those whose manner of dying left no body to be buried. Yelena had raised such a stone for her husband:

JOSEPH ALEXANDER MLOKOTE
1951–1983

His dates saddened me. 'He was so young.' He must still have been a teenager when Yelena married him.

'He died driving a truck along the corridor,' she said.

Behind his stone lay a plot full of tiny graves, which I assumed at first must be the graves of stillbirths. Yelena corrected me: 'They're for limbs,' she said.

The graves contained legs. Bits of feet. Knuckles of bone and sinew. There were so many little graves, so many piecemeal burials, I wondered where the cripples were. I had not see them on the streets.

'They work their fields,' Yelena told me, leading me to a larger mound of earth: an adult burial. 'What else can they do?'

'What about the mines?'

'What about them?'

I wondered if any cripples visited their own graves.

Then Yelena led me to the grave of her friend. There was no headstone. 'Kesi,' she said, to the mound, 'this is Saul. He was a friend of my father.'

I looked at Yelena. She smiled at me. 'I do not know why he has come to visit us, but I can guess.'

I had expected to find her unprepared for our meeting; to have the advantage over her.

'Your friend,' I said, so as not to show the hit, 'who was she?'

'A nurse,' she said. 'A citizen. According to her husband, she was six months pregnant when the *matsangas* attacked.'

I steeled myself. I was becoming familiar with the nature of these stories.

'They tore it out of her womb and threw it into her hearth-fire. Saul.' She took my hand.

From the swaddled shadows of her capulana, Yelena's son blinked at me.

'You know,' she said, 'I received your postcard. I know what brought you here. I know what it is you think I did.'

She walked me out of the cemetery and back up the hill to her house, and, as we climbed, she told me the tale of her brief, fatal involvement in world affairs.

'It was never supposed to go off,' she told me.

A devil's alliance of PIDE men and tribalists opposed to RENAMO were already planning Katalayo's assassination. When news of the attempt filtered through to FRELIMO, Yelena, Jorge's alienated daughter, saw an opportunity to play *agent provocateur* and make a name for herself within the movement. Playing up her alienation from her father, she sent the cabal the encyclopaedias I had sent her, and gave them the idea for the book bomb.

'You did this alone, of course.'

Yelena sighed. Apparently I was being boorish. 'FRELIMO is a big organization. There are factions. Groups.'

This faction of hers figured it would be an easy matter to follow the British seaman entrusted with the device; easy to lift it from him in Lourenço Marques; easy to arrange its disarmament at the hands of an old KGB operative, who for long months now had been twiddling his thumbs in some redundant field station in Lourenço Marques.

'So you were working for the Russians?'

Easy, once the bomb had been disarmed, to deliver it to her father: a present as harmless as it was terrifying.

I couldn't believe what I was hearing. 'Why on earth would you attempt anything so stupid?'

Why? Because, once Jorge Katalayo had *survived* his assassination, FRELIMO's leadership – this was the theory – would have been shaken into a more radical agenda and a more positive alignment with the Soviet Union.

Katalayo's daughter spoke with the melancholy of someone who, after years of interior struggle, has made peace with herself.

The bomb should have been intercepted, she told me. It should have been re-routed and defused, before ever being delivered. Only that, in her haste to get away while her mark was sleeping, the woman they'd hired to steal the bomb from the British sailor forgot where she'd written down the KGB man's address. After an hour's fruitless wandering, in a panic, she abandoned the parcel on a park bench –

– where, seeing the package, an elderly Portuguese man (this is what Yelena wanted me to believe) picked it up. He recognized the address, he lived out that way himself, and that evening he stopped by to deliver it. He must have been taken aback when the addressee turned out to be a black man. Perhaps he thought Jorge was a servant...

I could stand no more. I shut her up: 'You can't possibly know any of this.'

'Not the last part, no. We can't know how the bomb left the bench and ended up in my father's hands. The rest we know.'

'The woman who stole the parcel—'

'She was telling the truth.'

'You don't know that.'

Yelena threw up her hands. 'What is the point of this?'

'What was Jorge's address doing on the package in the first fucking place? It wasn't going in the mail.'

'What is the point?'

The point, as far as Yelena was concerned, was that the bomb was meant to fail. It was supposed to manipulate and to frighten. It was not meant to kill. She touched my hand. 'You know,' she said, 'if I could turn back time, I would.'

Well, let her have her dream of redemption. What does it matter?

From the sheetrock interior wall of a summer house, fifteen miles north of Maputo, a twisted pin untwists.

Damp plaster seals the hair-line crack, as the pin corkscrews its way out of the wall, and takes flight.

It shoots past the door to the kitchen, from which comes the faint but unmistakable smell of leaking bottle-gas – one of those signature smells, inseparable from evenings spent in holiday cottages – past bookshelves stacked with Franz Fanon, Georgette Heyer and yearbooks stretching back a dozen years: *Who's Who in World Trade*; UN Factbooks for this region and that; missionary society directories. The books sit up as the pin passes them, at a speed approaching that of sound, accelerating all the time. The books straighten themselves, lining up on the white-painted shelves. From the second shelf up, a second pin unwinds from out the spine of *The Wretched of the Earth*, and, coming free, flies off.

And another, and another. From out of the twill of the rag rug they come, hurling themselves into the air. From out of the walls and the ceiling. From out of the back of the room's centrepiece. Someone's head: unrecognizable.

Outside, the sand-lions are undigging their traps. Puffs of sand gather and cone in the air, then fling themselves into the hole where each spider frantically unburies itself before the retreating tide. On BOAC's night run from Dar to Nairobi, grain factors and irrigation specialists, bankers and fertilizer salesmen, carefully unblend the tonic from their gin.

The sun has unrisen beneath Zanzibar. To the gathering roar – a great re-threading – shavings of aluminium wire rise in a cloud above the sand. The lethal cloud unshreds everything in its wake, leaf and dragonfly and even bird. It hurls itself at the broken window – and sticks there, blasted and fused into a tight, mosquito-resistant grille, by a flash of pinkish light.

The bird unnotices the dragonfly.

In the room, at its precise mathematical centre, the unrecognizable head is repacking itself. The soft innards refold, suck up and re-smear their spilt lubrication; spit out stray shavings and turnings into the ever-faster, ever-hotter air. The head trembles. Vertebrae click and snap together. The meat within them turns from red to white. Sparks fly.

Julius at the door of his apartment in his slippers: 'What now, Jorge?'
A letter from the Phelps Stokes fund.
His brand-new American girlfriend naked.
His brand-new American girlfriend getting naked.
Samora. Marcelino. Alberto. Joaquim.
The head is not yet whole. It contains many minds.
A to K and L to Z.
The white man's magic!
General laughter.
'And you know, we have a paper shortage here.'

The head and body, of a piece once more, rise up: uncanny forward roll. The head snaps forward, a final, sickening crunch as linkage reconnects, vessels rezip themselves and the eyes, regaining their light, spit nails into the air, firing them with the force of bullets at the parcel there, on the desk before the window.

Within the parcel, a pinkish light.

The man – it is a man – crouches forward, and the chair tucks itself up under him. He reaches for the open box, and the pinkish light within; the smell of plastique.

The window mesh zips itself shut.

Jorge Katalayo sits at his desk, bathed in light.

The light unfingers his eyes, and his final thoughts form.

He knows what this is.

They offered him the north. Let's draw a line, they said. FRELIMO sits above the line, the Portuguese sit south – where all the money is.

So history repeats itself, he thought. Tragedy in Korea; farce in Vietnam; in Mozambique: pantomime.

He told them no. No north and south. No black and white. No rich half and poor half. All his life he has been sealing what should never have been split.

Dr Julius Nyrere in his slippers – they met at the UN – 'What now, Jorge?'

They talked till dawn. Geneva, Stockholm, Kensington Park. The money there for them, the friendly faces – the easy handshakes and their ruinous consequences. How many old friends lived their lives now behind tinted windows, gun-toting relations and foreign contracts?

We kept each other strong, Julius. Together, we kept our hands by our sides.

A Chinese delegate congratulated us on our self-reliant approach to revolution; on our belief in our own people's capacity for autonomous change.

We sent him away, too.

A life spent piecing together what should never have been split. What I could never get that oaf Kavandame to understand.

Kavandame, Mozambique's great resistance leader, now gone cap-in-hand – this according to yesterday's phone call – to Cabo Delgado's fascist governor: *Please sir, let me have my square of earth!*

As if clearing the whites out of his personal back yard will make a difference. Prick, thinks Jorge Katalayo, closing the book he has been sent, and the pink fire withdraws, unblackening his hands.

How funny, how apposite, that it should come in two volumes. That nice boy's present. Dictionaries do, of course. A to K and L to Z. We split things for convenience, then we mislay the half we need. Not a profound flaw. Not a complex human condition. We just bungle things.

Where's the cap to this pen?

Black and white. A split as deep as language. A split on which his early life was built.

'After my father died, my mother said to me: You must learn the white man's magic.'

He thinks: I wish to God I'd never come up with that line.

White man's magic! It's not even true. He'd been nervous – first time in America, big opportunity, the Phelps Stokes fund giving him a shot at the education the Portuguese authorities had tried their damnedest to deprive him of. Even to the point of a PIDE interrogation. *'You vill say uz vot you bin tot!'*

Makes me sound like an elf, he thinks, irritated, tying the string around the box. Wondering what's inside.

His brand-new American girlfriend is taking her clothes off.

His brand-new American girlfriend calls from the bedroom: 'Don't be long.'

Jorge at his desk: 'Just want to see what this is.'

His brand-new American girlfriend: 'Now?'

Jorge: 'Sure.'

His brand-new American girlfriend is on her way to the bedroom: 'You coming to bed?'

This is the house owned by a foreign woman, a friend of Julius Nyrere, where Jorge Katalayo comes in secret, under the very noses of the Portuguese, alone or with his girlfriend, to read, to write his speeches, to swim in the shallows and watch the herons and the bee-catchers. To think. Sometimes, when he can bear it, to remember his wife; which is, of course, to remember what his daughter, tiny and frightened and told what to do, did to his wife; and from there to remember what a ruin it all is, beyond hope of consolation, beyond the healing powers of any girlfriend, beyond the combined healing power of all the girlfriends in America, or even the touch of his grown daughter's hand, as they each grope blindly for a forgiveness neither can provide.

A box of books arrives.

*

Yelena's son was fast asleep by the time we reached the house. Carefully, she tucked him into his wicker crib, then went into the kitchen to make a pot of tea. She set the tray down before me. As she poured, she said, 'I'm glad you answered the call. I mean I'm glad that you're here. That you're helping us. That you came to be a *cooperante*.'

I said, 'The main reason I came was to find you. You hid yourself well.'

She sat opposite me. 'And now you've found me?'

'I don't suppose I was the only person upset by what happened.' If she could be suave, so could I.

'No. I don't suppose you are.' She was not afraid. 'Do you know I have been officially pardoned?'

'Does that make you feel more secure?'

She shook her head. 'No.'

Well, let her have her tragic mistake. What did it matter what she had meant to do? True, FRELIMO had slid more under Soviet influence, but who was to say whether the paranoiacs running South Africa would have treated their upstart neighbour any differently? It wasn't as if the Soviets ever achieved much in the region. They didn't even take Mozambique into their development zone, and the materials they exported in the name of aid were shoddier than even our own meagre home production. So really, in all honesty, what did any of it matter?

'I'm glad,' she said, 'that I've had the chance to tell you what really happened.' She imagined she had given me a gift. These days she'd probably say that she was 'offering me closure'. I was spared that, at least.

I said, 'You know I don't believe you.'

She shrugged.

'Do you want to know why?'

I told her what Jorge Katalayo had told me about her mother.

'He's off gallivanting across Europe, leaving you and Memory to rot in some *aldeamento*. He never mentions you. He has girlfriends. He makes one inflammatory speech too many, and suddenly – half a world away – there's a gun being pressed into your hands. Your mother's lying there on the floor, crippled and bleeding and screaming.'

'You don't know this.'

'I think you blamed him for that, just as much as he blamed you.'

'You're not one of the family. You don't have the right—'

'He made a speech once. About how the men and women of this country hate each other. You see, he understood. This is my gift to you. This is what I came here to tell you. He knew what was coming and he knew, when it came, it would be from you.'

'Samuel Calange says you're plotting to kill him.' I had thought our exchange was done, but I was wrong. As I was about to pedal away, Yelena had this gift for me.

'What?'

Yelena shrugged. 'He says you paid Redson to stage an accident with the earth-mover.'

I didn't know what to say.

'I wouldn't worry about it if I were you. There's nothing you can do.' She closed her door.

Now it was my turn to be creeping around town at sundown, looking for reassurance.

Naphiri's response? 'Never mind. Anyway, there's nothing you can do.'

President Chissano nodded glum agreement from half-a-dozen identical wall posters. Bleeding through the cheap, absorbent paper, like a bad dream resurfacing: 'RENAMO MOTO'.

The party administrator's office boasted seats now, of a sort – old pinto bean sacks stuffed with grass. Together, we demolished a half-bottle of Powers – Malawian cane spirit – paid for with the villagers' hard-earned *kwacha*. Another twist of the Goliata economic cycle.

'How much trouble am I in?' I had a creeping horror of the rural rumour mill. I had heard too many stories, from *cooperantes* and others, of people being driven into the bush on the strength of some stupid calumny.

'Trouble? None at all,' said Naphiri, and grinned. 'If your plan succeeds.'

She screwed the cap back on the bottle. 'First watch,' she reminded me. I fetched my gun and traipsed up the stairs onto the roof. The Italian's earth-mover was kept under constant twenty-four-hour armed guard.

Three hours on my own in the dark was more than enough time to convince me that I might be in serious trouble. Naphiri was complacent, full of crazy, romantic dreams about raising Goliata from the rubble: *All these streets will be cleared!* Sam on the other hand was a clever and experienced provincial politician.

It was a mistake solely to associate Naphiri with the party, Sam with the *matsangas*. If Sam was afraid, then there was something for us all to be afraid of.

Yelena and Naphiri had both told me there was nothing to be done. Of course there was something I could do and, once I had been relieved from my post, I did it.

4

Together, Samuel Calange and I made our silent way, under cover of night, towards our assignation. The crocodile of men following us must have made a strange, naive spectacle: fathers seeking news of missing sons; sons who, seeing the way things were going in this war, were thinking of performing a vanishing act of their own. All of us huddled close against the ghouls and vampires who, they say, haunt the graveyards here, so that a meal eaten in such a place is a kind of Hallowe'en.

Sam and I prepared the *braii*. When I had gone to see him and agreed to this meeting, something had passed between us: mutual cowardice, nothing more, but it was a bridge between us now, and it made talking easier. Sam told me how, when he lost Goliata to Naphiri and the FRELIMO government, he had expected to find a role organizing the political opposition – and while Rhodesia had control of RENAMO, that was still what RENAMO at least claimed to be. Now, though, under Johannesburg's 'Total Strategy', nothing was making very much sense. RENAMO wasn't even an army any more. More of a wrecking crew, commanded by *soldados simples*, grunts, amphetamine psychotics, hopping-mad buggers with silver marbles for eyes and muscular sprinters' thighs. 'So where is all this bouncing powder coming from? I am asking. Are they dishing it out like Navy rum now? Or dropping sackfuls from the air? Have they taken to dusting the jungle?'

I wasn't in much of a mood to discuss politics. The disfigured faces of the children I'd been teaching had taught me all I needed to know about this war. The villagers who had accompanied us had gathered nervously together a few yards off, where the hill fell away a little, giving them a view of Goliata's cane town. Sam called them to eat. They came and sat, his obedient flock. It was a strange reprise of Naphiri's feast and, for a moment or two, the similarities helped me tune out our surroundings: the gravestones, and beyond them, the little unmarked graves.

When they bothered to turn up, the forces of the *Resistência Nacional Moçambicana* proved a disappointing lot. The three adults wore burlap sacks over their heads to protect their identities. The effect was more pathetic than frightening. Half a dozen boys accompanied them; not one looked more than twelve. Presumably they had been press-ganged from other towns. They glared at us with a ferocity and a cynicism so extreme it looked rehearsed.

'Where are your students?' one of the hooded figures shouted. It took me a moment to realize he was talking to me. 'Why didn't you bring your students?'

Before I could answer, the hooded figure to his left piped up: 'His boots! He is wearing boots! He is in the militia!'

'They're my own boots,' I said.

'Where are your students? Why are your students not here?'

I was – absurdly enough – reminded of my mother. *('Have you done your university work? Have you much university work to do?')*

'Is this all?' The third ghoul was pawing over the food we had brought: flat baskets piled with roast chicken, *nsima* and relish, mangoes, tomatoes: 'What is this shit?' He squatted before the feast we had laid, his fingers playing over the dishes as though plucking some big, complicated musical instrument. 'Where is the meat? We told you to bring us *meat*.' His fingers were bony and pale: a skeleton's fingers.

'Where are the minds you have poisoned, teacher?'

I tried to shrug. The muscles wouldn't respond. I was shaking very badly.

One of the bandit children turned to the hooded figures, weeping with frustration.

'Can I kill him?'

'We don't want blood tonight,' said the tallest of the hooded men.

'Please. Just one of them.' There were tears running down his cheeks. 'Just him.' He pointed at me.

One by one, the villagers were running off. They knew what this was. They could see what it was turning into. I watched them kicking up these crazy zig-zags between the monuments, the wooden crosses; they were afraid of being shot in the back. Soon only Sam and I were left. I don't know about Sam, maybe he stayed because he felt responsible. I know why I remained: I didn't have the courage to run.

The boy begged and begged. 'Please let me kill him.'

'No.'

'Please.'

'You can take his boots.'

He stalked up to me.

'Give me your boots,' he said.

I smiled at him, the way you smile at a big, angry dog.

From off his back he pulled an AK half as tall as he was. 'Take off your boots,' he said, his finger tight on the trigger. He drove the muzzle into my windpipe. I grabbed it.

'Let go of the gun,' he screamed.

I raised my hands.

The boy pushed the cold muzzle into my throat a second time, much, much harder. 'If he doesn't give me his boots, can I shoot his head?'

'Of course.'

'What is this shit?' screamed the figure playing with our food. He got up into the middle of the feast and trampled it. He worked his way around every plate until he came to Sam. He did a little dance before Goliata's prospective mayor, kicking gobs of *nsima* porridge into his face. 'Is this all you brought? We will kill them all, you piece of shit! We will crush their skulls!'

A couple of the kids started shooting into the air.

Sam opened his mouth to speak, to excuse himself, to apologize.

With a striker's precision, the hooded man kicked him in the mouth. Sam's head snapped back like a boxer's punch-ball. Bones snapped.

I got my boots off at last. The child kicked them away from me and lifted the AK off my neck.

Sam scrambled to his feet. He staggered about the cemetery, groaning, his hands under his jaw, holding it together.

The child adjusted his grip on the gun and brought it down on my head. He was about ten years old but the gun was heavy. My whole skull flexed. I must have passed out for a couple of seconds. Something wet landed in my ear. It felt as though the blow had torn my scalp away, above my right eye.

There was blood in my eyes, over my face and in my mouth. I had bitten through my tongue. I wiped the blood out of my eyes and caught a glimpse of the boy before the red flow blinded me again. He had rejoined his friends. He had his gun in one hand, my boots in the other. I wiped his spit from out of my ear.

Far behind us, down the hill, in the town, came a scream, then some shouting, and another scream, then some children screaming. The sound didn't stop. It swelled.

The feast in the cemetery had only ever been a ploy, to separate us. By reducing the number of menfolk in the town, they had made Goliata easier to attack.

I took off my shirt, wadded it up and pressed it tenderly to my head. Unable to see, I was forced to listen. There was very little gunfire in the cane town. Whatever the *matsangas* were doing, they were doing it with knives and clubs. The villagers' screams were running into each other now: one long, continuous death-squeal. With a loud concussion that forced my eyes open, an orange fireball rose above the town. I blinked the stickiness away and stood up. Beside the fire, muzzle-flashes illuminated the roof of Naphiri's concrete blockhouse. The earth-mover was on fire. I watched the rooftop guns sputter, and thought of the miserable, dull nights I had spent on that roof, armed with a gun I hated and did not know how to use. One by one, the guns went out. Soon, smoke was pouring from the windows of the blockhouse.

Sam, wailing, blood pouring between his fingers, staggered towards the brow of the hill, fell against a gravestone and crumpled.

The hooded men wandered casually over to him. One grabbed him by the hair and pulled his head over the edge of the stone. Another sat on his legs, pinning him there. The third took out a machete and chopped his neck open. Then, muttering, blaming his tools, he tried to use his machete like a saw. The boys gathered round to watch.

No one was paying any attention to me. I edged away. The men at the gravestone separated and Sam fell to the ground. His head was still attached to his shoulders, but only barely. In the light of the *braii* we had lit together, preparing for the feast, Sam blinked at me. His tongue flapped uselessly. 'Gah,' he said.

They brought him over to me. I turned to run, trod with my bare feet on a sharp stone, fell over and grazed my knees. They dropped Sam in front of me. The boy who had taken my boots fired a clip into Sam's neck to loosen the linkage there. The sound tore through my wounded head.

Once they got it off, they played football with it a while, then passed it to me. 'Carry it,' they said.

By then it didn't look very much like Sam, or a head, or anything.

I picked it up.

'Watch this.'

. Two of us ran away in the night, another was shot trying to escape.

'Look at this.'

Three collapsed under the loads they'd been given to carry and were shot through the head where they lay. The *matsangas* used the seventh, Naphiri, for demonstration purposes, working at her strenuously until long after she was dead.

'Pay attention.'

We learned very quickly to obey the *matsangas*.

'Watch. Look at this.'

Whatever else it was, it was undoubtedly an education. Following their attack on the town on 15 October 1984, RENAMO soldiers had walked sixteen prisoners of war out of Goliata. Six weeks later, the nine of us who survived reached our journey's end.

The camp was not isolated. There were other RENAMO camps nearby, and even villages. Soldiers in misbegotten headgear rode downhill into camp on motorbikes, churned the site to a muddy slough and sped off again. Peasants walked uphill into camp, bearing food. Incredibly, once they had delivered their supplies, they were permitted to walk out again. The women weren't always so lucky, but among the girls forcibly 'made women' by the bandits, some seemed to have won back their freedom. They walked out of camp in the morning, and back in again at sundown. I wondered after a while whether I too might not be free to go. They were not even teaching me how to kill any more. Most of my days I spent with about a dozen others in a chicken coop, my hands behind my head. At sundown, we were allowed to take our hands off our heads. An hour after that, we were allowed to lie down. At first light, they made us kneel again and after a breakfast of *nsima*, with occasionally a relish of turnips or rotten fish, they told us to put our hands on our heads again. It was as if, after the initial excitements, our captors had run out of imagination. After a couple of months, they weren't even making us kneel.

I leaned my forehead against the wire of the chicken coop, looking out. No one seemed to be paying the least attention to us. Maybe we were not prisoners at all. It might be all in our heads, now. It was the logic of the place.

It was not too difficult a puzzle, working out where we were. Only Gorongosa boasted so many RENAMO militia. Mount Gorongosa was RENAMO's headquarters in Mozambique, a mountain fastness the overstretched FRELIMO military could not possibly overrun, and dead in the centre of the country, within easy striking range of the Beira Corridor. Only the Corridor could throw up the sort of spoils carried through our camp, uphill, to RENAMO's officer elite. Truck-loads of flour, crates of batteries, barrels of oil. Soldiers rattled back and forth in jeeps, in Toyota trucks, on motorbikes, on bicycles, even. They wore uniforms stolen from dead government troops. The uniforms often had tears in them, and terrible bloodstains. The soldiers grinned and strutted in the dead men's clothes, showing off their 'wounds'.

The RENAMO command proper rarely came down from the mountain, and preferred to communicate by radio. They surrounded themselves with camps of bandits. The bandits, in turn, buffered themselves with kidnapped villagers. The displaced villagers must in their turn have come to some unspecified agreement with the locals living in the shadow of the mountain, because everybody on the mountain got fed sooner or later.

Every few weeks or so a new batch of soldiers would come dancing into the camp and slash at their chests with knives – *zsa! zsa! zsa!* – and a man on stilts and a stylized leopard mask rendered them immune to bullets by splashing their wounds with a secret herbal preparation. Men without hands would enter camp to beg from the men who had mutilated them. The old man who fed the chickens had a scar the width of my thumb running right across his throat. A scalped girl shambled from one side of the compound to the other with her broom, intent, it seemed, on sweeping away the very foundations of the houses.

Then, just as I was getting comfortable, they moved me down the hill and I was placed in one of the villages nestling in the shadow of the mountain. Rather than raze it, RENAMO had decided to control it. I limped after the village's *régulo*, up to a drab cement blockhouse in a dusty, unshaded lot behind the marketplace.

I asked, 'What is this?'

He blinked up at me as though I were stupid. 'It's a school,' he said. He showed me inside.

On the desk at the front of the immaculate room sat an unopened box. 'What's that?' I said.

The *régulo* shrugged. No one told him anything. I opened the box. It was full of brand-new textbooks, printed in Maputo, ferried north at great expense, bound at one time for a place like Goliata. The books were another of RENAMO's spoils, plundered from some hijack on the Corridor.

I studied them. I turned to the *régulo*, incredulous: 'You want me to teach from these?'

The *régulo* shrugged. 'They're books, aren't they?'

Certainly they were books. History books, printed in Sweden, edited by an academic friendly to FRELIMO's socialist cause. There were whole chapters on Marx, Lenin, the evils of apartheid and the glory of the anti-colonial struggle. There was a foreword by FRELIMO's first president and chief political martyr, Jorge Katalayo.

I held my tongue.

Every day for the next seven years, RENAMO sent their children marching into school to have me teach them about Marx, Lenin, the evils of apartheid and the anti-colonial struggle. In all that time, no one ever questioned me or stopped me. Not the *régulo*. Not his minders. Not the dignitaries (RENAMO's honoured guests) who came by, once in a while, to witness the renaissance of learning in this liberated, liberalized, free-market corner of capitalist Mozambique.

They had never met a teacher before. They figured I knew what I was doing.

GLASS

1

The walls of the old iron bathtub rise around her, white and smutted. It is early Tuesday morning, 30 August 1983, and Stacey is getting ready for the funeral of her last grandfather, her mother's father, Harry Conroy.

She lies in the bath, staring down at herself, lost in contemplation of the way the water has split her in two. There is the upper part of her: her knees, her chest and her head, of course, mustn't forget her unseen head; this is the tanned, air-breathing part. Then there is the other part, the bigger part by mass, her back, her bum, her feet and halfway up her calves: the pallid, aquatic part.

She lies there, a little shaky. She is fourteen years old and they are burying her grandfather, the man who stepped in when Mo was incarcerated, who for eight years has been a solid presence in her life. But she is fascinated, none the less, by the way she can will this change in her nature, transforming parts of herself by lowering and raising them in the water.

She dips her hand in, slowly, watching her fingers tilt as they enter this other world. It looks as though her fingers are broken. She knows this is refraction because they have been doing this in class. Light entering water changes course. Light always takes the quickest path, and water, being dense, is slow compared to air. So light changes direction, bends, seeking the quickest way through the water. Light is clever.

Her body is too gross a thing, too meaty and massive, to finesse the water this way. It lumbers through air and water the same, insensate, especially now that the bath has cooled to blood heat. Her fingers can barely detect the difference between the air and the water – only this little tingle as her skin passes from one medium into the other. This trembling line like a blade held sensually, edge on, to the skin.

Her mother calls: 'Are you out of the bath yet, Stace?'

'Hang on!' Stacey shakes out of her reverie and reaches for the soap. Her mum says she spends too much time in the bath. It is one of those things that mothers say, but today is not a day to argue.

Stacey remembers how when she was little, for a special treat, Mo would let the bathwater run until it reached all the way up to her neck. She remembers looking down and thinking: this blue-green thing. It seemed amazing that this swimmy alien body was actually attached to her head.

Her name is Stacey Conroy. This is the name on her birth certificate, her mother's maiden name, the name she goes by at school. She does not like the name, and in her TV work she does not have to use it.

Stacey appears in advertisements, and has been doing so, off and on, since she was about six years old. Money has not been a motivation; Harry's wrestling promotion has expanded through syndication to the point where the two suits he employed to run it full-time don't even bother taking a salary any more. Stacey's own stock options – Christmas and birthday gifts from her granddad, held in trust until her twenty-first – will see her through college and long beyond.

Deborah, her mum, has not been pushy, either. If anything she has tried too hard to manage her daughter's expectations, discouraging her keenness for the camera. The push has come from Stacey herself. She loves dressing up. She has grown up among costumes, among capes and masks, the whirr of sewing machines, the sour flop-sweat smell of trailers and toilets and dressing rooms. She knows, and can identify by smell, every one of a hundred different make-ups, alcohol rubs, unguents and deep-heat preparations; let loose among the caravans on fight night, she has been found, come evening's end, wrapped in bandages like a mummy, in sequinned gloves and a padded sparring helmet several tens of sizes too big for her four-year-old head, weeping with frustration because she has got herself inextricably tangled in some visiting fighter's Stars and Stripes cape.

'The theatre is in my blood.' She says this in front of her bedroom mirror, wondering at this body that has always daunted her, like a boisterous pet she has no idea how to care for, this body, growing in maturity, which seems capable of no end of practical jokes, hair, farts, spots on the end of her nose.

Deborah comes into her bedroom without knocking. This is bad enough, let alone to be caught like this in front of the mirror, not even fully dressed.

'Are you OK, sweetheart?' Deborah wants her daughter to give her a very big hug. This could be made easier on two counts: mum could just relax a bit and stop pretending that She is Comforting her Daughter ('How are you feeling, sweetheart?' 'Are you holding up, pet?' 'Come here, petal, come on, poor lost lamb': all this in the last half-hour); second, she could take the goddamn chopsticks out of her *hair, agh,* that nearly went in my *eye...*

Deborah's kimono is black, or started out that way, though the black is hard to see beneath sequinned dragons and lotus flowers and thewed, half-naked samurai. Her face is panstick white, her eyeliner is red – art following grieving nature. Her fingernails, three-inch stick-ons, will have to wait till they get to St Patrick's because she still has to drive. They live out of Miami now, in Belle Glade, on the southern shores of Lake Okeechobee, well out of the operating range of the funeral home's cars. Deborah claims to be looking forward to the drive, that it will steady her nerves.

No one passing them is going to imagine they are on their way to a funeral. Deborah is dressed as a geisha; Stacey's own get-up is relatively conventional, but her wig is green, and Ben Donoso's charm is hanging on a silver chain around her neck. Pray it holds together for the day.

'Come along then, my poor brave chicken,' says Deborah, releasing her at last. Deborah is running out of endearing animals. In the driveway, waiting for her, a stab at her own father's brand of heartiness: 'Hurry up there, monkeybrains.'

Stacey's surname is Conroy. The name lacks conviction. It lacks truthfulness. It does not capture who she is. It carries no echo of the man she considers her real father, the man her mother married and visited in jail every month until he was released; who filled her first conscious memories, ages two to five, with light, and now is vanished, breaking his parole: the felon Mo Chavez.

In the car, Deborah winds down the window and lights up a joint. She wouldn't normally drive while smoking but it is getting late, the service is at two and she needs time to put her nails on. Also there is the question of dosage and timing: she is fifteen minutes late. Since 1969, when she and Mo stumbled upon its happy side-effects, Deborah has been using cannabis to self-medicate her epilepsy. Fourteen years of trial and error have taught her to respect her body and its rhythms: in excess, or taken at the wrong time of day, her smokes can trigger the very seizures they normally suppress.

Deborah maintains that Mo's marijuana runs were for her, more or less. The weekends he spent on his boat, the nights drinking with Nick Jessup, his so-called business partner; all this in the interests of Deborah's health and well-being, with no eye to the profit or the danger to himself. Stacey knows this is crap: a comfort story for a child who's missing her daddy, OK, maybe, but not a line you can expect to keep on spinning, year after year, into the child's teens. Her mother smokes regularly, it is true, but how much pot can one reasonably together woman be expected to inhale in one lifetime? Deborah forgets that Stacey was there with her in court, listening to the coastguard's testimony. When they lifted the weed out of Mo's hold, the boat rose a good two feet by the waterline.

The journey to the church has the clean lines of a proposition in mathematics: when you leave the town behind you're in farmland. The farms stop and the wetlands begin: an abrupt, engineered transition. A canalized river separates the wetlands from the suburbs. You have taken one road to get this far. The road is straight, the landscape is flat. This whole journey could be re-run in *Turbo* with virtually no loss of definition. *(Turbo* is the new Sega game in their laundromat, and Deborah thinks it weird that Stacey plays it so much.) From here the buildings rise in steps, and at a certain point – a point you have to learn is there, because there is no outward marker, no change of flavour or scene – you are in Miami.

Outside the church stands Michio Barondes, half-Japanese, half-Peruvian, the Yellow Peril, in joke-shop whiskers and a canary-yellow polyester cape, weeping into his embroidered sleeves.

The church is packed. There's Jackie Gleason, sat discreetly near the back. He must be seventy by now; his TV career has pretty much bombed but he still crops up in *Smokey and the Bandit* movies. The Mexican old-guard have turned up in their stage gear, and one or two of the home-grown boys have followed suit; Chuck Ryan, resplendent in his heel's garb, a Northwest Mounted Police parade uniform with white dress gloves, stands just inside the door to conduct the family to the front pews. Donoso the Vampyre delivers the oration, his white-face and blood-dribble ruined by tears, his thick black hair plastered down like lacquer. He leans on his best stick, the knob fashioned like a skull, red glass jewels for eyes.

Ben Donoso is a trainer now; one of the best. His fighting days are behind him. In 1980 a visiting fighter hurled him through a table. This was in the ring, a stunt both fighters had paced out a hundred, a thousand times. The table was mocked up the way it was supposed to be, each joint carefully weakened, the whole thing hefted and swung, tested for weight and balance. No one, least of all Ben, cared much about the prop's appearence. It was bright yellow, it looked good under the lights; no one, in the heat of preparation, thought to wonder what happens to linoleum veneer when it shears.

Donoso hobbles off the podium in tears. Harry was his friend, the man who used his own shirt to staunch the blood when Ben's femoral artery was severed, who rode with him in the ambulance as he faded out of consciousness, who was there with his wife and kids when he woke up. Harry funded the wrestling school he runs now, and from which he turns loose, each year, arguably the best fighters in the country; not just showman wrestlers but shootfighters, too, athletes and innovators.

Stacey hasn't seen Ben Donoso in a while. She has fond memories of him from when she was a little kid. Why else, on this day of all days, would she be wearing this weird mumbo-jumbo charm he gave her, back in Mexico? Since his accident he has not been around so much. He has the school to run. Also, things were not so easy with Grandpa. After the accident, Harry was not such an easy person to be around.

It occurs to Stacey, sat in front with a view of the coffin, that some of what she feels is relief. For a start, there is only one coffin; whereas there had definitely been more than one Grandpa, especially towards the end. There was the absent man, the man depressed by all the misfortunes he had failed to prevent: Deborah's childhood accident, Deborah's marriage, Ben's public and very bloody maiming. Then there was the smiling Harry, who was somehow worse: the man determined to shoulder every burden, prevent every misfortune, reliably accompany everyone he loved through every step of life, padding the world's every blow. The needy man. The drunk.

It's been nine years, following Mo's trial and sentence for marijuana smuggling – and, Stacey wonders, where was the snake Jessup while all this was going on? How slippy did he turn out to be, that all the shit was laid at her daddy's door? – nine years, then, since Harry stepped in to save the day, playing both father and grandfather to little Stacey. His daughter and his granddaughter were his burden, and he shouldered them gladly, dismissing every protest. He never let them down.

Ben settles into the pew a few places to the left of her, and she wonders if, sat before Harry's coffin, he feels the same secret relief she does. Ben was Harry's friend, but it must have been exhausting being friends to so many different versions of the same person. Absent Harry had no friends, had betrayed his friends, was a danger to his friends. He did not deserve them and did not know what to do with them. And needy Harry? The hospital bills, the school, could only be the tip of the iceberg: needy Harry would not have stopped there. Desperately wanting to be wanted, he was a smothering presence, his cheerful manner an unhappy, rum-fuelled fiction. No wonder Ben has been keeping his distance. Between one version of himself and another, Harry's been tearing everyone in two.

At home, at school, her name is Stacey Conroy. The name does not do justice to her Miami tan, and at the television studio, in her acting classes and on the billing for this amateur show, that student revue, Stacey uses the name she intends to adopt permanently when she is old enough, especially now that Harry is no longer around to be hurt by the change. A name to reflect her tan, her memories, hers and her mother's heart.

Stacey Chavez.

The priest's homily is rushed and nervous. Surrounded by wrestlers in wild costumes, perhaps he expects the service to climax in an eruption of spectacular comic-book violence. Stacey loves to watch the fights, not least because Deborah tries to steer her away from them.

Instead, once the service is done, everyone files meekly out of church, the men's costumes tawdry, the bodies beneath them lumpen and stiff and the worse for wear, the women thickened by childbearing, the children, in their best clothes, bored and whining, and one thought hanging over all their heads: is it over?

Have we been dreaming?

This good life: is it all over now?

The funeral tea and the wake are being held at Donoso's wrestling school, one of those white, ship-like Deco properties in Little Havana that the realtors get so excited about these days. Tables are set out front among the trees and flowerbeds. It looks like a rest home more than a place of sweat and strain – and before Harry took over the lease, this is exactly what it was.

The inside looks like some sort of political prison. A *Time* magazine photo special from darkest Latin America. Punchbags dangle from the ceiling, their khaki wrappers sweat-stained: complex, liquid patterns that lend the bags a personality. There are mats and weights. Stacey tries hefting a dumb-bell from its stand. The showers smell.

She has come to think about her grandpa, to lose some of the flipness that has been her armour and support during the service and the funeral; to cry, maybe; and to stay well away from the food Deborah has had catered in, weird English nonfoods made of filo pastry and frozen prawns and spit. Later comes the beer, the key lime pie, the hog-roast – probably in that order. Michio's sweating his guts out round the back of the property now because the kid he left in charge of his fire has let it reduce to smoulder and fizz.

She looks at herself in the wall of mirrored tiles, her hair a green cloud, her body broken, factored into neat squares. Like maps of hill country, flattened, idealized. All those damn bags of potato chips her mother kept forcing into her hands, every recess and pee break: 'Got to keep your strength up, little one.'

Throwing up comes naturally to her. She found that out in the courthouse. It was easy to do. Most of her friends at school use two fingers, three, hell, the entire hand, but she can do it with the tip of one finger: as quick and reliable as pressing an elevator button.

Her whole body trembles when she does it. Not to mention before and after. The tremble seems out of scale with the pleasure, as if her body is getting more out of it than she does. It's the same when she touches herself, and it's the same tremble she gets when she does it, if she has the patience, if she doesn't fall asleep or just get so damn bored and sore and what-really-is-the-point? She doesn't like to touch herself so much, because when it's really good it only reminds her of all the other tricks her body is playing on her.

She really ought to try and eat something, but by the time there's any real food around here, Deborah will have whisked them both through their quick-change routine and off to one damn starchy place or another for pine nuts, edible flowers and *ceviche*. Next week it'll be nuts and dried fruits from a post-Woodstock hole in the wall and the following week, God knows, some ethnic horror. One of the great things about your own sick, Stacey tells her friends, in her best, most urbane style, is the constancy of the flavour.

She walks out through the entrance hall, pausing to study the framed photographs: Harry, Harry's crew, Harry's empire: maybe this is why she cannot cry. It is virtually impossible to imagine that he is dead. There is so much evidence of him.

'Come along, little rabbit, eat a little something.'

Right by the door, there is Deborah, waiting to spring her trap. Stacey plucks a vol-au-vent from off the tray, palms the crumbly, slimy thing and secretes it, when her mother isn't looking, in the fork of a nearby tree.

Yesterday, tickling up her sick, she overdid it and hawked up blood. She didn't even know that this was possible. She wants to eat, but even if there were some real food here, she's too freaked out to put it in her mouth. After all – *blood*.

Who wants to throw up *blood*?

A man is watching the property from across the street. He is leaning against a beat-up cream Thunderbird. She spots him through the chainlink.

'Stacey!' Deborah is calling her. 'Jackie's leaving. Come say goodbye to Jackie.'

Stacey goes off to say goodbye to Jackie, and there is a little flurry as some other acquaintances take their leave. Rod Rodriguez – 'The Rod', another of Harry's early discoveries, rescued from a roadhouse outside Teponahuasco where Harry found him trading bouts for beers – is handing round the bourbon now, driving the event forward: Stacey can only imagine how things will be tonight: the wake's raucous, teary-drunk

341

conclusion. She wants to be a part of it. She deserves to be a part of it. She's *fourteen*, for heaven's sake, she needs release.

Deborah has other ideas.

Everyone who's leaving wants to say goodbye to Stacey and, by the time she returns to her tree, both man and car have gone.

2

Where Harry Conroy led, many have followed. Right now on TV a man in a black cape and mask is driving Hulk Hogan's head repeatedly into a table.

Transfixed before the screen, fingers up to the knuckle in her careful hairdo, Deborah absent-mindedly strokes the bald dent in her skull.

Following Harry's death, Deborah has returned to England with her daughter. She wants Stacey to know the old country. She also had it in the back of her mind that the schools are better here, but as things have panned out, Stacey's first love has won out over her studies; a full-time TV actress at sixteen, she does the very minimum the schoolwork regulations will allow.

Mother and daughter live together in Vauxhall, on a forgotten street, in an old Edwardian terrace house with high moulded ceilings. They have money. Deborah's stock options have seen to that, as well as the numerous financial provisions Harry made for his granddaughter. They have no attachments.

It has been a strange few years for Deborah. Out from under her father's heavy care, thirty-two years old, she had thought she might begin again, acquire a lover, travel; she even entertained a certain nostalgia for her last bid for freedom – the disastrous summer of 1968 when, smothered by her father's difficult affection, she ran away to London, just a kid, and fell in with a succession of unsuitable lovers: men who were never kind.

Four years on, 1986, she realizes that this kind of freedom is no longer possible. She is not a teenager any more. The life she has hankered for does not pertain to who she is now. Besides, the times are different. She is happy on her own, happy not to be travelling, happy to

sit and steer, as best she can, her daughter's career.

Now the Hulk has hold of the man in the black cape. He is twirling him around and around, over his head, as though he were spinning dough for a pizza. Even the very worst the world has to offer can be controlled now, with only a small loss of realism. Deborah glances at her watch and lights her joint. Although this ersatz world can never be hers, Deborah is glad Stacey lives surrounded by scenarios and mere appearances.

The Hulk is slamming the man down, head-first into the floor. The man's head connects with the sprung floor of the ring. He sprawls. He does not get up.

For her daughter's sake, Deborah will do everything she can to preserve the illusion that the world is harmless: a place of rules, prepared stories, angles and sleights of hand. Stacey knows that she used a walking frame until she was twelve years old. It is evident too that her life has been dominated by the threat of grand mal seizures. But the cause of it all, the details of the event…

To this day Stacey thinks her mum was in a road traffic accident.

Hulk Hogan stamps on his opponent's chest. Deborah expects the man in black to grab the Hulk's foot – to twist it, to rise, even as the Hulk falls. But the man does not move. A pause. Hulk Hogan steps away. Paramedics clamber into the ring and carry the man in black out on a stretcher. Impossible to tell whether this is part of the scenario or not.

Perhaps there was a time, as Stacey reached her early teens, when Deborah could have told her daughter the truth. How she had woken from a dream of God's white house to a blast of pain, trapped in the hollow metal dark of a car boot. To tell her this now – what would Stacey be able do with this information? She would only use it to psychologize her mother. To her mother's every check and word of reason: 'You only say this because of what some maniac did to you.'

How can Deborah admit her sufferings have no meaning? Her

broken skull; her stroke; her epilepsy. Her tongue bitten half away in excruciating increments, the struggle she had to prove herself a fit mother, baby Stacey so often nearly taken away from her; her husband's incarceration and subsequent disappearance; her father's slide into alcoholism, the way he punished himself to death. The fits themselves, their cruel variety. The way they cluster sometimes round her frontal lobe, twisting her moods. All the times she has sat frozen in her chair, staring into the middle distance, counting down, quite rationally and white with fear, to the end of the world.

Her daughter's early success – the speed with which the school soap *Grange Hill* has propelled her into the teen magazines and even the gossip columns – has robbed Deborah of those few moments when an adult intimacy between mother and daughter might have been possible. There is also the conviction – couched in the back of Deborah's mind, a small but certain voice like tinnitus – that she is not wrong; that the higher her daughter climbs, the more terrible the fiend will be who, with one blow of his hammer, will cast her down into the metal dark.

Hulk Hogan leaves and Captain America enters the ring with a bandaged knee. Even before he has finished acknowledging his fans, a man in a sort of beetle costume has wrestled him to the ground. When, Deborah wonders, did the world cease to be real?

She studies the girls surrounding the ring – the show's lean, muscular eye-candy in their swimsuits and cheerleader gear. It is becoming more and more difficult for her to feel easy with Stacey's looks. Even by these girls' streamlined standards, her daughter is becoming painfully thin. The columnists are whispering. Stacey and the rest of the *Grange Hill* cast are in America this week, singing 'Just Say No' for Nancy Reagan. She hopes someone's on hand to make sure Stacey eats properly.

Now the beetle is jumping up and down on the Captain's wounded knee.

Deborah will not always be here to take care of her daughter, so it is good that this new world has come to trivialize her pain. The world is

nanny now. Watching these choreographed atrocities, Deborah has convinced herself that this is how her daughter lives these days: the world scripting every line for her; weakening every table; padding every hammer.

Hands held behind her back to thrust her small bust against the cotton of her white school blouse, Stacey kneels on the tiled floor of the players' toilet cubicle and lets her co-star Darren slide his already rock-hard cock between her teeth.

An over-achiever in all things, she takes him all the way to the back of her throat, then, pulling back, she lifts his penis, pressing it against her face as she tongues his balls with a rapacity that is frankly frightening: he wilts.

It is Darren's dick in her face, but neither of them is in any doubt that Stacey Chavez is out to pleasure herself. She is known for this kind of thing, this athletic approach, as if she has something to prove. It does not take much to make Darren hard again. She dry-kisses the vein running along his shaft, pulls his foreskin back and tongues around the groove, then takes him in again. Darren thrusts a little against the roof of her mouth, unsure how much of this she will let him get away with. Stacey, determined to Win, to ruin him for all the others, grabs his hands, presses them to the back of her head and keeps them there, her hands on his, urging him to fuck her face.

The tiles are cold against her knees; her sensible school shoes pinch her feet. There is indignity in this, and perversity too, dressed as the schoolchild she never was; and Darren, in grey jumper and school tie, baby-faced Darren, at twenty playing fourteen-year-old heroin addict Biff McBain.

This American tour rides on the back of Biff's plot-line, for its poignancy has captured the imagination of a drug-paranoid world. Yesterday, at the White House, they sang for Nancy Reagan – Nancy's big on anti-drugs. Today they're in New York, half an hour away from

the game at Yankee Stadium, where they will perform their single 'Just Say No' in front of fifty thousand baseball fans.

When Darren comes finally, he ejaculates so far in the back of her throat, Stacey doesn't even taste his semen, only the musty afterbreath, mixing unappetizingly with the toilet's just-scrubbed smell. Still she sucks and sucks, taking him in, further and further, as he softens, Christ, what is she planning to do? *Bite?* Darren pulls her to her feet – a brave move, given she is a good four inches taller than him. Now he is kissing her, lifting her shirt, trying to wedge his head between her breasts, probably for balance, his whole body a-tremble with the aftershock of what is easily and for all time his best-ever blowjob.

She lifts her shirt for him. She doesn't wear a bra. She doesn't need one. Her breasts are so precise and tiny you can fit them in your mouth.

There you go.

Good boy.

She is eighteen years old – the age her mother was when she gave birth.

Deborah has always expected her daughter to do well. She has demanded it. At the same time, she is afraid that Stacey will make her mother's mistakes. So Deborah has set bounds on what her daughter can reasonably be expected to achieve. She has tried to manage her expectations. It is a strange sort of encouragement that begins 'Are you sure…?' 'Do you really think…?' 'Maybe, but…' 'Do not forget…' and its effects are equally strange.

For Stacey, these minatory utterances are not the soft upholstery Deborah meant them to be. They are chains and prison walls, tying her to her mother, this woman who has no life of her own but lives through her. They are goads, reminding Stacey of her own uselessness, driving her forward from one over-achievement to the next.

'I – I think I love you,' Darren stammers, pleasure-drugged.

Good. Meaningless as the words are to her, this is what Stacey wants to hear. This moment is what she has learned to manufacture. It is her

solace; otherwise she drowns, every waking minute, in the ghastly conviction of her own weakness.

A bell rings.

Quickly, they dress.

Stacey is first out of the gents', leaving Darren with his fly still undone, his school tie still askew. There are fifty thousand people out there, at the bright end of that tunnel, waiting to hear her sing. Thousands of men and boys who have yet to fall in love with her.

Nine years later. First-time Hollywood director Jon Amiel orders the crayfish. He has done what he can to persuade Stacey Chavez to order from the menu; Stacey is adamant, and has brought along her own muffin.

She has lost the part. There is no way Amiel is going to present the producers of *Entrapment* with such an obvious insurance risk, especially now he's had Zeta-Jones's agent on the line. But it would be tactless to let Stacey Chavez in on his snap decision during their very first face-to-face meeting. Besides, he likes her showreel, and life is long; he may be able to do something for her if she can get her head sorted out. All Brits go a bit crazy the first time they hit LA.

Tuesday, 9 May 1997. It is eight years since Stacey left *Grange Hill.* She has had her share of bit parts, a starring role in a more-than-dodgy Ken Russell B movie, a walk-on in *The Singing Detective.* The work that's really put her on the map is ITV's explicit reworking of *The Moth* – Catherine Cookson must have choked on her teeth, but enough critics looked beyond the carnal distractions and tissue-thin script to discover Stacey Chavez, her hunger, her fire. If she can only learn to harness it, her energy might make her great one day.

'I need a part that really *stretches* me,' says Stacey, lining up her knife. (Has she looked him in the eye once?)

Stacey has her meal planned. She doesn't need to look at her watch; she can count in her head. Every forty-five seconds she is going to eat a piece of muffin approximately the size of the first joint of her forefinger.

She will not tear this off the body of the muffin with her fingers: this method might suffice at home, but here it is too approximate. She will use her knife. A few seconds before she reaches for her knife, she measures the muffin against her forefinger, planning her attack. The conceit of cutting perfect rectangles from a round muffin is appealingly nonsensical, almost Zen. She maps this muffin's every crumb and bubble. Escape is impossible: this muffin is *going down*. Taking her hand away, she reaches for her knife, brings it over her plate and cuts exactly the shape she measured out. What I need, she thinks – because she is not beyond self-parody; like most anoretics, she knows what she is – is one of those vegetable slicers you find sometimes in Japanese kitchen stores. One stamp and hey presto! Every piece the same! Perfect bite-size muffiny chunks. She can even hear the exact note she'd hit, were she selling such a device, for such a purpose, on local TV, her first love.

Like this:

Per...fect (not too fast, build up slowly. Not too much of a smile; a note of suspense) *bite-size* (crisp and even here: nothing much else you can do. Just play up the consonants, the neatness of those two 'eye' sounds; careful not to drawl the 'z': this is no time to slacken the pace!) *muffiny* (a gift; would that every tag-line boasted such a word. You can really camp up kids' words. Big, big grin: hell, you just can't say 'muffiny' without breaking into a great big mischievous grin! Finally...) *CHUNKS*. (What a kicker! A real stamp-on-the-toes number. Heck, frighten them a little, even. Make them think about that sharp metal template hitting that dough. Not tearing it, not squashing it, not squeezing the life out of it *'which, as we ALL KNOW, happens TIME AND TIME AGAIN with INFERIOR CUTTERS'*. No, my friends, my ensofa-ed brethren, we are here today to talk about taking this muffin and CUTTING IT! Into CHUNKS!)

'Of course, the final decision lies mainly with the producers,' says Amiel, unable to keep up the pretence. He hasn't wanted to hurt her feelings, and because of this he is messing up badly. He knows this is

cowardly of him, placing responsibility for her eventual rejection at someone else's door. He knows that she will surely hear, at the back of these words, the most mealy-mouthed of excuses.

But she does not hear him. She cuts another bite of muffin free, places it on her tongue, presses her tongue to the roof of her mouth, and suppresses a groan of guilty pleasure as the morsel paps and melts, oozing between tongue and molars into the cavity below so that she must roll her tongue, gather the sweet bolus together once more, only to crush it, dizzy with pleasure, against her top incisors, then lick it off – another bite – and down!

'And you must meet Sam and Judith,' Amiel says. These are business acquaintances of his. A married couple with two kids and a dog. Or is it a kid and two dogs? Anyway it occurs to him that what she needs is some normal people around her. Ordinary dinner parties. Stuff. Because otherwise the sharks are going to have her. She's been here – what? two weeks? – and already she has an assistant and a personal trainer. She's been telling him, when she hasn't been worrying at that bloody cake of hers, all about her important LA lifestyle, and what began as an audition has degenerated, by this point, into something resembling intervention.

'You really must come,' he says.

Stacey isn't listening. What would make this meal complete is mustard. Lashings of mustard. Stacey loves that hackneyed phrase, *lashings,* so irredeemably naughty. It sums up everything she feels about mustard, the sour tang, the granular fascination of wholegrain, Dijon's fabulous range of shades, the melted-ice-cream texture of your everyday squeeze-bottle American blend.

She grips her hands under the table and counts the bones in her palms as though they were a couple of Chinese calculators.

This is an important meeting and the part is hers, she knows it, she can feel it. She is going to be a star. If she can just hold it together a little longer. She will not ask for mustard. She contents herself – when she thinks Amiel's attention is elsewhere – with another quick sprinkle of salt.

*

Monday 7 August: three months later.

Stacey Chavez has sacked her personal trainer. Instead, each weekday morning at 4 a.m., after a breakfast of celery juice and Fiberall, she drives to the beach and pulls up next door to a deep-bed Dodge with a Stars-and-Stripes on its roof and quarter of a million dollars' worth of gym equipment packed into its guts. For $400 a month, and if she gets there before the others, Neal Krantz, ex-Navy Seal, fitness record-holder for an unprecedented four consecutive years, 1983 to 1987, lets her pull the handle, and the truck, wheezing, unpacks itself like a *Transformers* cartoon: 3000lbs of barbells, two dip bars, four 300lb pull-down stacks, T-bars, pull-up bars, bell-bars, and six inclined press-benches in weatherized aluminium. Add a missile launcher to this arsenal, it would not look more intimidating.

Last week, during the most gruelling two minutes of her life, Stacey managed thirty sit-ups – less than half the number the Navy expects of its recruits. She drooled her way through fifteen push-ups, but Neal passed only three. She should have been able to do fifty-two. The demands of this new regime leave her exhausted and trembling. She dozes off in auditions. There's a phone by her bed and yesterday afternoon she slept through its ring.

Last week she flew around a two-mile course in just over twelve minutes, racking up her score; nevertheless, to be considered fit, she needs to dig inside herself for another fifty points. To begin with, the exhaustion worried her. She wondered how she would be able to juggle the competing physical and practical demands of her career. Now that the telephone calls have petered out, Stacey is beginning to leave these cheap anxieties behind. She has her mobile if her agent wants to talk. There's little point Stacey phoning her, she's always in a meeting.

It is dark and the sand is cold through the soles of her sneakers as she lines up behind the eight others in her group. Neal hands her a 30lb

pack – what he calls a 'half-weight'. It is standard armed-services issue, drab, with no waist-belt.

For ten years Stacey has been worrying her way up the career ladder. She has forgotten how to play, how to enjoy herself, even for a moment. She cannot stop. She does not know how.

Whatever she achieves can't, by her own impossible criteria, be worth anything, and so she snatches defeat from the jaws of every success. At twenty-six, faced with the first genuine stall of her career, Stacey feels old – as threadbare as a forty-something career woman grown grey and lined on a diet of *Cosmopolitan*.

Neal blows his whistle and they jog towards the dunes.

It seems to her that she has been dreaming her life: an anxious running-on-the-spot dream of unimaginable satisfactions forever delayed. The agent of this dream is her body, which will not let her be her best. It roots her in time and space, separating her from her goals.

The pack bounces from hip to hip, bending her into what Neal assures her is a sprinter's crouch.

Shed the body, and you shed the dream. So she has begun to rid herself of her body, ounce by difficult ounce, and she feels more awake now than she has ever been. Another whistle and they sprint. Another whistle and they drop into the sand for push-ups. Another: they jog again. The sun rises, and the sky does not brighten so much as gain in intensity, as though veils of atmosphere were being driven away, revealing a purer blue. Under this light, through the pain of new muscle, the intense self-centredness of Stacey's anorexia gives way to a spiritual sensation. It is time to shed the last scrap of her flesh. To distill herself down to the absolute.

They reach the foot of the dunes and Neal throws them each an ice-cold water-bottle from his stash. Beside the water crate there are metal ammunition boxes filled with wet sand. They form a line and pick up boxes, one in each hand. Another whistle and they trudge up the steep dune for a view of the ocean, then down again, no pausing, shoulders screaming, arms gorilla-stretched, around and up again.

The air grows thin and bitter. There is a dirty tin-foilish taste in her mouth, a flavour made from dead cells and stale fluids and chocolate Ex-Lax. Pain quarters her body, revealing its component parts. The arms have no solid connection to the skeleton. The shoulder blades float in a crossply of muscle. The calf muscles bend the leg. The quadriceps kick.

There is something electrical about the sky now, the cyan of a dead video screen, except that it is infinitely deep, a space of absolutes. They are running again. She is running into the wind. The front of her is chilled, the back half hot and clammy.

One mile.

A fever-line separates the two halves of her, a seam that shivers with every footfall, every arm swing, as though the halves of her are coming free of each other.

Two miles.

The halves of her lurch in opposite directions. Her prune-like heart misses a beat. Her joints tremble: she imagines the cartilage shrinking in every joint, rattling about in its sinovial bag so that her whole body becomes a baby's plaything: a tambourine of stretched skin.

Three miles.

She feels a shift inside her, nudging aside her dormant ovaries. Her shrivelled heart misses another beat.

Four miles.

This is it. The moment of departure. The sky is an electric blue. Goodbye, she thinks, expecting no answer from the dumb world of material things.

Goodbye.

Not her voice; someone else's.

Not her thought: *Goodbye.*

Five miles. Six miles. Ten miles.

It occurs to her that she is not going anywhere. She is still tangled in her body like a lobster in a trap. She is not leaving.

She sucks in air against panic and the air ripples around her, sending

a shiver around her which seems this time to be no mere hint of anything, but an actual unzipping. Stuff spills out of her like ectoplasm. Weightless, bound to no material law of motion, it ascends in absolute terms through the gridded blue that hangs above her in place of a sky.

'Come back,' she gasps, or thinks she does, but so much of herself has poured out, sound will not carry through her. In her terror she thinks this is what it is to be flesh. In this moment, she understands what has left her.

It is her spirit.

'Chavez!'

She had imagined she was a spirit, trapped in mortal meat.

'Drink this. Come on. Sit up. Chavez?'

But no. The soul is something else. Her soul is free, gone. But *she* is still here, tied to flesh. The irony is so fine – finer even than the cruelty – that she wants to laugh.

'Stacey. Chavez.'

She laughs, or thinks she laughs.

MODERN MEDICINE

1

Saturday, 11 March 2000. A rainy Chicago night. I am pressing my hands into the rucks and wrinkles of the bedsheet, searching for some piece of Stacey Chavez.

The room is in darkness and the curtains are open. Vehicles send ripples of light through the room's shifting blue interior. It feels as though we are coupling in an aquarium. She has pulled the sheet over her and around her like a shroud. There is a flash, a peal of thunder. What if the bedsheet is actually holding her together? I imagine unwrapping it, spilling her across the bed like a child emptying a parcel of presents. Disembodied laughter from a disembodied head.

Over the course of our meal at Lovell's I had expected to get to know her a little. The more we talked, the less of her I saw, the more I was confronted with Stacey Chavez, actress. Stacey Chavez, the fallen star, the recovering anoretic. If her recovery was so far advanced, how come she had turned up at the restaurant with a muffin in her handbag?

It had been my impression, returning from our meal, that we had not liked each other very much. Outside her Michigan Avenue hotel, I leaned forward to give her a perfunctory goodnight peck. She turned her head slightly so her lips met mine. Fold after fold of her coat concertinaed under my palm before I found her tiny waist. My fingers, indifferently splayed, ready for the wall of her back, cupped instead the secrets of her pelvic girdle, rising sharp against her skin. The bone whip of her spine.

After a minute of this she said, 'You can come in if you want.'

Stacey pulls the sheet aside, revealing herself, and bends forward to unbuckle me as I shed my shirt. I can hear her panting with the effort of it, the pain, the mattress stiff against her bones. Her legs are splayed,

the knees bent, the feet brought together, making a curious 'O'. When she leans forward to fellate me, her back arcs and her spine stands proud of the skin, a line under tension, and her ribs fan either side, the armature of an umbrella. It is impossible to describe Stacey's body without some resort to metaphor. Its radical thinness has robbed it of all familiarity. It does not look like a body at all. It looks like a hand: a delicate, alien hand with its unexpected points of articulation, its difficult, eloquent gestures.

When I woke up it was already light, and breakfast had been delivered to the room.

'I hope you like eggs,' Stacey said. 'You look to me like somebody who likes eggs.'

I like eggs.

Stacey had ordered a continental breakfast for herself. I watched her eat. She did not pick or slice or arrange or juggle. She did not guzzle everything in sight then run for the toilet. She ate: steadily, sparingly. I wondered how to reconcile her perfectly ordinary breakfast with last night's muffin dinner; was she fighting free of her old anoretic behaviours or re-learning them?

I was waiting on a call from the clinic, wanting to know the outcome of Felix's operation. Stacey, taking my edginess as interest, got talking about herself again. Her work.

SCTV: 'SC' for Stacey Chavez; 'TV' not for television, as I had assumed, but for '*tableau vivant*'. She was a long way from *Grange Hill*.

She had managed to place her work beyond casual notice, in a zone where her private obsessions were indistinguishable from the background: the migranous white-noise of the subsidized arts. She regarded this change in career, her successful dismantling of her celebrity status, as her real artistic achievement. The individual happenings – SCTVs one to four, her performances, *tableaux vivants*, whatever you want to call them – were more or less incidental to the central statement.

Stacey considered herself a conceptual artist who took celebrity as her subject. It was apparent that she had private means, aside from her earnings as an actress, and this was just as well, as her work was expensive to make. Her publicist had demanded two years' salary upfront, for fear of what Stacey's manoeuvrings might do to her professional reputation.

'I was doing everything wrong,' she laughed. 'Protesting outside the Turner Prize. Performances in church crypts in Oval and Hackney. The papers lapped it up.' One notorious performance of hers – it had a short run at the ICA in London – had her shoving fifteen Mars Bars down her throat then vomiting them into a bucket.

The business of erasure was more complicated than she had expected: 'That's why I had to pay through the nose for Vera.' Vera was her publicist; her anti-publicist now, sending carefully crafted details of Stacey's work to the usual diarists and media friends, ensuring that the tabloids became not so much frustrated with Stacey as bored and confused.

In spite of myself, I was intrigued. I too knew something about the business of erasure.

'So what do you do, Saul?' Stacey asked, throwing me a bone.

I saw no harm in spending another half-hour in Stacey's company, and, in order to answer her question safely, I did not have to depart very much from the truth. I had merely to talk as if my US business interests were as healthy as once they had been. I told Stacey that I ran an employment agency and from then on it was easy. Automatic, even.

Throughout the nineties it was expected of foreign aid workers settling in Maputo and Beira that they would fill their houses to the gills with domestic staff. It was the local custom, a useful source of employment and, in a city without labour-saving devices, the only practical solution to life's domestic demands. Anyone uncomfortable or embarrassed about employing servants was told, in no uncertain terms, and usually

by the Mozambicans themselves, to get over themselves.

Often, once they were rotated back to desks in Washington, these same staffers found themselves hankering after their old retinue, and this is where I came in. My operation, which was entirely above-board, exploited a legal loophole exempting foreign nationals from US labour law. By this means I was able to supply the apparatchiks of the UN, the World Bank and the IMF with cheap domestic labour. Better than that, I was pretty much able to guarantee the servants a goodish standard of living and a range of prospects far exceeding anything they'd find at home.

My eager young sub-Saharan jobseekers had all the right papers, and it amused me that the aid industry itself was the inadvertent conduit for their arrival in America.

It was the summer of 1996 before I let Noah Hayden catch up with me.

Nearly thirty years had passed since my lacklustre translations of Guy Debord's *La Societe du Spectacle* had graced the discussions of his New Left Reading Group, but Hayden was effusive. 'Do you remember those marches?' he exclaimed. This was one of the first things he said to me when we met again. We were both hitting fifty by then, and where I had shrunk and hardened, Hayden had acquired some considerable padding.

We were sitting in the garden of the Mount Soche Hotel in Blantyre, the commercial capital of Malawi, Mozambique's small, landlocked neighbour. I was here arranging domestic servants for the wealthier delegates at the Southern Africa Development Conference.

'Do I remember?' I thought I remembered. Voices like tides. The drunkard's walk we did: one miles-long, mutual jostle all the way to Grosvenor Square: *'Ho! Ho! Ho Chi Minh!'* These are the sorts of memories that manufacture themselves out of photographs, TV dramas, advertisements, celebrity reminiscences on *Desert Island Discs*; that widen the cracks between the flagstones of recall and smother them completely in the end. Cliché is a word we give to memories that don't need us to validate them any more. They have their own life.

I tried to show willing: 'I remember writing admiring articles about "Great Leader and Teacher Jack Straw",' I said. 'As I recall, my magazine was called *Letter Bomb.*'

Hayden grinned. 'Maoist.'

It was all bluster, all nonsense. I was worried we might run dry, anxious in case he mentioned Deborah. I didn't want to have to act out all those old lies again, years after the event. So I was boisterous: 'What the fuck's happened to Jack, anyway? Did he take something?'

'I think the question we are here to discuss,' Hayden said, 'is, have you?'

For years an industrious civil servant, Noah Hayden was now, by way of reward, a middle manager in the Department for International Development, with an impressive list of 'interests' to do with New Labour's foreign aid strategy. I knew what he was doing here. The Third Floor wanted a familiar hand to tug my leash. Noah Hayden was their man.

He was here to close me down, or at least, make a show of closing me down. So it was hardly surprising that I had gone into this meeting with a less than level head, teeth gritted against Hayden's complacency, his cereal-packet convictions, his infallible New Labour ideas about right and wrong.

As I saw it, Mozambique had held out against Rhodesia, then South Africa, and weathered all the blandishments of the Cold War, only to lose its independence at last to a handful of western NGOs. Every move the government made had to be countersigned by them or it risked forfeiting its aid. All around the harbour at Beira, international relief organizations were snapping up cheap real-estate. From inside their gated compounds, Scandinavian engineers, sipping imported beer, looked out upon our devastation with a speculative eye.

Although FRELIMO had clung on to power after the civil war, misfortune had softened it up nicely. In following the advices of the World Bank, it had had to defer indefinitely its promise of free universal education. Marxism-Leninism was abandoned. In Maputo, meanwhile,

the UN operation ONUMOZ had revived the local economy so that the daughters of famous Lourenço Marques streetwalkers – girls of fifteen, girls of twelve – were trading out of their mothers' old trysting places along the bay and promenade. When I finally shook myself out of my torpor and took a good, hard look at what my adopted country had become, it seemed obvious what career I should pursue.

For months I had being watching from my glassless tenth-floor window as, one by one, my fellow *cooperantes* had abandoned Katalayo's dream of independence for menial jobs in the aid industry. I wasn't ready to buckle under, but there was obviously no future in education, still less in government service.

The first people Nick Jinks and I ever 'trafficked' were families made homeless when the World Bank insisted on denationalizing Mozambique's rental market.

Hayden had neither the sophistication to understand nor the desire to conceal how angry and disappointed he was over my new line of work. 'Have you?'

'Have I what?' I said, teasing him.

'Taken something.'

'I'm sorry,' I smiled, leaving him shipwrecked on the shoals of metaphor, 'I don't follow you.'

Hayden had his alibi for this 'accidental' meeting already prepared, and when the direct approach guttered out, he treated me to the scenic route: 'The F.O.'s getting rather jittery about the spread of the Congolese mafia. You know they run the bus concessions around here?'

'I didn't know that,' I said. 'No.'

Noah Hayden smiled. 'But you have dealings with them.'

That my work so offended the sensibilities of men like Hayden wearied me. What would he rather I dealt in? Drugs? Diamonds? Ivory? Africa's export markets had been so spectacularly decimated, human beings were one of the few resources we had left to trade.

To trade in people? In Hayden's mind, I had fallen off the map in the

most spectacular fashion, abandoning FRELIMO and my principles. He couldn't see why I was so hostile to the charitable intervention he was here to promote. What was I kicking against? The truth – that I was still fighting Katalayo's revolution, shaking off the colonial yoke and flying the flag of liberty and self-determination when half FRELIMO had thrown in the towel – this was something Hayden didn't know how to respond to. If I was such an unreconstructed sixties throwback, how come I was so successful, travelling for business between my home in Beira, Maputo and the northern capital, Nampula; then abroad, as far as Kenya and Nigeria, Mali and the oil states of the Middle East? Or look at it the other way: how could a man claim political principles who provided under-fives as jockeys for camel-races in the United Arab Emirates one day, and rushed an ice-box full of human kidneys air freight to an exclusive clinic in Botswana the next? Of course Hayden didn't understand me. He imagined politics and crime were different things.

It pleased Noah Hayden to show himself to me. (Easy enough to imagine his home: cricket cups on the mantelpiece, music certificates framed in the bathroom.) It pleased him to know, from his extensive and industrious reading of the CIA *Yearbook* and who knew what other dry-as-dust public sources, things about the region that I appeared not to know. In his mid-fifties, Noah Hayden was still a puppy, eager to please, pleased to impress. Was he dangerous? Certainly – as a man is dangerous who is set in motion by others; whose actions are innocent of their effects. A man like that cannot be read.

A waiter passed our table. Hayden waved him over and handed him back his steak sandwich: 'Could you? The meat's a bit underdone. Thank you so much. Thank you.'

Hosting this year's Southern Africa Development Conference – the region's major annual political event – had thrown tiny, poor, lackadaisical Malawi into a tizz. Special SADC numberplates had been issued. Every bank in town had a dedicated SADC window, always open, for the negotiation of local currencies. Police and army

helicopters hovered precariously above the streets, trailing convoys of statesmen and dignitaries from the airport. Army checkpoints littered the streets in and out of major towns. In Blantyre, Christmas decorations cheered the only roundabout, and men in orange boilersuits were working around the clock to fill the worst potholes with sand and pitch. The town's hundreds of street traders had been banished to the derelict football ground.

Here we were, drinking gin and tonic in a country where life expectancy was plunging through the mid-thirties and the government had just voted to bury the country's former dictator in a gold coffin, and any minute now Hayden was going to start using words like 'human rights'.

'The trouble with you, Saul,' said Hayden, 'is you're political to just the right degree to excuse your cynicism.'

I blinked at him.

'I imagine you say to yourself: "They're better off where they're going than where they are now."'

'Not really,' I said, determined not to show a hit. Of course they were bloody better off.

'Why then?' It was his big moment. 'Why do you do what you do?'

Did he really think, for one second, that people like me were incapable of philosophy? That we had no idealism?

I didn't answer him. I had no wish to play politics, or to match his belligerence. And how else would it have come over? The world I live in. The world I have had a hand in shaping.

Each moonless night, hulks registered in Cambodia ply the seaways from Lebanon to Syria to Cyprus. Fishing boats from Somalia run aground on the beaches of Mocha. A whole mile from the Spanish shore, snakeheads throw children into the sea first so the women will follow; then they torch the ship.

The waiter came back with Hayden's sandwich; this time there was no steak in it. 'You said you didn't want it,' said the waiter, nonplussed, when Hayden complained.

The waiter was local. The following week the conference got started, and the hotel laid off every waiter, cook, bell-boy and maid, and hired South Africans in their place.

That same week, in the northern Transvaal, irate, unemployed locals were throwing Malawian immigrant miners out of speeding trains. In France, meanwhile, an Iraqi Kurd died after leaping twenty feet from a bridge onto the roof of a goods train, only to slip and fall across an electrified rail; six Russians stole a speedboat from a Calais marina, gunned the engine so brutally it exploded, and found themselves having to row across one of the world's busiest shipping lanes; and a middle-aged Lithuanian couple spent ten hours floundering around in the English Channel on children's toy air mattresses. When the English coastguard picked them up barely five hundred yards from the Kent coast they were still, somehow, in possession of a set of matching luggage.

What Hayden couldn't or didn't want to see was that this 'crime' he is so keen to stem is itself a kind of revolution. The vision of Franz Fanon and Jorge Katalayo is dead. Only has-beens like Mugabe believe in it now. So be it. The Third World's revolution – the *need* in the Third World for revolution – lives on.

This time, we are going to do things differently. There will be no attempt at, or expectation of, fair dealing. From our first meeting in 1992 to the operation's collapse in 1999, Nick Jinks and I arranged cross-border transportation for more than ten thousand men, women and children. Ten thousand pioneers, missionaries, merchant adventurers. Compared to the big distributed family networks, the trans-national combines, not to mention the refugee grapevines themselves, Nick and I were small beer.

Ten thousand mouths. The West wants to play by the market? Then so will we. It doesn't matter how many Noah Haydens there are in the world, chasing myopic agendas across continents they think still belong to them. We are going to eat the West, the way the West ate us.

*

'So what went wrong?'

Stacey was scraping up the remains of a dish of yoghurt. There was a mouthful of eggs benedict left on the plate in front of me. Numbly, I scooped it up, chewed, swallowed. It didn't taste of anything.

Through the plate glass windows of the hotel room, the bright sky was dirtied here and there with scraps of last night's raincloud. For the first time in my life I was making confession.

'Saul?'

I drank my coffee, and I told her. What the hell.

Friday, 12 March 1999. After nearly twenty-four hours of air travel, I booked into a Glasgow airport hotel, only to discover the circus had come to town.

Red Nose Day. For lunch, an unsatisfying encounter, interrupted by the maid. In the evening, Johnny Depp and Dawn French in a *Vicar of Dibley* charity special.

About ten to midnight, Nick Jinks finally phoned me. By his voice – it cracked like a crust of salt – I could tell he was crying.

He'd been supposed to call mid-evening, to tell me our consignment of fifty-eight men, women and children were safely delivered to the tender mercies of the Scottish casual labour market. Instead he was ringing me from a layby outside Carlisle to tell me he had killed them all.

And where the button was, to operate the fan on his T.I.R. trailer.

And where the levers were, to open the vents.

And where the vents were, which he closed before Portsmouth customs and forgot to re-open. On and on, round and around.

'Open the doors.'

Fear had made him stupid.

'Open the doors. Look inside.'

'Fuck,' he said, between inhales. 'Fuck you.'

'The ventilation is on, yes?'

'I'm not fucking looking.'

'Is the ventilation on now?'

'I'm not looking.'

'Tell me you've turned the ventilation on.'

'Fuck off.'

'Nick, turn the ventilation on.' I went to the window with the mobile pressed to my ear, and I looked up into the sky.

'Nick, listen to me, they could still be alive. Nick.'

There was nothing to see. No star shone fiercely enough to penetrate the airport's sodium glare.

Stacey picked up her coffee cup. It was empty. She turned it around in her hands, examining it.

I stood up. I caught the edge of the breakfast trolley with my hip and it rolled away. Cups rattled.

'Saul,' she said.

'I have to go.' I stumbled for the door.

'Saul.'

I rode the elevator down to the garage. I had no memory of where I'd left my hire car, but dumb luck led me to the right corner. I climbed in and locked the door. I dug my phone out of my pocket but my fingers were trembling so much, I kept fudging the numbers. The first available flight to Heathrow was at a quarter past three that afternoon. It would have to do. I booked myself a seat with a credit card, and swung by the hotel for my clothes and passport.

On the plane that afternoon, in the seat beside mine, already settled, fussing with her earphones, sat Stacey Chavez.

2

Stacey's apartment occupied the top three floors of a converted wharf in Wapping, a ten-minute walk from the City of London. White walls, mahogany-stained floorboards. The rooms at the front were shielded from the road behind linen blinds. Windows at the back looked over the Thames. If I leaned out and turned my head to the right, I could see Tower Bridge. The riverbank opposite was dark: a pub, a strip of park, a line of council housing.

Stacey's was the kind of life encapsulated on certain Finnish postage stamps. In the living room, back copies of the art magazine *Parkett* lay neatly stacked on the table by the flatscreen TV. Her bathroom cabinet boasted non-abrasive facial scrub and soapless soap. When I began staying over, she bought me some perquisites. This is what she called them. 'I've bought you some bathroom perquisites,' she said, and laughed. I added her purchases to the shelf she had cleared for me: perfumeless aftershave; scruffing lotion.

The top shelf held her medicines. She took small doses of Zoloft every day to balance her mood. 'I am better than well,' she would say, whenever the rigours of the day grew too much. 'Better than well.' And sometimes we went to bed, even if Jerom was there, tap-tapping at his iBook in the kitchen on the floor below. Jerom was Stacey's assistant. Jerom without an 'e'. He arrived early each morning before we woke. He had his own key.

'Hello, Saul,' he'd say. 'How are you? Sleep well?'

He wanted me to know that he was here.

'Good morning, Saul, how do you want your coffee this morning?'

He let me know, always nicely, that I was in the way.

Jerom had a double first from Oxford. When he spoke to Vera on the phone – Vera Stofsky, Stacey's agent, or anti-agent – he called her Vera. It was all first names with him. Phil was Philip Dodd, who ran the ICA at that time. Jeff was Stacey's New York dealer, Jeffrey Deitch.

It was a strange sort of work they were engaged in together: complex, carefully minuted, mediated through emails, websites, PDFs; there was always a biker at the door, collecting a DVD, delivering a printer's proof. At the same time, and perhaps because so much of this work was conducted in the non-spaces of the internet, I saw virtually no evidence of product – as though the art business were an abstruse strand of international politics.

Sometimes it was necessary for me to manufacture an interest; more often I was left to myself. I had my living to make, after all.

The US businesses were ticking over pretty much regardless of Nick Jinks's disappearance. Occasional work for the Chicago clinic supplemented the trickle of clients passing through my employment agency.

The UK was a different matter. After the accident, I had drastically reined in my operation, and for that reason my work had acquired a pleasing simplicity and immediacy: 'Two navvies this way!' and 'Three navvies that!' and 'Jump in the back of the van!' Each week another batch of new arrivals came to me, looking for cash-in-hand: navvies and hod-carriers, brickies and cement artists. Even for the ones who had no transferable skill – the ones for whom being a brickie meant making your own bricks, for whom lighting was synonymous with kerosene and lunch was bushmeat on a *braii* of stones and rusted cementation rods – I was usually able to find them casual work of one sort or another.

Most weekdays saw me plying the M25 in my 3-series BMW. Stabbing at my handsfree with nicotine-stained fingers, I deployed my network of white vans across the country, from Glencoe (cockles) to Glastonbury (mushrooms), Sussex (salads) to Sheffield (greenhouse produce). Most every labourer travels a long way for the privilege of trimming our leeks

and hand-selecting our beetroot. There are Lithuanians and Poles, Bulgarians and Turks. Most are legal, but a handful are not. These few are the invisible people, the wainscot people, the people adapted to live undiscovered up against the edges of things. My people.

It was a wrench, come Friday evening, moving from the brute immediacy of this life back into Stacey's orbit: her life lived between inverted commas. All those dinner parties: catty anecdotes about Vanessa Beecroft and Pipilotti Rist. Entire conversations consisted of nothing but other people's names. I did my best to act like a thug – mobile phone pressed to my ear, tales of congestion on the A3 arterial – but my heart wasn't in it.

I wanted her to stop taking the Zoloft. I wanted to know who she was without that crap in her system.

'No, you don't,' she said, and loosed one of her minatory laughs.

Every Sunday, Jerom insisted on filling the apartment with Sunday newspapers. Stacey never read them, and after a hard week's driving and dealing, I rarely got further than the TV listings. It was by accident that I stumbled, early that summer, upon an article about a little distinguished-sounding philosophical society near Malet Street – my first employer.

I showed Stacey the piece: a fragment of biography for her to play with. She said, 'That man looks like you.'

I leaned over to see. Accompanying the article was a photograph of one of the Society's former members.

'Look,' she said, 'there's going to be a party.' Stacey's enthusiasm for my past was something I had not predicted and did not want.

The picture was of Anthony Burden, the subject of *The Idealist*. This book – the author's first foray into biography – was, according to the paper, the surprise hit of the literary year. 'This is your chance to take me to something,' she said. She had opened up her life to me, but had seen precious little of mine.

Poised midway between Senate House and the Fitzroy pub, the Society had not only survived the years of my absence; it had flourished. Its combination of academic fustiness and public library had matured into something more eclectic and engaged. Its rooms were washed and repainted, the staircases stripped and stained ink-blue. The basement had been leased to a small juice-and-falafel chain called Open Sesame.

By the time we arrived, the party – to celebrate some literary award or other – had spilled onto the pavement. There was no one there either of us knew, but everyone recognized Stacey Chavez. I introduced her to Miriam Miller, the society's receptionist, secretary and general factotum. It was obvious Miriam did not remember me. When Stacey pointed out the uncanny physical similarity between me and the subject of her biography, Miriam blinked at her as though she was mad. She spoke to us for exactly three minutes, then passed on through the crowd.

I had expected a little happy reminiscence; at the very least, I had imagined wandering between the stacks of the library where I had worked for so long. But the collection had been sold off years before. So I watched with something like admiration as Miriam and Stacey, the two women in my life, the old and the new, worked their different and eccentric orbits around the room. At a loss, I hunted down the table where Miriam's book was piled high.

I read: *'Anthony Burden was as much fascinated by people as he was afraid of them.'* I skimmed ahead, looking for pictures. There were pages and pages of them: faithfully reproduced sketches of shells and ferns and matrices, natural patterns and what looked like, but could not possibly be, computer code. None of it seemed remotely fathomable, and I wondered how on earth Miriam had found a publisher willing to foot the expense of so many plates and photographs.

Miriam's stabs at exegesis seemed as stilted as the articles she used to write for the Society's pamphlets: *'Anthony Burden was as much*

fascinated by people as he was afraid of them. The patterns they made as they went about their business daunted him. Their movements seemed very unpredictable to him, and he imagined these movements were more complicated than his own. Society wasn't just bigger than he was. It was More.'

The nostalgia I felt while skimming this tosh was, I imagine, similar to the rush of feeling one experiences for a doughty elderly relative once they are past the point where they can damage anyone. I looked for more pictures of her subject. There were very few, and none which resemble me so closely.

Stacey passed behind me, chatting to a short, swarthy man in a T-shirt too young for him. 'We visited a hospital—'

I recognized, in her earnest cadences, the overture to one of her favourite anecdotes: the documentary she had made for Comic Relief. '... A regional centre for the treatment of landmine injuries.'

Manhiça, north of Maputo, this was. I followed a pace or two behind, listening in.

'... This half-human, half-plastic mass. All the ways they had of moving around. One stick. Two. Wheelbarrows. Skateboards made out of crates.' As though the more Stacey told this story, the more weight it would acquire. The truth, as she had told it to me, was that she had been very little moved by her journey. The suddenness of her arrival and departure, the technical difficulties attending the shoot, never mind her own disorientation, so recently released from the clinic, had conspired to place her at several removes from the things she had seen.

'I never expected it to remind me so vividly of the clinic I had just left. Its head-height mirrors and curtainless showers. But the cupboards stocked with limbs, the injuries, the burns. The little boy without hands.' She was speaking of the experience the way one speaks of a particularly gut-wrenching gallery exhibition. The pair paused to have their glasses filled by a teenage girl in a white smock. 'I was not upset,'

Stacey said. She noticed me. She held her hand out for me, drawing me in. 'I have spent so long among monsters,' she said.

Do Goliata's farmers, crippled by anti-personnel mines, ever visit the graves where their limbs are interred?

As summer wore on, I found it harder and harder to concentrate on my work. I lost whole days sometimes, driving for hours through the spoiled southern countryside of my childhood. When I came to, it was late afternoon, the low sun was dazzling, and the clean, mathematical shapes of the rolling hills stood out dark against the sky. I would take long glances out the side windows and in my mirrors, looking for a glimpse of the walls of this world, and the hills changed shape as I passed between them, remoulding themselves, tightening, relaxing, like graphs representing a series of mathematical formulae.

I can only explain these excursions as an attempt – late in life, and hopelessly – to evoke dim childhood memories: the South Downs above Horndean, their rolling, rain-soaked slopes, their valleys boxed off into tiny irregular rooms by overgrown hedgerows.

My past: my missing limb.

3

Saturday, 13 March 1999. I have not slept. I've tried calling Nick Jinks back but he isn't answering.

Around four this morning I found our lorry, abandoned in a lay-by outside Fort William. There was no sign of Nick Jinks. I hadn't the nerve to break the trailer's TIR seal and look inside. After so many hours, what would be the point? I drove our spoiled shipment south, parked it safely, hired a car and went to drum up some assistance.

Ferrer's Grange. The company name is spelt out in stainless steel letters fused alchemically to the granite. Underneath, scuffed into the stone, a sans-serif assertion: 'We Make a Meal of Farming'. In the yard, a fingerpost in white weather-resistant plastic points the way to reception, where the girls – school-leavers from faceless greenfield conurbations outside Spalding and Stamford – have the sallow patina of high-street travel agents.

From inside the Portakabin, with its cheap, crunchy carpet, I can hear the packing houses: the dentist's-drill syncopations of Lincolnshire light industry, plastic bearings squealing in the rollers of stuttering conveyor belts, the squeak-snap of table-top shrinkwrap machines. Every one a sound of protest, barely an honest rumble or clunk anywhere.

'Have you been here before?' the receptionist asks.

Oh yes, I know these places, these draughty barns stacked high with plastic trays, rolls of corrugated paper, brown, purple, green, reams of colourful print, dusky smiling island women, buxom farmer's daughters, headscarves, shell necklaces, *capulanas* slit to the thigh, cheap, badly registered three-colour pornographies of ripeness and increase; in another corner, industrial-sized bails of Clingfilm, boxes of sticky labels; underfoot a smeared confetti, Class I, Class II, Union Jacks, tricolores,

dinky little 'Farm Assured' tractors, *marques regionaux*; and beneath them, ingrained, immune to the twenty-four-hour schedule of broom and vacuum, blue-green crumb of broccoli, shred of carrot top, imprinted yellow leafshape of Brussels sprout, liquefaction smears, tomato pips.

The receptionist hands me a yellow plastic hard-hat, a dayglo jerkin, fluorescent gumboots and a laminated name badge: 'Visitor'. In this motley, nothing can mark me; they can always wipe me clean.

'I need a breath of air. I'll just be outside. All right?'

The fear these words plant on the receptionist's face suggests that hers is the sort of job where you have to account for every toilet break. She starts gabbling the company's safety policy. I might trip. I might slip. I might wander into an Orange Work Zone and, intoxicated into madness by the whirl of industry, hurl myself giggling into the shrink-wrap machine.

'I can surely wait outside the office?'

'Oh,' says the receptionist, and because I am already through the door: 'All right, then. Don't go far.'

Beyond the packing houses lies a crackled criss-cross of tractor and trailer tracks. And there they are, Chisulo and Happiness, picking Sweethearts out of the smashed earth.

Happiness is younger than her husband. Her skin is pale and freckled, her blood bleached by a globe-trotting Danishman, her fly-by-night dad.

Felix, on the other hand, is old and dark, and all his life in this country the *Azungu* – his old-country word for the whites he has grown old among – have congratulated him on his black twistedness. 'Like mahogany,' they say, which proves, he says, they are no carpenters.

Thorn would be a better choice; Felix is as twisted as though a mountain wind has sculpted him. When he sees me, he stands and smiles, because it is the custom of his people to smile. It signifies no friendliness whatsoever.

It is a strange sort of service I have done these two, and nigh-on impossible to explain to the natives of this merrie shopkeepers'

England, where making one's voice heard above the din has become the highest good. I have erased them – and as a consequence, there is much that Chisulo and Happiness cannot do. Banks refuse to handle their meagre earnings. Public libraries choose not to lend them books. On the other hand, there is much they cannot be made to do, and this, in their lives, was a welcome novelty – at least at first – for they came from a place where the State gives little, and asks much.

Happiness, working beside her husband, looks up, and though her freckled face is a blank, her eyes are full of stratagems. But this is, in turn, merely the customary look of her people, the people of Djibouti, that hell on earth where people chew leaves incessantly like cows simply in order to have something to do.

I tell them I have a job for them, and I pick a figure to turn their heads, but not too extreme: I don't want to scare them off.

Still they hesitate, for they have good work already here. Come the days of high yield, ordinary human sweat can earn them up to £1.50 an hour.

It's Chisulo who relents, finally: 'I'll go and fetch Asha.'

Asha is their daughter. An unwelcome complication, but I don't want to spook them now by saying she can't come.

Leaving Happiness to her pluck and drop, I follow Chisulo down the hill. The whole valleyside is one huge field, planted everywhere with melons, melons for every taste, here green stripy Sweethearts, there crazed yellow Passports, further down the hill the phallic wrongness of *Caroselli di Polignano*, towards woods the managers keep in the bottom for the shooting of great tribes and nations of grouse. (The company's recreation division call this venture 'The Lucky Brakes', but I doubt whether their city-analyst clientele know enough country lore to pick up on the pun.)

We enter the woods, deep enough so that the light begins to gutter. I can't imagine where their daughter must be, among these tangles and paths criss-crossing, these fallen trees.

Chisulo turns sharp left, past a fallen oak – and there is a caravan, a dilapidated Hurricane, abandoned wheel-less among the furthest

brakes, the plastic airstream bubble over its rear window long since smashed away, the trellis skirting round its bottom kicked in at precise intervals, suggesting the tantrum of a strictly governed child.

There has at some point in its history been a half-hearted attempt to paint the sides of the caravan Windsor green. Concrete breeze-blocks make steps up to the door, and from inside comes the laughter of children.

The concrete blocks wobble under Chisulo's feet as he climbs. He opens the door.

From the foot of the steps I glimpse children. One of them, a boy, his skin a curdled Balkan colour, is waving a metal contraption over his head, out of the reach of a black girl in a green polyester party dress with a silver ribbon round her waist, undone now and dangling, the ends scuffed and dull where she, along with everyone else, has trodden on them.

The girl hops, panting. This is a game, she is smiling. No, she is not smiling, she is panting, she is exhausted.

She is hopping. She only has one leg. The boy is swinging the other above his head.

Chisulo says something in a language I don't recognize, and smartly, without a trace of fear or embarrassment, the boy hands him his daughter's leg.

Asha hops to the door and Chisulo gathers her up in his arms and steps backwards, gingerly, down the breeze-block stairs. The boy swings the door shut. I catch a glimpse of the caravan's interior: its wallpaper, its mobiles, the pink tricycle, the space-hopper; empty boxes, piled into a half-hearted den.

Chisulo wants to put Asha's leg on, but there's no time. She wouldn't be able to walk across the field anyway, the ground is so uneven.

'We can put her together again in the car,' I tell him.

We ride the A14 – Happiness and the girl in the back, Chisulo riding shotgun beside me – and half an hour later I pull in 'to rest'.

So here we are now, staring numbly out of the window of the service station, blowing on coffee that is both scalding and tasteless. How am I supposed to say what I have to say with the little girl sitting here between us like this? I am still puzzling this through, muzzy from lack of sleep and too many hours behind the wheel, when Asha says, 'Chipsss. I want chipsss.'

I go and buy her some chips.

Then she says, 'Can I have ketchup with my chipsss?'

'Over there,' I tell her, sitting down again. 'See? Those packets over there.'

Asha returns with a fistful of sachets of tomato ketchup and a woman in a giant dishcloth smock running after her because she has not paid for them. They are seventeen pence each. I hand the woman a pound coin, but she says she has to put the sachets through the till – she means scan them. I tell her to use some initiative, pick a sachet from the can by her till and scan it through a few times, but she says she cannot do this, so I ask for my quid back, but she does not want to give me back my money, so I tell her to fuck off.

The till operator returns with the manager. The manager gives me change from my pound and tells me not to make further purchases from his food hall.

'Chipsss!' says Asha, eating them. Chips vanish without effort, without chewing – even without swallowing, it seems – down the little girl's gullet. Watching her, Chisulo's eyes grow grey and wet: windows on stormy weather. (Two years before, back home, Chisulo was studying law. But they were all something.)

'Carsss!'

Asha is done eating; now she pulls on her mother's sleeve.

'Carsss!'

I ask Happiness, 'What cars?'

'The games,' Happiness replies. 'The games, she means, downstairs, the games with cars. No, Asha.'

'The arcade games,' says Chisulo. He stands.

'Stay where you are. I want to talk to you.'

Chisulo sits but, as he does, Happiness stands: it is like they are being operated off the same pulley.

The girl takes her mother's hand.

'Go with her, then, Happiness,' I tell her, 'It's fine.'

'Carsss!' the girl chirrups, hand in hand with her mum, clunktapping away over the dog-hair-thin industrial carpeting towards the arcades.

'What is it, boss?'

I never expected to charge them so high a price for their freedom. But what can I do? Fifty-eight men, women and children. Imagine. The volume of human flesh. It is too much for one man to manoeuvre, let alone conceal.

Stripping, handling, wrapping, packing. Plastic and tape. After months spent trimming and stacking groceries at Ferrer's Grange, Happiness and Chisulo will find the whole process eerily familiar.

4

My hands frozen to the wheel, heavy with nostalgia, sick with it, I hacked back and forth over the South Downs, through villages with names like Hurtmore and Noning. The hills of my childhood had been scrubbed clean. It was a modern, monochrome landscape now. The soil was so thin, modern ploughs had cut great gobbets out of the chalk bed and left the fields flecked white and grey. From a distance, it was as though someone had gone over the land with sandpaper, revealing a grey primer beneath. The crops, when they came, were a sickly yellow-green, and rounded off the imperfections of the hedgeless hills, leaving them as smooth as the features on a golf course.

I could not go back. I would have to go forward. I thought about that.

I had grown bored of the modern arrangement Stacey and I had fallen into. Its lack of commitment was exhausting. I decided to do something selfless, if only for the sake of the change. I tried to make myself, if not useful, then present: a silent partner, someone for Stacey to turn to, to rely on.

But she already had Jerom, and how could I compete with him? Jerom had all the advantages: education, youth, a sense of humour, a missing 'e'. No sooner did I try to participate in their lives, than Stacey and Jerom set about seeing to my every need, hoping perhaps that I would leave them alone.

When I wrapped my BMW around a bus near St Katherine's Dock, Stacey took me to a showroom in Mayfair and bought me a replacement. 'What do you think?' she asked me as we drove back to Wapping along the Strand. I said something about the positive feel of the controls, the hard ride, the snugness of the seat: anything to paper over my wretchedness.

Just then her phone rang. Jerom dug it out of his pocket; Stacey never took her own calls. 'Well, *hello*, Jeff,' Jerom cooed, wriggling into the leather of the back seat. Since I had decided to be Stacey's best friend, Jerom never seemed to leave her side.

He was not so petty that he did not allow me to make some contribution to the household. I took charge of the coffee machine and the herbal teas. I kept house. I swept and tidied. I threw away newspapers before Jerom was done with them, wanting him to stop me, itching for an excuse. This was how I stumbled on the other key story of my year – though this was harder to miss; John Gridley's worn muzzle splashed across the front of a *Guardian* pull-out.

The senator for Illinois was familiar for his maverick politics: by and large a good Republican, Gridley was, at the same time, outspoken in his determination to get the Bush administration to grasp the nettle of foreign aid. Long before debt relief reached the international agenda, Gridley had advocated a unilateral writing-off of African debt. The terrorist atrocities of September 2001 only strengthened his old-school belief in the importance of winning hearts and minds abroad; above all, in being seen not to rip people off. A year ago, the critically ill senator told a *New York Post* interviewer that he would soldier on – and die in office, if necessary – until this 'vital pillar of national security' was enshrined in policy.

The year since had made a nonsense of the *Post's* valedictory. Not only had the senator's health improved to an improbable degree; there was now a better-than-evens chance that an international agreement would be struck on forgiving Third World debt.

Gridley's response?

Last week, he had declared his intention not to contest the next Senate race.

I was so nervous about what I would find in the *Guardian*, I couldn't even read the article at first; I had to scan it, hunting for tell-tale words like 'clinic' and 'kidney'.

Gridley was intimate, as few others are, with the economic disparity between rich and poor nations. Right now his only functioning kidney belongs properly to a former RENAMO lieutenant by the name of Felix Mutangi. That Gridley, hopelessly compromised, dared to continue his lobbying was admirable, I thought. The hypocrisy he had shown in buying a poor man's kidney, thereby saving his own life, was small beer by comparison.

The *Guardian* piece, after a lot of hand-waving, excused the Senator's resignation with a mere paraphrase of his own announcement. I could only hope its lengthy, saccharine approach would spike the story for other, more inquisitive editors.

I threw the paper in the bin and tried to forget about it. I emptied the ashtrays. I made a salad. I tried to straighten out the mess Stacey was making of her home.

One whole room was devoted to Stacey's wardrobe. There were shelves, floor to ceiling, stacked with her shoes, all in their original boxes. The contents of the bathroom medicine cabinet were sparing in comparison to the powders and lotions and mascaras and God knows what else cluttering her make-up tables; there were two of them, one in her dressing room and one in the bedroom.

Did I ever see her in the same outfit twice? In the unlikely event she ever ran short of cash she could have opened an agnes b museum.

Though the apartment was airy enough, I could never stay inside for long. I found the presence of all these Staceys hard to handle: Staceys hung up on the backs of doors, Staceys spilled from cupboards, laid out over beds and chairs, stacked in boxes, bottled, jarred. There were so many women Stacey could be. She could be anybody she wanted to be, now that she was nobody. She had rendered herself down to the bone. She was starving her life the way she had starved her body. Jerom's phone log in the morning; Vera's pie-charts in the afternoon; in bed, a man twice her age: what kind of life was this?

Similar thoughts must have crossed Stacey's mind, too, because come October she began to take lovers from among the students she met while delivering guest lectures at Goldsmith's and Central Saint Martin's. They were usually girls. The affairs would last a few days; never more than a couple of weeks. They shouldn't have mattered. Though we sometimes shared a bed, Stacey and I hardly ever fucked any more. Come night-time, we had our separate rooms. Still, it angered me to find myself cast in the role of an infinitely indulgent uncle. Someone who would pick up the pieces afterwards. This, my second experiment at living with a woman, had proved just as sexless as the last.

How could Stacey answer my disappointment? With pity, or with laughter? 'Sometimes I feel too delicate for cock,' she told me once, on her way out to a date. She stroked my cheek. She was trying to titillate me, to make me an accomplice in her adventures. A silent partner indeed.

Even when I hit her it didn't make any difference. The next morning I entered the kitchen, wobbly with remorse, to find Jerom taking photographs of her black eye. I couldn't work out if this was for her art or something to do with insurance.

5

Her tour. Imagine. *SCTV05*.

The walls of the bathtub rise around her, high, grey-white, and smutted. The brine supporting her in the bath is thick enough, salt is precipitating out of the water along the tideline, crystallizing wherever a smut greases the enamel.

Her tour begins late in the year in Milan, at the Inga-Pin gallery. The following week she participates in the closing days of the Venice Biennale. In the new year, the Neue Nationalgalerie in Berlin.

SCTV05. Stacey licks salt from her lips – naked, shrunken, she is not eating any more – as, little by little, the water in which she floats evaporates under the gallery's halogen lights.

The atmosphere at the Inga-Pin is business-like. Franca Sozzani, editor of *Vogue Italia*, arrives a few minutes before the end of the technical run-through. (There will be only two performances of *SCTV05* at each venue: once for the public, and once for the DVD.)

Sozzani has arranged for Helmut Newton to take a snap of Stacey this evening for the magazine; he wants to accompany her in person and write up the meeting.

Stacey nods agreement, shivering and dumb. She is not dressed yet. Fan heaters are going full-blast, three of them, plugged into the same extension lead. They have been arranged in a triangle, an almost-safe distance from the bath, and Stacey stands in the middle, scooping the towel up her outstretched arms in the shaft of hot air.

'The studio is half an hour by car,' Sozzani explains. He is struggling, in this white space and in the vacuum of Stacey's wide-eyed regard, to express his solicitude. His panic is palpable. 'We will be driving *north*.'

Nobody pays any attention to me.

Stacey crosses to the chair where her clothes are piled. Her flesh has retreated so far it has abandoned its defence of her sex. Now the gap at the top of her thighs is so wide, were I to put my fist between them, I doubt we'd even touch.

'Here.' Sozzani offers Stacey his coat and leads her from the gallery.

I wander over to the bath.

I dip my hand into the water. It is stone cold.

A jangle of keys.

Closing time.

This is the pattern of our days. By the time I wake up, Stacey has already left for work at the gallery. I throw on a dressing gown and I wander into the lounge to find the TV on, muted, and a line of orange Tic Tacs lined up, uneaten, on the arm of the hotel's easy chair. The suite is a sea of half-drunk bottles of mineral water. There is no Zoloft in the bathroom. She has decided not to take it any more, and because of all the stupid things I have said against it in the past, there is nothing I can say in favour of it now.

I leave the hotel and I look for something to do. More often than not, this is a waste of time. I am out of joint with Europe. I am too old to learn the tricks of Stacey's generation, these cut-and-paste people with their French-fried philosophy. Even their films leave me cold. There is more to life than entertainment, of course, but, having spent so long in Stacey's apartment, among Stacey's friends, drinking Jerom's coffee and listening to his end of complex, fruity transatlantic telephone conversations, I am not sure I can remember what it is. By the time Stacey gets back from the gallery, I am already slumped in front of the TV, hunting the channels for those game shows where the girls take off their bras. A nice hobby for a sixty-year-old.

The evening Stacey had her photograph taken by Helmut Newton, I found something else to watch instead: *Fox News Live* hosted by Martha MacCallum.

John Gridley, former Illinois senator, was dying of AIDS.

I reached for my phone, decided against it, went out into the street and hunted down a public booth. The lines to the Chicago clinic were engaged; a bad sign. I tried Felix and got his wife. Felix was out at work. She gave me a mobile number but I couldn't get it to work. I tried the clinic again.

There was no one there willing to speak to me.

How long had Gridley been keeping a lid on his HIV status? Was he clean last year, when he went in for his operation?

As he was carried into hospital this evening, Gridley's lawyer had issued a public statement to the effect that the senator's HIV infection had been contracted, not through sexual contact, but during the course of a surgical procedure. No journalist in America could fail to spot the invitation in that. The lazy ones would be waiting for news of a lawsuit. The more ambitious among them might notice, perhaps, that according to his medical notes, the senator, for all his troubled health the past few years, had not gone under the knife since his tonsils were removed in 1966.

His foul blood and failing kidneys – these were a matter of public record, so that the miraculous improvement in his health over the last year had been a source of grudging media celebration. But there was still plenty for him to tell. Gridley must even now be juggling offers for his death-bed confession. With a good ghost, you could probably make a book of it. Part One: the family's vain hunt for an appropriate donor. Part Two: and at last, *in extremis*, through discreet channels, via contacts in the overseas aid industry, certain parties are able to offer the dying man a final stab at life. An operation. A transplant.

What was Felix's HIV status now? What had it been, the day they gave his kidney to John Gridley? How could the clinic not have known?

Whether out of remorse, or to head off blackmail, or simply out of a dying wish to light the blue touch paper, and end his cantankerous career in a blaze of controversy, Gridley was getting ready to talk. The clinic's only hope, and by extension mine, was that the pneumonia

would get to him before *ABC News*'s dictaphone clicked on. Except that Gridley was a man of education and foresight; he would have prepared his confession already.

I went back to the hotel and waited for Stacey.

She got back from the photoshoot after two in the morning, knowing full well she was in trouble. She put on the bikini she had worn for Newton. It was leather. Expensive. Tiny. They had given it to her.

'What do you think?'

She tried to prance.

SCTV05.

Every so often, heads appear over the sill of Stacey's giant bath-tub. Imagine: the heads lean down and study her, their faces invisible against the glare of the halogen lamps. Stacey can only guess at their expressions.

Horror?

Desire?

Imagine: the computer-controlled canula at her left wrist releases a little of her blood into the water.

'No,' says a woman, looking down at Stacey, floating in water pinked by her own blood. 'No.' Trembling and tense. Her voice can't find the right register. 'No.' It sounds as though someone were offering her a canapé – something to which she is allergic.

'No, no.'

The head retreats. Poor hapless punter. Doesn't know much about art but she knows what she likes. Quick footsteps lead away, making little ripples in the bathwater that tickle Stacey's ears. Hunger twangs her gut like a piano string, and she struggles against the deadly urge to turn her head and drink the brine.

Everybody can see that she is dying. It isn't in me to save her. I know myself too well by now.

*

The Weight of Numbers

The clinic phoned me yesterday. A conference call. At least, they said they were calling from the clinic. Only someone used my real name. I cut the line and threw away the phone.

Today I'm phoning Felix again. Once more I get his wife. 'How are you, Lovemore?'

Anyone else buying a kidney transplant would have flown to South Africa or Pakistan for his operation. Not Gridley. Not in his position: the foreign travels of a gravely ill US Senator would not have gone unremarked. Gridley had insisted on shitting in his own back yard. From his deathbed, slowly murdered by the very kidney that saved him, he is even now giving statements to the FBI.

'How are the kids?'

Last year I set up Felix and Lovemore as my new caretakers for the northern states. I saw to their relocation, freed them from their files and police records, their government numbers and other bureaucratic spoors. In doing so, however, I have become the very world they would escape from. I am every policeman, every government official, every doctor, every care worker, every petty bureaucrat. So as I enquire, with a more than casual insistence, into the health of Felix's family – his wife, his two young sons – I must choose my words carefully.

In a couple of hours, the family's bank cards and mobile phones will cease to function. A couple of hours after that, a van will turn up at their door. I think they will cooperate. In any event their Chicago life is over.

If they phone the newspapers, if they tell their story, it won't make any difference: as of yesterday, my American business interests are not simply terminated; they never were.

The call goes as well as such calls can, and yet another SIM-card joins its fellows in the mud of the Arno. I am good at this, and I like to think I conduct myself professionally. I never resort to bluster or threats. The world is the way it is; Felix and Lovemore surely know better than to throw themselves and their children upon the mercy of US Immigration.

*

Venice in November. In the mornings, high water rises through the pavements.

We teeter along duckboards down flooded alleys, pausing distracted at this church or that, this paper shop, that stand-up patisserie. Rain ricochets off the brick walls of the alleys. Tourists in yellow galoshes huddle under the awnings of the ink-and-paper shops, the Murano glass outlets, the porticos of churches. We slip up like a couple of drunks on stone footbridges, their steps edged in marble slick as soap. Come rain or shine, summer or winter, Stacey tells me, the canals of Venice are always the same colour: the blue-green of plastic garden furniture.

(*SCTV05*. The gallery closes. The halogens go out, their glittery, schizophrenic light curdling for a second before it dies, blue to sepia to the brown-black of ashes.)

At lunchtime, from our table at Quadri, overlooking St Mark's Square, we watch as the lagoon water drains away – a clear foot of it, vanishing in minutes through tiny sink-holes between the flagstones.

In the centre of the piazza, a man and a woman in smart casual clothes trot in circles round and round. Every so often they point at random into the air, as though firing imaginary weapons.

Stacey is playing her 'Come here, go away' game with the staff. She wants the waiter to dry her shoes. She wants the waiter to bring her shoes back. She wants the waiter to bring her some dry shoes. Stacey wants a drink. Stacey wants the waiter to know, me to know, the world to know, that she can't be expected to just sit there with wet feet and no drink.

The couple's gestures are ungainly and unpractised. When I lean back in my chair to examine them, I realize I've been watching them through a flaw in the glass; that they are smaller and nearer than I assumed; that they are children.

Paulo, Eduardo: the names of Felix's sons.

I say to her: 'I don't think I can do this any more.'

MAPS OF THE WORLD

Monday, 17 July 2006

A despairing email from Jerom, Stacey's PA ('former PA', he styles himself), has led Moisés Chavez, criminal mastermind and underworld enforcer, out of his Guatemalan hiding place, across the Atlantic and up to the door of his adopted daughter's apartments in Wapping, near the City of London.

He rings the bell.

Jerom comes to the door. He has his jacket on already, his outdoor shoes. As Mo comes in, Jerom goes out, muttering something about an errand.

Mo knows Jerom won't be back. He can spot a coward by the smell.

Mo climbs the stairs up to Stacey's apartment; they issue directly into the main living space, no walls or doors.

It is a relief to find the room clean and well ordered. Jerom has done this much for her, anyway.

On the floor in front of a wall-mounted flatscreen TV, huddled under a Zambaiti blanket, Stacey Chavez kneads her PlayStation remote, slotting her virtual wheels through impossible gaps in her hunt for the closure of digital sunset in *Gran Turismo 4*.

Mo sinks to the floor beside his adopted daughter. This child twice abandoned. 'Stace,' he whispers. 'Stacey. Stace.'

He tries to look her in the face, but this is not so easy, because there is very little face left. It is all skull, the skin shining over the bone as though embalmed.

'Look at you.' Mo strokes his daughter's head. 'You can't even walk.'

He had not expected it to be like this. He had expected a fight, when Stacey found out about Jerom; the way Mo has been keeping tabs on her condition.

He strokes her head, her sunken cheeks, her neck, as loose and folded as the neck of a chicken. 'Please.'

He expected her to recognize him.

Stacey flexes her torso uselessly. Her head bobs and tosses.

Mo remembers playing with Stacey as a child. Her rough giggle. The way in the mornings she would clamber into bed to hug his head.

'It's a good place, Stace,' Mo urges her. 'Your mother went there,' he says, as if this were an inducement.

Through an anonymous account he will pay Coronation House for Stacey's care, as he paid for Deborah – this other ruin of a beautiful girl, the wife he abandoned, for her good, he thought at the time. For her good, and for the good of her child, because in 1983, with eight years of jail behind him and his youth fading fast, Mo knew there was no way that he could lead a legitimate life.

'They know how to help you,' says Mo, into his daughter's ear.

The truth is, he barely recognizes her. The last time Mo saw Stacey she was fourteen years old, wearing a black dress and a green fright wig on the day of the funeral of her grandfather, Harry Conroy. Mo was new out of jail, spying on the wake from across the street. Trying to come home. For weeks he tried. How many sharply truncated phone calls? How many drive-bys? But how could he come home? Knowing what he was now. Knowing the life he knew now, and what prison had taught him. Knowing what he was going to do.

Mo no longer smuggles marijuana.

'Please,' he says. He is reduced to begging. 'Please,' he says, stroking Stacey's shoulder. What there is of it. The bones.

Stacey whispers something, far too soft to hear. She is glued to the screen.

Mo follows Stacey's gaze, into the television.

Scenery rips past.

Only now does Mo see what his daughter is driving.

Inside the plastic PlayStation housing, inside the machine, a fractal math sculpts trees and mountains, throwing them upon the TV screen with the careless mastery of a potter. Each rock, each leaf, each twisted

branch is unique, an effervescent work of mindless art, no sooner glimpsed than gone. Clouds swell, glower, then disperse, revealing a low, late sun. Blue shadows spill from the hoardings and stands and the cheering, screaming onlookers, every one an extemporized original, as Stacey, made whole by games like these, made superfast, pumps the brake with a bony forefinger and thumbs the wheel around.

The world has come a long way since *Turbo*. The viewpoint skids and topples, then rights itself, as the game's forgiving physics bounce her off a wall and back onto the track.

Stacey has never got this far before. Her walnut heart shivers, and the game, sensitive to the moment, slackens its break-neck pace. The road straightens as it enters a beautiful park.

Deer graze beneath tall trees with foliage so rich and thick, it looks more black than green.

A dark lake flashes by.

Stacey hits the brake, turns the cream Thunderbird carefully around and, counter to the spirit of the game, retraces her route.

There are no pursuers now. She has fallen out the bottom of the game.

She wonders where she is now.

In the middle of the lake, a fountain sends a crystal jet into the air like a glittering whip, spreading coolness all around.

Stacey Chavez unclips her seatbelt. The cherry-red leather upholstery sticks to the backs of her legs as she reaches for the door.

The boy at the burger bar counter is sweating from more than chip heat, for he cannot hold medium chips and apple pie in his head without dropping the bacon cheese double. Neither can he operate the till: a twenty-by-twenty grid of buttons, their colour-coded subdivisions long since overridden by wear and spillage.

Fifty years ago, no one would have cared that this boy was dull-witted. Back then, being dim was neither a crime nor a catastrophe.

These days even operating a till requires a degree.

Anthony Burden takes his shopping-day lunch over to a table. He sits. He eats. The mush slides down easily enough. He faces the counter. He watches the boy. He feels something. Something he has no use for, no interest in. Something like compassion.

The net has been cast. Anthony Burden can see this. Though he is old and out of touch, though he has spent most of his life trying and failing to improve the lot of the poorer people of the earth, and though it is only the siren call of free health care and council housing that has convinced him to come back to the UK, he knows enough about the modern world. He knows about these places and how they work: how the till talks to the stock control computer, which talks to the email generator, which talks to the supplier's mainframe, and on and on and on. He can see, as though it were etched on the air, the self-stitching net that has been thrown over the world. He can see the struggles of people trapped within that net. He knows where the dreams of his youth have led.

As the boy struggles through his robot day, Anthony Burden realizes it has been given him, in these final years of his much-travelled and impecunious life, to witness something important. Here now, in a Portsmouth burger bar, he is witnessing the birth struggles of a world he has always dreamed of: a pre-wired, pre-fabricated world that has no need of people. A world already in control of itself.

Anthony Burden finishes his meal and leaves. He cannot remember the way home. Every street is like every other street. Every pavement is like every other pavement. Every hoarding is like every other hoarding. There are more connections in the human brain than there are stars in the sky, yet, by their chatter, all these connections go to make one singular 'I am'. So this city, webbed together with glass fibre and microwave, copper, coherent light and GSM, is one place now, one square foot of earth, and to walk through the streets of the city is to return to that square foot of earth continuously and reaffirm the city's great 'I am'.

Anthony Burden is lost, though there is nothing unfamiliar about his surroundings. On the contrary, everywhere he turns, he sees the same familiar scene. He is lost, and yet there can be no doubt where he is.

He is lost, as a man is lost who never leaves his home.

He walks.

This is the world he dreamed of: infinite trivial variations on a single theme. He walks, and the city rolls beneath his feet like a hamster's wheel, recurring endlessly.

His shopping bag knocks against his shin. Inside, his treasures: a bag of Young's frozen prawns (30 per cent extra free) and a half-price coconut. Anthony is going to weave magic tonight. Tonight, Anthony turns escapologist. He is going to make himself a pot of *caril de amendoim*, and taste his way to younger times and warmer lands.

When you have worked with as many anoretics as Professor Emeritus Lóránt Pál, it should be painfully apparent to you that their well-being depends less upon their physical condition as upon their outlook.

'Their *philosophy...*'

Lóránt Pál sucks his teeth, savouring his *mot juste*, but neither Stacey nor the man accompanying her seems impressed by his analysis.

He recognizes Stacey. He met her during her numerous visits to see her mother, and even then he had it in the back of his mind, given her radical appearance, that he might see her again – that she might one day self-refer.

Deborah, her mother, died here. They'd been unable to bring her out of her coma. An interesting case, if a harrowing one. Impossible to know for sure what caused the original damage. Stacey had told them it was a car accident, but Pál remembers the dent in Deborah's skull: it looked more like something made with a hammer.

'The anoretic constantly tests her body's limits,' Pál explains, sliding, out of bad habit, into an impersonal, third-person style of address. He spends too much time in the lecture hall these days, playing the Grand

Old Man of organic therapy. He flounders a second, experiments with an ingratiating grin and addresses Stacey Chavez directly: 'At least, while you're pushing your body as far as it can go, you're still engaged with it!'

Of course, the person he should really be trying to convince is her companion, this Spanish-looking gentleman in the ice-cream suit who claims to be the man behind the payments Coronation House received for Deborah. What on earth is his business with them, Pál wonders, that he wants Coronation House to treat yet another generation of the same family?

Once again – and is this by design, or by some malign chance? – he has acted too late. From experience, Pál knows just by looking that Stacey is a hopeless case. With the right treatment and surroundings the expert staff of Coronation House might sustain her for a few months more. But the heart is shrivelled beyond saving; the cold is deep in her bones.

Of course, he would not dream of saying such things to her directly. In fact, what can he say to her? What is he trying to say? One would think, at his great age, that Professor Loránt would have learned by now not to trip over his own professional enthusiasms. But it is his nature to be a bumbler in casual conversation. He prefers the lecture hall, and the freedom it gives him to shape a fully rounded idea.

'It is as well you came when you did, I think,' he says to them, euphemistically.

What he means is: Ms Chavez requires twenty-four-hour hospice care. Ms Chavez has passed the Point of No Return. Ms Chavez is dying. He can't disguise a helpless little shudder as he recalls the other ones – not many of them, but enough – who came to him too late.

Unwisely, he seeks to prepare them a little. He explains that the Point of No Return comes when you start thinking: What lies *beyond* the body's limits? *What happens if I let the body go?*

The couple stare at him.

With a sigh, Pál gives in, at last, to the inevitable. 'Well, perhaps I should explain what treatments we offer here,' he says.

The man's interest wakens straight away, while Stacey's sunken eyes burn with suspicion. Both reactions are predictable.

The working day proceeds as normal and by its end, as usual, Professor Emeritus Loránt Pál is left sitting on his hands, waiting for his taxi. Coronation House is profitable enough that he and his senior staff could each have their own driver if they wanted, but Pál, as senior partner, has set a very different tone for his flagship clinic. Not every client of theirs has a five-figure disposable income, nor is every outpatient immortalized in *Hello!*. One journalistic wit from *Vogue*, intuiting how the clinic used money from celebrity treatments to subsidize more interesting cases, compared the running of the place to an old-style grammar school. Pál and his colleagues sometimes stand accused of cherry-picking the most interesting cases. No one, however, can deny their excellent rates of success.

Pál uses the delay to open the day's non-urgent post. On top of the pile sits a large, heavy, brown padded envelope; Pál's thumb scrubs impotently at the flap. Even opening a letter is hard work, now that he is an old man.

After all his efforts, it is yet another 'courtesy' edition of *The Idealist*, this time with a flash on the cover announcing that Miriam has won the Elizabeth Longford Prize. God, is there no stopping this juggernaut?

Pál's feelings about the book are complicated by the fact that he misses and regrets Anthony Burden. He was as keen as anyone to learn what became of his client in the years following their psychological adventure. What he wasn't prepared for was Miriam's snide character assassination; the way she laid the blame for Anthony Burden's later life squarely, if subtly, at his professional door.

Of course he has regrets. What practitioner doesn't? Miriam is hardly the first biographer to judge the actions of the past by the *mouers* of the present. Young Pál leaps off the pages of *The Idealist* like a character out of early Harold Pinter.

Having to reassure people about that bloody book is getting to be an irritating obligation. 'Well, *of course* not!' he had exclaimed, that very morning, to the man in the ice-cream suit, that sinister fixer who would not give his name. 'Anyway, what the hell has ECT got to do with eating disorders?' His brain, catching up with his mouth at last, took over the reins: 'Look, what say you both come over to the clinic and meet our staff and see what we actually get up to here? What? Well, no, of course.' Polite laugh through gritted teeth. 'I won't be her actual *physician*. I am an old man now!'

No, no, no, my son, quite right, God forbid you should entrust your dearest to my hands, sullied as they are by over sixty years of practical experience—

Oh, but what's the use? Pál tosses Miriam's book aside. As if he hasn't memorized the thing already.

The great charm of *The Idealist* – or, depending upon your point of view, its great failing – is that Miriam has been unable to ascertain whether Anthony Burden is alive or dead. Her trail of her subject goes cold after Mozambique. Pál doesn't know whether he wants the book and all the attendant fuss to flush the old man from hiding or not. Obviously the mystery is good for sales. It has turned *The Idealist* into a sort of scientific-political *Donald Crowhurst*: the man goes overboard, leaving his writings to tantalize.

Still, can it be much of an Odyssey that ends so abruptly, and without any homecoming?

Pál wonders: if Anthony Burden was alive and they met again, what would they say to each other? Would Anthony blame him for the warp and weirdness of his life? Pál doubts it. After all, Anthony was there. He knew what happened, and why.

What would I say to him? Pál wonders. Would I say sorry? Certainly he has regrets. Of course he has regrets. He is an old man.

What would I say? Like a boy with a scabbed knee, Pál cannot help himself, but has to pick, pick, pick at his wound. He takes up the book

and turns with practised ease and heavy heart to chapter five. Miriam writes:

> *By the end of the Second World War, armed service medical personnel were being taught the fundamentals of 'ECT' – primarily as a palliative for schizophrenia – as part of their general training.*
>
> *Accordingly, in the autumn of 1939, the Society sent letters to the Italians Cerletti and Bini, inviting them to present a paper of their choosing to its Drill Hall open programme on Mental Infirmity and the Arts. The exigencies of war prevented the clinicians from accepting.*
>
> *Undeterred, the Society later played host to some lesser-known promulgators of electro-convulsive therapy.*

The cocksucker. For an old man Pál has surprisingly strong lungs. The stupid, dried-up old *vagina*. He never could stand that jumped-up receptionist. Those stinking cigarettes she used to smoke; those dreadful white blouses with the piping on them, like some kind of overgrown sailor-suit.

Lesser known. All right, so Loránt Pál is not the first name you'll hit when you look up the encyclopaedia entry. But what does that signify?

He closes the book and tosses it onto his desk.

He thinks: She'll outlive the lot of us.

In the driveway below his window, a taxi blows its horn.

The exigencies of war prevented them. How can she write like that and not want to fry her own face?

He eases himself down the stairs to the lobby. No lifts, no escalators for him; well into his eighth decade, he daren't let himself seize up for fear he might never get going again. Halfway down, a sudden convulsion seizes his hip. Frightening, insistent, alien – Good God, is this it? Is this how it ends? He imagines the clot in his thigh shattering into greasy brown shards, the shards racing helter-skelter for his heart and brain...

It is only his mobile phone, which he set to vibrate before this morning's staff meeting, then forgot to reset. Cursing, he wheedles the spiteful silver nugget out of his pants. Damned thing has nearly given him a heart attack.

'Hello?' he says.

This is the gauntlet that Pál runs now: the stuff of articles in the *TLS*; graduate papers on the internet; phone calls from 'freelance researchers'; an uncomfortable lunch or two with some gimlet-eyed bastard from the *New Scientist*, 'just to tease out wheat from chaff'.

Isn't there something, well, *unnatural* about all this? That Miriam Miller of all people, so much the Society's servant and retainer, should suddenly acquire her own voice, and at such a late date, suggests to Pál – a keen reader and re-reader of Dumas, *père* and *fils* – some long-nursed mission of revenge. Is it not treacherous, the way she has turned the Society's dull and muddled papers to her own account?

In any event, Miriam's unexpected foray into biography is stirring up no end of trouble for poor Pál. To begin with it had amused him to see how popular her long and tedious opus became. Whatever its stylistic limitations, *The Idealist* had somehow succeeded in awaking the forces of canonization in this nation that forgives failure so much more readily than success.

Now everyone wants a piece of Anthony Burden, the absentee genius, the prophet whose brain was so cruelly fried, who almost invented the computer, the network, the world-wide web; who set down the theoretical principles of virtual reality in the late forties, in a set of school exercise books that he never gave anyone to read.

Pál's own amusement cooled quickly. Watching this fad – this fascination with what might have been – coagulate in backwater after backwater of the public mind has become about as edifying as watching damp spread across a ceiling.

In response to enquiries, Pál has gone over his original notes again and again. He has reported faithfully and discussed candidly everything

he can about the case, in so far as it does not transgress his professional code. After all, Anthony Burden may still be alive. His privacy must be respected.

Nobody really wants to know the reasoning behind Pál's treatments, of course. People just want to believe that it wouldn't happen now, to them, to their children. People want to believe that medicine is *getting better.*

Better! And no sooner do we denigrate the therapies of our fathers, their shocks and surgeries, than we start *feeding amphetamines to schoolchildren*, for fuck's sake! *Better*, indeed! As if medicine could ever *get better*!

Whatever you say to them about what medicine really is – where it sits in the realm of social practice – all they want to hear is that you are sorry for what you have done.

Of course, Pál would not treat a man today as he treated poor Burden then. Then was then. Now is now: the AIDS-riddled, porn-infested Now. Why is this so hard to understand? To forgive? Truly, the past is another country, and old men are merely refugees. Go on, tell us to go back where we came from. Spit at us on the street, if you must. Kick us in the head. *I dare you...'*

A polite cough calls Professor Pál to order. The pleasant young man at the other end of the line experiments with a laugh: 'Perhaps I should call back at another time...'

Pál tries to swallow. Lord, what has he said now? He was never able to make much distinction between thinking and speaking, even at the height of his youth and powers. Old age has hardly improved him.

'I am an old man. I am an old man, do you understand? I am old.'

The fact of it is, he is being haunted by his younger self. 'I was a young man then. I was young. Do you understand? Now I am old. I am an *old man.'*

It is the irony of his life that he wasted his youth in pursuit of a certain notoriety. The best marks in his class? An assured future in

provincial medicine? What did he care for trivia like that? No, he had to throw all that up, of course, if he was ever to live a real life, following Cerletti and Bini around Europe, snapping at their heels like a crazy little dog...

'I AM AN OLD MAN!'

You can't end a phone call by slamming your mobile satisfyingly onto a surface. He has tried. Instead, obedient to the limitations of the new technology, Pál monkhouses his juddery thumb over to the little red telephone button. Right a bit... left a bit... up a bit... *there.*

Anthony Burden owns a hammer, but he no longer has the strength to wield it. When he raises it to strike – bones augmented, being extended, reach and strength increased, and every inch Tool-Maker Man – the hammer yanks itself out of his grip and goes clattering across the linoleum.

When his wrist has stopped ringing, he raps his bread knife across the coconut, once, twice, three times. The coconut rolls off the kitchen counter onto the floor – and does not crack.

He drops the coconut out of the window of his eighth-floor council flat. Then he goes to the elevator and presses the call button. What possessed him to buy this stupid fruit in the first place?

Classical music is being piped into the elevator to soothe the troubled spirits who tag the interior each week with yet another, seemingly innocuous one-syllable word: CHUTE, PUFF, VIM, DECK. Last week: BULB.

He is an old man, with an old man's mistrust of things and people, but tags and taggers do not rile him, even when the words appear on his front door. They are decorative enough, in a world that would erode all difference. If, as his neighbours claim, the tags mark some gangland boundary – well, then, so much the better: the old geography has not yet lost its power. When this machinic Eden shakes us off finally – the boy thrown from his till – perhaps we will go primitive again and treat this

chrome and concrete mess we've made as just another nature.

The lift stops. The door opens. Anthony explores the purlieus of the tower block, hunting his coconut.

It is lying on the grass, beside a cat turd. It is intact.

Burden picks it up and rides it back to his flat, scrubs it clean and places it on the floor. He tries to balance the leg of the kitchen table on top of the coconut. If he sits down hard on the table, the nut will crack. The nut keeps rolling away. He uses tins from the store cupboard to steady the coconut. The tins are not heavy enough to hold the nut in place, and now his back is singing and he has no strength left to lift the table.

He pauses, panting.

The music has followed him from the lift. A passionate piano; swooping strings. He recognizes it, almost. It jags against his ear, then goes swooping off again on a whim of its own. Rachmaninov? No. Tchaikovsky?

Then it comes to him, and all the mistakes of his life bubble up in his heart and he is crying for the first time in forty years. Poor Anthony, at his life's end, with nothing at all to show for his obsession with numbers, birds and bees.

It is the *Budapest Concerto*. The tears run unchecked down his cheeks as he leans against the table, sobbing, for what he has lost of himself. It is the work performed to extraordinary raptures, the night he first met his wife, Rachel, in the basement of the National Gallery.

What is it doing here? Is the lift stuck outside his door? A little recovered, Burden goes and opens his front door. The lift doors are closed, and the light above them indicates that the car is resting at ground level.

Are they piping music through the corridors, now? Are they piping music into our rooms?

Back in his flat, the music grows predatory: diminished fifths for the left hand scratch at the air.

Angrily, he wipes his face – stupid, stupid, ignominious, teary-eyed old age. I would be Lear, he thinks. I would rage rather than cry. But the piano is weeping and he sees himself for what he is: an old man in his bedsit, drizzling tears, and he knows where the music comes from now. It is in his head.

He goes into the kitchenette and picks up the coconut. He sets it down against the doorframe between the kitchenette and his bed-sitting room. He half closes the door, then stands with his back against it. He lets himself fall against the door. He loses his balance and falls to the floor. He cracks his head against the floor.

When he opens his eyes, he finds that something has gone wrong with the light in the room. Things have been sapped of their colour. A narrow, actinic light shines up into the room from sources far below, lighting ceilings and leaving floors in shadow. Streetlights. It is night-time.

Gingerly, he moves one limb at a time. He moves his head. Incredibly, nothing hurts. His head does not smart when he touches it. He sits up without a struggle. A dozen so-so movies replay themselves in his head: touching comic scenes in which a ghost gets up out of its own corpse, yawns and stretches, unaware of what it is. He thinks, I am dying, and he is filled with relief.

A piano, muted and passionate, sobs out a discordant cadence; minor strings put it out of its misery, then go spinning off.

The coconut.

It lies in two neat halves, one on the thin white carpet of the bed-sitting room, one on the black linoleum of the kitchenette. The husks are black, the flesh is white. Most of the coconut milk has run off into the carpet. A little puddle lingers in each scoop. Burden, crouched on the floor like an old cat, lowers his muzzle, and inhales.

Life's sweetness eddies through him, and away.

Weary, Burden staggers to his feet.

He goes to his chair by the window. Tower blocks rise around him, self-similar, peppered with trivial differences. In the street below, the new primitives are gathered: gangs of boys from Turkmenistan, Havant, Albania, Portsea, Nigeria, Hayling Island, Congo, Cosham, China, Horndean, Iraq, Waterlooville, Afghanistan. They smoke cigarettes. They ride their mountain bikes in circles in the road. They shelter mysteriously in doorways, then wander off, as though grazing.

Burden sighs: these are merely the movements of livestock. He would have tribes in bright colours clashing in the streets! But over the years some vital human thing has been invested in this chrome and concrete nature; something that cannot be retrieved. He is glad he has never had children.

A woman in a mackintosh and a white headscarf appears. She is heading for his tower block. She is old, he thinks, watching from his eighth-floor eyrie. She is as old as he is.

The longer he watches her, straining his eyes, the more she resembles a loop cut from a film. It is as though she were super-imposed: there, but not there. Fascinated, his hands white claws, Anthony watches as the woman nears.

The boys spot her. They agitate around her, vaguely threatening. One of them throws a lit cigarette at her back. It strikes her mackintosh. There are sparks.

Oblivious, she keeps walking. She pulls away from them, and they have not the energy to follow her.

She disappears from sight. He imagines her below him, walking the last few yards along the asphalt path. He imagines her climbing up the stairs to the main entrance. She taps in the entry code. She opens the door. She steps inside. He has seen her somewhere before.

He imagines her rising through the building. In his mind she does not take the lift. She climbs the stairs. Though she is as old as him, she climbs the stairs smoothly, mechanically, as though the stairs were a scale in music. Music surrounds her, as it surrounds him. The *Budapest*

Concerto. The walls, the floors, the ceilings of this structure are made of music.

Of music. Suddenly he knows what this is. He knows what is happening. After all these barren years it is happening again.

The woman leaves the stairwell and passes Burden's open door. She pauses, turns; gingerly, she knocks. 'Hello?'

She waits. When there is no answer, she leans into the room. She sees an old man, weeping with frustration.

'Is everything all right in there? Only I saw the door open. I thought maybe—'

'Hello?

'It's just me. Don't worry. From eight-oh-three. Are you all right?'

He does not turn round. He watches her in the window's reflection. She steps into the monochrome room. She is out of place here, but so is everything else. Everything is disordered. She is no more absurd than the coconut lying broken on the floor, or the bag of prawns he left to defrost in an empty fruit bowl. Stripped of context, every object shines.

She shines. She does not appear to be moving. She appears instead to be expanding. She fills the glass. She fills the room. He feels the air compress as she steps beside him.

She follows his gaze through the window, beyond the towers, out towards the invisible sea.

'Hello,' she says, patient, insistent. 'Hello. It's Mrs Cogan,' she says. 'Kathleen Cogan, just across the hall in eight-oh-three.' He still does not answer, so, gathering her courage, she takes hold of his hand.

The piano swirls. It capers. Anthony imagines temples, aqueducts, arenas, embankments, kiosks, statuary, railways, theatres, formal gardens, vistas, bandstands, playgrounds, fountains, amphitheatres, parades...

Kathleen shifts her hand in his. With a fingertip she traces the scar across his thumb.

'Hello,' he says, at last. 'Hello. Thank you, Mrs Cogan. Thank you, Kathleen, for looking in on me.'

He turns and takes her by the hands. 'I am quite well,' he says.

Outside, lights play over Portsmouth's last remaining marshes. Helicopters belly in the air.

Grade Seven civil servant Noah Hayden, disappointed, exhausted and soon to retire, comes to a nameless mud track between Portsmouth's few undeveloped reed-beds and climbs with trepidation from his car. Above him, police helicopters quarter and dice the landscape with their floodlights, tearing the hot night to shreds.

Today's anonymous tip-off has disturbed them, the way you might disturb a wasps' nest with a stick.

Hayden steps away from the car, testing his footing at every step. There are old moorings among the reed beds. The oldest have long since vanished from view, leaving only holes behind, where the wooden piles have rotted away. The holes have a petrolish sheen over them where nothing grows.

What fills these holes is an essence of rotted wood and the microscopic carcasses of whatever fed on it, mingled with the liquefied remains of whatever fed on the microbes – and on and on, who knows how long a food chain? Though water covers the holes for much of the day, what fills them has very little to do with water. It has the consistency of porridge. Dogs have been known to disappear into them. One or two children. So Noah Hayden treads carefully, and even though there is a line of plastic police tape to follow, it takes him a good five muddy minutes to cross the fifty feet or so to the burial site. The police team, forewarned, are waiting for him.

He is close. Saul Cogan, who was Hayden's room-mate at Cambridge, and his friend. Who stood him a steak sandwich in the Mount Soche Hotel in Blantyre, Malawi. Saul Cogan: gangmaster and entrepreneur; trafficker (this is known, but not yet proven) in men, women and children.

He is blurred. In the files, the tax records, the police tapes, the depositions of foreign governments and the internal inquiries of

411

international aid agencies, nothing adds up. There is no Saul Cogan, or there are too many Saul Cogans. He is nowhere and everywhere, a ghost in the globalized machine.

The helicopters have their lights trained on the work of recovery. The result is a kind of shifting, multi-angled daylight. Shadows leap about as if with a life of their own. Perspectives wheel and collapse. It is impossible to say what are two reed-stalks nearby and what are four reed-stalks far away. The policemen are dressed in identical waders and paper masks, and Hayden finds it no easier to focus on them. How many men are here? How many holes? How many jetties? How many helicopters? Is he going to faint?

The bodies so far recovered are lying in a row to one side of the burial site. In their anaerobic resting place, they have come to little harm. Through the greasy plastic, each horror is still recognisably human.

Why did they call him out here? To what end? He did not have to see this. He passed on the email, didn't he? He made no fuss when they took away his computer. He answered all their questions. He kept his temper when they insisted on interviewing his wife and even his children.

'Who do you think sent this to you?'

Well, really, it hardly took a genius to answer that one.

'Why?'

'Because he can afford to.'

'Meaning?' They were very excited.

'Either Saul Cogan knows you will find him, or he knows that you will not find him.' Hayden could not resist a little smile as he added, 'I suspect the latter.'

No, they did not have to make him see this. It is spite. Punishment for his smile. The Third Floor is spitting blood. All over Europe, the nets are tightening, the gates are swinging shut. The whole northern hemisphere is swaddled in meshes of infra-red and ultrasound. Still, this one man eludes them. Try as they might, they cannot pin him to their

card. Saul Cogan, pooping and farting at the new world order, refusing to fit in their file.

At what point, Noah wonders, did I start to like him again?

He heads back to his car. The reeds before him sway and hiss. They tickle his hands, the back of his head, his groin. Reeds spring up between him and the police tape he must follow, back to dry land and his car.

The tides. He imagines the waters encroaching, the little patch of dry land around him shrinking, shrinking. His footing gives way...

Perhaps he has been here before. The place reminds him of the bilharzia-ridden shallows of the Shire River. He has seen the Shire only once, as a functionary for the Department for International Development, when he toured the camps thrown up to accommodate refugees, Mozambican and Malawian, dispossessed by the 2000 floods. The river, which had marked the border between Malawi and Mozambique, was rife with rumours of Saul Cogan and his operations. Diligently, Hayden reported these back to his friends on MI5's Third Floor.

But it is impossible, at such a remove, to imagine what, if anything, they had made of them. Cogan's men stealing food aid. Cogan's men distributing food aid. Cogan, the lender of tractors and ploughs, collector of tithes and tribute.

Saul Cogan, *régulo*.

Yes, this might be any break along the Shire, where starving skeletons of men cook bushmeat on little fires, wary, as easily put to flight as the animals they hunt.

Might two such different places not be one place, after all? Hayling Island, the Shire River, Mozambique, Malawi, Britain – there is no difference. All places are the same place. How close are the walls of the world? Unnerved, he turns around and returns to the place where Saul Cogan has buried his dead.

Up comes another. A helicopter hovers directly overhead, winch spinning, lifting the corpse free of the mudlark's hole. Noah Hayden,

craving company, re-enters the circle of men surrounding the hole. The light and sound of the recovery operation are at their fiercest here. Everything shakes in the downwash, vivid in magnesium light.

Up it comes, through the pink-blue skein, through the interface between worlds: the corpse in its plastic wrapper.

Over fifty dead have already been recovered. Men, women, children. Where are they from? What happened, that there are so many?

The black, poisoned water settles. A metallic film forms over the hole. Pastel colours shoot and swirl across the black water, until the black is hidden.

Hayden knows these colours. They belong on maps of the world. Throw a stone into the water, he thinks, and all these pretty colours will disappear.

This is one for his friend.

Throw a stone.

EPILOGUE

Christmas Eve, 1968

Each time their link with Mission Control hissed out, without drama or fanfare, Apollo Eight command module pilot Jim Lovell was reminded of a journey he and his wife once made, driving their car through lonely Florida countryside to Lake Kissimmee: how the radio stations faded out, one by one.

Apollo Eight has not landed on the moon. It has flown by, tantalizingly close, less than seventy miles above the surface: a reconnaissance mission. Altogether, Borman Anders and Lovell have made ten lunar orbits. Each took two hours, and every other hour – when the moon got in the way of their radio communication with Earth – they spent the time in silence, taking it in turns to look out of the window at the Moon's dark side: a secret face no one had ever seen before.

The first thing Jim Lovell noticed about the Moon, seen this close up, was its lack of colour – though why this should have startled him, this self-evident fact, he cannot say.

Ten orbits; twenty hours. All the while they looked at the Moon, their eyes were tuned to the colours of home. Looking on this other world, they saw nothing but shades of grey. For Jim, it was as if the place was holding something back. As though a vital datum were being withheld.

Apollo Eight's purpose is to prove that the dream can be realized: that men can travel this far away from Earth and come home safe again. When they emerged from behind the Moon for the tenth and final time, Mission Control welcomed the crew back on air with more fanfare, relieved for them and proud of themselves. Now, hours later, the Apollo Eight spacecraft is starting its journey home, and it is time for the astronauts to speak to the waiting world.

Jim says to the world, 'The vast loneliness is awe-inspiring.' He tries not to wince.

'It makes you realize just what you have back there on Earth,' he says, wishing he did not have to listen to the words coming out of his mouth.

Lovell's words are weak. His carefully chosen, utterly inadequate words. They lack fuel. They lack thrust. He launches them and watches, helpless, as they struggle and stall and plummet back to the cold, unmeaning ground.

He has been up here often enough – with Aldrin on Gemini Twelve; before that on Gemini Seven, with Frank Borman – to know that he will never find the words. The words do not exist. All he can do, over the course of his career as an astronaut, is to encourage as many people out here as he can. Floating together, they might think up some new words, unearthly words – divine words, even – to do the job he cannot do like this, the TV camera in his face (another Apollo Eight first) and too little time.

'For all the people on Earth,' Bill Anders says, 'the crew of Apollo Eight has a message we would like to send you.'

Frank Borman sticks the camera in Bill's face.

'In the beginning,' says Bill, 'God created the heaven and the earth. And the earth was without form, and void; and darkness was upon the face of the deep. And the Spirit of God moved upon the face of the waters, and God said, Let there be light: and there was light. And God saw the light, that it was good: and God divided the light from the darkness.'

Jim wonders: How did God divide the light? Did he divide it, like Newton, with a prism? There are no colours here. Jim has looked at the far side of the moon, and he cannot imagine that moonlight contains any colour. Pass it through a prism, every band will shine bright white.

Now the camera is in Jim's face. It is his turn. They have practised this. 'And God called the light Day,' says Jim, 'and the darkness he called Night.'

He takes the camera and points it towards Frank Borman. After the broom-cupboard that was Gemini, the Apollo command module feels as spacious as an ordinary room – until you start throwing TV cameras around.

Frank Borman: 'And God said, Let the waters under the heavens be gathered together unto one place, and let the dry land appear: and it was so.'

And were the waters blue? Jim wonders. Was the land grey, or brown, or sandy yellow? Or green with verdigris, or rusty red from all the iron in the earth? He thinks, there is iron in the Moon, but it cannot rust.

It comes to him that nothing is being withheld them here: it is simply that they have come out here with the wrong sort of eyes – eyes that see the colours of earth. They are blind to the colours of space, whatever they may be.

'And God called the dry land Earth; and the gathering together of the waters called he Seas: and God saw that it was good.'

Jim is thinking back to their last lunar orbit: the way the Earth rose over the Moon as they swung clear of the far side.

Earthrise. Above the grey of the lunar surface, the Earth was a colour. The Earth was many colours. Red and yellow in the blue. The different blues of ice and ocean. Green in there somewhere, too. Colour belonged nowhere else but on that ball.

Jim shifts the camera away – it's in the script, they've practised this – up to the window and in, filling the homes of Earth with the first ever television image of their planet. As he does so, a simple thought strikes him: it is only on the Earth that colour makes any sense. Away from Earth, colour means nothing: neither ripeness, nor rot; neither springtime, nor fall. Of course there is no colour out here. There is no one out here to benefit by it.

He thinks: We have no need of colour now. We must let it go. This kaleidoscope, this bauble of our childhood. We must lay it down, Jim thinks, and look about us at the world as it really is. We must press on

into the greater world, the real and terrible world we have found beyond our little corner: the world of black and white. ˙

And he finds himself transported back, imprisoned in that jet again, the Banshee, a lonely dot over the Pacific, and his instruments are out and his lights are out and there are no stars and there is no *Shangri-La* and he knows his fuel is low and it is so dark the sea might as well be above him for all he knows. The sea might be above them, beside them and below them all at once, behind them and in front of them.

Rising in a calm black ocean, this bright little bubble of ape hope.

'And from the crew of Apollo Eight,' says Frank Borman, wrapping up transmission, 'we close with goodnight, good luck, a Merry Christmas and God bless all of you – all of you on the good Earth.'

ACKNOWLEDGEMENTS

For their hospitality and good advice I owe many thanks to Patricia and Chris O'Dell, the Barclay family, Susie Tiso, Rhidian Davis, Geoff Ryman and Nancy Hynes.

Without my agent Peter Tallack and my editor Louisa Joyner, this book would be much the poorer.